The
Shattered
Cross

a novel

MICHAEL JOHN SULLIVAN

PERMUTED
PRESS

T0019435

A PERMUTED PRESS BOOK
ISBN: 978-1-63758-211-4
ISBN (eBook): 978-1-63758-212-1

The Shattered Cross
© 2022 by Michael John Sullivan
All Rights Reserved

Cover art by Cody Corcoran

PERMUTED
PRESS

Permuted Press, LLC
New York • Nashville
permutedpress.com

Published in the United States of America
1 2 3 4 5 6 7 8 9 10

The Shattered Cross

For you, the reader, for taking this time travel journey with me. Thank you always for keeping me good company.

Book One – *Necessary Heartbreak*

Michael Stewart has weathered his share of hardships: a troubled childhood, the loss of his mother, even the degradation of living on the city streets. Now he's raising his teenaged daughter, Elizabeth, on his own and doing the best he can at work and at home. But he's turned his back on his faith—that is, until the morning Michael and Elizabeth volunteer for a food pantry at their local church.

While storing boxes in the basement, they step through a tunnel…and find themselves in First Century Jerusalem during the tumultuous last week of Jesus Christ's life.

Book Two – *An Angel Comes Home*

The prequel to book three (*Everybody's Daughter*)

The mysterious George Farmer from book one and three is revealed. Farmer, an old man who is found on the streets of Northport by the police with a suspicious fatal wound, discovered the tunnel leading back to First Century Jerusalem before Michael Stewart did. What was George's background? What was his purpose to the story? Why was he found dead?

Book Three – *Everybody's Daughter*

What if you had a chance to ask a loved one for forgiveness after they died? What would you say?

Would you give up your own lifetime of happiness for someone else?

Michael Stewart confronts these questions as he travels back in time through a mysterious tunnel in an old church when the Romans ruled with brutal violence and Jesus preached his peaceful message.

His teenage daughter Elizabeth soon follows Michael but is surprised to discover that her father is nowhere to be found. Little does she know that Michael has returned safely to the present, leaving her to battle a vicious Roman soldier.

Separated by centuries, Michael is trapped to fight his own battles in the present day. Elizabeth's disappearance and the discovery of her blood in his car ignites a rush of judgment as the FBI focuses on him as a person of interest. Michael's only hope for saving his daughter rests in the hands of his best friend—a local pastor with secrets of his own—and a mysterious old journal containing tales of miracles within the walls of the old church itself.

Book Four – *The Greatest Gift*

Michael poses as a Roman soldier, takes a sea journey with an Apostle, and hears what it is like to be with Jesus during his teaching days.

In present time, Hewitt Paul, an embittered FBI special agent, seeks solutions to the mysteries surrounding Elizabeth and Michael's disappearance.

As faith collides with cynicism and compassion faces off against cruelty, these three people will encounter the unimaginable in ways that alter their lives forever.

Chapter 1

Smoke seeped down into the tunnel. Michael Stewart stopped running, exhaling an exhausted breath, coughing. "Do you see this, Elizabeth?" he asked his daughter. Fear and an ominous sensation chilled his thoughts. *Where are we?*

He pointed to the bright red, unfamiliar etchings and words on the surrounding walls as a putrid scent assaulted his senses. An eagle with wings spread out long caught his attention. The words *The drums beat loudly while our hearts rage in silence* were below the eagle. "Elizabeth, do you see this?"

She nodded.

"What does it mean? Any idea? You're up on pop culture. You know. You're on that tic tac." Michael looked back at her.

She frowned and shook her head. "Tik Tok, Dad. Tik Tok! How many—"

"I know, I know. I get it mixed up with those mints," he shrugged.

"What about this one?" he asked her. It was a picture of two tomahawks crossing each other. The words carved below stated,

The ground on which our ancestors stood is soaked with blood. Do not trample it. Revere it. Heal.

"I have no idea what any of this is," Elizabeth said.

"Are we in the right place?"

"What other tunnel is there? Are there any other tunnels here on Long Island?"

Elizabeth sidled up beside him. "What is that awful smell?" She wrinkled her nose. "Let's hurry back home. I want to update my social media. No one's going to believe what just happened."

"You're not telling anyone this time." Michael looked around, wracking his brain, trying to figure out if they were indeed in the right tunnel leading back to the old church's basement in Northport.

Elizabeth distracted him. "Why can't I post a picture? Just one. Please."

"No, no. Absolutely not. Remember all those kooks knocking on our door, asking crazy questions?"

"Yeah, there was that."

"We also put Pastor Dennis in an embarrassing and awkward predicament with all the nutjobs tearing the church apart to get into the basement."

Elizabeth sighed. "Yeah. He wasn't too happy about it."

"Especially when that nosy reporter wrote that article about us time traveling to First Century Jerusalem, encouraging even more crazies to drive the Pastor to the point—"

Elizabeth interrupted him. "Well, was the reporter wrong?"

Michael frowned.

"Okay, I get it. Message received, loud and clear," she said. "No updates. No pictures. No videos."

"Did you do Facebook Live?" Michael asked, panicking.

Elizabeth laughed. "Geez, Dad, think about it. No satellite dishes or wireless communication in the century we just left. Pretty barren for any Generation Z female."

Michael shook his head. "I wanted to make sure because I never know what you're going to do in this wacky world of technology."

She rolled her eyes. "Even I can't rig up any modern technology in ancient times. C'mon, let's keep moving."

Michael took several steps toward the stairway, the odor growing stronger. "This place smells like rotting fish."

Elizabeth held her nose. "Smells like Thanksgiving at Grandma Bertha's."

"What are you talking about?" Michael placed his wrist over his nose. "She made delicious turkey and stuffing that was to die for."

"'To die for' is the right way to say it."

"Keep thinking of the potatoes, gravy, and stuffing smell to get your mind off whatever this stench is."

He climbed the first few steps, and a cold breeze hit him in the face. "It's freezing up there." He glanced back at Elizabeth. "That's weird."

"Maybe Pastor Dennis is running the air conditioner?"

"At the start of Spring? From what I remember, it's supposed to be cold today."

"It's Long Island, Dad. We could have four seasons in one day."

"I suppose." Still skeptical, he climbed two more steps and gazed at the surrounding land beneath the star-studded sky. "Woah."

His daughter joined him on the steps. "What the…?"

Michael let out a surprised gasp. "Where is the…"

"Church?" said Elizabeth, finishing his thought.

She grasped his arm. "Are you seeing what I'm seeing?"

"We're not dreaming, are we?"

"No," she said. "I don't think so." She rubbed her eyes. "No. This is no dream."

Michael made it to the top step and looked around several times.

"Dad, what else can you see?"

"I see nothing.... I see absolutely nothing."

Elizabeth climbed the remaining steps, looking to the left, the right, and then behind her. "I think we ran through the wrong tunnel."

"Maybe there was another tunnel?" He shook his head. "No. Maybe. I don't know. How could we? This is the only tunnel we know of."

"That's just it," she said. "That we *know* of. Perhaps…"

Michael climbed out of the tunnel and stood outside, his feet sinking into the wet terrain. "Where in God's name are we?" He turned back toward Elizabeth, reflecting on what happened during the last week of Christ's life. The encounter with Pontius Pilate. He grimaced. "What have we done?" He fell to his knees. "Elizabeth, what did we do?"

Elizabeth climbed out of the tunnel, her head swinging around, taking in the landscape. "Where is everybody? Where is everything? Where's the toy store? The streets? The lights? Where is…"

Elizabeth shivered. She tried to speak, but a thick vapor came from her mouth instead of words.

Michael trembled.

Desperate, Elizabeth approached Michael, reaching out for him, struggling to move forward. "Dad…what's…happening to…?" She struggled back toward the tunnel's entrance. "Can't see you. Where are you? Help me!"

"No, no, no," Michael yelled, straining to grab her hand as Elizabeth vanished high into the air. "Nooooo!" He looked upward, jumping several times, grasping for her image.

He crawled down the stairs, shouting. "Elizabeth, can you hear me? Where are you? Shout so I can find you. Are you down there?"

The only sound he heard was the beating of his heart, pounding painfully against his chest. "Elizabeth!" He yelled her name over and over until he lost his voice for a moment. He struggled to clear his throat.

He wept into his hands with the image of his daughter's hallowed, distraught eyes ingrained into his mind.

"My Lord, what happened to my daughter? Where did she go?" He looked up at the opening at the top of the stairs, fearful of the reality of what he had witnessed.

A chill ran through his whole being, cold enough to make him shiver with panic. "My God, what have we done?" he whispered. "What have we done?"

Chapter 2

———◈———

Michael often read about the Romans and the rule of Pontius Pilate in school, and now history stood before him, stimulating his curiosity with joy and intrigue.

Pilate paced around the marble-made room, commanding the attention of the guards and slaves serving him. Michael stared at his garb, a bright red toga draping him to his ankles.

"Slave," Pontius Pilate said. "Fetch me water."

The woman wearing a threadbare cloth limped toward him, carrying a ceramic bowl filled with water.

He dipped a torn towel into it, and the moisture tipped over and fell to the floor. He washed his hands and the bottom of his neck, his eyes never leaving the woman's stoic gaze.

Pilate pointed to another slave. "Fetch me food."

Another woman dressed in white garbs with gold chains dangling from her neck appeared holding a big bowl of fruit. Her eyes were ocean blue, much like the color of the sea Michael saw on his trip to Malta when he met the apostle, Paul.

He was briefly mesmerized until Pilate stood before him, pumping his hand with force into his chest. "You are not from here. What is your business with the Roman Empire?"

Michael took a few steps back. "My daughter is in danger. Your soldiers informed me that a bandit named Barabbas has taken a girl like my daughter against her will. And he is asking for gold for her return. I have nothing, Prefect. I am a poor man here."

Pilate bit into a slice of fruit, frowning. The juice splattered down his chin. He waved at the woman, and she hurried to him, handing him a clean towel. Pilate snatched it and methodically wiped the sticky substance off his face. "So, you are not a rich man here? Do not expect pity from me. Are you rich in another part of this land?"

Michael reflected for a minute before answering. "I have a better gift than gold."

Pilate let out a mocking laugh. "Better than gold?" He opened his arms wide and cornered the slaves waiting in the far corner of the room, their heads lowered in submission. "What can be better than gold? Are you going to give me all of Rome? Perhaps the power to rule the entire world? What do you think?" he asked the slaves.

With their heads bowed, both women let out a nervous sounding laugh.

He turned to Michael. "Tell me, are you a prophet? Are you going to tell me I need to repent for the sins of myself and the Roman Empire? Will I be banished to the blazing fires of hell? Will I be removed from power? Lose my authority here?"

Pilate paced, not making eye contact with him. "Tell me, stranger, will the Jews drive us out of their Holy City?" He snorted. "Do not fill my ears with such fables." He shook his head, not allowing Michael to respond, and continued to riddle the room with Roman philosophy. "Whoever you are, I have heard it all. I have all. I have had prophets, kings, wise men, and fools from here and from afar tell me how my heart must change or how I should get on my knees to repent."

He gestured toward a table topped with gold and silver jewelry and trinkets. Pilate picked up a woven basket and turned it over. Roman-made coins fell to the floor; the clanging noise echoed throughout the high ceiling structure.

"Your legacy will be important and recorded for all future generations and mean much more that any gold or jewelry or any basket of money you may claim," Michael said. "I know it is important to you. I know how you desire to be remembered like the Greek gods. I know how your mind thinks, how your heart beats."

Pilate looked fascinated in what Michael was saying. "How do you know all of this about me? You know how my mind thinks, more than anyone close to me? More than my guards. How?" His lips curved into a devious smile. "Are you a prophet? Enlighten me."

"I am not a Prophet," Michael said. "I am a student of history."

"History is for idiots looking into the past," Pilate said. "Prophets predict the future. Which are you?"

Michael struggled for a response, looking down at his torn sandals and his bloodstained left pinky toe, a result of walking hundreds of miles to elude the Romans. He bent and touched his foot, allowing him more time to gather his thoughts. When he straightened up, Pilate stood close to him with a menacing scowl.

"Answer me, Jew. Which are you?"

"I am both," Michael said, hoping he sounded convincing.

Pilate punched him in the face.

Stunned, Michael backed up to the opening of the room, rubbing his bruised chin.

"Do not talk in mysteries to a Prefect," Pilate said. "I asked you a question, and I demand an honest answer."

Michael took a deep breath, staring at the ceiling. "I do not always speak with answers that can satisfy you, Prefect. I am like any other man in this land who loves his daughter. I made a promise when she was born to protect her from any hardship."

Pilate's glare was more threatening.

Michael tightened his shoulders and took a deep breath, gathering courage. "You are about to crucify an innocent man in Jesus of Nazareth."

"Who?"

"Jesus of Nazareth."

Pilate reached into a ceramic bowl sitting on a small wooden table and bit into another piece of fruit, the juice once again dripping from his chin. He gestured to the women slaves. They all brought a towel. Pilate held out his arms. The women frantically wiped away the sticky drippings. He pushed one of the women aside, and the rest scurried back to the corner, lowering their heads.

"I am thinking," Pilate said. "Leave me be. I need my rest."

"Are you going to help me?"

"I demanded to be left alone, stranger. Do not test my patience."

Michael followed the women out of the room.

"Wait," Pilate said, halting Michael's exit. "What do you know of this man, Jesus of Nazareth? Does he have much gold? How many followers does he have? Are they loyal? Do they have weapons? What is his purpose? Are they looking to revolt? Are they planning to kill me?"

"He is a peaceful man, a man of love. He has no riches. He has some followers, but they do not have weapons because he does not believe in violence, nor is he looking to start a revolt." Michael sighed, worried he may have said too much. He knew he hadn't answered most of the questions accurately, but they were true to what ideology was in Pilate's time. He also knew it was a revolution, and Jesus and his followers were armed but not in the Roman way.

Pilate snorted. "Then why should I be troubled? Where is the danger? A meek man cannot battle me. My Empire is the greatest in any civilization. Do you not know this?"

"I do."

"Peace is not the way of life here, stranger. We will overrun any man who kneels before us." He gave a disbelieving glance. "Why would a man such as you describe need to be crucified? You do not make any sense. Your lack of logic puzzles me."

"There isn't logic here. I tell you on my daughter's life that what you think isn't possible will happen. And it will be written for all the civilizations. It will happen soon. The leaders here will come to you and demand it."

"Your language is not from this land. Or any land I know of."

Michael reminded himself mentally to not use contractions when he spoke. "Why?" Pilate asked, his voice again mocking Michael. "Why would anyone want this to occur if he is a peaceful man, not armed, not interested in starting a Jewish revolt. Is he not a Jew?"

"He is."

Pilate circled him, rubbed his chin, and glared. "Why should I trust you? A strange man who speaks strange words. Strange words I have never heard before. Why should I, the greatest Roman Prefect, or anyone—woman, child, or peasant or even a Jew—believe what you say?" His voice sounded sharper. "Answer me, stranger."

They glared at each other, ironically much like the stare-offs he used to have with Elizabeth during one of her rebellious teenage days.

Michael took an anguished breath. "Because he is the son of God."

"What? Did you say what I thought you said?"

"He is the Son of God."

"Stranger, you lie. Or you are plain crazy like the rest of the Jews here."

Michael clenched his fists, wincing at the thought of telling such a scourge the truth. "He is Jesus of Nazareth, the son of God. It will be written."

"Written? Where? Where is this written?" Pilate glared. "Where is this Jesus of Nazareth written as the son…of what god?" He slapped Michael's face. "You lie. Show me where it is written. What book?"

Michael rubbed his stinging cheek. "It hasn't been written yet."

"If he is the son of God, why doesn't he strike us all down here?"

"It's not like that." Michael raised his tone.

"Tell me, stranger. How is it? How is the son of God not able to free himself? If he is to be crucified, as you say?"

Michael faced Pilate, angry at being mocked. "You do not understand, Prefect."

Pilate cornered him and grabbed his arm. "What do I not understand, stranger? Tell me, oh great Prophet, enlighten me."

"I have told you the truth."

Pilate shook his head.

Michael backed away. "It is up to your heart to accept it or not."

"Give me a truth that only you would know about me."

Michael paused for an extended moment. Pilate grew impatient. Finally, Michael answered. "You have hidden many cruelties, taken bribes, and stolen from many…so Tiberius will not find out."

Pilate sneered. "How dare you!"

"You know I speak the truth."

"You do not know what I do or who I do business with. Give me a truth that is not known and has not been written."

Michael dug deep into his memory, pulling out the Roman history lessons he was taught in high school and college. "You will ask Marcus Gaius Sejanus to be your daughter's husband."

Pilate's eyes widened. He stayed silent for several minutes, giving a look of concern. "Are you spying for Tiberius or another Roman governor?"

Michael pulled out a lie, forcing himself to look confident. "You are right. I am a prophet."

Pilate froze, then paced around the room, circling Michael three times before stopping. "And you know all about this man, Jesus?"

"I do. You will be ridiculed for thousands of years."

"Years?"

"I mean sunsets."

Pilate's veins popped out of his neck; his face contorted in anger. "Perhaps it is you who needs to be crucified and not this Jesus."

Michael backpedaled toward the door's opening, his heart racing from imagining himself tortured and dying and not being able to save his daughter's life. Fear gripped him. "Prefect, I only want to save my daughter. I gave you the future. The future only you and I know about your daughter." He dug deeper into his history lessons. "Your daughter is much like my daughter. I worry about her with a husband. Would you not worry if that bandit, the man who murdered a Roman soldier, hurt your daughter?"

Pilate turned his back on Michael for a few minutes, taking time to finish off the fruit. He again called upon a slave with the water bowl, cleaning his hands and face of the leftover moisture. "When does this happen with this man, Jesus?"

"Tomorrow, Jesus will be handed over to the authorities."

"I will send him to Herod."

Michael grimaced. "He will send him back to you."

"How do you know?"

Michael grew frustrated. "History will record it."

"And what if this does not come true?" Pilate asked.

"If what I say is a lie, you can kill me." *I can't lose Elizabeth. Half my heart was taken when my wife Vicki died. I can't go through this again.* "Kill me if I'm wrong." *I won't go back until I have her with me. God, please. Please help me.* "I am pleading with you." He remained quiet for a few seconds. "My life is fruitless without my daughter. I have no other way to help her. I would help you if your daughter were in danger."

Pilate pointed to a slave. "Bring me another wet towel." The slave brought him a small cloth, and he wiped his eyes and yawned. "I grow tired. I need to rest. We shall talk some more. Later." He waved to the soldier, standing guard by the opening.

"Help this man to a room so he can rest. Do not let him leave. Attend to his needs. If he starts any trouble, kill him."

Kill me?

I will kill you if need be.

Chapter 3

A Roman soldier pulled Michael up off the concrete bed, tightening his grip around his neck.

Michael flailed at the soldier, belting him in the face. Another soldier joined them, and they clamped their hands around his chest, dragging him away. Michael struggled to free himself. Another Roman jumped in, lifted Michael sideways, and threw him on the ground.

Michael rubbed his back and staggered to his feet. "If you are so tough, why are there three of you against one of me?"

He massaged the lower part of his legs, leaning down as the crackling of his bones ignited sneers from the soldiers.

The guards, dressed as history previously recorded them in steel armor and long spears, stepped aside as Pilate walked into the room. "Did my guards tell you how much I missed you?"

"Could have fooled me. Why the rough treatment? I'm...I mean, I am trying to help you."

"You are trying to help you. Let us be honest with each other."

Michael winced from the strain of taking a few steps. "I cannot be any more honest than I have been with you."

"How did you know about my daughter and who I want her to marry? My wife does not even know this. Are you a spy for Tiberius? Has he given you gold?"

Michael rubbed his stinging arm. "I told you. I am a prophet."

Pilate shook his head. "How do I not know of you? I know all the prophets in this land."

"Obviously, you do not know of my land."

"Where is your land?"

"It is not important, Prefect. What is important is that I have given you information only a prophet would know."

Pilate threw his hands in the air. "You lie. I know all the prophets here."

"You do not know me. But now you do."

"My guards watched you last evening. They said you did not say much. You were in thought. What were you thinking?"

"I was not thinking."

"Yes, you were," Pilate said. "They said you walked around the room many times. When I walk in such a way, I am always thinking, always planning, always." He glared. "What are you plotting?"

Michael scrambled for a safe answer and exuded confidence. "I am not plotting. I do not need to plot anything. But I will act if I need to."

Pilate looked confused. "You should be plotting. Did you not inform me that your daughter is being held by that barbarian Barabbas?"

"Yes. I believe so. But I may not be right. One way or another, I will not give up until I find my daughter."

Pilate seemed to ponder that thought, rubbing his forehead. "If what you state is without lies about this man Jesus, then why would any man and father not be plotting to rescue his daughter?"

Michael wasn't sure where Pilate was going with this line of questioning. He knew this was a method practiced by authorities in the Roman Empire. He straightened and shot what he hoped was a menacing glare, deflecting some of the impact by looking upward at the high ceilings. He noticed the uniqueness of the tiles and how they were layered. *No wonder these structures lasted to our time.*

Michael spoke in a convincing tone. "Of course, I'm plotting," he lied, trying to show Pilate he wasn't weak. "I have a couple of plans. I suggest you understand this fully."

"Are you threatening me?" Pilate took a couple of steps closer to him. "Are you plotting to overthrow the Roman Empire?" His voice filled with anger. "Or worse, plotting to overthrow me?"

"If I needed to rescue my daughter and that was my only choice, I would, Prefect. We may be strangers, but we are much alike. You would do the same. I know how much you love your daughter. How much you want to protect her." Michael clenched his fists and met Pilate's angry glare. "I will not be stopped."

Pilate grasped his fists. "Do not raise your hands to a Prefect."

Michael relaxed his clench.

"Your eyes and hands tell me you are a desperate man." Pilate smirked. "I enjoy meeting men who are desperate." He strolled around Michael like a shark prepares his prey for an attack. "What happens if I let this preacher from Nazareth be crucified?"

"Then the scriptures shall be fulfilled."

"I do not care about your scriptures," Pilate said. "Your scriptures are false—a lot of fools writing lies, filling the minds of men and women and children with falsehoods. There is no god. Look around. The Romans are their gods. We have our gods to worship."

Michael remained silent.

"What will become of my legacy?" Pilate put his arm out and growled, moving toward the opening, demanding silence from men and women outside passing by the room. "Tell me now. What will become of me and my decision to crucify this man Jesus?" His face was red with anger. "Answer me. Do not lie to me. Or I will hunt down your daughter with every Roman soldier available, and I will make certain you witness her torture."

Michael rubbed his forehead and stared at the blood-stained ground. His sandals made a sticky sound as he paced toward the door. The room confined any massive movement, its barren walls giving it a hospital type of feel. "You will forever be known as giving the order to kill the Son of God. You will be mocked. Admonished."

Pilate gestured to a soldier standing nearby to fill a cup of wine. He approached Michael and handed him the drink. "You have a tale to tell me."

"Was my prophecy about your daughter a tale?" Michael asked.

Pilate turned to the soldier. "What do you think?"

The soldier did not answer, perhaps out of fear for his own life or knowing that it was not proper protocol to respond to Pilate orally.

"Tell me another tale," Pilate mused. "Woman, I need a drink to listen to such fables." One woman scurried from the room.

"It is not a tale," Michael said, inwardly panicking that Pilate didn't believe him. "You can deny what I have said but know I have given you more truths than any other prophet."

Pilate turned his back to him.

Michael approached and said in a lower tone, "Your name will be infamous for thousands of years to come. Even worse, you will be ridiculed for all time."

"Like Caesar?"

"Like him but worse."

"I will be mocked?"

Michael nodded.

Pilate waved him away. "I have been informed of this man, the so-called king of the Jews. That my decision will forever be written and remembered."

"My words of truth for you are the only weapons I have to save my daughter," Michael responded. "I will find her. You can make it easier for me."

Pilate took the cup of wine the woman gave him. "Drink with me. I do love tales."

Michael took a brief sip from the cup, wincing from the sour taste. "I will battle you or any Roman who steps in my path."

Chapter 4

Michael paced the stone-carved room with vigor, raging about the delay in getting an answer from Pilate. The Prefect had not been seen in hours. The urge to ram the soldier with all his might was seething in his heart. His anger could not be tempered any longer. *What more does this dictator want? I've given him information no one has, including his wife. Jeez, I wonder if Pilate is married. It's never been written he was but assumed.*

I don't trust him since lies can be written into history, and I can't give him any more proof. He either helps me, or I take matters into my own hands...with weapons.

It was Thursday, or so he thought judging by how many sundowns he witnessed. It was the night of the Last Supper.

The soldier guarding the door slumped several times; his helmet lay near his feet. Michael yawned, and the soldier did the same. *It works here too. Maybe I don't need to use force. Really, force? Keep dreaming. Do what's necessary.* Michael yawned once more, holding his mouth wide open for several seconds, exaggerating.

The soldier did the same. He took a deep breath, and Michael could see his arms relax, the spear dropping to the floor, alerting him. The soldier shook his head several times and rubbed his eyes.

Michael yawned again.

The soldier sat, the back of his armor scraping the concrete wall. "I need to rest."

"I do too." Michael sat and closed his eyes, faking exhaustion.

Several minutes later, he heard the soldier snoring short, loud sounds.

Michael leaped over the soldier, partially leaning into the opening of the room, and without making a sound, he scurried through Pilate's mansion. He heard faint background noises of people speaking. He knew he was a marked man if he left, but he would be dead man if he stayed. He had to concentrate on his end game: find Elizabeth and get back home.

Michael snuck by the last remaining guards as the evening commenced in Jerusalem. He raced past a cluster of Roman soldiers drinking and laughing wildly, their boisterous boasts of maiming or killing the locals screeching, disturbing the silence of the night.

Michael was dressed in his dull red garment he wore on his last trip to Jerusalem. It was dirty, grimy, and faded in color. He ignored his split pinky toe, still oozing blood through the dirt-covered foot. He darted up a back stairway as another group of soldiers—sober, he determined—drew closer. Michael watched them from a second-floor balcony and hid behind a short concrete barrier.

He breathed a sigh of much-needed relief and refocused his emotions to gather up a revised plan to rescue Elizabeth. He stood quietly, still jittery over being spotted, and listened for any distractions or chatter. He heard only quiet and turned to his right and ducked his head into the room, his ears picking up a man's voice. He took a few steps down the dirty hallway and, with one ear, peeked into the room.

Can it be? One. Two. Three. Four. Five... Eight, nine, ten... Wow...is that...it is...it's Jesus!

Michael stared. Men sat silently at the long concrete table, stunned. Peter and Paul flanked Jesus. *Peter. My goodness. That night we talked. After he denied Jesus. He's going to go through hell tonight. Again.* Michael took a deep breath. *Paul. The trip we took. All those conversations. He won't even remember meeting me.*

Jesus held the chalice, and Michael could see he was talking. Michael bowed his head as he had done thousands of times when praying. He took a couple of steps closer, his entire body now in full view. Bam.

Judas slammed into Michael and glared, his eyes raging with contempt. He pushed Michael to the floor. "Get out of my way," he said. His eyes flashed evilly. Judas struck him again in the chest.

Judas glanced back toward Jesus and the apostles and ran.

"Judas!" Michael shouted, realizing he could grab some money from him to help rescue Elizabeth.

He rushed out of the room after Judas. He zipped and zagged through the narrow, curvy streets of Jerusalem before coming to a rest for a moment. *Where is he?* Michael breathed deeper. "Wait," he said, while taking a couple more steps in a less enthusiastic fashion. "What do I do if I catch him? What do I say?" he questioned in a whisper.

He heard a commotion and ran toward it, breaking his trance. "There he is," Michael said out loud. "Hey, traitor."

A group of men handed Judas a cloth bag. It jingled as Judas grabbed it. He grinned an evil smile.

It was all going to begin again. The whippings. The blood spilling. The crown. The thorns. The mocking. The beatings. More blood. Pain. Suffering. Sadness. Tears. The images jolted Michael back to reality.

He had witnessed it before when he traveled through the old church basement in Northport. It was still fresh in his mind. *Why did he have to suffer so much? What was the point of this?* Michael questioned for far too long. He reflected some more, observing the crystal evening sky above him that was filled with shooting stars. A noise nearby made him dance behind a tall concrete wall. He watched several men walk toward the Garden of Gethsemone near the Mount of Olives. It was dark, so dark all Michael could see were heavy, defined shadows milling around the Garden. Michael moved closer. *There they are! The apostles!* Michael waited. His heart pounded, waiting for Judas to arrive. Adrenaline surged through him. *Stay awake! He needs your help.* Michael breathed a sigh of frustration, turning back away from the Garden, pinned against the concrete wall. He spun back a few minutes later, noticing most of the apostles were sleeping. Jesus prayed. Michael watched and wrestled with the reality.

The only way to rescue Elizabeth is to pay people off. Gold and silver speak in this time. My God, I'm sorry. I can't lose Elizabeth. I can't go through that agony again. Lord, please forgive me. I need Judas' help.

A crowd arrived, surrounding Jesus. He looked forlorn, expectant of what was to happen. A tear dropped onto Jesus' cheek. He stared at his traitor. Judas approached. Jesus did not move. "Do what you need to do."

Caught off guard, Judas wavered and glanced at the Roman soldiers, then back toward Jesus.

"Why do you hesitate?" Jesus asked.

Judas stepped away, unsure.

"Do as you have been paid."

Michael yelled, "It's blood money!"

A Roman soldier was alerted, and Michael hid, then peeking out.

Judas approached Jesus again.

Jesus winced.

The kiss.

The apostles awoke from the commotion, brandishing swords and knives. One soldier lost his ear, and it fell to the ground, gushing blood.

Jesus picked up the ear and placed it unscarred back on the soldier.

The Roman soldiers gasped.

"Arrest him!" shouted the high priests.

The Romans grabbed Jesus and hurried him away as the apostles scurried in different directions.

I hate Judas, but I need him.

Michael followed, stalking him as he watched the fallen apostle from a distance, figuring out what to say and what to do.

Judas ran to an abandoned field, grabbing a long piece of rope loosely attached to a fence, holding a gate closed.

"Give me the money!" Michael shouted.

Judas stormed toward him, placed his two hands around Michael's neck, and tightened his grip.

"Stop!" Breathless, Michael kicked at Judas, shaking away from his grasp. "Give the money back or give it to me."

"No," he said. "It is too late. The Romans will kill him. I have killed him."

Judas threw the bag of money. Michael gathered up the silver, and Judas placed a rope around his neck.

Michael held his hand up. "You don't have to do this."

Judas' eyes glistened. "Leave while you can. Before you are taken with me."

The ground shook under Michael's feet.

"What the...?" He picked up the rest of the coins and sprinted back to the Garden.

It was empty—as if nothing had happened.

Michael had no choice but to run back to Pilate. Perhaps the money he retrieved would convince Pilate to give him some help—any help—in finding Elizabeth. Maybe Pilate's sympathy toward him as a father would motivate his feelings.

Maybe.

He remembered Pilate was a macho type too, his ego clearly more of a threat than his desire to enrich his finances even more. Pilate had hopes of moving up in the Roman Empire, as Michael recalled from his previous research.

Elizabeth came first. He was a dad. Always. It's what defined him from the day he watched his first wife die. He had an obligation, a duty, even if it meant he had to die for Elizabeth.

He waited nearby, out of sight.

Pilate better accept my offer. If not...I'll take him hostage. And demand the biggest ransom, so much money Barabbas will free Elizabeth.

If Barabbas has her.

Perhaps I better look elsewhere to find help.

Chapter 5

Alarmed by a disturbance, Michael raced to see what the commotion was. All his senses were on high alert, the adrenaline surging through his tired body. He scouted the noisy event by sneaking behind a tall pillar holding up a small structure.

He recognized one man in the crowd, his face barely shown as a droopy brown hood covered everything but his mouth. Michael knew who he was from a previous encounter, from another time, yet ironically during this same time. This man wasn't any ordinary man. He was wanted. Perhaps one of the *most* wanted men in Jerusalem. Hunted by all authorities, his face was familiar to most Romans. Fear was now Peter's only companion.

Michael watched in sympathy for the plight the apostle was about to suffer. He always wondered when scripture described Peter's traumatic situation, why would he risk his own life congregating in a public place? Perhaps he thought it was easier to blend in among the people than hide.

He shook himself out of his trance, realizing Peter may be able to help him find Elizabeth. Peter always had his ear amid rabble-rousers and renegades. He would know.

Michael had to seek anyone who could help him.

Even Peter.

It was risky—dangerous even—to be seen with Peter. There was a heavy price on his head, Michael assumed. He knew if the angry mob that was gathered believed he was a friend of Peter's, his chances of survival were as low as Jesus'. Though it's not like they'd put up wanted posters with his picture on it.

He approached Peter quietly, hunched over and barely taking a breath. He shimmied up from behind and tapped gently on his shoulder, barely grazing his thick brown garment.

"Peter," Michael whispered. "Peter."

Peter stayed silent, his body frozen, stooped over.

Michael nudged him a bit harder yet still slight. "Peter," he said in a higher tone.

Thump. Peter struck Michael in the chest with his elbow.

Michael's hands bunched into fists, raised his arm, and stopped, rethinking his unplanned response. *Woah. Wait a second. Is this wise? Take a good hard look. Do you see what I see? Yeah, plenty of crazies looking for blood and a piece of anyone. Rebels and seasoned fighters just itching for a brawl. No. This is not wise.*

Still stinging from the blow to his chest and furious, Michael grabbed Peter's elbow. "Look at me."

Peter winced.

"Either you talk to me now, or the conversation here is going to get really loud. And I do not think you want that, do you? I know who you are. And what you're about to do."

Peter turned, lifting his brown hood slightly off his face, his eyes piercing and filled with raging anger, the moon's light painting a most treacherous look. "Sir, you do not want to challenge me on such an unholy night."

Michael did not back down from Peter's threat, remembering it was him who was in trouble the most. "Sir, you do not want to deny me what I need to ask of you."

Peter grew angrier. He glared, raised his hand as if to strike Michael.

Michael grasped his fist. "You are trying my patience. This will not end well for you. You are a wanted man. I am desperate for help."

Peter wrestled his hand from his grip and grabbed Michael's throat. His breath smelled, polluted from wine. He released his hold and moved back, standing slightly, and looked around nervously.

Peter then gestured to him to meet behind a small building nearby, pointing in the direction. Michael nodded and went to the agreed-upon place. Peter pulled down his hood.

"Sir, I do not know who you are, but leave here while you can. You are in danger. As am I."

"I cannot leave. Not yet," Michael said.

"Do you welcome death?"

"I don't," Michael said. "I mean, I do not. But I will give up my life for my daughter. She is in danger." Michael hesitated. "She may not be alive. But I have to find out. One way or another..." His words trailed off.

Peter looked away, staring at the mob gathering in the square. People were drinking and shouting, and small skirmishes broke out in the middle of the throng.

Peter was stoic, resigned perhaps to his fate. He would never live in anonymity again. He would always be on the run, looking to see who was behind him. Michael felt sympathy for him.

Peter rambled some words Michael could not understand. He paced back and forth several times, mumbling incoherently, even to a faint whisper. Michael heard the name Judas, betrayal, and we are all going to die. And little else.

"Peter." Michael took his hand. "Look at me."

Peter stopped pacing, his eyes filled with tears and sorrow.

"I want your help," Michael demanded. "Help me, and I promise I will do whatever it takes to help you as well. I promise." Then Michael became impatient and said what he thought was impossible, not really believing what he saying. "I will help you save Jesus."

Peter's eyes widened. He then frowned. "Lower your voice," he said in dismay, clutching Michael's arm. "Do you want to get us both hung? The Romans have spies everywhere, men looking for people like me."

"I just need your help. Or anyone's help. I do not know this town or the people like you do."

Peter laughed in silence and turned his back. "Do you think I can trust anyone now?"

Michael remained quiet because the truth would not give him any hope.

Peter faced him. "Do you? Do you really believe I can go to anyone around here for help or protection? I am a dead man."

"Jesus has many friends. Right? You do too. We need to go to your friends. I have money." He jingled the silver.

Peter clamped his hands, glaring, eying it. "How is this going to help my brother, Jesus?"

"I can bribe the Romans, pay off a few soldiers, and convince them to help Jesus escape."

Peter paced again, his fingers pulling at his scrawny brown beard, little streaks of gray peeking out. "How?" he asked, shaking his head. "How is that possible?"

"Sit. This may or may not work, but I need your word you will help me no matter what happens."

Peter nodded. "Go on. Speak, stranger."

"You know rebels, many of them. You know where they are. What it would take to help my daughter. What it would take to find her. I have the silver to make this happen. Please. Help me."

Michael was not sure if Peter was convinced. He sat and let the apostle reflect, pray, meditate. Peter gave a pensive look, giving Michael some mental relief, if for a moment.

"Where's your daughter?" Peter asked.

"I am not sure," Micbael said, standing. But I believe Barabbas has her."

Peter shook his head. "You are mistaken. I hear the Romans arrested him. There was no woman with him. But that does not mean..." Peter didn't finish his thought.

"Are you sure?" Michael asked.

"I heard from one of Pilate's guards that Barabbas is in prison. Your information is wrong."

Michael shook his head.

"I would know," Peter said.

Michael was distraught. Had he been so wrong? Was he deceived by the man who gave him this information? Michael had been duped by a few men who seemed honest on his previous trips. It was possible. He knew this. *Maybe the man had his own motives? Maybe he was a thief or even a murderer like Barabbas? What do I do now? Maybe Elizabeth has escaped? Be positive. Do not fall into this mental trap. You need to get back too. But I will not go back until I find out one way or another. Yeah, Elizabeth probably escaped. She's smart. Young. Strong. She's been here before. She knows her way around. Maybe she went back to Leah? She certainly knows the town and knows the safest places to hide.*

After deeper deliberation, Michael came to a hollow, inconclusive conclusion. So, he theorized out loud, pondering out-of-the-box solutions, making sure Peter could hear them in case he had something to contribute.

"My only chance now to find out where my daughter is…is to go to Pilate."

Peter grimaced, taking a deep breath, and Michael noticed his eyes moistened. "If Pilate has her, he will have her…" The last word trailed off, piercing Michael's heart. "…killed."

"No. I am not going there," Michael said, putting his hand up and looking away. "I do not believe you."

Peter stood and faced Michael. "You do not belong here. And if you do not belong here, your daughter certainly does not. You are running out of time, stranger. You best be on your way and seek other means besides running to the Roman butcher. You walk among evil. Good here is snuffed out, extinguished, hung until the last bit of love never sees the light. Darkness has covered us all. Run. Run, stranger, run until your legs cannot carry you one more step." Peter sat back down, his hands covering his face. "I cannot bear my heart to hurt anymore. I must go back before anyone suspects me being with you." He looked up at Michael, his gaze ghostly and staring off into the great beyond. Peter stood again, brushed off some dirt, and walked away.

"Run, stranger," he repeated. "Do not wait any longer. Run."

It's going to happen. Again.

Chapter 6

Several Romans surrounded Peter. A mob grew, shouting at the apostle. Michael walked closer, pulling his hood halfway over his eyes. "He was with the King of the Jews," one man said, slurring his words.

"I saw him too," yelled another man.

"I am not a follower of this man," Peter said.

A cock crowed.

"Are you sure?" asked one Roman soldier.

"You have me mixed up with another man," Peter said.

The cock crowed again.

"I am sure," a man said, turning to the Romans. "He is a follower of Jesus."

"This man lies," Peter said. "I do not know any man named Jesus."

The cock crowed thrice.

Peter pushed the man aside.

He ran.

Michael chased him.

Peter ran down the narrow streets.

Michael hunted him. "Stop, Peter."

Peter looked back, staggered a few steps. He collapsed and fell to his knees, covering his face.

Michael reached him.

Peter sobbed uncontrollably.

Michael went to him and looked down, ashamed of the critical views of Peter he held when reading the gospel accounts. He even boasted these disapproving thoughts to friends and judgmental ears—to anyone who would listen.

I'm ashamed. Peter is broken and destroyed. Who was I to be so shallow? All these years, I called him out to friends. I called him a coward and a fake when I am similar to him, as I would have also denied Jesus too, as I have rejected him many times before.

Michael's eyes stung from long ago tears unshed. He remembered his own fragileness that awful moment when the thought about ending his life consumed him.

My friend needs me, much like that dreadful night when I needed a forgiving heart.

Oh, what a terrible night it was.

What awful thoughts pierced my broken soul.

My God, what was I thinking? Was it you who knocked on my door that night? Did you knock to stop me from taking that belt, from tightening it around my neck?

Was it you who knocked a second time? Then a third? And fourth?

Was it you who kept banging on my door? Was it you who was there although I couldn't see you? Was it you who left that seashell on my doormat? Was it you who left it knowing how much I love that seashell because it reminds me of my favorite place, the beach?

My God, thank you.

It was you.

Are you calling upon me to help my friend?
If so, I am ready.

Peter continued to bawl, muttering incomprehensible words through his tears. He removed his soaked hands from his face. "My brother, what have I done? I am no better than Judas. My God, how can you ever forgive me for what I have done? How can you? I will never forgive myself, never, never...."

Michael took a few steps toward him. "We have to do something right now." He placed his hand on Peter's shoulder. "I am sorry. I truly am. I wish you could change it. We can help each other. Let me help you so you can help me."

Peter looked up, eyes red and moist, dripping into his brown beard. "Sir, what do you need of me in this most shameful time?"

"I can help you," Michael said. "We can change all of this. Help me help you. Please. Help me."

"You do not need to help me. I am a man who has committed the most horrific sin," Peter said. "I have denied my brother." His head sunk into his hands. "Jesus said I would deny him. And I did."

"I understand," Michael said. "But you are human. I've drank too much. Swore too often. Cursed God for the hurt I've had. Hated the life I was given. I gave up thousands of days blaming God, blaming loved ones, pushing away friends. All because I did not know how to appreciate the love I was given. Oh, Peter, if you only knew how many sunsets I have looked away."

Peter lifted his head. "Have you denied my brother too?"

Michael grimaced. "Yes, I have. I felt rage toward everyone when my Vicki died. I blamed and hated my God and my family and friends. I was filled with a bitterness not long ago when I thought I had lost my daughter. I hated God more.

I've hated how my father treated me, demeaned me. So you see before you a man who has fallen more times than I have stood. Hate and rage have been part of my life and also crushed with regret and remorse. That's what humans are all about; that is who I have been."

Michael knelt beside Peter. "Look at me."

Peter did.

"I have denied Jesus many times. I am ashamed too. So often, I hate myself. Can you believe even in the most beautiful moments I have been given, I feel I do not deserve such joy? I have spent too many days wishing I wouldn't have another."

Peter gave a puzzled look. "When did you meet my brother? I do not remember you. I would have remembered you. When? How? Where?"

"When and how and where are not important," Michael said in a quiet tone. "What you need to know is as bad as you think this is, you will heal. You have many sunsets ahead. You have many important sunsets in which you will reach people like me struggling with their lives, their faith. And you will teach and inspire and make an impact and carry everywhere you travel the word of love and forgiveness. You have much work to do. Important work. For all the rage and hate I had, today I stand before you a much better man, a man who loves in the true sense of the word. A man who forgives. A man who has finally forgiven himself for all the mistakes I made. Our brother would want us to do this."

Peter took a deep breath and wiped some lingering tears off his face with his sleeve. "How do you know this? Are you a prophet?"

"I am not. What you see is what I am. Frail at times. Scared. Angry. Happy. But most of all, I am hopeful. I am hopeful because of you. Because of our brother."

Peter sneered. "You are a false prophet. Leave me be."

"I am not a prophet," Michael said. "But what I say is true. I need your help. I need to find my daughter. She may be in trouble."

Peter dismissed what Michael asked. "I do not know you. You could be a Roman spy. Be gone."

Walking away, Peter paused and faced Michael. "Leave, stranger. This night is unholy."

Chapter 7

Michael moved with determination, grinding a short piece of metal, scraping the tip of one end into a grooved, sharp point, creating blips of fiery hot flashes. He admired the visual theater, delighting in his new level of valor. He tested the edge against the palm of his left hand, drawing a trickle of blood. Michael watched it zig-zag down his fingers and onto the ground, giving him immense satisfaction.

He slipped the makeshift weapon inside the inner lining of his garment, somewhat proud he found a secret room away from the Garden to manufacture it, the location given to him by Peter before they departed. He moved expertly through the darkened, narrow streets of Jerusalem, tiptoeing past several drunk, comatose Roman soldiers sleeping off their nightly hangovers.

The simmering torches, which lit some sparse sections of the street, were putting out their last flickers of light, barely illuminating the entrance to Pilate's fortress.

Much to his surprise, there was no chatter he could hear, not even sporadic conversation or banter among Pilate's usually gossiping guards. He waited until there was a change of shifts, snickering as he watched the sober guards help the others to their rooms. The timing was perfect.

That must have been some party.

He climbed the steep stairway leading up to Pilate's bedroom and stopped halfway.

A rat bigger than the ones he dodged in the New York City streets scampered toward him as if it was commanded. Michael gazed at the creepy rat as it crawled up his leg. *Spectacular. Of all the challenges I have to face in this forsaken, crazy world, now this? Okay. Enough. Time to show this rodent who's the boss.*

Michael flailed at it. The rat raced behind his leg and to the middle of his back of his garment. He could feel the sharp claws digging into it. He fell back on the stairs. *You've got to be kidding me.* Michael stayed calm, whispering to himself. "Okay, let's stay quiet. No need to panic. There's a rat on my back." He stood and spun around, twirling several times. The rat tightened its claws, burrowing into his shirt. Michael felt a pinch and a drop of blood.

He spun around many times, accelerating on each 360. The rat fell off, hitting the ground, stunned. "Stay away from me," Michael said, pointing at the dazed rodent. He raced to the top of the stairs and froze.

Michael watched the rat sprint up the leg of a soldier sitting on chair. The rat rested on his body armor beside him. "No." Michael put his hand out to try to halt the rat's ascension. "Stop."

The rat continued to climb, tickling the solder's arm, slightly awakening him as his eyes fluttered like shades going up and down in a cartoon. Michael sped behind him, tied a piece of cloth inside his mouth, and clubbed him in the back of his head with his hard object. The soldier fell sideways, still sitting in a chair. Michael pushed him up against the wall so he wouldn't tip over.

He breathed in deeply, his heart racing. He took a big gulp of courage. Michael barely regained some composure, the adrenaline flowing as he grabbed a weapon from the soldier. He straightened up, long spear in front of him, and approached Pilate.

He leaned down, holding the sharp edge of his weapon close to Pilate's heart. He thought about Elizabeth for a moment and slightly backed away. *What if...what if this isn't the best way?* He took two steps and pondered his choices.

Chapter 8

Michael immersed himself for a brief moment, gazing at the décor of Pilate's bedroom. The bed railings were gold, its mattress two King bed sizes put together, a silk cloth covering it. There was a table filled with gold trinklets and jewelry, pitchers of wine and fruit on another table. Pilate lived as he pleased.

Despite the grandiose setting, Michael's rage built as he lowered the sharpened edge, touching the flesh surrounding Pilate's heart. The Prefect's snores deepened. Visions of Elizabeth imprisoned flooded Michael's mind, adding more agitation and anger. The tip of the spear pricked Pilate's skin. Pilate stirred, his eyes flickered, and he turned over, undisturbed. He gagged and coughed a couple of times and sat up, his hand covering his mouth and his other hand pressing against a small pillow.

Michael turned and noticed the guard stirring. The Roman struggled to stand, woozy, holding his head as he fell back onto the wooden chair. He tried once more to regain his balance.

No, you don't. Michael raced to the soldier and swatted him across the back of his head with the blunt end of his weapon. The guard fell face-first onto the chair and then to the cement floor. *Good. That should hold you there for a while. Sleep well, swine.*

Michael took a relaxed breath but was short-lived when he heard Pilate yelling at him.

"What are you doing here?"

Michael faced Pilate and didn't answer, his mind searching for something plausible. Pilate stomped closer, trickles of blood dotting his garment as a glimmer of light from the torches donned the room.

"I asked you a question, stranger," Pilate asked, his eyes bloodshot and strained. "What are you doing in this room?"

Michael stood straight. "I'm here to rescue my daughter."

"She is not here. Now get out."

"No." Michael could smell the alcohol on Pilate's breath as he moved closer. "I need your help. Now."

Pilate looked incredulous. "At this time of the night?"

"My patience is running out," Michael said. "And remember this: there is no other prophet like me. I have proven this to you. I am here to collect my payment. Your help. Now."

Pilate took a few steps toward the lone window in the room. "Do you know who you are talking to? I could have you killed."

"Yet you have not," Michael went to him. "I know exactly who I'm talking to. I know much more than you think I do. I know more than all the people living in this forsaken town."

Pilate kept gazing at the clear dark sky, its landscape decorated with bright blue stars and a full moon so brilliant it illuminated all of the Prefect's frame. Michael was behind him.

"Answer me. Are you going to help me?" Michael asked.

Pilate turned. "And what if I do not?"

"I will have no choice."

"What choice would that be?" Pilate pushed him aside. "There are many more desperate men in this town. Some are spending their last sunrises. Would you like to be one of them?"

"Do not tempt me, Prefect, to give you the same justice you give to so many others."

"You are rather brave. A fool. But brave."

Michael ignored the rush of adrenaline flowing to his head. "Prefect, there is no other person here to help me. You are the most powerful man in this town. You will be a hero to save a young girl from those savages."

Pilate turned, his eyes glassy and sad. "I have indeed heard it all." He walked back to his bed. "But my head aches from your woes and some sour wine. I need to rest. We will talk at the next sunrise."

Irritated, Michael agreed.

"Is it your practice to knock out my guard with that weapon of yours?"

"I will do whatever I need to do to get my daughter home safely."

"Even kill me?"

Michael hesitated. "Of course not, Prefect. I cannot recover my daughter without your assistance."

Pilate smiled. "I am glad to hear you say that. I might need you to do something, though I am not sure you would be willing to do it."

"I will do anything," Michael insisted.

"Good."

Michael went to him. He had read in some history books that, while Pilate had a mean streak, he had some elements of compassion inside of him. "Anything, Prefect. Anything. Whatever you need me to do, I shall."

Pilate waved him away. "I need my rest. At sunrise, come back here, and we will talk."

"Yes, Prefect."

As Michael left the room, Pilate shouted, "Prophet, keep that so-called weapon away.... You are not like the prophets in this land. They do not believe in force. I am glad you are like me." He paused. "But do not even think about using any more force on my soldiers. They will not hesitate to kill you if you dare to use that weapon again. But you amuse me. So here I let you stand before be."

Pilate scoffed.

Michael mocked him. "Do not test me. I will not hesitate either, sir."

Chapter 9

Michael lay on a clean concrete floor surrounded by several tall pillars, its surface perhaps prepared for Pilate's arrival, brightened by three torches lit and held in equally impressive stands attached high in the hallway. Pilate was not far, resting on the next floor. Michael knew he needed patience and deceit in dealing with the Prefect. Pilate was an impatient man, violent and without accountability, sometimes spontaneous, and obsessed with power.

Hungover Roman guards sleeping nearby temporarily comforted Michael, for he knew as long as they were unresponsive, he wouldn't have to defend himself. Still there was apprehension swooning over him, his mind restless and rambling with many gruesome scenarios. *What will Pilate demand? What task could he possibly ask in this treacherous town? Will he ask me to steal for him? Spy for the Roman Empire? What if...no. He wouldn't ask me that. He already stated prophets are non-violent. But I already showed him I can be violent.... Oh, great. Stop. Stop this thinking. Try to rest.*

Michael stared up at the smooth granite ceiling, admiring the structure and design. *Must have cost a fortune. No surprise. They're perpetual thieves. They take what they want, whether it's gold or flesh. No wonder these thugs are admired by dictators everywhere. Doesn't matter whether you live in the 1st century or the 21st century.*

His mind swirled again with wild consequences. His body was provoked by waves of adrenaline, and he swelled with anxiety so strong it gave him the urge to march in a circle, stopping briefly to slow down the dizziness. Michael leaned against the wall and slowly slid down, his back scaping its rough surface, and closed his eyes to rest for a moment.

He felt someone tap him on the shoulder, and then hands touched his face. "Michael, wake up," a voice said.

He rubbed his eyes with the sleeve of his grimy shirt. "Who is that?" He sat up. "Who is there?" He squinted and tried to make out the face. "Is that you, Pilate? I'm sorry for dozing."

"No. It is me."

Michael's eyes widened. "Is this a dream?"

"You are not dreaming," the voice said. "Lower your voice."

Michael wiped his eyes one more time. "I must be dreaming."

Chapter 10

L
eah hugged him, holding him tight. Her smile widened.
Michael was surprised. She led him past a lone guard,
who looked the other way.

"How? What just happened? Did I see right?"

"I gave him some gold," Leah said. She stopped outside the
Jerusalem wall, holding his hand.

She leaned down and sat next to him.

"How did you know I was here?" Michael asked.

"Word spread in my village that they saw you heading to the
city wall. Your story about where you came from still puzzles
me. But I see you as an honest man, Michael. A good man. We
shared much talking on the rooftop."

He forced a smile. "We did share our hearts. Our losses.
Our grief." He sighed. "I'm happy you came. Your neighbors
are good people."

"They saw how happy I was when you were staying with me.
They thought we were together." Leah smiled again and blushed.

"Oh. I am sorry."

Leah shook her head. "There is no need to be sorry. I explained you were a long-lost cousin who was visiting me."

"I am grateful we met."

"As am I," Leah said. "Where is Elizabeth? Did she leave when you departed? I want to say goodbye to her. She is the daughter I never had. So young. So energetic. So loving."

Michael's head hung. "I do not know. Somehow, I lost track of her—of where she went. She has her own mind. Her own ambitions. When we were taking our trip here, we were overrun by these bandits. They took everything we had. I was knocked out, and when I regained consciousness, Elizabeth was gone. They left me a note to bring gold to get her back. I do not have any gold."

Leah gave a sorrowful look; her eyes cried. "What are you doing here?"

"Pilate said he would help me if I do him a favor," Michael said, trying to convince himself this was his best option to find Elizabeth.

Leah shook her head again. She didn't need to say anything. Michael knew.

"I know," he said. "I know. I have no other choice."

"Have you tried other ways?" asked Leah, holding his hands.

"I have tried every way my mind can think of."

Leah sighed. "You must find another way. Pilate is a murderer. He will murder you once you give him what he wants. And who knows what he will want from you?"

"I know the risks," he said. "But the risks are worse if I do not try and hear what he has to say. Maybe he will be sympathetic to me."

Leah shook her head again. "He has no heart. No soul."

"I know all about Pilate," Michael said. "I have read much about him. I know about his daughter and the man he wants her to marry."

Leah backed away, giving a confused look. "Are you a Roman?"

"Oh, no. No, no, no."

"Then how would you know this?"

"Remember what I told you about where I come from?"

"Yes…"

"I have acquired knowledge unfamiliar to your world. I just know. But anything I say will only complicate what you can understand."

Leah returned to him, caressing his face with her hands. "I may not understand what you say. I do understand who Pilate is and what he has done to my people."

"I don't disagree…I mean, I do not disagree."

"Then you know he will betray you once he has everything."

"It is my only choice, Leah." Michael tried to banish those words from his mind, for he knew this was a one in a hundred chance of making this work with Pilate. Yet, the one he knew he had was better than anything he possessed now.

"This is no place for a woman of my faith," Leah said, standing back up. "I will find you the next sunset and only in the dark."

She kissed him on both cheeks and smiled. "I am filled with joy to see you are alive and healthy."

Michael hugged her. "I am too. You touched my heart. I need your help."

"What do you need?" she asked.

"I need a weapon. Big enough to kill. Small enough where I can hide it under my clothes."

Leah gave him a confused look. "Why?"

"Do you really want to know?"

Leah nodded. "Is it the Roman soldier? Marcus?"

His eyes widened. "Marcus? The soldier that wants to marry Elizabeth?" Michael paused. "It's all making sense. I thought he was killed. No. I'm back in the same time. When he is alive. Has he been by your home?"

"He has. He showed me a wedding ring he said was yours."

He still has it.

Chapter 11

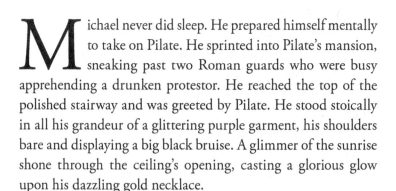

Michael never did sleep. He prepared himself mentally to take on Pilate. He sprinted into Pilate's mansion, sneaking past two Roman guards who were busy apprehending a drunken protestor. He reached the top of the polished stairway and was greeted by Pilate. He stood stoically in all his grandeur of a glittering purple garment, his shoulders bare and displaying a big black bruise. A glimmer of the sunrise shone through the ceiling's opening, casting a glorious glow upon his dazzling gold necklace.

"My friend, I see your bravery is at a high peak. I hope you slept. Were you comfortable?" Pilate smirked and stalked toward Michael. "Come, join me in private. I believe we have much to discuss."

Michael followed him and entered a beautifully decorated room, its four concrete arches neatly stretched apart, condensing an otherwise spacious area. Pilate went to the lone window and faced him. Michael could see the wrinkles under his eyes were more defined, his eyes were weary and drawn, and perhaps there was even some powder on his face. *Do I see what I think I do?*

Really? Pilate? A man's man? Violent. Ruthless. Makeup? Really? How vain. Look into his eyes. Show him you're not intimidated by his power. Don't blink. Keep staring. Romans respect strength.

Michael glared, his fists clenched, his mind ready to instruct his hands to grab his weapon Leah had given him. He walked to Pilate, inches away. "I am here to find my daughter whether you help me or not," he said in a demanding tone.

Pilate's eyes widened. "Is that so?"

"You're wasting my precious time. What do you need me to do?" Michael asked.

Pilate walked past him. "You will go to the prison basement."

"Yes. And?"

Pilate leered. "You are determined, my friend."

"I am not your friend. What do you want me to do so you can help me find Elizabeth?"

"Elizabeth. What a lovely name. She must mean the world to you?"

Michael fingered his knife, gripping it. "She is everything to me."

"And you will do anything?" Pilate asked.

"Anything." Michael's voice rose. "I'd give up my life to spare hers."

"I am impressed with your resolve. Though the way you talk alarms me."

Frustrated, Michael gritted his teeth. "I may use different words than you, but I love my family like you love yours. I would defend my family like you defend yours."

Pilate strolled a few yards into another room and Michael followed. Pilate grabbed a piece of fruit from a bowl sitting on a ceramic table. He threw it up in the air and let it crash to the floor. He mashed it. "You know, when you are Prefect you have to be prepared for every situation."

"I understand."

"And you are correct," Pilate said. "I have had to defend my family. There was a time not long ago when my wife was assaulted. She was badly hurt. Thankfully, she has recovered. But I knew that she was hurt because of my decisions. It is one of the toughest things to go through—leading the people when your loved ones are hurt because of what you have done."

"I know," Michael said.

"You know? How does a man of your stature know this?"

"I know about loved ones paying for my decisions."

"In what way? Curb my curiosity, if you will."

"It was my decision to visit a friend here, and I took my daughter." Michael finally realized the truth of his actions. The hallow words crippled his heart. "It was my fault. You have made mistakes. Right? I read about the time when…" Michael stopped, realizing what he was about to say about Pilate's eventual downfall hadn't happened yet.

Pilate hiked his thick eyebrows. "What were you about to say?"

"I misspoke."

Pilate sneered. "You seem to do this often."

"Prefect, how can I convince you?"

"It is a time when a man becomes desperate when we are confronted with such hardship. I took vengeance. I got revenge. I made sure anyone who might have done this to her met their god. I did not care about the consequences. Would you do the same? Take vengeance? Not care about the consequences?"

Michael hesitated, unsure what Pilate was trying to convey in his ruthless, violent thought. "Yes."

"Hmmm," Pilate said. "You do not sound sure."

"I am sure. I would take vengeance. Tell me."

Pilate grinned. "What if I told you Barabbas raped your daughter?"

"I would rip his tongue out and cut his—I would kill him, ten times over."

"Kill him and do for your daughter what I did for my wife. Kill him twice for bragging about it. Kill him three times for doing it night after night while you were looking for her."

"Where is he?"

Pilate summoned a guard in the hallway. "Come here."

The guard bowed.

"Show this father to Barabbas, the man who raped his daughter and had the audacity to encourage his other murderers to do the same."

The guard nodded and straightened up.

"Give him your spear. Let him leave his blood on a Roman weapon. No one is to know your task. These are my orders." Pilate pointed to Michael. "Take your vengeance. Let him know no man, especially a thief and murderer, can put his hands on your daughter. Let him know this as you plunge that weapon into his heart. I will see your daughter is found and returned when you have done this."

The guard instructed Michael to move toward another stairway at the far end of the hallway. "This way." He pushed Michael down the stairs.

"Remember your daughter," Pilate shouted from the top of the stairs, his words echoing. "Remember how he touched your daughter. How she cried. How she pleaded for him to stop. How that murderer raped her."

The thought infuriated Michael and anger raged inside his heart, and his soul blackened as he was led away and down into a sweltering dungeon. The smell was putrid and pungent, usually repulsive to him. His fists tightened, and he struck the concrete wall with both hands.

"Give me your spear," Michael said, clutching the weapon so tight his knuckles turned white. He held it up. "I will take every last breath out of that rapist monster."

Chapter 12

I mages of Elizabeth and Michael decorating the Christmas tree dashed through his fragile mind. Watching her play the flute and then the violin at the school concerts. Celebrating her first goal in soccer. Tearing up as she walked with her classmates at the high school graduation. He smiled, then grew sad, despairing living those days knowing she was not with him anymore. *Oh, God*, he thought. He lurched forward, remembering how the grief was too unbearable. How he was ready to rip the world apart piece by piece. How he spent years on his knees in front of that grave weeping, inconsolable, dismissive of Leah's offers to help him. How he remained in their world to make sure Marcus was killed. It seemed so long ago, yet felt like it didn't even occur...and it hadn't.

"Kill him," the soldier implored. "Do what the Prefect orders. Take revenge for your daughter."

Michael clenched his long sharp weapon in both sweaty hands. Moisture from his forehead dripped down to his nose and slivered to his lips from the oppressive heat of the jailhouse dungeon. He glared at Barabbas; rage rose inside him.

The soldier sneered. His teeth, yellow and chipped with one missing at the front, distracted Michael for just a moment.

"What are you waiting for?" The soldier took a big gulp out of a water jug, eliciting a sound of satisfaction. "Kill him."

His voice annoyed Michael. The soldier continued to laugh and take surges of swigs, three or four at a time. The smell of whiskey polluted the air, adding to the already foul odor of blood and death. Michael measured his weapon as Barabbas finally stood, his thick black beard bounced, and his eyes menaced him.

Think like a Roman soldier.

"Sit down," Michael yelled, drawing a big laugh from the soldier and an equal one from Barabbas.

"Hey, Roman," Barabbas said. "You sent this to kill me?"

"Shut up, murderer," the soldier shouted. "You are fortunate he is going to take your last breath. If I was given this honor, I would make sure you suffer."

The soldier took a long gulp. "Kill him," he repeated, wiping his whiskey-stained lips. "Your spear is long enough to reach his heart."

Michael thrusted the spear toward Barabbas, who quickly moved away from it, mocking him.

"Ha! You will never get to me," Barabbas said with an evil and confident smile.

Michael swung his spear wildly, banging several times against the metal bars protecting Barabbas. Some of the wicked clangs ignited short flashing sparks. He chased Barabbas from one side to the other several times, like a windshield wiper swatting a bug. Michael's face pressed up against the bars, pushing the spear closer and closer. Barabbas laughed louder until Michael pierced his shoulder, drawing blood.

"You will die for this," Barabbas said.

"The only heart that will stop here is yours," said Michael. "You are about to meet your devil in hell."

Michael darted back and forth, slipping and sliding a weapon toward Barabbas, occasionally catching a piece of his body. Exhausted, he stood back for a few moments, panting like a dog on a hot summer's day. "There has got to be a better way than this."

"There is not," the soldier yelled. "My orders are for you to kill him this way while he is in his cell."

"Why?" Michael said. "Why does it matter how he is killed?"

"I do not ask the Prefect why," the soldier responded. "I just do. So do as he says, or I have orders to kill you both."

Michael turned toward the soldier. "Try me."

The soldier picked up a nearby long spear and sword.

Michael gathered his breath, sighed, and held the spear chest high and pointing forward. Barabbas raced toward him, and he pulled the spear back, falling down. The soldier laughed, bending over. "You are going to have to do better than that. Let me show you."

The soldier carefully demonstrated how to hold the spear, approach the cell, and slide the weapon from top to bottom utilizing different angles. The soldier nailed Barabbas in the stomach, drawing a bigger gush of blood. Barabbas fell to the ground, hands on his fresh wound. "That was for my brother," the soldier said.

Barabbas laughed and groaned. "Your brother was a bandit just like me, so I rid the world of him. Less competition for me." He flashed a wicked smirk.

The soldier grew angrier and poked Barabbas again, just below his waist. Barabbas winced and fell sideways, moaning.

Another soldier hearing the uproar ran over and pulled the soldier away from the cell. "Leave him be," he said. "The Prefect was clear it must be the stranger that kills him."

"Why does it have to be him?" the soldier said in a sinister tone.

"The Prefect has his reasons. Do what the Prefect has ordered, and you will be rewarded."

"My brother is right," said the soldier, dropping his weapons. "It is you who should be given the honor and duty of killing this murderer."

The other soldier gave an encouraging tap and walked away.

Oh, the irony of this, Michael thought. *The irony of it all. The irony of this town and time.* Barabbas did not move. Michael slowly slid his weapon through an opening, directly toward Barabbas' heart.

"Kill him," the soldier said in an excited voice.

In war, we kill. In defense, we kill. No one will ever hurt my daughter again in this world. Let God judge me if need be. I accept my judgment.

"What are you waiting for?" asked the soldier, moving closer to Michael. "Do it now. Do it for your daughter. Do it to the bastard who raped your daughter."

Barabbas was still breathing, somehow smiling, goading Michael to come after him with his hands.

"What are you afraid of, stranger?" the soldier asked. "He is like a pigeon without wings."

Michael moved closer.

"Kill the bastard," the soldier whispered in Michael's ear, his tone chilling his heart. "Kill. That. Rapist."

The last three words blackened Michael's soul more.

He took a deep breath, pulled his spear back, and whacked the soldier in the head. The soldier staggered a few steps away. Some blood trickled to the floor. Michael followed him and from behind, smashed his head with the blunt part of the weapon.

The soldier fell face first, a most dangerous thud that echoed in the dungeon. *Move. Quickly.*

Michael took a quick glance to the left and right. He fell to his knees and rummaged through the soldier's clothing, grabbing the keys. He unlocked the cell door and stalked Barabbas, his weapon ready to attack.

"Tell me where my daughter is." Michael pressed the tip of his spear into Barabbas' heart. "Tell me now, and I will let you live. Do not tell me, and I will take your last breath."

"Does she talk strange?" Barabbas asked.

"Yes."

"Is she young?"

"Yes."

"Her name is Elizabeth?"

"Yes."

Barabbas played with his beard for a few moments, drawing Michael's frustration. "Where is she? Tell me." Michael pressed deeper on his chest.

"Let me think," Barabbas said, wiping some blood off his hands. "The name is familiar...how did she cry?"

"What?"

"Did she cry like this?" Barabbas made a mocking sound. "Or did she cry like a baby? Like this." Barabbas squealed in a higher tone.

"Stop! I will kill you."

"You will never kill me. You are not from here. My friends will find you if you do. Then they will kill you and your daughter."

"One last time." Michael pierced his skin. "I will kill now."

Barabbas slowly got up. His bloodshot eyes widened. He grinned, and the blood on his teeth sickened Michael.

Michael glared.

"I will never tell," Barabbas said.

Furious, Michael pressed the tip of his weapon deeper into Barabbas, drawing even more blood.

Barabbas sent him back against the metal door with swift kick and raced toward Michael. Michael raised his weapon, and Barabbas plunged into it.

Barabbas gasped as he fell backwards, the spear impaled in his neck, creating an open wound. He fell to the ground, drowning in his own blood, breathless.

Michael pulled the weapon out of his neck, and Barabbas gagged, blood dripped out of his mouth, and his eyes glazed.

Michael heaved a heavy breath. "Burn in hell forever."

Chapter 13

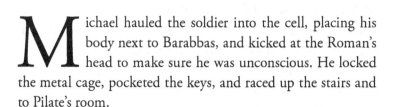

Michael hauled the soldier into the cell, placing his body next to Barabbas, and kicked at the Roman's head to make sure he was unconscious. He locked the metal cage, pocketed the keys, and raced up the stairs and to Pilate's room.

Pilate was engaged with a scantily clad woman, her bronze earrings dangling as they conversed in a hush. He had changed his clothes and was wearing a bright red outfit. A thick necklace sparkled with sprinkles of gold glitter.

Michael did not wait for Pilate to finish his discussion. "Prefect," he said in a defiant tone. "I have done what you have requested."

Pilate turned toward him and smiled. "Prophet, you surprised me. You are unlike any prophet I know in this land. Many condemn me for my love of brutality. I did not think you possessed the courage to carry out such a task."

"Prefect, you must live up to your part of the deal." Michael noticed how young the woman appeared, her dark brown hair without any strands of gray.

Pilate whispered some words to the woman, and she gave him a kiss on the cheek, touched his hand, and left. He faced Michael. "You must forget what you have just seen."

"I don't care about that. What about your promise?" Michael asked.

"I live up to my word," Pilate said. "Where is my soldier?"

"He is sleeping off his obsessive drinking," Michael said.

Pilate frowned. "I have grown tired of my guards being derelict of their duties. He will pay the consequences of not fulfilling this important mission."

Pilate walked to the opening of the room and called for another Roman guard. He waved Michael over. "Soldier, you are to take my new friend through the tunnel." He turned toward Michael. "Give him a description of your daughter."

"About this high," he said, pointing to his chin. "Hair to her shoulders. Blue and purple colors on the tips of her hair."

The soldier gave an incredulous look. "What?"

"I know. It's the style."

"Where is this style?" the soldier asked.

Pilate interrupted. "Enough." He gestured to the soldier to leave. "Take him as far as you can and return. We need everyone here. We can expect a rebellion upon announcement of that rat's death."

The guard straightened up and saluted.

The soldier turned to Michael. "Follow. Do not leave me."

"I wish you much fortune in your travels, my friend," Pilate said, shaking Michael's hand.

"We are not friends."

"So be it. I wish you and your daughter good health."

Michael sighed. "If we find her."

Pilate smiled. "You will. Listen to my soldier. He knows the fastest ways to find her."

"I hope you are right," Michael replied, displaying some doubt.

"I am never wrong," Pilate said. "Right, soldier?"

"Yes, Prefect," the guard shouted back.

Michael was unable to find any reassurance from Pilate's perceived confidence. Numb from the intense encounter with Barabbas and the soldier in the dungeon, he was anxious to leave.

As he walked with the soldier, Pilate called out, his eyes menacing. "Never come back, my friend. For you will be a marked man." Pilate laughed, but Michael was too entrenched in his thoughts about Elizabeth to care even a little.

I know all about what happens to you. You will deserve every bit of pain you will suffer. Oh, how I wish it was much more than history has written.

The guard took him down another stairway in a secluded part of Pilate's mansion. The area was well lit with torches hung on magnificent stanchions placed strategically every ten yards or so, its walls made of shiny, polished marble.

Michael marveled at the architecture of such a time before recapturing his composure. "Where are we going?" he asked the guard, who was moving at a brisk pace.

"To a place only a few have gone and many have not returned," the guard said.

"Now, you are talking in riddles," Michael said. "Can you not answer such a simple question?"

"You speak oddly for a man who lives here."

"I do not live here. I live far away."

The soldier stopped. "Does the Prefect know you are not from here?"

"Keep going," Michael said, waving him on.

"You do not give me orders," the soldier said in an agitated voice. "My Prefect gives me orders."

"Not for long," Michael said, letting a subconscious thought finally slip out verbally.

The soldier gripped his spear tightly. "What is your intention?"

"My only intention is to find my daughter," Michael said, trying to defuse the situation.

"Then think this only," the soldier replied. "Only this."

Deep beneath Pilate's palace they went, the air thinning out as each step down they took. Sweat poured off Michael's forehead to his face. "How much farther down are we going?"

"We are here." The soldier removed his metal helmet and wiped the sweat off his face. "I need a moment to catch my breath."

Michael wandered a few feet away, finding a long, vast hallway dimly illuminated by some flickering torches. He could not see where it led but knew there was a long walk ahead. He returned and pointed in that direction. "Is this where we are going?"

The soldier put his helmet back on, picked up his spear, and nodded. "Yes. Follow me."

So Michael did. For many steps and what seemed like miles. "How much farther?"

"Until we find your daughter." The soldier turned around and smiled. "Is this not what you want?"

"Of course. Is she nearby?"

"Not far from here."

Michael jumped in front of the soldier. "So you know?"

"Move, stranger." Michael stepped aside. He became suspicious. They had not seen anyone during the long journey. Not even a rat. Not even a bug. Nothing. Absolutely no living creatures but themselves.

"How much further?" Michael demanded again.

The soldier stopped. "I am tired of your questions. I am thirsty. I am hungry. I have taken you as far as I can go. I need to protect my Prefect. It is the most dangerous time. Here is where I leave you."

Michael grabbed the soldier's shoulder. "I do not know my way down here."

The soldier struck Michael in the side of his head. His ear felt the brunt of the end of the weapon, and he bled. His head ached, and he caught droplets of blood in his right hand while his left hand comforted his ringing ear. He stumbled a few steps and leaned his shoulder against the wall—the Roman left in the opposite direction.

"Why are you leaving me here? Where do I go? How do I find my daughter?" Michael shouted above the sharp, high pitch screeching in his ear. "Please," Michael continued, trying to run toward the soldier. He fell. Bloodied and out of breath, he closed his eyes for some comfort. "Please, sir. Please. Help me…Help me find my Elizabeth."

He was not sure if the soldier heard his pleas. He got up and held onto the wall. Michael regained his composure and shook his head several times, trying to silence the ringing. *Now is not the time to worry about this.* So he walked forward and walked and walked until he heard some muffled chatter from above. He stopped and strained to hear what was being said, placing a hand over his damaged ear.

He continued to walk until he could not go any further. He swung the lit torch side to side to see if he could find any opening. Michael sighed and took a few steps back from the end wall. He again swung the torch side to side, searching for any hint of a door. He then held the torch high, checking the ceiling first, then forward and backward.

Michael noticed a slight crease several yards away from the end wall to his left. He gently put his hand on it and pushed. It opened. He peeked through and saw a stairway. Sliding his body through, he made sure he closed the makeshift door, leaving no sign he was there. He did place a thumbprint near the door and in the shadows as a marker.

Michael walked up the filthy concrete stairway, taking brief breaks from the strenuous climb. He lost count at sixty steps upward and grew frustrated as he gasped for some breaths in the dusty, grimy, thin air.

Am I still in Jerusalem?

Chapter 14

Faint chatter from above sounding like voices singing in unison drew Michael up several more steps. A slight sliver of light slipped through an opening from above, encouraging him to think the treacherous trip was almost over. The singing grew louder and louder and louder, and the glow shone brighter and brighter. The words echoed. *Jerusalem. Jerusalem. Mighty hearts unite in the night. Mighty warriors gather for the fight. Victory is nearby. Bloodshed can add fury to our fire.*

He finally reached the last step and rested. Weary, his heart was beating as loud as a heavy metal rocker's drum.

He took several deeper breaths, fingered a sharpened rock he had pocketed on his crazy climb, and pushed on the opening. He rose into a room, believing himself unseen. Michael stared ahead, unconvinced his eyes were seeing what was before him. The tiny room, shiny marble walls surrounding him, was inundated with several tables with piles of gold, silver, and trinkets.

Michael moved swiftly to the next room. The singing grew louder and became familiar. Something he heard Leah sing when they sat on her rooftop at night.

"Do you wish to pray?" a man dressed up in holy garb said, entering the room.

Michael stumbled in his response, barely audible. The man repeated his question louder.

"I do," he said, disguising the truth.

The man waved to him, leading Michael to a large area. "This way."

Men and women were gathered, some in silent reverence, others whispering prayers. A tap on his shoulder startled him. "Michael," a voice said in a hushed tone. "Pray with me."

He turned, mystified. "Leah, what are you doing here?"

"Come with me."

Leah led him out of the area to a secluded room and touched his hand. "Why did you come here?"

"I had no choice," Michael said. "Pilate had a soldier take me into a long tunnel."

"Tunnel?"

"Yes. I came up from it and into this place."

Leah kept looking behind her to see if anyone was listening. "As you can tell, this place is our Temple."

"I realize that now."

"Not many know of our tunnel," Leah said.

"It's how I got here and past everyone. I will show you."

"No," Leah said, gripping his arm. "You must leave. You are in much danger. You being here is putting us in danger."

"Why?"

"You do not know?"

Michael shook his head.

"The Romans were just here and asking about a stranger who is searching for his daughter."

"I guess I am a stranger, and I am looking for Elizabeth. But how do they know it is me?"

Leah tightened her grip on his arm. "Do not deny what is real."

"Tell me."

"Shhh. They will hear you." She looked back at the opening of the room and spoke in a low tone, almost a whisper. Michael leaned closer to her, his arm around her back. "You are wanted for killing a Roman soldier and a hero of the people, Barabbas."

Michael scowled. "I did not kill a soldier," he said in a slow, measured pace.

"Did you kill Barabbas?"

"I had no choice."

She pulled on his arm. "We must get you back home now."

"Not without my daughter."

Leah shook her head. "You need to go. Pilate is devious. He has set you up. If you do not leave, you will be killed."

Michael yanked his arm away from her. "I will not leave until my daughter comes back with me."

"Do you know if she is even still here?"

Michael frowned.

Leah sighed. "I know. I will try to help you. I know someone who can locate her....if she is here."

"Why didn't you tell me the last time we saw each other? And who is it?"

Leah hesitated. "You were talking strange. You confused me. I did not know if I could trust a man whose memory was short."

Michael slowly nodded.

"We need to go now." Leah led him swiftly from room to room, stopping where the gold, silver, trinklets, and treasures were stored.

"We need gold to rescue Elizabeth, if my intuition is correct," Leah said. "Gold talks here, Michael."

" But is this is stealing from the house of God?"

"No, it is borrowing," Leah said. "We are getting Elizabeth back in return."

Chapter 15

Leah led Michael down another tunnel, grabbing two torches hung near the entrance of the Temple. She held his arm as they navigated the musky, dark walkway, littered with wet dirt and multi-colored pebbles. Michael flinched a couple of times, remembering the days of being a single parent and stepping on Elizabeth's Legos. For just a moment, Michael recalled how he used to implore her to pick up those annoying pieces.

"We have a long walk," Leah said, breaking up Michael's short foray into yesteryear. "Take your steps slowly. When you need to take a breath, let me know. Keep your torch to the side. I will keep mine in front so we can see where we are going."

Michael nodded, not even knowing whether Leah saw him do so. "Are you sure this will lead us to Elizabeth?"

Leah hushed him. "I believe so. Keep your voice low. We are traveling beneath many Roman buildings. They are looking for people like us."

"People like us?" Michael said. "What do you mean, people like us?"

"Like you. Like me," Leah said, turning to him, her light blue eyes twinkling in the fiery light from the torches.

"I do not understand," Michael said. "I am not like anyone here."

Leah shook her head. "You are more like us than us."

Michael sighed. "You are talking in riddles now. I am from another land. Another time. Another culture."

Leah laughed. "Now you are talking in what you call... riddles?"

Michael was uncertain of how to respond. "How much further do we have to go?"

"Stay calm," Leah responded. "These people do not know who you are or what you have done." She paused. "I am hoping that is the situation."

"Why is that important?"

Leah kept walking and stayed silent.

"Leah, tell me," Michael pleaded, moving in front of her. "We never keep anything from each other. Tell me the truth. I can take it."

Leah took a deep breath. "Michael, you were made a fool. Barabbas was a hero to the people."

"I know he was a hero to some, not all."

"He was a hero, Michael, because he fought the Romans. He was not afraid to kill them and risk his own life. The Romans are brutal oppressors. They had you do their dirty work." Leah held his hand. "Now the Romans will chase you, hunt you like they hunt us rebels. They will do this to show the people they will protect them against people like you. Even a bandit like Barabbas."

Michael shook his head. "I had no choice."

"It does not matter. Pilate knew you were desperate."

Michael sighed. He released her hand and walked a few steps forward. "It is what it is. I cannot change it now."

Leah caught up to him. "That is not the problem."

"What do you mean?"

"We must keep walking. Faster," Leah said. "We are losing time. Think of a plan in case they find out about you."

"Leah, stop, just one moment," Michael said. "Tell me what you know."

Leah stopped, put her fingers to her lips. "Listen closely. Elizabeth is with a group of rebels, people like Barabbas. People who want to overthrow Pilate and the Romans. And they will not stop until they kill Pilate."

"So you know. Is she safe?"

"Yes, for now," Leah said.

"What does that mean?"

"It means you must let me help you, or neither you nor Elizabeth will make it out of here alive. Can you not be stubborn for once and let me handle this?"

Michael was silent and nodded slowly, not sure if he was just doing so to placate Leah.

"Good. You must listen to everything I say. I will go to where she is. I will find out how much they know about what happened to Barabbas. I will get Elizabeth out of there when it is safe."

"But that's dangerous for you and Elizabeth."

"It would be dangerous for you too. You are not only a wanted man by the Romans but also by the rebels. Do you want more danger to fall upon you and your daughter?"

Michael froze in the thought of not being able to take action to help Elizabeth. He had gotten to know Leah on trips to Jerusalem, but he didn't know who she was now. She'd changed from being a meek widow to someone involved with an underground element, fighting Pilate and the Romans.

He was not sure what to believe or if he had any more confidence in Leah than he had in himself.

Chapter 16

Leah guided Michael deeper and deeper below the city of Jerusalem. What once were big bursts of crowd cheers and jeers above became muffled, then whispers, then dead silence. The air was thin, musky, and dusty from the dry dirt being kicked up from their brisk pace. The torches, still raging, gave sufficient light as Michael labored to keep up with the younger Leah.

She was much fitter than Michael thought; her gray over-dress covered her frame. Some wrinkles had even disappeared from what he remembered from his last trip. She was different, somehow. More elusive. He was older. Yet she wasn't. Or perhaps he was just misreading it all. Time travel was taking its toll on him and not her.

Michael leaned over. "I need to catch a breath."

"We cannot stop—we are running out of time."

"One minute. I'm not as young as when I first met you."

She turned around. "What are you talking about?"

"We are older. Older than the first time I saw you."

Leah gave him an anguished look. "I do not understand. I do not know you from another time. Are you confusing me with someone else?"

Michael rubbed his forehead, some dust smeared as it mixed with sweat. "I'm sorry for the confusion. I keep forgetting."

Leah shook her head. "I have only known you and Elizabeth for a few sunsets. I only know what I heard from the other rebels who told me about this strange girl from another town. I am guessing it is Elizabeth."

Michael winced. "We are back, back for the first time meeting you. Just in different circumstances."

Leah gave a puzzled look.

"Yeah, I know—no need to discuss this any further. I keep getting mixed up. Sometimes a light bulb goes off and on, and I lose my place with my slow-moving mind." He laughed. She didn't.

Leah pulled him forward. "Let us keep moving."

"How much farther do we have to go?"

She reassured him with the touch of her soft hand. "Not long."

A deep sorrowful feeling engulfed him. Who was Leah really? Could he trust her? All of these spontaneous thoughts leaped at him, spinning the worst of possibilities that she was leading him into a trap.

It struck Michael as odd and at the same time frightened him as to why she was assisting him. "Why are you helping me?"

"Why?"

"Why are you helping me, a stranger from another land, another time?"

Leah looked confused. "I thought it was apparent."

"Enlighten me. I am a bit nervous with someone I do not know. Or I do not know as well as I thought."

Leah moved closer, her eyes piercing his. "You are a father looking for his daughter. I feel your anxiety in my heart. Come closer to me."

Michael did.

"Closer."

Their lips almost touched, and Leah took his hand and placed it against her heart.

Michael could feel the rapid beating.

"Do you feel this?" she said, pressing his hand harder.

"Yes."

"What do you feel?"

"Your heart."

"Yes, I know you feel my heart. How does it feel to you?"

Michael hesitated, unsure where the questioning was going. "Fast."

"I am scared to be with you as I am a widowed woman living in oppression. But we have spent some sunsets together and shared some of our pains, so I know you are a good man, a good father who loves his child, his daughter. This is enough for me to help you. Enough to help your daughter."

Michael nodded.

Leah grabbed his hand and pulled him forward. "No more stopping."

"Perhaps I can call us an Uber?"

"What is an Uber?"

Michael laughed.

"What is funny?" she asked.

"Someday I will explain it to you."

A faint pinging sound could be heard, making Michael curious. "Do you hear what I hear?"

"Of course. I am not deaf. I am able to see, hear, and think."

Yes, that's Leah. He smiled again, making sure she did not see him do so.

The pinging sound grew louder and louder each step they took. It shrieked, echoing slightly in the tunnel. Leah turned to him. "We are almost here. Let me do the talking." She put two fingers on his lips. "Hush. Do not identify yourself. I will do so. Do you understand?"

"I do."

"Good. We cannot afford to make any mistakes." She turned to him again. "Or you, your daughter, and I will not make it out of here alive."

Michael affirmed the seriousness of her statement with a thumbs up.

She gazed at him and shook her head. "You are from another land…."

"I am ready to do what is necessary."

"Whatever you do or say," she said, gripping his hand hard. "You do not acknowledge her as your daughter."

"Why?"

Leah gave him a frustrated look. "Please. Just do what I say." She tightened her grip on his.

"Okay, okay, I understand. Whatever you say."

"Good." She released his hand, and they climbed a short stairway. The pinging sound was blunt but loud like metal striking metal. Leah and Michael were met by a shaggy-looking guard grasping a long, sharp spear. He pointed it at them. His dirty, dark black beard with some strands of gray was scraggly and going in all directions.

"Woman, stranger, what is your business here?" he asked, his dark brown eyes ominous.

Leah bowed, and Michael did the same, leading to a quick startled glance from her. "We are here to help the cause. Remove the oppressors. Kill Pilate. Kill every Roman until they are gone."

Woah. What the...? Michael's heart raced. *What am I getting myself into?*

The guard disappeared into an adjoining room. Intense heat swept over Michael as a gust of wind suffocated his common sense. Sweat poured off his face. He wiped his eyes, removing some of the moisture. His heart pounded; he could feel some of the beats skip. *Oh, great. Now is not the time to lose control. Calm down.*

He spun around to see if there was a place to sit down. He staggered to a lower step. Dizziness struck, and he held onto the gravel wall with both hands.

"Michael, Michael," Leah said, her voice faint.

He turned, and she faded into darkness.

Chapter 17

M ichael struggled to breathe. He gasped and choked and coughed and waggled his arms like a lone desperate kayaker paddling upstream in a hurricane as a couple of men dumped buckets of water on him.

"No more." He wiped the moisture from his face. Three men, their hands bloodied and dirtied, smiled, their chipped and missing teeth startling him. "Stranger, what is your name? What are you here for?"

"What?" Michael said between coughs. "I don't understand."

One man waved away the other two. "Bring the woman," he said forcefully.

Michael tried to straighten up more but felt lightheaded. So, he leaned back to stretch, gaining some composure. Leah was brought in; her worried face gave Michael a grave feeling. "Is this your sister?" the man asked.

Michael finally cleared his eyes. Leah gave him an approving glance.

"Yes."

"You are here to help our cause? To kill the Romans. Drive them out of Jerusalem? Kill Pilate?"

Michael took a short glimpse at Leah. Her response was fleeting.

"Yes."

The man smiled and grabbed his arm. "We welcome you, my brother. We have a big battle ahead. Prepare yourself. Make your weapons."

"What? Where?"

"Come with me," the man said. "What is your name?"

Michael again locked eyes with Leah. She gave no facial expression or sign. *Now what. What do I say? Think. Think. Think quickly.*

Michael feigned coughing, held his chest, and grabbed his throat. Holding up his right hand, he staggered. "Water," he managed to say. "Please. Water."

He fell sideways. "Help. Please. Help. Please...."

"Someone help him!" Leah screamed, running over.

The man ran out of the room. Leah leaned down, her eyes watering. "Are you all right?" she said, rubbing his back.

Michael looked up and smiled. "Give me the Oscar. Let me take that walk on the red carpet now."

"What?" Leah stepped back in disbelief.

Michael stood and bowed as if he was acknowledging imaginary applause from an audience. "What do you think of my acting performance?"

Leah struck him in his right cheek.

"Woah," Michael said, touching his bright red face. "That hurt."

"Good," Leah said, her eyes throwing bullets his way. "Do not scare me like that. I thought you were in ill health. Even worse, I thought you were dying."

Michael felt his face blush, ashamed like when he faked he was ill to his Mom in third grade so he wouldn't have to take a test. "I'm sorry, Leah. I didn't mean to frighten you."

"Well, you did. Do not ever do that again. Or if you must, wink."

"I was not sure what name I should give them," Michael reasoned.

There was a moment of silence between them. Leah then nodded. "They do not know you."

"So I just say 'Michael?'"

"Yes. For now."

"Why?"

Leah looked behind her. "Pilate has told his soldiers to kill any protestors. They want to make an example out of you to appease them...us. People like us. All of us here."

"What is here?" Michael asked, trying to figure out who knew who and what group he was involved with now. "And where is Elizabeth? Is she here?"

"She is," Leah said.

Michael put his hands on her shoulders. "Where? Tell me? Now."

"Keep your voice down," Leah pleaded.

"Where *is she*?" Michael demanded an answer. He grimaced, his shoulders tightened, and he straightened up.

The man came back into the room with a bucket and a ceramic cup. Michael faked some light coughing.

"Here, my brother," the man said, handing him a cup of water.

Michael looked at the cup, noticing some slight dirt residue sticking to the bottom.

"Drink it," Leah demanded, her eyes widening.

Michael gave an anguished face. He took a sip.

"Drink it all," Leah pleaded.

"Can I get something to eat?" Michael rubbed his stomach. "I haven't eaten a good meal in many days…um, sunsets?"

"Do you think you need…" Leah started to ask.

Michael put up his hand, rubbed his stomach again. "My brother. I can use a piece of bread or two."

The man nodded and left.

Leah approached him. "What are you doing?"

"I need to get rid of him, so I can get some concrete answers."

"Do not agitate the people here," Leah said. "If they find out who you are, you will be killed."

"I am not," Michael said. "I want to see Elizabeth. Does she know I'm here?"

Leah shook her head. "She is a strong woman. You should be proud. The men here respect her for what she has done for us."

Michael gave an incredulous look. "Done?"

"Yes."

"What has she done?"

The man returned, interrupting Leah's answer. He had two pieces of bread, its mold visible to Michael.

"Oh, my," said Michael, lurching forward.

"Eat it," Leah said.

He touched it, repulsed by the hardness. He broke off a small piece away from the green part. *Do I have to eat this?*

"Would you mind if I can have a cup of wine?" Michael asked.

The man gave him an exasperated look.

"You do not need to do that," Leah said, with a frown.

"It will give me the energy I need to kill those bastards. I will need it to fight the Romans and kill that dictator Pilate." The man smiled and left.

"What are you doing?" Leah asked again, measuring each word, her eyes piercing his.

"I could care less about fighting the Romans or killing Pilate. My only worry is Elizabeth. You can either help me or leave."

Leah shook her head. "You do not know what you are involved with now. You just cannot take your daughter and escape. It is much more complicated. If I left you, you surely would die."

"Then tell me, Leah. Tell me what I should expect. And tell me where my daughter is."

"I cannot take you to her. I am not a fighter. Your daughter is."

Michael was furious. "No. Elizabeth is not a fighter. She doesn't believe in violence. Or fighting. Or killing."

"You may think this is so where you live. But where we live, this is our way of life. You have to kill or be killed."

Michael put his head into his hands. "You are mistaken. It cannot be her. I refuse to believe it." He looked up. "Please let it be somebody else."

Leah moved closer, her head sideways to his, her mouth to his ear. "Listen to me. Do what they say. They are planning to kidnap Pilate. When you go with them, you will find her. Leave when you can. They want revenge for Barabbas' murder."

"But I did..."

Leah put her hand over his mouth. "You must never..." she paused, "never, ever admit you had anything to do with his murder."

Michael's eyes widened.

"And you must never show you know Elizabeth. Never."

Leah continued, "Never even say Barabbas' name. Do you understand?" She removed her hand from his mouth. "Do you?"

Chapter 18

I *see this man. Not like any man I have met or seen here.* Leah watched Michael rest. *He tells me he knows who I am. How, though? Where have I met him before? Was he sent by Yahweh? To comfort me. To heal me from my loss. Would the Romans send a spy like him? He does not look like a spy. Yet he speaks in a foreign tongue.*

He is kind. Loves his daughter. Speaks of his family fondly. He also speaks of a wife he has lost. I guess he found another wife? Did he take the sister of his wife like we do here? He did not say so.

His land he speaks of is unfamiliar to me.

I will watch him.

Make sure he is sleeping and not spying.

I must be careful. The Romans are everywhere.

Looking for his daughter.

Leah shook her head and looked away from Michael.

God, give me peace.

God, give me strength.

God, give me courage.

God, give me courage to kill...if necessary.
And kill a Roman.
For I demand my justice.
Please forgive me God.

Chapter 19

The sound of metal striking metal greeted Michael as his newfound brother in war encouraged him to make his weapons. He expertly sharpened a long spear. After his own spirited effort, Michael was escorted to a fiery furnace where all sorts of battle aides were made and prepared.

Men of all ages customized their weapons of choice, each bragging that the blade they had forged would kill the most Romans. Many knives were made thick, and fewer were thinner. "Like this, brother," a young man with barely any stubble on his face instructed. "The thinner, the better."

"Why are many making them thicker?" Michael asked.

The young man gestured to him to move closer. Michael did.

"They want to make sure the thickness pierces a Roman's heart. The elders say a man who murders many Romans will find a place in God's Kingdom."

"Isn't that the objective?" Michael asked. "To kill?"

The young man flashed a devious smile. He lowered his voice. "Sure. But I would rather have it thin, so I can pull it out and kill many more."

Michael didn't respond.

The young man showed him a shortcut to make the blade narrow, sharp, and small enough to keep hidden. "We can kill more Romans with this." He raised a thin knife, its tip jagged and sharp. He held out his hand. "My name is Saul," he said.

"I'm Michael. I mean, I am Michael." They shook hands.

"Glad to have you here, brother," Saul said with a big smile. "You are new here?"

"Yes."

"Ask me anything," insisted Saul. "Let me give you some battle advice. When you engage with a Roman soldier, come up from behind." He demonstrated the maneuver.

"Then go for the neck," Saul added. "Over here in front, they are protected with steel. The easiest way to kill is from behind, and you slit their dirty throats. Frontal attacks are ineffective."

Michael was unsure whether to thank him or just be afraid. His thoughts went to a previous battle with a Roman soldier on another trip to Jerusalem. *Marcus. That Roman soldier. The one who will not stop chasing Elizabeth...me...Leah...I wonder if I will see him. He's around somewhere. I may have to kill him again. Another battle. More bloodshed. But necessary. It's the only way to make it back safely. Marcus can be beaten. I've done it before. I will do it again.*

He strolled around the big, heated room, occasionally wiping some perspiration off his forehead. *Finding Elizabeth should not be hard. How many women are here? I don't see any. I could ask about her, but that may expose me, her...and Leah. Be careful. Like Leah said. She's lived here longer. Put away your ego.*

Michael gave a thumbs up to Saul as he came upon him, hiding his weapons. Saul gave him a puzzled look and kept placing the rest of his short knives in areas only a skilled warrior could.

Could Leah be with Elizabeth? I do not see Leah either. Looks like every rebel in Jerusalem is in this room.

He watched the men working at a fast and furious pace. They seemed to be blinded with faith that their weapons and manpower would be enough to take on one of the most ruthless and brutal armies in human history.

Do they really think they can battle Pilate and his soldiers? Michael shook his head in disbelief.

Make sure you blend in with these rebels. Keep your talking to a minimum. Do not let anyone know that you know Pilate. You will be seen as a traitor.

Michael kept his eyes everywhere, looking sideways, behind him, and straight ahead while engaging with Saul. He liked his new friend. Seemed like a decent guy. Normal. For here. In this time. In this town. Someone he'd go out for a beer with back on Long Island.

They each made four weapons. Michael followed Saul's advice of making the knives sharp, short, and thin. He prepared himself mentally for confrontation. *I will have to kill if need be. I know, I know. It goes against what you believe. Then again, I killed Barabbas. What you were taught. Do not battle yourself with this, or you will never find Elizabeth. But do everything to sneak away and find her. Anything.*

Michael made two more small knives and managed to pocket them without it being noticed. Saul was impressed and gave him an encouraging pat and some last-minute instructions.

"Do not hesitate to use your weapons," he said in his most solemn tone. "Your life is most important. They are crooks. Scoundrels. Rats. Lower than bugs. Kill them, brother."

His voice picked up more passion. "They have killed our children, raped our women, and then murdered them. Ruined our temples. Stolen our hard-earned gold and silver."

Saul took a breath. "Kill them. Make them suffer the way they make us suffer. Make them bleed. Show no mercy."

Michael waited for Saul to say more. He did moments later. "Never show mercy," he repeated. "Mercy is a weakness here. The Romans devour weakness. Do not let them see you as weak."

Saul paused. "Do not..."

"Show mercy," Michael said.

"Time for some killing," Saul said with a burst of enthusiasm.

Michael followed Saul to another room, relieved he was out of the heated area. They came upon a bigger group of rebels forming a circle. In the middle, a man with a cane was surveying them. He appeared to be the leader, though fragile and elderly. He spoke in a forceful yet measured tone as he mapped out the intended plan.

"Group one will cause a distraction. The goal is to draw the Romans' attention. Make this distraction as loud as possible, as real as you can make it be. Draw each other's blood to give it credibility." There were a few seconds of silence. "Are you group one?"

Several men shouted, "Yes."

"Group two," the man continued. "When the Romans move to break up the distraction, move quickly and attack them from behind. This will draw the next section of Roman security to help their fellow rats. Once this happens, run to the outside wall and keep running. This will make the next group's task easier. And run in different directions. Discuss this among yourselves. Give me a show of hands on who is in group two."

Many hands went up.

"Good," the man said with a burst of pride. "That is the perfect amount of manpower. Here is the most important part of our plan. Once that stairway has been cleared of most of the Roman soldiers, you must fight. Fight until your last drops of blood are spilled. Until we have a free path to Pilate."

Oh my. Michael's mind wandered back into this wicked world.

"You are to take Pilate," the man continued. "If he resists, make him sleep with force. Take him back here, and we will wait them out for a while before we give our demands. We cannot fail this time. More importantly, do not let our people down. Our women and children need us to be victorious."

Wow. This is suicidal. We are all going to get killed. How do I get out of this madness? He glanced at Saul. Michael saw a face of glee—no fear. His eyes were filled with anger, devoured with the thoughts of revenge.

Michael scanned the room to see if Elizabeth was here. He could not locate her or any female.

"Who is in group three?" the man asked, shaking Michael out of his mental demise. The man raised his cane in a show of strength. Only four men, including Saul, raised their hands.

Saul turned to Michael. "You are with us."

"Me?"

Saul pointed at him. "You."

"Oh…"

"Raise your hand," Saul said.

Michael did so.

"There you are." The old man hobbled over, smiling, showing two missing front teeth, causing Michael to relieve himself of some anxiety with a chuckle.

"You are a brave man to volunteer to take this big role. May God be with you. May Moses and Abraham provide you courage for your soul. May David be in your heart."

The group cheered wildly. The old man raised his cane and kept shaking it up and down, drawing a bigger response. Michael was bewildered. He rubbed his eyes. Faded images of fuzzy, twinkling stars showered him. He bent over, feeling the jagged edge of one of his hidden knives. A trickle of blood snaked its way down his leg.

He gathered a deep breath.

"Are you all right, Brother?" asked Saul.

Michael waved back. "I'm fine."

"You do not look fine."

Michael wasn't.

We're committing to a death sentence. They don't know any better. They're crazy. The Romans will massacre them. How am I going to stay alive? And find Elizabeth?

Chapter 20

Under the cover of darkness, the band of rebels navigated the short, narrow roads of Jerusalem, stopping every five or six streets to scout any danger. Michael could tell the members of his unit were nervous. They were young. Some were boys. Their faces expressed angst. Some were likely heading into their first battle. Perhaps they'd never fought a Roman before—only heard about it from the older warriors. They weren't a ragtag company, but the experience was limited.

"Keep your eyes in the back of your head," encouraged Saul in a whisper. He went to one boy. "Noah. This is your time. You will avenge your brother's death. Are you ready?" he asked, holding Noah's shoulders tight.

Noah barely blinked and nodded.

"Good." Saul pushed him back. "Take your vengeance, for it is much deserved."

Saul turned to Michael. "What about you, brother? You look like a man with experience—a man who has killed before. Are you?"

"Why do you ask?"

"I noticed that you ran more backwards than you did straight ahead. How odd you did that. Why? Is this some new military ploy?"

"It's a habit I've developed over the years."

Saul scrunched his thick eyebrows. "Where did you develop this habit you speak of?"

"In New York City. People tend to do that after growing up there."

Saul looked confused. "Where is this New York City?"

"The Big Apple. Broadway. Big buildings. Noise. People walking fast."

"You are a warrior unlike any I have known."

"I realize what I have described is odd, and maybe one day, I shall explain. But right now, do not worry about me," Michael said. "I will fight, and I will follow your lead."

"One day, I hope to understand some of your words."

The rebels in front of them moved, so Michael and Saul did the same. It was almost sunrise. Light peeked out slightly. The attack was strategically timed as outlined by the leader, the old man with the cane. "The Romans are lazy. They live their lives for gold, silver, women, and drink. We will be ready, more prepared after our sleep without any indulgence," he preached. "They will not be ready with the poison in their blood from the parties. We are better prepared than the Romans, and that will enable us to kill them and drive them out of our city."

Michael knew the strategy was the most effective in battling such a fierce army given his knowledge of the Romans and his previous encounters. He knew the Roman soldiers were notorious boozers. Pure drunks, many of them—intoxicated most nights. Michael was surprised the rebels didn't try at an earlier hour.

The rebels halted their march not far from where Pilate and his entourage were sleeping. They rested behind a small concrete building, two large light red arches rising high to hold a wider ceiling. It looked new to Michael, though he struggled to decipher the markings on the front.

Michael's vision challenged him at this time of the morning. "Saul, what do you see up there?"

Saul sneaked a quick glance around the side of the building and shook his head. "I do not see any Roman dogs."

"Well that is good." Michael felt hopeful that the rebels would retreat since the plan didn't call for attacking if the area was vacant.

Saul looked solemn and more dejected as time moved on without any signal from the leaders in the front.

"What's going on? Is something wrong?" Michael asked.

Saul peered toward the front and sighed.

Sitting across from him, Michael noticed his pensive expression. "Talk to me. What are you thinking? Be honest. Our lives are at stake. We need to know." Michael gestured to the others in the unit.

Saul stood and rubbed his forehead. "I will let the top group leader decide what to do."

"That's not a good answer. What are you worried about?"

Saul hesitated and again took a peek. "I am a paranoid man, Michael," he said, his back to him. "So my thoughts are not the best to listen to. At least not at this time. Someone wiser than me has the power to choose what we do." Saul faced him. "My brother, sometimes I am cautious. I have been told this. Mensah has encouraged me to take risks. Because without risks, we will not be able to regain our right, our city, our way of life. It is why Mensah makes the important decisions and planned our strategy. He has seen more battles than all of us. He knows the Romans better than me or anyone I know. I trust his plan. I trust Mensah."

Michael put his hand up and measured his words. "I get it. That's all well and good, but if you think something is wrong, then you should say something. Your thoughts matter too. You and I and all of us are putting our lives on the line. As far as I know, we only get one life, Saul. Just one life. You have to say something."

Saul didn't respond.

"I come from a place where we work together and help one another." Michael grew impatient. "My daugh—" he caught himself before finishing his thought. "Go talk to the leaders. You have a right to express your worries."

Saul left without saying a word.

Michael stepped out in full view. "Where are you going, Saul?"

Saul waved his hand back at him, gesturing to remain where he was. "Stay with the others. Wait until you see my signal."

Minutes later, the rebels in front of them fled forward. Michael looked at the three other men, their boyish faces masking fear, eyes wide open. "What do we do?" Michael hoped they would offer suggestions since they knew Saul better.

None of them offered guidance, and Michael's heart raced with trepidation. "We need to make a decision."

No one answered as they all clenched their weapons in silence.

Paranoia flooded his body. "Someone needs to decide. We can't let the men in front of us not have backup. They will be slaughtered if we don't. Hurry. We need to catch up to the next group."

They sped through the streets, pausing only once after hearing a nearby voice shouting something that prompted a nervous laugh from the three boys. He was just a drunk staggering to get home. They finally caught up to group two. Michael and the boys rested, catching a needed breath, not out of exhaustion but of anxiety. He also gained a vantage point to Pilate's residence. "Where are you, Saul?" he said in a whisper. "Where are you, Elizabeth?"

Group one went ahead and did what was planned, causing a distraction. Yet there was no Roman response.

So the groups reconvened on the side of Pilate's mansion. "We attack now," the main leader of the rebels said. "The Romans are likely too exhausted from their boozing and women to engage us with a fight. We can catch them by surprise."

Michael still could not locate Saul in the group of about sixty. *Where did he go? This is strange. Something's not right. I have a bad feeling about this all. The Romans may be drunks and women chasers, but they haven't stayed in power this long because they weren't prepared for any battle. No. This feels like a trap. The Romans were class A military strategists.*

The men were disorganized. The groups were mixed now. Rebels lost fellow members, and perhaps some had left. The leaders shouted out names to reorganize their units. A ruckus erupted in the distance. Several rebels had gone ahead. Shouting and screaming reached a high pitch, piercing the once peaceful morning. Romans came from the front and sides, surrounding and spearing the rebels the way they had sought to attack from behind.

The battles became hand to hand combat, the Romans in their protective armor, utilizing longer, sharper, more effective weapons. One rebel managed to grab a Roman, pull his helmet off, and threaten to slit his throat. A group of Romans surrounded him.

Michael snuck to another room adjacent to the stairway leading to Pilate's bedroom. *I have to stop this madness. I'll reason with Pilate. Too many are going to die. No. I can't stand by.* Blood was sprayed all over the stairway. Bodies lay everywhere—mostly rebels. A Roman soldier gurgled and pulled off his helmet, holding his throat. He pleaded for help.

Michael gasped at the horror of seeing bodies face down in puddles of blood and took deep breaths to settle his pounding heart. Adrenaline squeezed every bit of oxygen he needed, forcing him to rest briefly.

He could hear a commotion ahead and above. Michael gathered up enough strength to race up the last steps two by two. He stopped at the edge of Pilate's bedroom.

His mouth dropped, and he grabbed a knife from his pouch. "Saul. Elizabeth."

Chapter 21

Elizabeth was dressed like a character out of a Rambo movie, a piece of ripped cloth tied around her forehead, her arms bare and tense. She choked Pilate in a headlock. "How does it feel, Prefect? A woman has power over you. Feeling emasculated? This is for all the women you abused and hurt. I'm going to make you suffer the way you made others."

Pilate struggled to maintain his balance, his feet sideways. He gasped for air. Elizabeth dragged Pilate a few feet toward Michael.

"Dad! You're alive?"

Michael, bewildered at what was before him, stood stunned. "Of course, I am."

"This murderer told me you were killed."

Michael approached Pilate. "You liar. I helped you."

"Why would you help this killer, Dad?"

"I had to make a deal to find you," Michael said. "Are you part of a gang?"

"No, I came here to find you," Elizabeth replied. "This piece of garbage had me convinced I would never see you. Said you were hunted down because you killed Barabbas. I was ready to leave. But Leah…she told me…" She tightened her hold on Pilate. He squeezed out a couple of coughs.

"Now what? Do you have a plan? We are here with one. Right, Saul?"

Saul remained quiet.

"I…" Pilate fingered his neck, "…demand…you…" Pilate gasped, "… release me."

"You don't do the ordering around here now." Elizabeth pierced his neck with the tip of her knife.

Pilate wheezed for more air. "I will find safe passage for both you and your father if you take away that knife."

"No," Saul said. "Kill him. His blood shall spill where many of my brothers and sisters have shed blood."

Michael moved toward to Elizabeth, still shocked to see his daughter having a stranglehold on Pilate. "Lizzy, please. There's been enough killing. There are bodies everywhere. If I had my way, they'd be all Romans. There's more to this. History…"

"Screw history. Don't you think it's too late for that speech, Dad? Don't you know what this rat has done to the people here? How his regime kills and maims and intimidates the poorest of the poor. He is the worst of the worst. You know your history. You know this."

Michael wished he could dispute his daughter's assertions. He thought for a moment and took a deep breath, only wanting to diffuse an already horrific situation. "This is not our history," he said. "Not our place to be part of it. Eventually, Pilate will be overrun and exiled."

"What?" Pilate said.

Michael approached him. "It will not be long before you are removed. The rebels will throw you out."

"Is this because of the man, the Jesus prisoner?"

Michael didn't answer. "Let him go."

Saul jumped in front of Michael and challenged him, pulling out a knife. "If she will not kill this swine, I will."

Michael grabbed his arm. "Mensah said to take him as a hostage back to your hideout! You said you trusted his judgment."

Saul reflected, staying silent for several moments. He looked down and then up at Michael. He nodded. "Where will you go?"

"Home. Never to come back," said Michael.

"If you give me over to this enemy," Pilate said. "I will have my army track you down." His eyes seethed revenge.

"You are fortunate I have asked for mercy," Michael said. "Eventually, your army will be thrown out of Jerusalem."

Michael looked at Elizabeth. "Give Pilate to Saul," he told her. They exchanged Pilate. Michael and Elizabeth hugged. "Thank God, you are all right."

Elizabeth didn't answer.

"What's wrong?" Michael said.

She pulled away from him.

"Did they hurt you?"

Elizabeth shook her head, her eyes transfixed behind Michael. He turned slowly. Saul lay on the ground gurgling, struggling to get to his feet, blood pouring to the floor. He slipped on it, trying to regain his balance.

Michael ran to him and checked his pulse on his neck. "Oh, no."

"Leave now before your blood is shed. You are fortunate I have taken mercy on you." Pilate sneered as the blood dripped from his knife. "Go now. For you will be hunted and chased until they shed your blood and your family's blood."

"Why did you have to do this?" Michael pleaded to Pilate.

Pilate smirked then gave a surprised look, his eyes glazing over. He staggered forward a few steps and fell, a knife in his back.

Elizabeth twisted the blade.

Michael raced to Pilate, kneeling. "Help, Saul!"

Pilate stared, whispering some words.

Elizabeth went to him. "Saul's dead."

Michael stood. "We must go now, Elizabeth."

They raced down the stairs, passing hand to hand battles.

Three Romans spotted them leaving.

Michael shouted, "Pilate is in trouble. Help him."

Chapter 22

Michael and Elizabeth kept a brisk pace, avoiding big crowds, sure of where they were going: to the tunnel. Chaos surrounded them as combat spewed onto the streets. Men old and young fought the Romans in all their armor and weapons. The scene was brutal with blood splattering the grimy stone streets of Jerusalem.

He glanced at Elizabeth's scary stare as they approached their escape location. One lone Roman stood on top of the tunnel entrance.

Michael bent forward. "Let's take a moment to think about how we are going to get past him."

Elizabeth grabbed a knife from under her shirt. Michael looked up. "This is how."

Michael managed to straighten up. "There has to be a better way."

"From what I can see out there," said Elizabeth, taking a few steps in front of him. "This is the only way to get out alive in this place and time."

Michael's eyes widened, surprised at Elizabeth's conviction and bluntness. "Let me think. Just give me a moment."

"While you are thinking about some plan that may or may not get us home, we're losing valuable time to escape this crazy city. We will be spotted sooner rather than later."

"Enough is going on to keep the Romans occupied," Michael countered, trying to sound convincing. He turned to watch a fight between a Roman and rebel, each flashing sharp weapons. The Roman had a sword while the rebel had a rather lengthy knife. They ended up behind a building out of Michael's view.

Elizabeth was quiet. She pulled another knife from under her shirt tucked neatly below her beltline.

"Geez, how many do you have there?" he asked.

"Enough to get us out of this filthy madhouse," she said. "These people have no regard for life or peace."

"No different."

"No different from what?" Elizabeth said.

"Do you think this time and place is any more humane or civil, as you put this, than our time?"

Elizabeth pondered her father's thoughts. "I guess in some ways," she finally answered, "it isn't. In other ways, it is."

Michael stared at the podium where he first saw Pilate during their initial visit to Jerusalem. *I guess Pilate will not be there today to cast judgment.*

"It is Friday, right? Today?" Michael said to Elizabeth.

"What do you mean? Why?"

"Friday. Good Friday. From what I gathered in seeing the events of the last couple of days, this is Good Friday."

Elizabeth waved her hands in the air. "I wouldn't know. I've had a lot more things on my mind without trying to figure that out. You know, getting home. Finding you. Worrying whether you were alive or not."

Several fights spiraled out of control in the distance. Faint shouts and cries could be heard, and one Roman knocked a rebel down, then plunged his long spear into the chest of the fallen man. Michael winced and looked away.

"Dad, now is our time to do this," Elizabeth said.

Michael pulled a knife from beneath his shirt. "I will go first," he said. "If I do not make it, do not wait for me."

"Oh, no," Elizabeth said in a defiant tone. "We go together or not at all."

"Can you just listen to me for once?" Michael asked.

"When I listened to you last time, how did that work out for us?" said Elizabeth with a bewildered look.

"Touché."

Elizabeth hugged him. "We need each other. No more talk about separating."

"Oh, no...no, no, no," Michael said, pulling away from her.

"What?" Elizabeth said.

Michael pointed behind her. Elizabeth turned around. "Wow. I didn't think we'd see her again. But she came."

"She came?"

Elizabeth nodded slowly. "I told her where our tunnel was. She wanted to come with us."

"She can't come. She will never fit into our time and town. You know that."

Elizabeth sighed. "It was the only way I could get her to give me information and the only way I could get her to help me find you."

Leah was walking toward the Roman soldier, who appeared to not have a care in the world that this small woman was approaching him. The soldier even took his helmet off and greeted Leah with a smile.

"Okay, that's the signal," Elizabeth said.

"What signal?"

"Her hand, Dad. Her hand. She's waving it behind her back."

"She told you this?" asked Michael, unbelieving.

She turned to him. "We go. Now."

Michael joined Elizabeth, moving stealthily toward the distracted Roman and Leah. They stopped just about ten yards from them. Leah took several steps away from the soldier, smiling and talking, drawing him away from the tunnel.

Elizabeth jumped out. "Wait," Michael said in a high whisper. "We..."

She ran swiftly toward the soldier and blindsided him with a belt to the head. The soldier staggered, holding his head, mumbling. Michael knocked the Roman to the ground with the blunt part of his knife, and Elizabeth cut the soldier's hand, holding his weapon.

The soldier pushed Michael off. He rose slightly. Leah drop-kicked him in the groin. He fell. Leah struck him again, this time in the head. "Let's go," shouted Michael.

Elizabeth delivered three more blows to the soldier's head, knocking him unconscious. "Now we go."

Michael pulled the grate up. "Go. Hurry. Don't wait for me. Run."

Elizabeth went first. She waited for Leah. "Now," Michael shouted.

Leah jumped.

Michael followed her, quickly pulling the grate over the opening. "Keep moving," he pleaded.

"I cannot move that fast now," complained Leah.

"Why?" said Elizabeth turning around.

She pointed to her stomach. There was a gash. She pulled a sharpened knife from underneath her long attire. It was bloodied. "I am not well."

Leah crumbled to the ground.

Chapter 23

Michael and Elizabeth had become familiar with this trek in their back-and-forth visits. Secretly, Michael had taken two more visits to see Leah. But carrying an injured Leah was burdensome for him. He rested twice, out of breath.

This journey was also different, unlike the first trip he had taken. The tunnel was unfamiliar, and the terrain didn't seem right. Odd paintings and symbols inundated both sides of the walls.

The smell of the tunnel was musky and ripe, similar to a rotting, dead carcass. Michael stopped halfway through to catch his breath. "Keep pressing on that wound, Leah."

He glanced at Elizabeth. "We must get help," he said.

"Why?"

"We can't risk having her come up on the other side," he explained, bending over for another deep breath. He laid her on the ground. "The time when that Roman soldier came back... Do you remember?"

"No," Elizabeth said. "What happened? I thought you killed him."

Michael shook his head. "Nope. I told you that to keep you from being scared."

Elizabeth gave a frustrated look. "I'm not going to be scared. What happened?"

"I turned to see him coming up to the church basement. And voilà. He was dust."

"He was what?" Leah interjected.

"Dust," Michael repeated.

"Oh," said Elizabeth. "Yes. Leah. Stay here."

"You stay with her," Michael said.

Elizabeth nodded. "Bring water. Something for her wound."

"I will be back as fast as I can," he assured.

"I wonder if my phone works now," Elizabeth said. She pulled it out of a side pocket from her long garment.

Michael shook his head. "You are addicted to that thing."

Elizabeth shooed him away.

"Be back as soon as I can."

"You already said that. Go," Elizabeth demanded.

"We'll get it taken care of, and you can go back."

Leah gave a half smile.

Michael continued to move forward, searching for a security stick and lighter he had left behind in case he needed it. Aging eyes caught up to him. His vision was fuzzy in the dark, prompting him to stash some aids. He slowly took the next steps, falling to his knees eventually, pawing at anything he could get his hands on during his crawl.

Maybe I put it somewhere else. Further back? Further ahead? I am sure it was near this part of the tunnel. But this tunnel doesn't even look the same. Oh, I hope we didn't take the wrong one. Would there be another tunnel?

He grew frustrated, taking baby steps with his hands flying in all directions, touching stones and pieces of the terrain. *Maybe Elizabeth moved them? Perhaps someone else found this tunnel? I thought I had camouflaged the entrance well.*

He finally stood, giving up on his search, and wiped some dirt and what appeared to be soot off his knees and hands. The tunnel started to narrow. He kept his hands on to the walls to gain stability as his knees weakened from the many steps he had taken. Light illuminated a portion of the tunnel ahead. *I wonder what is going on today? Maybe there's an event? The weather has been good lately. Well, it's always good to see children and adults out instead of playing video games inside.*

"I'm almost there," he shouted back in the direction of Elizabeth and Leah, not knowing if they could hear him. "Keep pressing on the wound. And stay there."

He waited for a response but never expected one, the actual purpose being to take another short rest. Michael began his climb back up the stairs, leading to the church basement. He stopped briefly to look at some of the drawn images. *They must have done this while we were gone. I don't remember any of these when I came through last time. Maybe I'm losing my mind like Lizzy says. Or how does she describe it? Oh, right. Yes. I'm oblivious. Yes.*

He shook his head. *No. I'm not losing my mind. I would have remembered these images.*

Michael kept climbing until he reached the last few steps. He stopped before he got to the top, disgusted from the foul smell. *What is that? Is there some food festival going on? Has to be. Nothing that bad could be anything else.*

Man. Enough. Keep moving. Get help. Clothes. Water. Ointment. Something to eat…check.

Michael kept repeating it to himself. He made it to the last three steps from the top and stopped. "What the…" he mumbled.

It was near sunset. He looked to the right, then to the left, and spun to look behind him. Michael stumbled back down the steps, staying out of sight. He rubbed his eyes and shook his head.

"Am I seeing right? Did we come back in a different tunnel during a different time and in a different place?"

He sped up the stairs, peeked out again, and just as quickly went back down. "Oh, my goodness," he said to himself. "This isn't right at all. *Think, Michael. Think. What do I do?*

He went back up to the top step without any reason. "Where's the church, Main Street…the toy store? There aren't any streetlights."

Michael stood in a vast field. Corn stalks rose high for many yards in front of him. He squinted to get a view of the Bay. It was still there, giving him some sense of relief. He could see outlines of what appeared to be boats or fishing vessels, but he wasn't totally sure.

Michael retreated down. *I better talk to Elizabeth.* He half ran and half walked in a furious pace. Upon seeing them, Elizabeth greeted him in exasperation. "What happened? Where's the water? The meds? The food?"

"Stop. Let me speak," Michael said. "Something's not right."

"Yeah," Elizabeth said. "You don't have anything you were supposed to have."

"I'm not sure we are back where we are supposed to be," Michael said. "Maybe we came back at another time. I don't see anything familiar except for the Bay."

Elizabeth expressed disbelief. "What are you talking about?"

Michael waved his hands in frustration. "We aren't where we should be. That's all I know."

Elizabeth sighed. She grabbed onto his arm and dragged him forward. "Let's go," she said.

"What about Leah?" he asked.

Elizabeth turned to her. "She's fine. The bleeding has stopped. Rest, Leah, and we'll be back to help you. Whatever you do, stay there. Don't follow us."

Elizabeth pulled him forward some more. "We're wasting time, Dad. Are your eyes playing tricks on you again? Did you have something to drink before we went to the tunnel?"

"Granted, my eyes aren't what they used to be, and I get that blurriness every so often, but…"

"But what? You need to get that cataract surgery when we get back. ASAP. Ugh. Keep up with me."

She moved at an ultra-fast pace. They made it to the end in record time. Elizabeth climbed the stairs and reached the top step, joined by Michael.

Chapter 24

"Elizabeth?" He looked around, yelling, pleading, "Elizabeth, talk to me! Where are you? Please! Please, say something!"

He took a few steps forward toward where the corn stalks stretched high. His head swung like a swivel stick for several seconds. "Oh, God, Lizzy, where are you? Please, answer me! Can you hear me? Call out to me if you are trapped."

Billows of dark smoke rose high. A cool breeze whipped the toxic smell toward Michael. He stood silently, stunned, bewildered by what he just witnessed. He backstepped down the tunnel, eyes dazed, baffled at the vacantness of the surrounding landscape.

The sun had set and the early stages of darkness prevailed, casting an eerie glow from the first wandering waves of light from the moon. He tried to rationalize where Elizabeth might have gone. *No, I know what I saw. She disappeared into thin air! I am not dreaming. Right? Am I right? Did my eyes deceive me?*

He shook his head several times as if it would change what he saw. It didn't. He sat on the seventh step from the top of the entrance. Michael placed his head in his hands and talked to himself. "Let's be calm and think this out logically. We just came out into a different time. It has to be. I know we went down the right tunnel, and we are where we are supposed to be—where we should be. This should be Long Island. But where did everything go? Where did Elizabeth go? It doesn't make sense. Where in God's name did the church go?" He sat for a couple of minutes in silence.

"Leah…maybe she can help? How, though? What could she possibly do or say to help me?"

Michael retreated into the tunnel, and after more mind-confusing analysis, he walked briskly back to Leah. She was standing looking much better than before. The wound was gone. *How strange. Maybe she had something to heal it? The ointments she always spoke about on my trips. Maybe she wasn't exaggerating? The balms could have incredible treatment powers.*

"Michael, I feel different," she said, running to him. "Look. This is so strange." She appeared flustered, out of breath, showing him where the gash was before. Not a trace.

"My, you are healed," Michael said.

"I know," she replied. "I felt this deep shiver—cold, like my body had been in the sea. Everything went black. I thought I fainted. I could not see my hands or legs, but I know I was still here. A big wind swept me up."

"Up where?" Michael said.

"Into the sky."

"The sky?"

Leah nodded.

"What happened after you felt that?" Michael asked.

"I could see you. My wound was gone. No bleeding. No mark."

"Wait," Michael interrupted. "You didn't put any ointment on your wound?"

Leah shook her head. "I was waiting for you right here. I never left. Never took a step forward or backward."

Michael took a deep breath and leaned against the wall, then slid down to a sitting position.

"Where is Elizabeth?" Leah asked.

Michael shook his head. "I don't know."

"You do not know?" said Leah, pulling at his arm. "What happened?"

He gathered himself to his feet. "I have no idea."

"Go after her," Leah said, standing, shaking his arm.

"I don't know where to go."

"Go where you saw her last."

Michael sighed. "I did. I looked everywhere. And when I say everywhere…. It's all different back home. Nothing that was there before is there anymore."

Leah gave a baffled look. "What are you talking about?"

"The town I lived in for almost thirty years…I mean, where I lived in for many sunsets…is gone. Vanished. Everything. It should all be right up there." He pointed to the stairway.

Leah stayed silent for a moment. "You are not in the right town. You are mistaken. Confused. Retrace your steps."

"I believe I'm in the right place. It's just that the town is not in the right place."

"You must go find your daughter," she demanded in a solemn tone. "I must go back to my home. We must do what we always have done. Be with our families."

Michael could not muster up a response or any reasonable thought that could convince her or, more importantly, solve his dilemma. He pulled away from Leah's hug, giving her a soft kiss on her cheek. "Till next time, if there is another time," he said. She clenched his hand and kissed it. "Safe travels, Michael." They departed, walking in opposite directions. He tried to put the sequence of events in order, making another mindful effort in coming to some sort of rational explanation or even an idea of a plan. Yet no matter how much logic he gave to his thoughts, he had no answer for what he had seen or heard. Michael was no closer to having any concrete conclusion.

He walked back outside, stunned, feeling he was playing the part of a character in *The Walking Dead*. He headed straight to the Bay, wondering who he might find wandering by the boats. The dock was empty when he arrived. The statue honoring 9/11 victims was gone. The park where Elizabeth spent so many hours on the swings and slides was no more.

I'm in a different time—no doubt about it. My eyes do not deceive me. But what period of time am I in? The boats look modern. There's nothing I could say is from many centuries ago.

Darkness had settled in, and he stumbled upon a deep hole where the canopy once stood. The smell was pungent. He turned away from it. *What is that?* He broke a couple of sticks off a nearby tree, remembering his days as a scout. He rubbed and rubbed until a flame ignited. He grabbed a thicker piece of stick—longer too.

He held it for several seconds under it, finally giving himself some light. He leaned over and looked down, horrified. He jumped back. "My God. Where am I?" he said. "This can't be my town."

He took a few steps back to the deep hole, held his nose, and looked down once more. "Oh...my...God, it cannot be."

Small bodies lay on top of each other. Skeletons of bigger bodies were beside them. Fleas and flies and ants crawled everywhere. A pack of wolves not even aware Michael was looking chewed and pulled on the skin of a man, his mouth and eyes open in horror.

My God. Susan. Paul. My family. Michael raced up a hill at a frantic pace. He was confused, the landscape unfamiliar. It was lush with fewer roads—mostly long dirt paths where concrete and neatly manicured streets once were. He saw small huts with chimneys—no more two- and three-story houses which lined his neighborhood not long ago. He looked for the electric plant which donned the Northport sky, its red flicking lights utilized by airline pilots as an indication to turn toward the local airport. He did not see it.

He guessed where his old, dirty shingled home might be, wandering for a couple of hours in many directions. A lone deer spooked him, then sprinted toward the Sound. He believed he finally found the big hill he so often climbed, slipping and sliding those winter nights after taking his dog Little Brother out for a walk. The golf course that surrounded his neighborhood was gone. It was just trees shaking from the swift wind generated by late-night brisk breezes. He stood where he thought his old three-story house was.

It wasn't.

He could see the ocean not far away, no longer obstructed by tall trees. He could smell the salty air and feel the sporadic gusts pelting his face. Michael was where his house should be. He did a 360 at a methodical pace, whispering, "Where...where... where are you?"

He raced toward the water then stopped, rubbing his eyes. Confusion and fear swept through his body. *What is that? What flag is that?* He moved closer. A flag flapped in the brisk wind coming off the ocean. He squinted and stopped.

Am I in the wrong country? He rubbed his eyes once more. *Are my eyes playing tricks on me? What time am I in? Am I on Long Island? I have to be. That's the Sound.*

Chapter 25

M ichael came upon numerous men, women, and children near a barn fire raging where the Crab Meadow beach playground once stood. It was a favorite place of Elizabeth's. She spent countless hours maneuvering the monkey bars, the twisting tunnel slides, and swings.

"Higher!" Elizabeth would implore her father in her toddler voice.

Michael would cautiously push her a bit more skyward, frustrating Elizabeth. She was fearless even as a child. But his worries were worse, always consuming him, so much he would play the role of the overprotective parent. So he would try to outwit Elizabeth. As she got older and wiser and caught on to his strategy, Elizabeth eventually got her wish, being guided higher and higher until Michael could not take it any more. She would laugh hysterically. He would sit down, nervous from imagining his worst fears.

He remembered the time when Elizabeth fell off the monkey bars, landing on her face and stomach, knocking the wind out of her. She raced to him, arms outstretched, panicked, hugging him tight. He held her for several minutes, trying to subdue her tears.

Instead, he cried, and at that moment, he grieved for the loss of his first wife, who was not there to help console Elizabeth. Michael wiped a lone tear from his eye, realizing what was part of his past was now a vacant piece of beach.

He slowly approached the people by the fire. A cool, gentle wind jetted off the Sound into his face, sending a shiver through him, his clothes sweaty and ripped from his trip to Jerusalem.

"Hello," Michael said with a half short wave.

No one answered. No one looked at him. They sat in stone cold silence, not even making eye contact.

"Hi," Michael said, trying once more.

An old man, his hooded head tucked in his hands, slowly looked up. His face was black and blue, and a deep gash under his eye was covered in dry blood. "Why are you speaking that language?"

Michael gave a confused look. "I don't know what you mean."

"The way you speak," the man said, his tone angry. "Where are you from?"

"Here," Michael said. "I live in, um…I used to live not far from here. I speak English." He pointed back.

"English? Only spies speak that language. Are you a spy?" the man asked.

"A what?"

The old man stood. "You are a spy. We honor the Umbras. The Umbras are our means of survival. We are dedicated to the Umbras."

"What are you talking about?" said Michael. "What are the Umbras?"

"Sit," a woman holding a small girl said. "You have spoken too much."

"Shush," he scolded back. "We believe in the Umbras."

The woman, wearing a dirty, oversized brown coat, hid her face, holding the child tight, and turned her back on them.

"What do you need?" the old man asked. "We have nothing. We've given everything. I will do whatever the Umbras want me to do. Please do not harm my unit. They have lost many in their unit." He gestured to the child. "She is all we have left. We cannot suffer any more loss. If need be, take me. I will go to the camp."

Michael shook his head. "What are you talking about? What camp?"

"I am committed to helping the Umbras. I will do whatever the Umbras ask."

The woman turned around and looked up, fear in her eyes that pierced Michael's heart, and she pulled the old man down to sit beside her. "Stop," she demanded. "No more."

"Please, please, leave us be," the old man said, his voice fragile. "Please have mercy on us."

Michael stood in prolonged silence, puzzled. He backed up several steps, welcoming the warmth of the fire but uncertain as to what to ask or do next. He spotted a small boat on the far end of the beach; men with nets were casting them. He went to them. The men stopped working.

"Hi, I'm trying to find out—"

The men jumped in their boat and paddled away, using long wooden oars. "Wait, wait," Michael shouted, running into the waves coming ashore. "I need your help. Stop."

He stumbled several yards into the Sound. Water crashed against his chest. He swallowed saltwater, coughing. "Stop, please, stop."

They disappeared into the darkness as a slight fog formed. He looked to his left and saw the lighthouse still stood, though dramatically different from what he recalled. Michael ran to it, hoping he would find someone who could give him much needed answers to what time period it was.

What little paint was left on the lighthouse was chipped and grimy. The building was empty, barren of life—any life. It featured a big red fist painted onto the part facing the ocean. A light mist built into a steady rain. He pushed open a rusty door and shouted a few hellos. Michael rubbed his hands together, trying to fight off a shiver. He sneezed.

A noise above alerted him. He climbed the spiral stairway one step at a time, stopping on each step to decipher any more sounds. He did not. He reached the top and peered out the window. It was scratched, and a broken piece at the top right allowed a soft breeze to sweep through.

The fog had taken a deeper hold, impacting visibility, and the rain pelted the lighthouse exterior in spurts, some drips trickling in through the slight opening. A lone bed was unmade behind him. He sat, his body and mind exhausted. Michael replayed his conversation with the old man. "Nothing makes sense. What are Umbras? Who is he speaking about? No. Nothing makes sense, nothing. That flag—I've never such a flag before."

Michael opened the only window and peered up toward the top, catching a glimpse of the flag flapping hard from the ocean's breeze. It was too dark for him to get a good look at what was on it, so he backed up and closed the window.

Michael pulled the only blanket off the bed. It smelled of cigar smoke.

He wrapped the blanket around himself. He looked down and picked up a torn book, its cover title barely legible. It read "Rules of the Umbras."

Michael slowly flicked through it. There was a series of guidelines written in English and in a language he had never seen before. He lay his head down on the flat pillow and began to read.

His eyes widened as he sped through a list of punishments suggested for aliens and citizens who did not obey.

The word "death" inundated the pages.

Michael's eyes weakened and wandered. He tried to shake off the exhaustion. His mind traveled to a better place and a better time, where Elizabeth, Susan, and his family spent their first Christmas together. He struggled to exit the mirages.

He could not.

Chapter 26

Thump. Michael waved his hands in front of his face. His eyes were bleary and his body strained to sit up. He rubbed the side of his head, feeling a lump. A man dressed in an old military uniform stood before him.

But he didn't look like a soldier from the history books he studied in high school nor those described to him by his Uncle Ed or Uncle Frank. He wondered if his eyes were failing him again.

"Get up," the man shouted in an accent Michael had never heard before. The man, his shoulders thick, rippled the top part of his uniform. He pointed a long, thin blade attached to an old-style rifle.

Michael put his hands high. "I honor the Umbras."

"Sure you do," the man said, coughing and grabbing a towel from near the window. He dried his wet hair and held part of his hand to his mouth, spitting.

"I swear. I do."

The man threw the towel away, approached Michael and pushed him back on the bed. "You speak fluent English. You are not from here. Where are you from?"

"Back there." Michael pointed behind him.

"Back where?" the man questioned.

"There!" Michael kept pointing behind him.

"You lie. What are you doing here?"

"Looking for my family, my daughter, my town…"

The man gave him a disbelieving look. "Are you a spy for the Umbras? Are you checking up on me? I do my duty well."

Michael shook his head. "I don't even know what the Umbras are."

"What do you want from us? We have nothing. You have it all. I give you my life. What more do you want?"

"What are the Umbras?" Michael raised his hands in bewilderment. "I don't know what you are referring to. Believe me. I just want to find my family. Do you know the Stewarts? We live up on the hill. Near the golf course."

The man backed away.

Michael approached him. "Sir, I need help."

The man leaned back, resting his rifle against the dirty wall. He pulled out another knife and did the same.

"Why are you here, in this place?" he asked. "What is your name?"

"I needed to rest. I'm exhausted. And confused."

"Are you so confused you can't remember your name?" The man picked up the rifle again and pointed it at Michael's throat.

"My name is Michael Stewart. I am telling you the truth! I used to live not far from here. Up on the hill." He waved his hand to where the three-story colonial house once stood.

The man wielded the rifle and glared.

"I'm just an average American."

"What is an American?" the man asked.

"People born in this country. You. Me. Everyone here," Michael responded.

"There are no such people like that. American? I have never heard of such a person. What are you hiding?"

Michael sighed. "Nothing. Forget that. Can you help me?"

"You need to leave. Go back to the Umbras. Tell them I have done my duty well and passed the test."

"Please. I mean you no harm or confusion. I just want to find my…"

"Yes. I heard you. Your family," the man interrupted him. "What is a family?"

Michael shook his head in disbelief. "Do you not have any family?"

The man frowned. "Family? What is that?"

"A wife. Children. Someone you spend your most of your time with, sharing and loving." Michael took a step toward him.

"Back off. I have a unit. Or I did have a unit." He grabbed Michael by the neck and threatened him. "I can easily slit your throat and dump you in the water. What is your choice?"

"My choice is to find my family," he said, gasping.

The man released his grip.

"Do you not have a family?" Michael asked with urgency.

The man grimaced and moved closer to him. "I do not know what you are referring to. I had a unit."

Michael backed away. "Okay. Okay. Do you know where I might find my family?"

"I do not understand."

"Um…unit. Yeah. Where would I find my unit?" he asked with hesitation.

"Likely in the camps. That's where many have been taken."

Michael gave an exasperated look. "What camps are you talking about?"

The man's eyes widened. "You cannot be from here if you do not know."

"Believe me, I am from here. But I do not know."

The man walked to the window and took at quick glance out at the darkened sky. A slight rain moistened the sand below. He turned around, still brandishing his weapons. "I do not trust you. Yet you have no weapons. You are not threatening to me in any way, but I don't trust you. How do I know what you say is true?"

"You don't. I wish I had a better answer. But I am from here with no weapons. Only this." He pointed to his heart. "I have no harmful intentions."

The man fingered his weapon and paced around the small room several times, his eyes never leaving Michael. "I am not worried about you. I worry about what you might say to the leaders of the Umbras."

"I am not with those people," Michael insisted.

The man sat on the bed and stared at him for what seemed like an hour but what was most likely five or six minutes. He reached under a pillow and looked at a book.

"Dickens!"

The man nodded. "Yes. One of my favorite authors."

"Mine too."

"I have all of his books."

"You have A Christmas Carol? It's my favorite."

The man gave him a confused look. "I never heard of that book."

"What?! How do you not know his most popular novel? Short, certainly, but it made one of the biggest impacts."

The man shook his head. "No. He never wrote a story like that. I have all his works. What is Christmas?"

Puzzled, Michael scrunched his eyebrows and searched for a response.

The man stood. "Enough of this silly talk about Dickens. I know what I know."

"But...A Christmas Carol. Christmas. Jesus born. It's named after Jesus—Christmas. December 25th every year. It's what inspired Dickens and this great story. How do you not know about this work by Dickens?"

The man glared and stood silently, eyeing Michael from the top of his head to the bottom of his torn shoes. He shook his head several times, then paced a couple of steps back and forth.

"How do you..." Michael started to say.

The man interrupted him. "Stop. No more about this book. You're not telling the truth. You're trying to confuse me."

"I'm not. Please believe me. I'm confused too. I have no idea where I really am. Can you help me?"

The man softened slightly. "I'm Adriel. What garments you see are only for show—a way to survive, a way to deceive the Umbras. We need to go before you are spotted. Any man who walks into this area either doesn't know how dangerous it is or is just plain crazy."

"I'm not crazy," Michael said.

"This is my area to guard against intruders who would harm the Umbras or disrupt some of their trade. I am obligated to kill anyone trespassing, and if I have to kill you...I will. I have killed many here. I have no worries in doing so again." He turned to the window. "That flag sickens me."

139

Michael approached him.

"Back up," Adriel said, hoisting his rifle forward.

Michael raised hands in surrender. "Relax. I have nothing to fight you with except my bare hands."

Adriel glared. "Your hands aren't strong enough to fight me."

"I know," Michael conceded. "That flag. The one up on the top of this lighthouse. Is that real?"

"As real as the dead bodies in the ditches around here are."

"By the Umbras?" Michael measured his words. "Is it a country?"

"Countries," he said. "Or parts of some countries. It's hard to tell."

Michael sighed. "How do you tell?"

"Sometimes you can't. They hide in the shadows. You don't think there are many, but they are a big army. Their way of life has been passed down from generation to generation after the last big war."

"World War II?" Michael said.

"That's the big one."

"That doesn't make any sense. America helped win the war."

Adriel faced Michael. "America? This America you speak of was never in the big war."

Michael gave a baffled look. "I don't understand."

"You better understand this. The Umbras could be watching us now. They have devices that watch and listen to what we say. I've already debugged this place five times."

Michael looked around, nervous of what was already being said. "You never heard of the United States of America?"

"Not even in a Dickens story."

"None of this is making sense."

Adriel lowered his rifle. "This America you speak of. What world is this from? Is it from the other side of the world?"

Michael shrugged.

Adriel took another quick peek out the window. "There are NO friends here. Only survivors. Which is what we need to do." He paused. "We need to leave before we are both taken to those camps."

"These camps, where are they?" Michael asked.

"You do not want to go there. You will never be able to leave."

Michael scowled. "I need to find my family."

Adriel gave a puzzled glance.

"I mean, my unit."

"Go back from where you came, if you can," Adriel implored. "It is not safe for you or even me. Go home."

Michael took a deep breath. "But I am home." He went to the window and sighted a large boat not far from the shore. "That vessel, Adriel."

"Yes, what about it?"

"Where is it coming from, and where might it be going to next?"

"To Europe. That is a cargo ship. It comes here to pick up and leave supplies."

Michael nodded. "I'm guessing on this. But my guess is the only plan I have. It's a big guess and the only way I can find people I might know, since no one I know is here anymore…I guess I'm going to be cargo. Can you help me?"

Adriel didn't answer.

Michael continued. "What about you? Want to take the trip with me?"

Adriel stayed silent for several minutes, frequently taking brief looks outside. He gripped his rifle and stared at Michael.

He leaned back on the wall and remained quiet for a few more moments. Then he straightened up and pulled open a small dresser drawer, grabbed a black and white photo, and tucked it inside his military uniform.

He gestured with his rifle once more, pointing it straight at Michael's heart.

"I understand," Michael said.

Chapter 27

Michael stayed below deck while Adriel loaded the ship with various oats, corn, and animals. He was among mixed company—sheep, dogs, deer, elk, and cattle. Hay was spread throughout the lower level. The smell was putrid from the animal waste.

Michael peered through a pin-like hole in the wooden ceiling leading up to the main deck. Laborers were beaten until they were bloodied if they didn't work fast enough. Some who fell were picked up, dragged with a chain attached to their necks, and then thrown overboard if they could not get to their feet. One gray-haired man struggled in his frailty to carry a case of corn to the far end of the deck. He collapsed face first. A soldier poked him several times, encouraging the older man to get up. He didn't.

The soldiers left him there until all the cargo was neatly stacked and then went back to the old man, his face sheet white. He mumbled a few words and pleaded for mercy. The soldiers attached a piece of cement to his leg, and a group of six picked him up and tossed him into the ocean.

Michael backed up away from the small hole and put his hand over his mouth, stunned. He gathered his senses and went back to look some more. He winced and flinched as another man met his fate through a long sword. A drop of blood spilled through the hole and into Michael's eye.

Oh my. I must find Susan. She's not here. She better not be here. Our house is gone. Maybe Susan and Paul escaped? Maybe they are somewhere else? Maybe Susan went home. I'm guessing, but it's my best guess. And Elizabeth. What about her?

Distraught, Michael hung his head.

Adriel joined him moments later, kicking him. He put two fingers to his lips and whispered, "Hey, pay attention. We are almost ready to leave. Stay quiet. Do not go above. If you need anything, let me know. Our first stop is in London. Does this help you?"

Michael nodded. "I hope so. My mind is swirling with the possibilities. I'm taking a big-time guess. It's a risk."

"No," Adriel said. "You staying behind is a risk. You do not belong here."

Michael frowned. "I did…or I thought I did. I'm not sure where I belong."

"Well, it's not here," Adriel said.

The ship jolted and inched its way out of port. The animals stirred, and Michael befriended a lone husky. He gave the dog a piece of what was left of his meal. The husky was grateful, and Michael had a new friend. The husky lay its head in his lap.

"Don't get too close to the dog—he might be your nicest enemy," Adriel said.

Michael patted the dog on his head. "How can this dog be an enemy? A dog is man's best friend, and I need all the friends I can get."

The ship picked up speed. "How did you end up at the lighthouse?"

Michael wasn't sure how to answer.

"Was that a difficult question?"

"There's not a simple answer."

"Only the truth will save you," Adriel said, glaring.

"I come from the town we just left. Except it wasn't my town anymore. What was there not long ago is gone, vanished. Nothing is what it was…." Michael's words trailed off.

The creaking of the ship unnerved Michael. He stood, stretched, petted the husky's head again, and tried to release some nervous energy. "This is one crazy place."

"We live in tragic times," Adriel said. "Men killing men. Women are taken from their units. Their children forced into labor camps. We live in total oppression. It's why my people have fled to the mountains."

"Why didn't you go to the mountains?"

"I had nothing left. Nowhere to go."

Michael stretched his arms, his hands hitting the ceiling.

"Stop that," Adriel demanded.

Michael paused for a few moments. "Why the lighthouse? The uniform? The persona?"

Adriel looked away. "I do not claim to be proud of what I do, how I act, or who I keep company with. But it is my only way to survive. I try to find some purpose to life. My life. This is my only joy. Traveling. Getting away from the pain. Away from the hate. This helps me find peace."

Michael took a deep breath of the ocean air, which reminded him of his love of the sea, of the sounds and smells and images of Crab Meadow Beach back on Long Island and the wonderful memories that were clear as a gorgeous blue sky on a summer's day.

145

"I can see why you do this," Michael agreed.

He peeked again through the small opening. The deck was quiet with just a few men resting and chatting and another small cluster of soldiers playing cards.

"How long will it take for us to get to London?" Michael asked.

"Depending upon the crosswinds and weather, five or six days most likely. Maybe a bit longer," he said.

"I don't have much time."

"I have all the time in the world," Adriel said.

"In my world, time ran out."

"That sounds hopeless. You need to give yourself a chance to have a life."

Michael shook his head. "I have no life, the way the world is right now."

"You cannot fight this world."

Michael took a deeper breath, inhaling a gust of wind, its salty air making its way down below. He was momentarily refreshed. The breeze picked up, rocking the medium-sized vessel. Michael held onto a piece of wood sticking out of the ceiling.

"The toughest part of the trip will be upon us soon," Adriel warned. He slapped Michael on the back, snickering.

"I'll be fine," Michael reassured, trying to sound convincing. He sought to settle himself, so he sat, allowing his husky friend to find more human comfort. He closed his eyes and drifted while Adriel kept guard. Michael drifted deeper and deeper until reality faded.

Vicki appeared, nursing a newborn.

"Who is that?" Michael asked.

"Why, silly, it's Elizabeth…who else would it be?"

"But that doesn't make sense, Vicki."

She smiled. "It's not supposed to make sense. Look around. Does anything make sense?"

Michael sighed and shook his head. "Where are we?"

"We are somewhere, and we are nowhere, somewhere in between."

"I don't understand."

"You're not supposed to."

Michael grew frustrated. "You're talking in riddles."

Vicki placed Elizabeth over her shoulder and rubbed her back, causing a burp. "You are making it complicated by over-thinking. You do this often, sweetheart."

"I need your help," Michael pleaded.

"How am I going to help you?"

"Give me some guidance, something that will help me find Susan."

"Who is Susan?"

"My wife."

"What? Who?" Vicki gave a sad look.

Michael avoided eye contact. "I wanted to move forward. Make another life. I waited for a long time. For…"

"For what? For me to return. Here I am, Michael."

He stayed silent.

"I miss you every day. I miss Elizabeth. Did you ever miss me?"

"Of course."

He hugged her. "I know. I was angry for a long time. I needed to give up my rage."

"I was lonely while I carried our daughter. You were too busy with your work. Your writing. Your books. Was it that important to you? More than our daughter?"

Michael didn't respond.

"Was writing that novel more important than you coming home that night?"

Vicki gave a forlorn look.

Michael was hoping this was all a dream.

He opened his eyes.

"Was your work more important than Elizabeth?"

Chapter 28

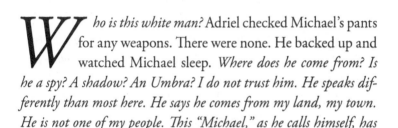

*W*ho is this white man? Adriel checked Michael's pants for any weapons. There were none. He backed up and watched Michael sleep. *Where does he come from? Is he a spy? A shadow? An Umbra? I do not trust him. He speaks differently than most here. He says he comes from my land, my town. He is not one of my people. This "Michael," as he calls himself, has no knowledge of what has happened to us here. How does he not know of the oppression and evil that thrives against us? What man or woman does not know of what has happened to us here?*

He talks about his family. What is he speaking about? I have never heard such words. Does he mean unit? Perhaps he is a good man. He carries no weapons. He is not strong enough to fight me. Yet why do I fear him so much? Maybe it's the fear of the unknown my ancestors told me about when I was small. Fear of not knowing this white man's intentions.

Why does he not know of the Umbras? He has to be spy. I've seen many like him. I will make him feel like I want to be part of his unit.

There have been many good men who are cloaked in deception and lies. No. I cannot trust this Michael.

I will watch him closely while in London. I will test him to see if he is a man with a brave heart or one who seeks the treasures of this world. He says he has no money. No means of transportation. No food. But how does he survive? How does he look like a man who hasn't starved?

He is not a hunter, he claims. If he is not a hunter, how does he eat? Oh, this is what a spy does. They deceive. If he lives among us, why haven't I seen him before? If he lives near the Lighthouse, I would would know him.

This Michael is strange. I will let him talk more. Perhaps he will show what is true in his heart. And this other world he speaks of… it's what I have read in those novels. Dickens' type of stories. And this book he claims Dickens wrote? Such a lie. Oh, yes, a white lie.

And what is this America he speaks of? This strange land. He speaks of his unit living here. No one like him lives here. There are more questions about him than answers.

And who is this Jesus? I will dig deeper into his mind. Maybe this Jesus is his imaginary friend. Like the young members of my unit dreamed of when they played together.

My unit. Oh, my unit. Why was I not there to defend them? Why? Oh, I can never forgive myself. I will kill every last one of those Umbras. I cannot bear how they took our loved ones. I promise this to you. To you, my unit. My forever unit. I will get my vengeance for you and for our nation and people. I will not stop until I have my revenge.

And this Michael will not stop me either. If he tries. I wonder…I wonder. He says he is a man of high standards. A man who doesn't steal and kill. How does a man who claims he is from here…

survive? I do not believe him. It is those who pretend to be someone else who are the most dangerous. A wolf in sheep's clothing. I will be on guard. He will not interfere with my reprisal. I will kill him too if need be. There will come a time. I promise you this, my unit. Someday I will go to the mountains and lead us back to our rightful place. We will all be together. Perhaps not here. But we will howl like the wolves that came before us and protect us all high up in the sky. We will avenge our losses with their blood.

I will watch this Michael. I will watch him like an eagle circling his prey. My eyes shall never leave him. Even in his sleep I shall be ready. Always. I promise you this. I promise this to my ancestors. Get sleep. He's sneaky. Do NOT trust him. Sleep. But keep one eye open. Always.

Fences crawled high into the sky, their metal arms thick with steel, entrapping humans transformed into zombies, as they robotically dug deep ditches to dispose of the day's deaths. Adriel stood stoically, sentenced to an endless trance, his eyes gazing out to the great beyond, devastated from the loss of his unit.

His weapon at his side, his feet immersed into the moist terrain saturated with blood and tears, he performed his survival séance…for time was no longer real.

"Adriel, check on barracks number eight," a commander shouted.

He walked the mile or so past cages of surrendering souls soon to be human skeltons—some whispering, some whimpering, others crying, most in stary-eyed silence. Adriel could barely raise his weapon, a long thin rifle with a shiny, silver knife protruding a foot for so forward. His vast shoulders slumped, burdened by the countless calculating murders he witnessed and was forced to execute with the Umbras.

"Adriel!" a commander bellowed. "Take this one to the Lighthouse. And do what is required."

He managed to straighten up and give a brief yet heartless military salute. "Sir, may I request a week or two at the Lighthouse for some R and R? Maybe travel, too."

"Why is this needed?" the commander answered, his devious glance all too familiar to Adriel.

"I am exhausted from the twenty-hour shifts. I can continue to carry out your orders more effectively there."

The commander fingered his weapon, an impressive long-barreled gun. He looked dismayed, which oddly didn't bother Adriel one bit.

I am too tired, you bastard, to even care if you shoot me. Go ahead. Take me out of my misery. I have nothing.

"Commander," yelled another man in old military garb rushing up to them. "There's been a breach in one of the underground tunnels. They saw a man and a woman from one. Oddly dressed, too. Could be rebel spies!"

"Did you arrest them?"

"We were too far away to do so."

"Go after them!" The commander turned back to Adriel. "What was your request again?"

"Sir," said Adriel, approaching the commander. "The lighthouse…"

"Go, take all the time there. Give me weekly updates. I like that we have someone like you. Like me. There."

The commander moved closer, his eyes bleeding blood. Adriel flinched, unsure of what he was seeing, perhaps hallucinating. "Your eyes…"

"What about them?"

"They're…"

The commander inched even closer. The blood trickled down his cheeks, then gushed to the ground, forming a big puddle.

"Adriel, what's wrong?" the commander asked.

Adriel stayed frozen. The commander slapped both sides of his face. "Snap out of it!"

He stayed in his trance. The commander belted him again, three times, four times, five times, six times, seven, eight, nine, ten, eleven, and twelve."

Adriel turned and dragged the prisoner away.

"Remember, I want a weekly report. Do not let anyone touch our shores, coming or leaving."

Adriel continued the slow march toward the Lighthouse. The sky darkened more with each step he took. He let the prisoner go from the chains and opened the Lighthouse door. The prisoner, his face battered and tattered with dark blue and black bruises, waited outside as the wind whipped furious waves against the outer walls of the Lighthouse.

Adriel climbed the small, narrow stairway to the top. He looked in the mirror, then tried to wipe away the blood from his eyes. There was none. He looked at his bloodstained hands. He went to the bathroom to wash it away. He saw nothing. *Have I lost my mind? Did I see what I saw back there with the commander? I must be going crazy.*

He went back outside to retrieve the prisoner. "Where did he go?" he said in a soft whisper. "The man could barely walk."

Adriel took a deep breath to gather himself. The salty air invigorated him for a brief moment. He walked in each direction about a hundred yards. *Maybe he was rescued by my brothers? They could have been that man and woman they spoke about coming from the tunnel. It's the only way the prisoner could have left or gotten far.*

Adriel heard the Lighthouse door creak. He turned but saw no one. *I am losing my mind.*

He sat down on the beach and watched the tide crawl its way up the shore. He lay his weapon down, grabbed a shovel from the side of the Lighthouse, and started digging. He dug and dug in a furious fashion, then took a tape measure out. *Good enough.* It was deep. Deep enough, he thought, to do the job. He was quite skilled at it now, having done it so many times for the Umbras. Adriel was always the first one they called to dig the holes. *What a job to be so good at. I'm going to hell for it.*

The ocean waves rushed up more, tumbling into the hole. He jumped in, the frigid water refreshing his soul. He slowly lay down. *Have mercy on me, my brothers and sisters for abandoning you and this fight. I have nothing left. My soul is black, my heart is cold, my mind sickened, my body has surrendered. Forgive me because I have nothing left to live for...*

The water piled over him. He closed his eyes and opened his mouth, gagging as the saltwater leaked in. He coughed and spat some of it up. He lay down again. The water rushed in some more, stinging his eyes. He rubbed them, his bleary and blury. He thought he saw a shadow stretched high on the exterior of the Lighthouse sneak by. *Who is that? What was that?* The water rose to head level. He choked as the ocean became unforgiving. The Lighthouse door creaked again. *What is that?* Adriel sat up, catching a breath and heard footsteps climbing inside the Lighthouse. Adriel didn't move for several minutes, pondering his fate while the water rose to neck level. The sand started to collapse on him. He finally climbed out of the hole and brushed himself off. *Was that one of my brothers?*

Adriel shook himself out of his dream as Michael wrestled with the chains to find a comfortable position to get more sleep. "Knock it off," Adriel said.

Michael closed his eyes. Adriel did not this time.

Five Days Later

Michael awoke chained and bound, his legs buckled together. Adriel sat opposite him, staring, bleeding above his right eye, his face bruised.

Michael shook his legs, the clanging sound of chains irritating him. "What's going on?"

"Isn't it obvious?"

"No. Nothing is obvious."

"You're a prisoner of the Umbras," Adriel said. "I tried to persuade them to let you go. I didn't succeed."

"Are you sure you tried?" Michael questioned.

Adriel glared.

"What happened to you?" asked Michael, gesturing to Adriel's face.

"Just a little skirmish," he said, his front tooth noticeably chipped.

"Now what?" Michael said, trying to stand.

"We wait until we dock. You will be taken by me to a London labor camp under the Umbra's authority."

"Oh, I can't let that happen," Michael said. He peeked through the hole and noticed men pushing crates of food to the far end of the vessel.

"You will do what I say," Adriel demanded.

"And if I don't?"

"I have no fear of dropping you overboard for the sharks to feast."

Michael didn't respond.

"We will pretend I am taking you to a labor camp."

"Are we close?" Michael asked, turning toward Adriel.

"Not long before we are there, and we must be ready. Listen to me. Do what I say. We need to make a move at the right time once we are off this ship."

Michael could feel the vessel slowing down to a crawl. The boat creaked, and some of the cargo below slid forward against the far wall. The animals sensed the end and stirred. The husky leaned his head against Michael's leg.

"Where are we really going?" Michael asked, bending down to rub the husky's gray face.

"To the outskirts of London, away from the crowds and craziness. It's dangerous for both of us. You want to find your unit, right?"

"You mean my wife. She's outside of London, about an hour north."

"Wife? What is that?"

"Are you kidding me?"

Adriel didn't answer.

"A wife. Partner. Someone you have a relationship with. Church. Exchange rings. Make a family...anything familiar to you?"

Adriel remained stoic.

"Um...unit. Live together."

Adriel shrugged. "Do you know where this unit might be? You need to be sure, so we don't waste time. We need to catch the next ship back in a couple of days, or the Umbras will notice I am missing. Then I'll be a wanted man."

Michael hesitated. "It's my best guess."

The vessel stopped, and activity blossomed on the deck as men pushed cargo off the ship at a frantic pace.

"Stay in front of me." Adriel unlocked some of Michael's chains. "Do not speak unless I speak to you."

Men were being whipped for not pushing the crates fast enough off the ship. Adriel slowly walked Michael away from the chaos and into a nearby narrow street. He stopped by an abandoned storefront, looked behind and to the sides, and pulled Michael inside.

The store was empty, musky, and dusty, the floor red-stained and grimy. "What is this?" Michael asked.

"A safe haven."

"Safe for who?"

"Us. Let me remove the rest of the chains. We have much traveling to do if you are to find your unit. Keep your head down. It's dangerous."

"More dangerous than where we just came from?"

Adriel removed the last of the chains from Michael's legs. "It's a matter of perspective. When we travel through London, act like you belong and do not make eye contact with any soldier. Follow me and do not lag behind." Adriel handed Michael a small knife. "Use this when necessary."

Michael didn't respond and shoved the knife inside a side pouch. They walked past a marketplace where men and women and children were peddling a variety of fruits and vegetables.

Adriel snuck two apples into his pockets. "Grab what you can."

"That's stealing."

"So starve." Adriel shrugged his shoulders. "It's your choice to either eat or die of hunger."

Michael stole an apple and enjoyed the crispness and sweetness of it.

"I thought you would make that choice." Adriel moved toward a narrow street where a stairway to a tall stone building was drenched in blood, and children mopped away the bloodstains.

"What in hell goes on here?"

"That's a good way to describe it," Adriel said. "You really don't know?"

Michael huffed out of frustration. "I have no clue."

"Religion. Or what they call religion."

"Christianity?" Michael said.

Adriel scrunched his brows. "What's Christianity?"

"Seriously? Is there any religion here?"

Adriel nodded. "Educate me. Can't wait to hear this story. You seem to be a great storyteller."

"Jesus was crucified by the Romans, and he died on the cross." Michael dug into his pocket, looking for the chain and cross Elizabeth had given him years ago. He pulled it out. "This helps me talk to people in another time."

Adriel laughed. "Sure. Sure it does."

"It's a symbol of the sacrifice Jesus made by dying on the cross."

"Oh, this Jesus guy again. Christmas. Sure. Sure. Whatever you say. You lost me. I never heard of the man Jesus or anything about him."

"That's impossible," Michael said.

Adriel ignored him. "Stay vigilant. We do not want to end up part of their festival here."

"Why?"

"Do you enjoy keeping that head of yours?"

"My God. What is that?" Michael asked, pointing to a store.

"Religion. Or what they say it is."

Michael moved closer to the store window and peered in for a better look. A woman's head was mounted onto a gold stick, her eyes open wide and mouth expressing horror. He jumped back.

Adriel laughed.

"That's not funny. It looks so real."

"It is."

Chapter 29

A driel and Michael dodged out of a soldier's view and slipped into a back alley. Adriel pulled some clothes off of a long line and promptly undressed, then redressed to look like a civilian, tossing the World War II uniform into a garbage bin. He pulled Michael into a nearby store, pretending to be browsing as an elderly woman slowly made her way to them. "Good day. Would you like some tea?"

"No, thank you," Michael said.

"Yes, ma'am." Adriel smiled. "I'd appreciate a cup."

The woman gave Adriel a toothy grin. "I'm Onakan."

Adriel gave an alarmed look.

"Looks like you've been traveling for a while," Onakan said. She smiled. "How did you get here?"

"The usual way."

Michael turned his head sideways, eyeing pens and notebooks as he usually did in any store. He was suspicious of Onakan's questions.

"Where are you coming from?" Onakan asked.

"Not far away," Adriel said.

"You're from this town then?"

Adriel looked at Michael. "You could say that."

"Do you have a unit here?"

"Yes." Adriel sighed. "Ma'am, please excuse me, but I sure could use some tea."

Onakan went to the back of the store. Michael watched her leave in the mirrors stationed high above under the ceramic ceiling.

"Let's go," Adriel said.

"What?"

Adriel showed him a map. "I got what I wanted. I sent her away so we can get a head start."

"On what?"

"This place will be swarming with soldiers."

Michael ignored Adriel. He stole a pen and ripped a piece of paper out of a notebook.

Onakan returned with a cup and saucer. "Do you want any sugar or milk?"

"Yes, ma'am. Three spoonfuls of sugar and a splash of milk. If you have any honey, oh, how sweet that would be."

Michael gave him a puzzled look.

"Let's get out of here," Adriel said once Onakan left.

"I'm right behind you."

As they approached the door, Adriel put his hand out.

"What's wrong?" Michael asked.

"Too late. An Umbra is heading this way."

Onakan handed Adriel a cup of tea. "Here you go, sir."

Adriel grabbed it and put it down on the counter near the cash register.

Onakan strolled behind the counter, reached down, and pulled out a gun. "I think you should wait and drink your tea."

Michael looked at her in disbelief. "You've got to be kidding."

"Do I look like I'm kidding? I may be old, but I can handle myself. I recognize an expensive piece of property when I see one. Or should I say two." She pointed the gun at Adriel. "Both of you turn around or I'll blow your beady eyes out."

They turned around and Adriel grabbed a rubber ball in a plastic bucket. "Get down," he said.

Michael fell into a cluster of soda bottles piled high. The bottles tumbled; some broke. The sticky liquid squirted everywhere.

"What are you doing?" screamed Onakan.

Adriel flung the ball, clocking her in the face.

She backpedaled and tumbled into a display of gum and candy.

Adriel lifted Michael off the ground. The front door swung open, and an Umbra soldier entered, pointing his gun.

"Onakan, where are you?" the soldier shouted.

She gasped for breath. "I'm back here."

Adriel and Michael headed through the back door and out onto the street. They ran and ran and finally stopped when they were out of sight. "What just happened?" Michael asked.

"Are you braindead? I was trying to buy us some time with the tea until I could take the map."

"How did you know she was…?" Michael asked.

Before he could finish his question, Adriel interrupted. "When she opened the register, I saw some Umbra money. Most of the locals here still refuse to take it."

Adriel pulled out some paper. "Look at this. If you see this, run. Don't wait." It was light green with three heads together, all with menacing looks.

"Who are these three heads?" Michael asked.

"They are of the three leaders who began the repression of the world. Evil. Pure evil."

"Who can we trust here then?"

Adriel opened the map wide. "We can't trust anyone. Treat everyone as if they are with the Umbras. Their money talks here. Big time for some."

Adriel continued to study the map.

"This place is archaic. Don't you have GPS?" Michael asked.

Adriel gave a look of disbelief. "Not here."

"No cell phones?"

Adriel sneered. "I wonder whether you are from this world or not. Only the rich have those."

Michael shook his head. "This is crazy. Where I come from..." He stopped, realizing what he was about to say wouldn't even make sense to Adriel.

"Where do you think your unit might be?" Adriel asked.

Michael pointed north of London. "St. Albans should be right about here. That's the town she spoke of where her grandparents came from. I think I can find her or someone from her family who can tell us where she is."

Adriel analyzed the map and pointed to a particular spot, his big forefinger pressing down. Michael joined him, examining it. "No such place as St. Albans. That's Mosso. I believe that's it. Right?"

Michael shook his head. "I know that's St. Albans. I never heard of Mosso."

Adriel gave a frustrated breath. "It's Mosso. From what you see on this map, is this where she might be or her relatives might be?"

Michael hesitated. Adriel grew impatient. "Yes or no?"

"Yes."

"Then that's where we go," said Adriel.

"How do we get there?"

Adriel pulled out a compass, one that looked like Michael had as a kid. "We walk. Like my ancestors."

"Didn't your ancestors use horses?"

"That they did," Adriel said. "But we don't have horses here."

"Maybe we can hitch a ride?"

Adriel shook his head. "It's not safe. We won't know if they're a spy with the Umbras. Think, Michael. Watch the shadows. They are lurking everywhere."

They left the city limits and wandered into the spacious, ascending green hills of the countryside. Michael knew Susan's hometown rather well because she often spoke of her growing up there as a child. The restaurants. The pubs. The cathedral. All of this made St. Albans a pleasant town to raise a family. Or so he thought it was St. Albans.

Adriel kept one eye on his compass and his other eye on the surrounding area. There was a herd of cows blocking the road, a lone farmer yelling to his dogs to move his livestock along. "Don't make eye contact," Adriel warned Michael. "Look away. Like me."

"Got it."

Michael got caught between three cows nibbling at his grass-stained shoes. He froze, holding his hands up in the air. "Adriel, I need help."

"Stay still," Adriel said. "They will move at their own pace. Do not touch them."

"That might be impossible. They're on top of me."

Adriel tried unsuccessfully to shoo the cows away.

"How long will this take?"

"You're on cow time," said Adriel, laughing.

The farmer yelled to his dogs to untangle the three. The cows moved, and Michael ran to rejoin Adriel. "I see you're amused."

"You are so out of this world. You're not even in the same galaxy as me."

"Glad I could be of some entertainment value," Michael replied, not sure if he should be offended or not.

The sun began to descend, casting a majestic looking sunset over the steep grassy hills. The night was calm, and the evening landscape glittered with beautiful mosaics of star clusters.

"That is nature in all its glory," Adriel said, reveling in a rare quiet moment.

"Can't argue with you there," Michael said. "I enjoyed many of these types of nights with Susan…and Elizabeth." He sighed, feeling profound sadness wash over him.

"What will you do if you can't find your unit?"

Michael remained quiet.

"Do you have another plan?" Adriel asked.

"I don't."

"It's always good to be prepared for all possibilities."

"I can't think of any other ideas right now. This has to work."

"You are a man who seeks extreme solutions to even a simple problem," Adriel reasoned.

"My problem isn't exactly an everyday situation." He paused. "You think the way I talk is strange—I have never heard someone like you who speaks this way."

"It is the way my ancestors spoke. It is the way of our land. My ancestors often speak of the old country. Our old country is gone forever." Adriel continued, "No matter what language you or I speak. It is what you make it. And you prefer to welcome a storm instead of looking for the rainbow after it."

They came upon a pub called Shannon's. "Keep your mouth shut. I'll handle this," Adriel said, opening the door.

People were chatting—mostly men swigging beer and downing shots. Music was playing loud on a jukebox, and a group of female Irish dancers tapped their way across a small, makeshift wooden stage. Lovely young women were serving food too.

"This is festive," Michael said.

"What was that?" Adriel asked, turning around, putting his hand to his ear.

"Very festive," Michael yelled.

Adriel shouted back, "We're not here to party. Lower your head. Now!"

Two World War II-clothed soldiers dragged out a young man and woman. Several patrons shouted and screamed, pawing at them. Another man wearing a green hat and black coat swung at the soldiers. The man was stabbed with a bayonet and tumbled back into the arms of a couple of men.

They took him inside. The Umbras left.

The bar was quiet. The man was taken to the back of the bar. Music was still playing. The conversation began again.

Michael pulled on Adriel's arm. "Is this place safe?"

"Keep your hands off of me."

Michael stared straight ahead.

"Snap out of it," Adriel said, whacking him hard on the shoulder.

"I'll get us some drinks," he continued. "Fit in. Grab that table in the corner. I'll ask around. Susan? Right?"

"Yes. Susan…Stewart."

"Stewart. Susan. Right."

Michael sat, taking a napkin out of a wooden rack and wiped the table clear of leftover beer stains. He looked up, and a young lady stood before him. She had beautiful green eyes and bright red hair.

"Well hello, handsome."

Michael blushed.

"Don't be shy, sweetie. I won't bite."

"Now I feel better," Michael said, his face turning red.

"Are you local or stopping by?" she asked, sitting down next to him.

Michael moved over nervously.

"I told you, honey, I don't bite."

"I know, I know."

"What's your story? You're alone. Anyone who is anybody has some sob story."

"My story is way too complicated to tell."

The woman smiled, and her eyes sparkled. "I'm Colleen." She held out her hand.

Michael shook it. "Michael Stewart."

"Ah, such a good Irish name."

"Really? I didn't know that."

Colleen gave a look of disbelief.

"Seriously," Michael said.

"I believe you," Colleen replied, brushing a stray red hair away from her eyes.

"Do you know the Horns?" Michael asked.

Colleen inched closer and whispered, "Are we done with our flirting?" She leaned back and laughed. "Lighten up, sailor."

"I'm not a sailor."

"I know. I was busting your cajones."

A couple of men brushed past Colleen, one grabbing her backside. She flinched and smiled. "Be nice, boys."

Another man standing at the bar shouted, "How much are you charging that lad, Col?"

She turned around and gave him the finger. The crowd watching from the bar roared in laughter.

The man approached Colleen. "You've got something more to say, whore?"

"Woah," Michael said, standing up. "No need to say that to this lady."

"She ain't no lady," the man said, pushing Michael back into his chair.

"Take it easy, Jimmy. I'm just entertaining an out of towner."

Jimmy backed away, his face red, his eyes thundering.

Colleen turned toward Michael and without losing any momentum said, "Do you want me for the night?"

Michael freed himself away from the flirting. "I'm looking for Susan Stewart. You may know her as Susan Horn. Do you know her?"

"I sure do know her. How do you know my cousin?"

Michael paused, hesitant in how to respond. "Oh. Your cousin."

"Did she jilt you? Did she take you for your money? Without putting out? She does that to a lot of men around here. She plays the field pretty good, if you know what I mean."

Michael shook his head. "I don't know what you mean."

Colleen sat next to him. "Look around, stranger. What do you see? Men wanting women. Women making a living."

"Not my Susan. No. She wouldn't. She isn't like that."

"You may have the wrong Susan. My cousin is sweet when a man gives her some Umbra money."

Michael kept shaking his head in disbelief. "I…I…don't believe it. Where can I find her?"

"How long have you known her?" Colleen asked.

"Almost my entire life."

"Your whole life? Now you are pulling my leg. Are you sure you are looking for my cousin, Susan? The town's most desired bedmate? She's never mentioned a Michael Stewart to me, and we're very close. You may not have the right person."

"I don't know what Susan you are talking about, but the Susan I am looking for has beautiful red hair, has a heart of gold, and is kind to everyone—animals too. Loves her fur babies."

Colleen laughed. "Oh, you so don't have the Susan you are seeking. My cousin is not like any of what you described."

Adriel sat and placed a beer in front of him. "Seems like all the lasses around here are friendly. Who might you be?"

"You can call me Colleen. And you?"

"Adriel." He stuck out his hand, and Colleen shook it, holding onto to his longer.

"Well, Michael says he's looking for my cousin, Susan," Colleen said.

"That he is. Can you help us?"

Colleen released her hand hold and got up. "My cousin is always on call. Like me." She winked at him.

"Your cousin isn't my wife I am looking for," Michael said.

"You mean unit. Are you sure, Colleen?" Adriel asked.

"Well, there's only one Susan Horn in this part of the woods, and she stays at a boarding house not far from here. Make sure you have money if you want to see her. There's a price for everything here." She winked again. "Umbra money gets you much more." She laughed.

"Michael, only one Susan Horn here," Adriel said.

"I don't believe it's her."

Colleen grabbed her purse off the table. A big-sized man with a short blue jacket rubbed up against her. "Hey sailor, do you need some company?"

The man pulled out some Umbra money.

"Perfect," she said.

She smiled at Adriel and Michael. "Have to go. Say hello to my cousin if you go see her. She's not far from here. Near a hotel. You can't miss it if you take a left and walk a couple of meters or so."

"Thank you," Adriel said.

"Just beware, Susan has three—"

"Yes. Susan has three brothers. I know them well," Michael said.

"Oh. You do?"

"Sure. Shane, James, and William."

Colleen gave a big smile. "My big cousins are the best."

"Where does she live again?" Michael asked.

"She's past a big farmhouse and by the hotel."

"Colleen, it was nice meeting you. You seem happy," Adriel said, flirting.

"Why, yes, you could say that."

"I just did."

"Are you in town for long?"

"No," Michael interrupted.

"Mmm…perhaps. You'll be here?" Adriel asked.

"Every night." She gave Adriel a long hug and backed away. "Don't forget about me."

Adriel winked. "I won't."

They walked outside. Michael stared into the night, the music blaring and yet muffled to him. He watched men and women dancing through the big front window. People drank and laughed. It was all a blur. So surreal.

"Why were you flirting with that woman?" Michael asked.

Adriel smacked him in the chest. "You need to fit in. Be part of this culture. Or you will get us both killed."

"This culture is repulsive," Michael countered.

"Embrace it. It's how I've survived."

"I'd rather not."

Adriel pushed Michael away from the bar. A woman barreled through the door, chased by a couple of men. She screamed. "Stay away from me."

She fell and one man grabbed her hair, dragging her several feet, laughing while swigging a beer. Michael jumped him. Another man swatted at Michael with his bottle, cracking the back of his head.

Michael fell to the ground, wincing, dazed. He looked up to see Adriel manhandling one, picking him up and tossing him like a rag doll. Michael staggered to his feet, picked up the loose bottle, and smacked it against the other man, knocking him to the ground.

Adriel lifted the woman up. "Go. Don't come back."

The frightened woman sprinted away.

"Let's get out of here," Adriel said.

Michael threw the bottle against the bar door. It broke into several pieces.

Chapter 30

Michael and Adriel sought shelter at a local inn. Still hurting from the brawl, Michael lay down on top of a tiny wooden bed. Its mattress was rock hard, but he hardly noticed, gazing out to nowhere.

Adriel stayed silent for much of the evening until Michael got up, restless. He looked out of the only window in the room.

"What's on your mind?" Adriel asked.

Michael shrugged.

"I know," Adriel said. "I know...it's crazy here."

"What's with the old World War II uniforms? Why..."

Adriel jarred him out of finishing his thought. "Shush!" He leaned down. "Never mention those uniforms. The Umbras wear it to honor their ancestors. It's their sick tradition. Nothing more. Just plain evil."

Michael didn't respond. He sighed and stared out at the vast fields that surrounded the three-story bed and breakfast. The sky was dark and clear; there was a crispness in the air. Michael opened the window slightly, gazing at the twinkling stars. The moon's light illuminated a peaceful landscape, ironic indeed in these times. Michael couldn't care less. "There's so much beauty in this world, yet so much ugliness." He took a deep breath and turned to Adriel. "What you went through is horrible, cruelly horrible, and I don't know whether to cry or be outraged and seek revenge for you," he said. "But what I have seen here... so many have a right to be scared. I'd want to take revenge. I couldn't just stand and watch and do nothing."

Adriel gave a perplexed look. "Revenge might not be the answer, at least right now," Adriel said, his face looking drawn to Michael, wrinkles seemingly forming deeper since their travels. Or perhaps it was the moonlight's glow slicing through the only window streaking across his face that struck Michael most. "Revenge needs to be taken at the proper time. Be careful when you seek it."

Michael took a couple of steps toward Adriel. "I've done something that changed time, changed my town, altered my life...maybe even yours—your children, your wife, I mean... your unit. This repulsive world. I've done something terrible..." The words trailed off. Michael sighed and hung his head.

"You're talking crazy," Adriel said. "One man can't change this world. Many have tried. But it can't be done."

"That's not true. One man can change many lives. Millions even. Can change how the world looks at this life we are given. Can change how we look at life after we take our last breath. And you don't even need a sword or weapon to do it."

"Ha! You live in a fantasy world for sure. Are you sure you're not writing a novel? Am I going to be in this out of this world story?" Adriel laughed again.

Michael paused, reflecting for a brief moment. "I know it's hard to believe. But I could visit places and events from the past," he continued to explain. "I was back in first-century Jerusalem. Is there even a Jerusalem?"

"Yes, there is," Adriel said.

"How about that…but there is no United States. No churches. No Jesus. Right? You never heard of him?"

Adriel shrugged.

Michael gave a forlorn look. "I need to figure out what went wrong and where it went wrong." He looked up at Adriel. "And how to fix this."

"We do not have much money left. We need to keep moving, or the locals will become suspicious," Adriel warned. "Anyone who isn't anyone here will be taken for monetary gain and sold to the Umbras to be slaves. Do you want to end up like my unit? Many men have given themselves up, so their units didn't have to be enslaved."

"What happened to you? Did you have no choice?" Michael asked.

Adriel looked down and grimaced. "I didn't know they were taken until it was too late. I was out trying to find safety to avoid the camps. By the time I returned, my unit was gone."

"How do you know they were taken?"

"I saw the blood. The stuffed animals left behind. Our journals. They would never leave any of that."

Adriel continued. "Local governments are desperate for funds and looking to appease the Umbras to avoid punishment. We would fetch some a lot of Umbra money."

Michael shook his head. "This world has gone mad."

"It's always been this way. And you have not seen the crazy parts yet," Adriel said. "What your eyes will see will devastate you, ruin you, destroy your heart."

Michael sighed. "There isn't much left of my heart." He paused. "I'm not sure I want to see those parts."

Adriel sat back down on the bed. "You have no choice. It's best you get as much rest as you can."

Michael lay down on the bed, still lounging on the top of the covers.

"Do you want to see that woman?" Adriel asked.

"'That woman' meaning my wife?" Michael said.

"Whatever. But you saw how the women here are."

Michael waved his hands at Adriel. "I don't want to hear it," he raged.

"Okay, okay, I get it. Keep your voice down and contain that temper. We need to be civil here. We are strangers in their town."

"I understand. But this frustrates me."

"Perhaps we shouldn't go see her then," Adriel suggested.

"We leave at sunrise." Michael asserted, managing to pull part of the top blanket over his legs.

"Let's see how you feel in the morning."

"I'm not going to feel any different in a few hours than I feel right now."

"Do you want to take her back with us?"

Michael sat up. "How?"

"By the way we do things in this world. It won't get done doing it your way."

"Go on."

Adriel tore a piece of bedsheets away. He put it around his mouth. "Like this," he said in a muffled tone.

Michael's eyes widened. "Are you saying we kidnap her?"

"I'm saying we do what's necessary."

⁓⁓⁓

Michael arose with vigor, anxious to see Susan and what her life had become and wary over what he witnessed last night. *Would my son Paul be there? Maybe Elizabeth?* He could sense Adriel wasn't as excited, noticing he was taking his time packing up.

Perhaps he knew much more about Susan and her life than he admitted. Adriel was a man of this world. Surely, his instincts were better than his. Yet somehow Michael remained hopeful Susan would remember him. There was no logic in any of this, so why should he think otherwise?

Adriel pocketed a long silver knife. "Are you sure?"

Michael pointed at the weapon. "Yes, and do you need that?"

"You're naïve," Adriel frowned. "You have had a soft life. One without violence. Pain. Blood."

Michael shook his head. "No. That is not true. I've seen my fair share of tragedy."

Adriel paused a moment and continued. "Then act like it. I have spent much of my life grieving over the loss of my unit. And I had no idea how to live through it. We are forced to live their life of beliefs. Worshipping many gods. It seems to inspire their occupation. Their drive for military might." He went to Michael. His eyes were sorrowful. "I tried suicide four times, and each time something in my heart told me I needed to see another day. I could never figure out what the reason was until recently. Until now."

"Me?"

"Not just you," Adriel said. "But your unit. I could help you find them, the ones you love. Then I'd have a reason to live one more day. I know you would do the same for me."

"I would," Michael finally extended his hand. Adriel grabbed it with firmness.

"I'm ready," Michael said with a burst of enthusiasm.

Adriel paid the clerk at the front desk. "I own you big time," Michael said.

"Do you even have any credits?"

"What I have wouldn't work here. It would only make people suspicious."

They were greeted with a cold morning and overcast skies. A feel of rain was in the air. There was a commotion not far from the small hotel. Michael stopped and squinted. "What's going on by the bar?"

"It's not our business."

A woman screamed, her shrieks echoing on the damp morning.

"Someone is in trouble," Michael said.

"We should move quickly," Adriel insisted, ignoring him.

"Are you listening to me?"

"I heard you. Let's get out of here before it's too late."

Michael continued to walk toward the crowd gathered in front of the bar. He reached the outer portion of the mob. Men and women surrounded Colleen. She lay on the ground, her hands covering her face. Michael pushed his way through to her. "Colleen, what's going on?"

She removed her hands from her face.

Her eyes were black and blue with gashes on her cheeks and above her eyes.

"My goodness!" Michael said, trying to help her up. A stone smacked Michael on the back. "Hey! Who did that?"

One burly looking man stepped forward, holding a stone. "Get away from this whore. You are obstructing justice."

Michael stood and confronted the man. "Don't you dare."

The man grabbed him by the bottom of his jacket and flung him into the crowd. A melee erupted. Michael covered his head, and the mob kicked at him. He rolled away from the swatting. "Get out of the way," Adriel said, tossing bodies aside.

Michael felt a hand lift him off the ground. "Have you had enough fun?" Adriel said, his face displaying rage.

Michael went to Colleen. She was bloodied and unconscious. He knelt beside her to feel if she had a pulse. She didn't. Michael opened up and started breathing into her. He tried and tried… and tried until Adrien leaned over. "We need to go."

Michael got up and turned to the mob. "Are you happy? She's dead. You're all murderers!"

Adriel whispered to him. "This isn't our town. This isn't our battle."

The crowd split. Whistles screeched. "The Umbras!" a woman shouted.

Adriel grabbed Michael and led him away. "Run! The shadows are coming."

"Where to?" Michael yelled.

"Follow me!"

Chapter 31

Michael and Adriel rested in an unattended barn. Cobwebs decorated an area where horses used to be held. He was in one stall while Adriel was in the one next to him.

"Let's wait a few minutes before leaving," Adriel whispered.

"Why didn't you want me to help Colleen?"

"Because I knew it was a lost cause."

Michael shook his head in disbelief. "What were they doing?"

"Giving her town justice."

"By stoning her to death?"

"That's justice."

Michael slammed the stall wall.

"Hey, keep it down," Adriel said in a firm whisper.

"What did Colleen do to justify being stoned?"

"Anything the Umbras can think of."

Michael sighed. "So they give out punishment to the people here like what the Romans did by sending the Christians to the lions?"

"Christians?"

"Yes. Christians. Lions. Romans."

"Don't know what you're talking about."

Michael became frustrated. He stood. "I'm going."

Adriel joined him, pulling him back before taking a peek out from the barn. "Not so fast! Okay, wait...wait...wait...okay, the coast is clear."

They walked and walked and walked, measuring their steps, deep in reflection, though likely only Michael was more pensive after what he saw. It wasn't long his heart raced as he could see a diminutive woman hanging laundry on a long line in a spacious backyard complete with swings and slides and monkey bars.

"What do you think?" Adriel asked.

"About what?"

Adriel turned and smacked him on his right shoulder. "The weather," Adriel said, laughing. "The woman! Is that her?"

"I need to get closer," Michael said, squinting.

They walked several more yards. A heavy mist settled and drops of rain descended from the heavens. The woman grabbed the boy and girl by their hands and dragged them inside the farmhouse.

"Oh, great," Michael shouted. "Now what?"

"We go to the house and knock on the door."

"No."

"No? You didn't drag me out into the countryside to not meet her."

Adriel gripped Michael's left arm and pulled him down a final embankment. The house was slightly lit. Worn, red wooden frames barely stretched around two big windows in the front. Rain rolled off the steep roof, a tile fell from the brisk wind, and some water filled several buckets below, reminding Michael of the homes in first-century Jerusalem.

Adriel let go of Michael's arm. He stood in front of the window, peering into the house. Michael stood behind him.

"We should leave now," Adriel said, turning around quickly.

"Why? What's wrong?"

Adriel grabbed his arm again and Michael jerked it away. "No. I want to see."

Michael walked to the window. Rain pelted him sideways, its moisture dripping from the top of his head to his nose and mouth. He spat some of it away and stared.

"We should leave," Adriel said again.

Michael stayed silent, still fixated on what he saw inside—women entertaining, some sitting on laps of older men, one red-haired woman leading a man into another room. Michael pounded on the door. "Susan, Susan!"

"Stop!" Adriel said, pulling him away. "What are you doing?"

Michael pushed Adriel away. "Stay out of this!"

Adriel put his hands up in a surrender fashion. "Okay. I understand."

"No, you don't," Michael countered. "You have no idea what this feels like."

Adriel shoved him. "Don't tell me what it feels like. I've lost much more. Seen more blood and death. Don't you ever lecture me on what I do and don't feel."

Michael took a deep breath. He slammed his clenched fist on the door four more times. "Susan! Answer the door!"

An elderly woman opened it. "Mister, what do you want?"

"I want to see Susan, the red-haired one I just saw with another man."

"You'll have to wait your turn."

"I don't think so," Michael said, pushing the woman aside.

"Michael!" Adriel said. "I'm sorry, madam. He's had too much to drink."

Michael turned back as he began to climb a stairway. "I have not. I am here to take my wife back home."

"Nebid!" the elderly lady shouted up the stairway. "We need help."

A man appeared with an automatic weapon at the top of the stairs. "Back away. You wait your turn."

Michael climbed a few more steps.

"Don't do it," Adriel implored.

Michael took two more steps.

Nebid locked his gun and pointed it at him. "Last chance, hero."

Chapter 32

Michael backed down the stairs, half putting his hands up.

"Smart choice, hero," Nebid said, walking down the stairs.

"We don't want any trouble," Adriel said.

"Nor do we," the elderly lady added.

"Maddy, what do you want me to do with these two?"

Adriel stepped toward Nebid. "He's had a bit too much to drink. We apologize. We support the Umbras. Always."

"What?" Michael said.

"We support the Umbras," repeated Adriel, glaring at him.

"Keep your hero under control," Nebid said. "I won't be far. Maddy, any more trouble, say the word."

"Thank you, Nebid," Maddy said. She turned to Adriel and Michael. "Are you going to give me any more trouble?"

Michael didn't answer, furious that Adriel surrendered his pride.

"There will be no more problems," Adriel promised.

"What about the hero?" she asked, buttoning up her bright red sweater to the top of her neck.

Adriel glared at Michael.

Finally, Michael relented. "All good here."

Maddy smiled. She brushed away some gray hair, twisting it into a long pony tail. She stood up straight, perhaps trying to appear taller than her diminutive frame. "You want to spend time with Susan?"

"Yes," Michael answered.

"That's a big price. Susan is one of our most asked for."

Michael sneered.

"How much?" asked Adriel.

She went to him and whispered some words, "Whatever you have we will take."

Adriel pulled out some money. "Is this enough?"

"It will do. You boys rest in the waiting room." She pointed in the direction where it was. Michael and Adriel went to it. Adriel sat down. Michael stood, enraged. "How can you just sit there while this is happening?"

Adriel shook his head. "Do you want to see her or not?"

"What kind of a question is that?" He slapped at Adriel's shoulder.

Adriel shot up, grabbing Michael's neck. "I told you before. Keep your hands off of me."

He released his grip and Michael backed away. "I just can't sit there while another man touches her. Can you understand that?"

Adriel sat back down. "She won't even know you."

"How do you know that?"

"Because if she did, she wouldn't be giving herself to another man."

Michael's face reddened. He jumped Adriel and they fell to the floor.

"Halt!" Nebid shouted, pointing his gun at them. He tugged at his fatigues briefly, then adjusted his dark green hat, bits of gray peeking out from his long sideburns.

Maddy joined him. "Oh, boys, stop acting like children. Susan is available for both of you."

Adriel and Michael got up, pushing each other away.

"I have no interest in this woman," Adriel said. "I will wait here."

Maddy nodded. "Susan is cleaning up. She will be ready in five minutes."

Nebid pushed them both into their seats. "Next time, I'll put a bullet in both of you."

Adriel shrugged.

Michael glared.

Nebid backed up, twisting his cap backwards for a better view. He rolled up his left sleeve, his arm coiled in a weight lifter's pose. "Try me."

Chapter 33

Maddy guided Michael to a room on the third floor. It was dimly lit, candles hovering above, flickering from the breeze of a small fan circulating. The light pink walls danced with shadows of first Michael and then Susan entering the room. "Hello there, are you a sailor or a soldier?"

"Neither," Michael responded.

Susan appeared tired, her eyes drawn and mourning, clothes scantily covering her body. She smiled slightly. Her fingernails cracked in several places, some red underneath a couple of fingers.

"Susan, do you know me?"

She shook her head. "Should I?"

"Yes."

"Where do I know you?"

Michael drew a frustrated breath. "What happened to you? Why this?"

Susan moved closer. "Who are you?"

Michael didn't answer. "Why? Why are you doing this?"

"Do you want me to attend to you?"

Michael went to Susan, holding her hands. "No. Why are you doing this to yourself?"

Susan pushed him away. "Are you here for me as you requested or to bore me with your questions?"

Michael went to her again, clenching her hands. "Listen to me. We know each other. From another town. Likely another time."

"What are you saying? You scare me."

"I don't mean to."

She pulled away from his clench. "You should leave. You're not interested in me."

"No. I need to know why you are doing this. The Susan I know is intelligent, a strong woman, someone who would look at this profession as beneath her. You are a fighter against such an injustice."

Susan went to the stairway. "Maddy, this man is done."

"That was quick!" Maddy replied, laughing.

"My quickest one."

Maddy giggled more, and Michael joined Susan at the stairway. "You don't have to do this."

Susan turned to him. "I can see this is not a place for you. Your eyes show kindness, not like the meanness I see in all the other men. Leave while you can. Nebid takes his revenge on anyone who displeases us."

Susan left and went back into the room. Michael peeked in once more. He went to her. "Your cousin was stoned this morning."

Susan didn't respond.

"Did you hear what I said?"

"I heard."

"And?"

"You best go now," she said to him. "While you can."

Michael gathered up a deep breath, annoyed. "Your cousin. Colleen. She's dead."

Susan looked away.

"Does this not bother you?"

She turned to him, her face forlorn. A tear dropped from her eye. "Leave while you can. Never come back."

Michael went to the doorway. "I plead with you. Meet us in two hours. Make up any excuse. We will make sure you have a better life."

Susan stayed silent.

Michael went back downstairs, meeting Adriel at the front door. Maddy slammed the door shut. "What happened?" Adriel asked.

He hung his head and slid down the front door, taking some loose paint chips with him. He curled up like a baby in his mother's stomach and buried his head with his hands, weeping. He knew Susan didn't recognize him. He knew he had lost her forever. His thoughts went to Elizabeth. *Where are you? Are you gone forever?* Michael agonized more. *My Elizabeth.* "My Elizabeth," he screamed.

Adriel leaned down. "Don't make me bend over. I'm too old for that," he said, giving a slight laugh.

Michael took a deep breath and wiped his eyes. "You were right. She had no idea who I was. I tried to convince her to leave with us."

"What?" Adriel said, giving a look of disbelief.

"I offered her a chance at a better life."

"You need to wake up. It's a great profession for a woman. What else would a woman do here to make some good money?"

Michael shook his head. "Are you kidding me?"

"There is no better profession for a woman here than what this Susan is doing."

Michael scowled. He wasn't sure whether to belt Adriel or break the door down and kidnap Susan. The rain gained some steam, and he could see Adriel becoming impatient.

"We have more traveling ahead," Adriel insisted.

"Where?" Michael asked, confused.

"I have an idea," he said, his eyes lighting up much like the Christmas trees Michael remembered.

Michael was conflicted about leaving. The urge to knock on the door again swept through him. Adriel tapped him on his shoulder. Instead, Michael retreated from the thought. "What's your idea?" he asked.

"You said you had a first unit. Right?"

"My first wife."

"A unit," Adriel said.

"Whatever. Yes, my first friend or partner or unit or whatever you want to call her. She died the night Elizabeth was born," Michael said in frustration.

"Exactly."

Michael looked at him, digesting Adriel's happy face and his words. "Oh, my. Do you think?"

Adriel's eyes widened. "A guess."

"But a good one."

"Where to?"

"Not far from here," Michael said.

Chapter 34

Michael arose feeling dreadful. He'd struggled throughout the night to ward off a nightmare. Perhaps what he saw was just a dream and he was just waking up from it all? It didn't take more than a few stretches of his aching arms and legs to realize it was all too real. He suppressed the extreme depression after meeting Susan and seeing what she had to do to live. He convinced himself that desperation would be his best medicine to survive. To go on. To battle. *What will be of Susan? And Paul? Our child? I guess there is no Paul since we were never together. Is there anything we can do? Help her. No. She didn't want our help. What about Vicki? Oh, I can't even bear to think about this anymore. No. I refuse to believe she is living the same life. I need to change this. For everyone.*

He looked at Adriel. *I wonder if it would change for Adriel too? Would he be able to save his friends or family or whatever he refers to them as? Maybe have a different life? Perhaps find another home? Again. Maybe we are supposed to be together. To help each other. There are so many ways it can go. But which way? Which way is the real way? The real way it's supposed to be for everyone. How am I supposed to know which way is the right way?*

He then thought about Adriel's story of contemplating suicide and the reasons why he gave Michael to fight one more day. Perhaps now Adriel was Michael's reason to do the same. Perhaps they met each other for bigger reasons than they both ever comprehended.

Yet guilt swept over him like it had done many times before. Guilt was all-consuming because Michael let it overrun him in every part of his life.

The emotional torture of seeing how awful Susan's life was and the anticipation of possibly meeting Vicki again rattled his soul. Would Vicki be living the same way? Like Susan. Oh, what a terrible, dreadful thought. His mood swung much like the pendulum in that eerie Edgar Allen Poe's horror story, and he wondered what he could do about Vicki, if anything. Adriel tried to settle him and failed.

"You need to get a hold of yourself," Adriel said, trying calm him. "She doesn't know you. It's better she doesn't from what it sounds like your previous life was with her…though this still confuses me." Adriel gave him an unconvincing look of belief and shook his head.

"Stop it!" Michael yelled. "I don't want to hear about it anymore. Your confusion. Whatever you believe. Whatever you think how a woman needs to live here. *To make a living…*" he said with deep sarcasm. Michael lashed out to no one in particular. "I don't care what your beliefs are or what society wants you to believe or how you've been *brainwashed* to think a woman should be here!"

Adriel approached him. "I never said a woman should—I said it is what they needed to do to survive. And I'm not brainwashed. I am a survivor. Susan is a survivor."

Michael dismissed what he thought was his warped logic.

Adriel continued. "What do you think Vicki will be doing to survive? Have you thought about that? Are you prepared to see her like Susan? You better wake up here. This isn't some novel you read or wrote."

Michael ignored him. He focused on getting to Vicki's possible destination. "Suffolk. My recollection is telling me to go there. From what she told me of where her family...unit came from, it's near the coast."

"Beautiful territory. Shouldn't be a problem with authorities. We need to steal some means of transportation," Adriel added. "If we are to get there."

Michael hesitated. "We would be at risk from the Umbras. Would we not? What if we were caught?"

"You need to stop," Adriel said in anger, rushing over to him. "Your world is not real. Or the world you think this is. This world will devour you like lions in the jungle if you act like a lamb. You'll get slaughtered. And one thing is for sure: I will not get slaughtered because of you."

"Don't you have any more credits left?" Michael asked, his tone more conciliatory.

"We have just enough to get back."

"Oh."

"Yeah. Come and join me in this real world."

"What are we stealing?"

"Those," Adriel said, pointing to two chained up, rusty looking bikes by a grocery store.

Michael shook his head. "How in God's name do we take them?"

Adriel smiled. "Have you ever stolen anything in your life?"

"Well, a package of Twinkies…and when I'm in Jerusalem, plenty."

Adriel gave a confused look. "What are Twinkies?"

"An artificial delight of sugar and sponge," Michael said.

"You come from one weird world, if you are telling me the truth," Adriel replied, moving in a brisk pace toward the bicycles.

"Slow down," Michael pleaded.

Adriel pulled out a small ax.

"Geez, where did you get that?"

"I took it from the whorehouse's garage."

"When did you do that?" Michael asked.

"When you went upstairs to see Susan."

Adriel swung his ax fast and with force twice, breaking the old chains in seconds. He pulled the two bikes away. "Which one?" he asked Michael.

"Doesn't matter. Do any of them even ride?"

Adriel grabbed the blue colored one and gave the smaller pink one to Michael. "Oh, great."

"You said it didn't matter. Besides, I'm bigger and heavier and certainly stronger than you. This one looks sturdier than the other one."

"Sure."

"You said it didn't matter."

"Okay, okay. Take a chill pill," Michael said, putting up his hands defensively.

"You are starting to drive me crazy," Adriel said, hopping onto the bike.

Adriel looked away and began to pedal. Michael did the same, catching up to him. "I'm sorry, Adriel. It's a verbal reflex for me to say something like that. It's in our culture."

Adriel didn't respond.

"Please accept my apology."

They continued to pedal in silence for several minutes. Michael reached over and rang the small bell on Adriel's bike. He continued the annoying ringing until he saw Adriel break into a slight smile.

"Ah, you love me ringing your bell?" Michael said with a smirk.

Adriel shook his head.

Michael rang the bell again.

Adriel swung at him and missed.

"Ring my beeelllllll, ring my bell."

"Stop."

"Oh, you don't love my bell ringing?"

"No. Your voice. It's like knives scraping concrete...." He looked at Michael. "No more."

"Are we crazy in love?" Michael said with the biggest grin.

"You are testing the boundaries of my patience."

They both pedaled faster, gaining a bit of energy from their playful banter.

"How much longer do we have to get to Suffolk?" Michael asked.

"Not long. It's a pretty town. Many tourists go there for the ocean."

"How difficult will it be to find Vicki?"

"I don't know. We got lucky in that bar finding out where Susan lived. Luck usually doesn't come around twice, at least for me. What about you?"

Michael took a deep breath. "I actually got lucky twice."

"Well, in this world, it's not likely to happen. We are probably going to have to take more time finding her."

Michael nodded. "I'm persistent. I've dreamed of seeing her many times."

"Even while you were with the other one?"

"Yes. Even when I was with Susan."

Adriel gave him a confused look.

"You never forget your first love, your first wife—I mean your first unit. We had plans. Goals. To raise a family together. To travel. To make a wonderful life. Then I was betrayed. By a friend. And I had to learn how to forgive. I'm not sure I have."

They stayed silent for the rest of the ride, only to be interrupted with an occasional bump until the brimming evening lights of Suffolk greeted them.

"Let's find shelter," Adriel said. "We will have to sneak into a room."

Michael barely understood the words, his mind wandering into yesteryear, half asleep. Adriel jolted him out of his trance, showing him a short metal rod. Michael surveyed the vacantness around him, giving him initial comfort. In the vastness of it all stood a lone, small structure, its windows on the second floor, blackened.

Chapter 35

There was no one at the front desk. Adriel put a couple of fingers to his lips. Michael nodded. They tiptoed through the small lobby, arriving at a lone elevator. Adriel pressed the up button. "We'll go to the top floor. Hopefully it's vacant and we won't have to worry."

The elevator stopped.

A bell rung.

The elevator door opened up.

"Well, hello," said an old man, his half smile unnerving Michael.

"Uh, hi," Michael managed to say.

"Looking for a room?"

"Indeed," Adriel interjected.

"Come with me."

The old man pulled out a decrepit looking notebook and paged through it slowly. "There we are," he said, looking up at them. "Do you want the executive suite or standard?"

"Exec—" Michael said.

"Standard," Adriel interjected, placing some Umbra money on the desk.

The old man stared at it.

"What's wrong?" Adriel asked.

"I'll never get used to it."

Adriel sighed. "I hear you. I use it to stay safe."

The old man nodded and handed them a key. "Room 304. Smoking allowed."

"That won't be necessary," Michael said.

"If you wish."

"I do."

"Thank you, sir," Adriel said.

As Michael turned, he watched the old man open another drawer. He saw a gun. It looked like a Glock. He tapped Adriel on his shoulder.

Adriel ignored him. "Keep walking."

"What's wrong?"

"No one is allowed to have guns here," Adriel said. "Except the Umbras."

Adriel and Michael came back downstairs to seek some much-needed food. There was none, the clerk said. Yet he was in a mood to talk—perhaps lonely since it appeared only Michael and Adriel were staying the night.

The clerk said his grandfather had come home from World War II, depressed and angry from his country losing the war. To the Umbras. The three evils, as the clerk put it. "He hated living. He hated what his country had become. He hated people." The clerk looked down, shaking his head. "He was ashamed.

He eventually took his life so he wouldn't face working in the camps."

Adriel nodded several times and stopped Michael from disputing the old man's historical account. "You weren't there," Adriel scolded him. "Were you?"

"No, I wasn't," protested Michael. "But my country won that war. After what happened at Pearl Harbor. We were bombed while all those men were sleeping on the ships. In Hawaii. December 7th, 1941. Roosevelt's speech. A day in infamy."

"What are you talking about?" scolded Adrien.

"I'm telling you the truth. I swear. The US dropped the bomb to end the war. Had to do it twice before they surrendered. D-Day. V-Day. Churchill."

"Pearl Harbor? What is that? What does USA stand for? Churchill?" The old man laughed. "Biggest bust for our country. He got hung on that big clock tower—Big Ben. What a disaster he turned out to be."

"The bomb?" said Adriel. "Are you talking about the nuclear bomb?"

"Yes."

"The Umbras have the bomb."

"Never bring up the name Churchill here either," the clear behind the desk cautioned.

"What are you talking about?" Michael said. "Churchill was the reason the English withstood all the bombings at night."

Adriel shook his head. "You never learn, do you? Please forgive him. He is lost with his fictional account of history."

"You don't need to forgive me," Michael roared. "I know what I know."

The clerk put up his hands defensively. He winked toward Adriel.

"I saw that," Michael raged.

Adriel laughed. The clerk laughed.

"Now you're both laughing at me. Great," Michael added.

Adriel slapped him on his back. The clerk smiled. "Perhaps you need a bit of tea to calm your nerves," he said, his smile much like the Cheshire Cat in *Alice in Wonderland.*

Michael rolled his eyes. "I don't need your tea. I don't need you. And I don't need you either." Michael glared at Adriel.

Adriel was unfazed. "Don't be mad at me for trying to stop you from disputing true history and facts."

Michael sighed. "Can we have the keys to the room?"

"No keys necessary here," the clerk said.

"Terrific. What kind of place do you run here?"

The clerk looked to his left and right and leaned over the old wooden desk. He whispered. "One that abides by the rules of the Umbras," the clerk said, continuing to look around.

"What in God's name—"

"Stop," the clerk demanded. "There is no God. We do not believe in God. Never, ever mention God. Ever."

Michael was frozen. Adriel gave a sheepish grin.

"Why is that rule of not allowing to have keys for a room important to the....um...the so-called Umbras?" Michael asked.

"The kind where they can sneak into any room to punish those they feel are disloyal."

"Your world is truly messed up," Michael said, dropping his voice.

"And where might be your world?" the clerk asked. "The moon?"

Adriel laughed.

Michael gave him a dirty look.

"Chill," Adriel said, slapping Michael in the chest.

"My country put the first man on the moon," said Michael with pride.

The clerk and Adriel looked at each other.

"What? Did I say something inaccurate? Again?"

Adriel and the clerk stayed quiet.

"Hello, Earth to Adriel? Hello to the cranky clerk behind the desk."

Adriel shook his head, and the clerk walked away.

"Tell me what's wrong."

Adriel walked Michael up two flights of stairs to their room and closed the door. He pulled a chair forward and shoved it under the doorknob. He then dragged a big dresser and placed it against the door.

"What did I say?"

"We don't ever mention the moon or anything in the sky," Adriel said in a hushed voice. "We don't dare even look up at the sky."

"Why?"

"Two reasons why. Number one, the Umbras execute you if you look toward the sky because they believe you might be praying to God. Second, the Umbras have been reducing the world population in their most threatening places by sending people into the sky, never to come back. To die."

"Get out of here," Michael said.

"Rumor has it. People are disappearing."

"You have no proof. And that's an expensive way to reduce the population."

"Whether you believe me or not, don't look up because there are shadows watching everywhere. And do you think the Umbras care about money? They have all the gold in the world.

They have all the materials and water. I can only tell you what others have told me."

"I don't believe you. No way. There are other ways to do it, unfortunately."

"And how would you know?" Adriel said.

Michael sighed. "I just know."

"Care to tell?"

"No. I don't even know what I know is true."

Michael woke to a new day, catching Adriel's eye as he stood peering down at him after his bath. He wasn't sure whether he'd even find Vicki or what he would say or do. But he had to know. If she was okay. If she was safe. Not hurt. Not entrenched in this culture. *God forbid if she was part of…*

Adriel waved at him, disrupting his cruel thought. He mouthed. "Let's go."

Michael gave a thumbs up.

Adriel returned a confused look.

"I'll be right down," Michael said, not even knowing if Adriel could hear or comprehend his mouthing of words.

Michael moved his stolen Glock under a towel. *Yeah. I can be a badass here too. While the cats sleep, the mice play.* He smiled and waved at Adriel, who gave him a gesture to come right now. Michael mouthed, "Five minutes." He held up his hand, showing five fingers.

If he dares to cross me, I'll take him out. Michael pulled the gun back out, examining how many bullets he had left. *Enough to plug him in the heart. If he gets out of line or causes me any trouble, I'll leave him behind. He'll be fine. This is his world. I need this to survive here. Make sure you keep it out of sight. It looks like very few have a chance to defend themselves here.*

Michael gave another fake wave to Adriel, who turned around and prepared his bike. *That's right, Adriel. You are right. I'm not your friend. The only friend I need is this.* Michael put the gun under the towel again.

He looked for some deodorant and only found some small bits of broken soap embedded on the sides of the tub.

This will have to do. Vicki will be there. Maybe. Please be alive. Don't be...or be with any man. Or taken. Or...like Susan. Oh, Susan. I'm so sorry. I'm sorry this world has done this to you. Please, God. Help me. I have no more options. If anyone who can help me, she can. I know. I know this in my heart.

Then cold reality crushed him.

"What if we didn't meet? Like Susan. And what if...what do I do? What do I say? How will I convince her to leave?" he said in a despondent whisper.

Chapter 36

Michael straddled the bike, finding a comfortable way to rest on the narrow seat. He pressed down on the pedals and stretched his back and arms. He dug in for a long bike ride. He'd filled a makeshift container with tap water for the journey, though the water was murky and grimy. Once he'd been moving forward for several minutes, he cursed silently the strenuous feel of the transportation and yet marveled at the pristine beauty of the English countryside.

He saw green everywhere, and it was entrancing. It wasn't long before they wrestled with a thick, out-of-this-world-dense fog. Michael followed Adriel for a couple of miles to stay together, for the visibility was nil.

It was typical English weather. The wind was temperamental—sometimes sweet and inviting, sometimes wicked and fierce. The ferocity of it knocked Michael off his bike twice, leading to big bursts of laughter from Adriel. It was funny the first time to Michael but not so much the second.

He allowed his grieving heart to remember the romantic times he shared with Vicki. Their honeymoon in Aruba. Slow dancing in their only home after learning Vicki was pregnant with Elizabeth.

Michael's heart wept and swam in joy all at once as the bitterness and anger he had embedded in his soul so skillfully after Vicki died still lingered, biting at him. If only he could have completely let go of that rage that he'd temporarily buried after marrying Susan.

Adriel was strangely quiet, though Michael never would have noticed until his tire went flat.

"Houston, we got a problem."

"What does that mean?" Adriel asked.

"It means I have a problem."

Adriel gave a frustrated look and rolled back to Michael. "Wonderful."

"Now what?" Michael threw the bike down in anger. "Maybe we can borrow another one somewhere."

"You mean steal."

"Borrow."

"Steal."

"Whatever. Can we steal or borrow or whatever name you want to place on the action someplace else?"

Adriel shook his head. "Look around. What do you see?"

"Green."

"Precisely." Adriel took out a knife and plunged it into the remaining three tires on Michael's bike.

"What are you doing?" Michael asked.

"So no one else can use it and follow us."

"Are you serious, or have you lost your mind?"

"Perhaps a little of both," Adriel said. "Get on."

"Get on where?"

"Behind me, or do you prefer riding on the handlebars?"

"There isn't much room," Michael said, trying to reason with Adriel.

"Get on," demanded Adriel. "Or you can walk the next twenty or so miles."

Michael didn't protest anymore. He mounted the scrawny seat and wiggled his way on what space was available. "You know I'm not eight years old."

"Really? Are you sure?"

"Ha ha."

"Another wise word from the prime minister of weird world."

Michael tapped the top of Adriel's shoulder. "Am I frustrating you again?"

"Don't touch me."

"Then how do I stay on the bike?"

"Pray. You like to do that. Right? Pray for your life," Adriel said.

Michael couldn't tell if Adriel was bantering or being dead-on serious. He wrapped his arms around the lower part of Adriel and held on tightly. "We are a unit, right?"

"No. We aren't." Adriel looked back, glaring at him. "You are a pain in my everything."

"Pain in your everything? And you say I'm from a weird world."

Michael continued to tease and unnerve Adriel for the next couple of miles. "If I am part of your unit now, perhaps we can take our next trip together soon. But where to? South America? Nepal? The Himalayas?"

Adriel stopped the bike suddenly, and Michael was hoisted off and rolled down a hill a few feet. The Glock fell out of his pocket.

"Where did you get that?" questioned Adriel.

Stunned, Michael didn't answer. He wiped some grass and dirt off his clothes and glared. "You did that on purpose."

"Yeah, I did. How did it feel to fall on your brains? Do you have any more left?" Adriel roared in laughter.

Steamed, Michael raced toward him and shoved Adriel off the bike. "Don't you ever do that again."

Adriel got up and struck Michael in the head, knocking him back to the ground. They somersaulted down an embankment, switching places on top and bottom, grasping and pawing at each other like hangry cats and dogs.

Bloodied from a cut on his nose, Michael punched Adriel in the head. He winced, rolled over, and lay silent. "Geez, I'm sorry, Adriel, so sorry," Michael said with remorse. "I lost my temper. Let me help you up."

He nudged Adriel. He didn't respond. "Oh, God. What have I done? Help. Help," he yelled, his voice echoing.

Voices screamed out and Michael froze, trying to regain his feet. Before he could do so, up he went, lifted by several hands, squeezing his neck and arms. "Help my friend," he pleaded, choking and pointing to Adriel. "He's hurt."

Michael's hands were pulled behind his back and cuffed. "Hey, what are you doing? It was a friendly fight. Just two guys sorting out some of our differences. Help him. We are in the same unit. We support the Umbras!"

Two men came from behind. They wore long beards, their eyes covered in sunglasses. They were tall and muscular. They picked up Adriel and dragged him into a big white van with a large three faces similar to the money embroidered on the doors.

Michael watched Adriel struggle with the men. He managed to flee for a moment into the dense fog and didn't see anything more. Michael kicked at one of the men, knocking him flat on his back. A man faced and confronted him, displaying a machine gun.

Michael kicked once more, striking the man in his groin.

It wasn't long before the man recovered. He took off his sunglasses and placed them in his pocket.

He glared at Michael and swung his machine gun at him.

Michael grabbed it, and they tumbled to the ground. They struggled and rolled several yards.

Michael tried to break the finger on the trigger. He bent it back as the man screamed.

A shot echoed and rippled through the vast landscape.

Chapter 37

S tinging swats of small balls stung Michael.
The metal pellets dug deep. He winced and struggled to
stay on his feet.

One blow penetrated his lower back near his spinal cord. He
held onto the blood-stained wall.

He faked mocking his tormentors as a matter of pride and a
badge of courage showing he could not be broken.

The eerie touch of blood slithering down his back and legs
felt like a cobra ready to devour him.

Lightheaded, his vision was fuzzy. Michael slumped down,
ready and desperate to pass out.

His tormentors would not let it happen. They shot big bursts
of water out of cannons, smashing him around the tiny cage cell
like a cat chasing a mouse.

He regained his footing, took several steps like a drunk in a
bar during the last call, and crashed into the metal door. Michael
opened his eyes; water poured down into his face. He smiled.

"You can't beat me," he said within a measured, soft tone.
"You can whip me, flog me, bloody me, starve me, belittle

me. But I still have him." He pointed upward. His tormentors laughed and mocked him, calling Michael the man from space. "And you never had him. Or you never will have him."

He stumbled to a back wall and held onto it for a few moments like he often did as a child, clinging to the wall for fear of being taken on midnight rides for punishment. He wiped away more moisture from his face, took a deep breath, and fell to the floor. He lifted his head, relieved to find his tormentors were gone. Weary, his eyes barely open, he lay against the wall, sitting upright. He struggled to keep his eyes open, blood dripping into them, obstructing his vision. He relented and closed his eyes. He allowed his mind to find some rest.

His exhaustion helped him drift off into a dream, one he often had after he lost Vicki. He would take her sledding on the hills of Northport. The first Christmas Eve they spent in their new home, the skies provided a light snowstorm, enough to coat the hills with sweet sledding conditions.

He made hot chocolate and poured it into a thermal jug for them to enjoy. Michael put on his favorite winter coat, wrapped a scarf around his neck, and grabbed a pair of thick, black gloves.

Vicki looked adorable that night. She wore a heavy pink coat and matched it with a pink ski hat, scarf, and gloves. Her hand in his, they strolled down that icy, snow-covered hill to the Crab Meadow Golf Course.

The sixth hole with its steep inclines was an inviting target for sled enthusiasts of all ages and skill levels. Michael gave Vicki a soft kiss, placed the sled down, and sat in the back. "You can drive," he said, his smile as big as the snowflakes tumbling down.

"Wow. What an honor," she said, teasing him in the way only she could.

Vicki smiled and sat. Michael wrapped his arms around her. "I will never let go," he said.

Down the hill they went. They roared in laughter as the sled came to a slow stop, only a few feet from banging into a thick oak tree. "Stewart, you are one crazy man," Vicki said with a big grin.

"Yes, I am," he agreed. "Crazy in love with you."

"Well, you are my crazy man. Forever."

"Forever."

He tightened his grasp on her hand, tickling it with one finger, playfully bantering with her as they walked back up the hill. Then they sat in silence, relishing the picturesque sight before them. The landscape was like a beautiful painting, looking just like Thomas Kincade had created it. The solemn silence of solitude was something Michael had feared all his life. That night, it was different.

He was not alone.

They sipped their hot chocolate, and while they were quiet, they were talking, touching without touching, kissing without kissing, making love without doing so.

"This is majestic," Michael said in a soft tone, looking out over the landscape.

"Perfect," agreed Vicki.

Michael was weak, dehydrated, and broken, yet resilient. He slept some more—only for a short while though. He awakened flinching, grasping at air, thinking he saw Vicki.

He would race to the image, only to hug the putrid smell of the air he breathed. Death was all around him, in his mouth, throat, nose, eyes. It was so oppressive he threw up, and in hunger and fear of retribution, he crawled to his mess and ate it.

What am I doing? Where am I? Where's Vicki? How come she hasn't picked me up from work? Am I at work?

"Vicki, are you here?" he said to no one in particular. "Were you even born? Was Elizabeth born?"

She was dressed in all black with the heart earrings dangling, the ones he gave her for Christmas after their engagement. They sparkled in the evening moonlight, exciting him. Her lips were inviting, colored in a light pink shade. Her fingernails, neatly manicured, shone a darker pink.

She looked fabulous, like a movie star from the 1940s walking the red carpet.

Michael once again rose and walked toward her. His eyes danced with joy, and his body stirred with unconditional love.

"My love, I missed you. I need you. I love you. Please don't leave me. Help me find Elizabeth. Your daughter. Our daughter. Help me. Please, Vicki. Help."

Michael staggered a few steps. His eyes filled with tears as Vicki stood before him, arms stretched wide.

"This world is so cruel. I can't do this alone anymore."

He leaned his head on the door, holding onto the bars. Michael straightened up and cleared his eyes once more. He strained to see who stood before him. "Who are you?" he asked. "Are you here to hurt me? Guess what: I can't be hurt anymore. Tell me, who are you?"

There was no answer.

"Is that you, Vicki?"

There was no response.

"Can you help me?"

Michael wiped his eyes again. He strained to see who was before him. The image of a woman was distorted. He leaned in closer and opened a wound at the top of his forehead. Blood snaked its way down on his nose and mouth and dripped to the floor. He spat some of it away.

"Help me, please."

The woman unlocked the cage.

"Run," she said. "Run until you see no more Umbra soldiers."

Chapter 38

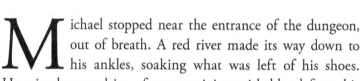

Michael stopped near the entrance of the dungeon, out of breath. A red river made its way down to his ankles, soaking what was left of his shoes. He wiped away drips of sweat mixing with blood from his eyes. His back stung, the welts reminding him of his previous brutal encounters.

He heard a woman's voice call to him in the distance. "Don't stop. Keep running."

Michael, still gasping for a deep breath, put his hand up in surrender. "I need to find Adriel."

The woman grabbed him by his arm and escorted Michael out of the dungeon. The sun felt warm and bright on his skin, but Michael couldn't see it. The images he saw were double and triple before him. He could hear birds chirping. A soft wind gave him a slight shiver.

He squinted and wiped more sweat and blood from his eyes. The wound at the top of his forehead still gushed. He grappled with stopping it with no success. A woman, her face dirtied and hair tied in a short ponytail, pulled harder on him.

"Sir, you must go with me, or we will both be caught," she insisted. "If I must carry you out of here, I will. But I will not let myself be captured again."

"But, my friend—my unit…"

"Forget your unit. We need to get you to safety, and then we can talk about your finding your unit."

Michael stooped over, catching a breath. "Where to?" he asked.

"Stay with me," the woman demanded, her blonde hair bouncing as she moved swiftly down a hill. Michael stumbled and fell, tumbling several times before coming to a stop, exhausted from the beatings he suffered and unable to sustain any kind of balance for more than a few steps.

"You're going to have to do better," the woman pleaded.

"I'm going as fast as I can."

"Well, go faster."

Michael stood again, wobbly. "Okay. Okay."

The woman put her shoulder underneath his and walked him for some distance to a small house, hidden in the deep brush of a forest. It was broken down, the front door without a screen.

"What is this?" Michael asked.

"A place to heal and get ready for the next trip."

"Oh, no. I am not going anywhere without Adriel."

The woman bent down to Michael, who sat against a wall in what he assumed was the living room. "I admire your loyalty," she said. "But our safety comes first. If you are healed and want to play hero, that's your choice. But we don't even know where this Adriel is."

"Don't say that," Michael said, trying to get up. He fell just as quickly. "He's alive. I know he is. He's stronger than me. Stronger than you. Smarter. Tougher."

The woman stood and began building a fire. "I hope he is for your sake," she said with skepticism.

"I won't be able to go on without him."

She turned to him. "You may not have a choice."

Michael didn't respond. He crawled over to where the fire was, warming himself. He lay flat on his stomach, avoiding any contact with the stinging gashes on his back.

"Let me try to treat your wounds," the woman said.

"I'm okay."

"You're not. You're still bleeding. Drop your inflated male ego and let me help you. I won't think any less of you."

Michael was too exhausted to debate. He closed his eyes. The woman gently pulled his shirt off, dropping the blood-stained and drenched clothing to the side.

He felt the cool compresses the woman placed on his welts. He flinched several times. "Forget the pain. This is the healing part," she said several times.

Michael closed his eyes and relaxed.

"Vicki, wake up, please," Michael pleaded.

She lay in a hospital bed, motionless. Elizabeth was nearby, held and coddled by a nurse, crying like she'd swallowed the raging sun.

Michael held Vicki's hand, kissing it several times. "My love, please open your eyes. Please. Talk to me. Look at our daughter. She's here. She's here for both of us."

Vicki didn't answer.

"Give my wife her daughter," Michael said. "Now!"

"Mr. Stewart, please," the nurse said.

"I said give Elizabeth to my wife. Now."

"Mr. Stewart, please…."

Michael looked back at Vicki. "They won't give you Elizabeth, my love. What am I going to do? Please wake up. Please."

He wept. "Tell me. I'll be lost without you. I won't be able to go on. Please stay with me. We need you. Elizabeth needs her mother."

Michael wiped away his tears.

"Mr. Stewart, we should go," the nurse called over, still holding Elizabeth.

He stood, yelling, "I'm not leaving my wife."

A chaplain came in and put his hand on Michael. "It's time for me to administer the last rites."

Michael swatted his hand away. "Don't you dare! She isn't dead. Get away from her. Get away from me!"

"Son, let me help you. Let the nurses help you."

"I'm not your son."

"I understand."

"You understand? What do you understand? Tell me what words of wisdom you have for me while my wife dies—tell me!"

The pastor stepped back and bowed his head, saying a prayer.

Michael lay his head on Vicki's shoulder. "My love, I just can't go on. I can't."

Michael awoke, sitting up, his hands swinging.

"Woah, settle down, sailor," the woman said. She placed a wet cloth on his forehead. "Sit back."

Michael struggled to stay up.

"Lay back."

"Who are you?" Michael asked. "Are you an angel?"

The woman gave a slight smile. "You could say that."

"Why did you help me?"

"Because you looked like you needed it."

Michael sat up, wincing. "I can see now."

"You had a lot of blood that soaked your eyes. So it's no wonder you had trouble with your vision."

The woman looked about his age. She had a scar on her right cheek, and some wrinkles were forming under her eyes. Her hands were rough and without any long fingernails. She had the hands of someone who lived outside.

"Looks like you've been through a few battles," he said.

"More than you can imagine."

"Is this something you do all the time?"

She rinsed the bloodied cloth into a plastic bucket. "What do you mean?"

"I mean rescuing people."

"You could say that."

"I'm glad you rescued me."

The woman smiled, sending chills down his spine.

"My name is Michael."

"Nice to meet you, Michael. My name is Vicki."

Michael's eyes widened.

She looked away, taking a quick glance out the window. "Did you know another Vicki? You were calling for her when I opened your cell."

Chapter 39

Adrenaline rushed through Michael like it had the first time he met Vicki many years ago. Yes, these circumstances were a world apart—literally. It was her eyes—her green eyes—that convinced Michael it was her yet wasn't her. His mind scrambled for some simplicity, and he knew that where he was it wasn't just possible.

Michael knew he could not inundate Vicki with too much information about what he did in Jerusalem or feed her his memories of them as a couple and lovers. She would think he was crazy. She would leave him or perhaps even worse, turn him in to the Umbras for a favor.

Who would believe him anyway?

Adriel still doesn't believe me.

Michael thought perhaps Vicki and her friends would have some resources to help him find Adriel. He couldn't afford to push that possibility away with his mad story.

Then his romantic side engulfed him. His previously extinguished feelings that he buried for so long surfaced. Could he and Vicki get back together again? *And what was with the blonde hair? Maybe she isn't Vicki. My Vicki.*

Michael shook himself out of the brief confusion and semi-fantasy. He approached her. She was resting, pensive, her eyes open wide, gazing at the burning flames from the fireplace.

"Um, um, um...Vicki," Michael said, his heart beating fast, unsure of what to say just like he was on their first date.

Vicki pulled on her hair and removed a wig.

It is her.... or am I losing my mind and seeing what I want to see?

She turned and smiled. "For deception purposes...by the way, my name's not poison. You can say it."

Michael smiled nervously.

"Are you okay? Your face is red. This isn't a date, you know." Michael laughed though he wasn't sure why.

"I thought you might be like...I mean, I saw this woman, someone I knew a long time ago. She wasn't the person I knew back then, and..."

Vicki eyed him. "Who did you think I was?"

"I don't know. I've seen things in this world that I've never seen before."

"Are you new to this part of the country?"

Michael took a deep breath. "Yeah you could say that."

Vicki joined him. "I don't judge any man or woman. We do what we have to do to survive. I have done almost everything to stay alive."

Michael gave a forlorn look. "Everything?"

"Yes. It's why I am here today. To rescue you. To save you. To give you another chance."

Michael nodded. He reflected on what Vicki said, putting it into context of the world he now existed in at this moment.

He searched to change the subject, not wishing to dwell in any more of the thoughts flooding his mind regarding the hardships women endured. "Um. You have a pretty name."

"Pretty gets you nowhere in this wicked world."

Michael sat next to her, remembering all the fireside chats and cuddles they had when life was so simple and they were young and innocent, discovering their love for each other. He didn't know whether to feel sad or exhilarated. He was more forlorn, resigned to this cruel fate.

"Vicki…"

"Yes."

"Um, do you…I mean, are you…with…"

Vicki laughed. "Are you asking me what I think you are?"

"Oh. No…what do you think I was asking you?"

"Aren't you a smooth talker?"

"I'm not really."

"I know. It's a bit of English sarcasm."

"Oh."

She laughed again. Michael's ego was bruised.

"Hey, relax. I'm not committed to a unit. Wasn't that what you were going to ask me?"

He nodded and sat in silence. *Now what? No unit. Good. No children? Maybe? Who knows what they call it? No Elizabeth. Not good at all. Now what?*

There was another period of awkward silence between them.

He feigned, clearing his throat. "My friend…I mean my unit…"

"Yes, Adriel," she said. "You spoke of him often, even when you were delirious."

"We have to find him."

Vicki pushed some logs into the center of the fire, ignoring Michael's suggestion.

Michael moved closer. "Vicki…"

"Adriel, right," said Vicki. "I know."

"I don't have many friends like him. He's the one. The only one. In this world."

"You can count on me."

His face went red. "Always did."

Vicki gave him a confused look. "What?"

"I mean, yes. You've proven that to me."

"Listen to me. Hate to squash your male ego, but you're a lost puppy in this wacky world. Any man that gets captured by a group of native thugs and sold to the Umbras needs help."

Michael nodded. "What made you decide to do this?"

She stood and stretched, yawning. Michael admired her figure. Her legs and arms toned. She had that familiar curve. His heart raced.

"Survival. One of my former units was captured, sold, and raped. We decided as a group if one of us is taken by the Umbras, we'd help one another. It was a bond and will never be broken. We must always be on the run from the Umbras too. While we are a fractured unit and not committed every day, we are there for each other when needed." She paused. "We all have hefty prices on our heads."

"Do you ever rest?" he asked. "Have any sort of relaxation? Go to the beach? It was a favorite of ours…I mean of mine."

Vicki turned toward him. She touched the tip of his hand, and he closed his eyes. He wanted to embrace her, but he knew he'd receive a negative reaction.

"I would have loved to have a forever unit, a loyal unit…a life other than this. This isn't any kind of life for any man or woman.

I'm tired from the running and fighting. Someday I hope to be rid of this nightmare. All of this hate and killing and destruction is senseless. I'm exhausted. Drained. Sad. Even depressed."

He felt an emotional connection with her building every time she said his name. Could he fall in love again? Should he? Would she? His romantic side kicked in once more, and he twirled around emotionally in the fantasy world for a few seconds.

If we didn't meet, then…I have to believe Elizabeth isn't here… or nowhere….

Chapter 40

The crackling sound of firewood splintered the air. Michael scowled, stretching. His mind would not let him rest or even find any peace. He was having a hard time recalling memories of Elizabeth. *What's happening to me? Why can't I recall Elizabeth's graduation? I remember bits of it. It's like I'm not who I was before. I'm losing everything and every day of my past life.*

He dug deep into his subconscious while listening to Vicki's soft snores. *Our wedding day. I remember us going down the aisle. Where did we take our honeymoon?*

The blanket didn't completely cover Vicki's entire body, so he gently pulled it down to cover her exposed feet.

How he longed to touch her, kiss her, hold her, and rub her feet like he had done many winter nights while living on Long Island in their wedding house. It was repeated thousands of times, sometimes with the aid of a hairdryer.

In this world, there was no hairdryer to warm her feet. Or time to even snuggle.

This was different. Profoundly surreal. Shocking. He shook himself out of a trance. *Focus. Rest. Heal. Find Adriel. Make it back to the tunnel.* Change whatever needs to be changed, if possible. What happens if I do change it back? Does Vicki die again? Would Elizabeth be born? Would life be what it was before? Oh, God. I would lose Vicki, and Elizabeth would be here. Oh, God. No. What would I do?

He could feel a cold breeze sweeping down the chimney. He shivered and stood, wrapping a short blanket around himself, covering the top part of his body. He put on his blood-stained shoes and went outside in search of some loose wood to keep the fire going.

The moonlight cast an eerie light as if he was in a prison yard and the guards were shining a spotlight on him. He looked back at the house and wondered about its history. *They must have built this a couple of hundred years ago. Looks more like a log cabin. I wonder what year?*

Michael walked several yards toward a pile of loose wood near the edge of a tiny stream. He leaned down and cupped several gulps of water, quenching his thirst. He relaxed and kneeled beside the streaming water. *I wonder where this leads to....*

He let his body take a brief break from the constant anxiety, absorbing a few moments of comfort noise, the sound of the water making its marathon run. Michael gazed at the clear black sky littered with blue illumination from the thousands of stars. His mind wouldn't rest long as images spun around like a wheel of a car in a NASCAR race. *Is this my decision? Or is it not my decision anymore? If not, and I do try to change it back, I...I can't bear this. I can't bear losing Vicki again, knowing I put her through that horrible day...but Elizabeth, she's young, so much to live for.... Oh, God...can you take me and let them live? Please, let them live…and this world…how cruel and awful and bloody and deadly it is for everyone must change. This is so much more important. This world…this world needs to change. Not for my sake. But for the billions that will come later and after I'm gone.*

The distraction temporarily blinded him from reality. Michael didn't know whether to be happy or not. He was still alive but sad because his once-settled life was no more.

"Michael, Michael, help me!" Vicki screamed from the house. He was jolted out of his thoughts and grabbed several pieces of sharp wood and raced back. The door was open, and he sprinted in, spotting a man who was pointing a bayonet at Vicki. Michael struck him from behind, pushing a sharp, thick tree branch into his back. The man yelled words which he didn't understand.

The soldier turned with his bayonet, and Michael thrust another long stick into his heart, twisting and turning it until he saw his eyes surrender. The man collapsed, falling face first and onto the branch. Michael stepped on his head to be sure he was dead.

Vicki tried to sit up but fell back, lying beside the fire. Michael jumped over the dead body and to her. "Where did he get you?"

She mumbled a few words. Her eyes flickered and opened and closed a few times. Then they shut. Michael tried to sit her up. He ran outside with a bucket and filled it with a pile of mud. He slabbed it beneath to give her a makeshift band-aid and mushed it into the gash. He ripped a piece of Vicki's pants and tied it.

Relieved for just a moment, he went to the man with the bayonet. He checked his pants pockets for identification and found none. He placed the weapon near the fireplace and dragged the body outside, dropping him for a moment to catch his breath.

Michael took a deep gulp of cold air, picked up the man's legs, and continued to drag him through the forest. He saw the river and followed its path until it hit its apex, an embankment where the rushing water fell one hundred feet or so into a big basin. He tossed the body over the side, believing no one saw him. He returned to the house and checked Vicki's pulse. *Still beating.* He went back outside and grabbed more firewood to keep the fire going. Michael touched her forehead and thought she had a fever. Returning to the river, he bought back a bucket of water. Occasionally, he lifted Vicki's head up, encouraging her to drink.

She did, if only slightly.

Michael found another blanket in a small closet. He placed it over her and rested by her side. Exhausted, he surrendered himself and closed his eyes, his hand on hers.

Now what. What do I do if she doesn't recover or can't go on? This is only getting worse. I need Adriel. Yes. I need to find Adriel. This is his world. Her world. Not my world. They know what to expect, where to travel, and how to avoid the Umbras. Adriel is a survivor. A warrior. Unlike any I have known. I'll have to be like him. Here. It's the only way to get out of this mad world.

His mind quieted. He examined Vicki again, demanding she drink some water. She struggled to take a sip.

Michael stood and looked out the broken glass window. He could see his aging reflection, the wrinkles underneath his eyes prevalent from the moon's illumination.

He lay again beside Vicki. He touched her hand. *I never stopped loving you. I need you—more than ever. Please get better. Fight to live. You always have. You taught me how to fight. I need you. Your daughter needs you.*

Chapter 41

Every hour, Michael placed his hand on Vicki's forehead to see if she still had a fever. In between nursing Vicki and catching a blip of sleep, he would stalk the broken window, even taking a few turns around the house.

Paranoid, Michael carried the bayonet with him, keeping it in a ready and upright position for possible unfriendly encounters. He wondered why Vicki didn't have any type of weapon on her. Not a fan of guns in his other life, Michael became one in this world.

He kept it nearby and was prepared to defend them both to the death. Michael didn't have a macho feeling of any kind but rather one of love like he felt so often back on Long Island.

Vicki rolled over, still sleeping. Michael watched her take each breath, his heart skipping beats in unison. He could hear the strumming of guitars on a rainy night in Paris, remembering their first vacation together as a married couple. He longed for a slow dance again beneath the Eiffel Tower as they had done before. A chance to feel her against him for even a brief second.

He knew it wasn't possible or necessary, but nevertheless, he desired it.

Vicki somehow made Michael forget about the physical and emotional abuse he suffered as a child. Michael had sought solitude under the bunk beds he and his brother shared. He'd turn his back and grip the bedroom wall in desperation. On other nights when his father discovered his hideout, Michael would seek the closet and huddle on top of the safe, not saying a peep when his father came looking for him with the belt.

Many nights, he'd fall asleep only to be awakened by his mother's calls from downstairs that breakfast was ready.

It was Vicki who gave him joy and love and confidence and faith finally in his life. She provided what no one else ever had—she made him feel worthy of love.

Now here she was again.

The world in which they had first met was much different. This world was cruel. Chaotic. Unforgiving. Violent. Vicious. Without purpose.

Yet Vicki was Vicki in every way. From what he could see right now.

Michael wiped a tear with his sweaty shirt. The fire was fierce, and the heat drove him back a few yards. Beads of sweat formed on Vicki's forehead. There was a kick to Michael's energy level. *That's it. Break a sweat. Break the fever, Vicki. Come on. You can do it.*

Vicki turned over and opened her eyes slightly. Michael dried her sweat with a piece of torn cloth. He lifted her head. "Drink this, sweetheart," he misspoke. "Um…I mean, drink this, Vicki."

He wasn't sure if she heard him. She was bleary eyed, out of it, and still suffering from the ravages of the high fever and dehydration. She did drink, finally taking a few gulps. Michael lay her head back down on a makeshift pillow. "Rest, Vicki. Rest. Michael is here. To protect you. I mean, help you."

He watched her fall back asleep. Michael felt some peace and wiped her forehead again.

"Like old times," he whispered and didn't care if she heard him. He smiled. "Like old times. Just me and you. Together. Us against the world."

Chapter 42

Michael shivered as he returned from bringing in some more wood. He dropped a couple of pieces into the fire, satisfied with the warmth it provided. He rubbed his hands together. "Hey, Vicki, come here. I have a great fire going, like other—"

He caught himself. *Not yet. Give it time. Don't be anxious. It's going to take time. Remember, she's not the Vicki you knew back on Long Island. Man is she not that person. This world really hardens a heart.* He bent over and put his hands to the fire, basking in the warmth, feeling toasty.

"Vicki." He stood, looking toward the bathroom. "Everything okay in there?"

There was silence. "Vicki?"

He knocked on the bathroom door. "Vicki. You in there?"

Again, there was silence.

His heart pounded. "Vicki!" he shouted. He went to another room, a room so dusty and dirty he had to cover his nose and mouth, coughing. There were a couple of raggedy, broken mops in the corner with two empty metal buckets and nothing more.

"Vicki," he said in a higher tone, leaving the room. He stood gazing at the raging fire. *Where did she go? I was only outside for a few minutes. Maybe she's going to get some water and food?*

Michael darted outside and prowled around the exterior of the building, repeatedly calling, "Vicki, are you here?"

Frustrated and feeling his anger building, he broke off a long branch from an aging oak tree and sharpened it against a thick stone. He added three more of the same and went back to retrieve the bayonet.

He could not find it.

"How about that?" he mumbled incredulously to no one in particular. "I help her get better. She leaves me alone and runs off with the only weapon."

Michael kicked a metal bucket in a rage; water spilled everywhere. "Son of a…that hurt like a—"

"My, oh, my, what child have we here," said Vicki, who appeared behind him at the door. "How mature are we?"

"Jeez," yelled Michael, jumping back, thrusting his sharpened tree branches at her.

Vicki laughed. "Simmer down, my big warrior. There'll be plenty of time for that. Why are you jumping like a cat who saw a tiger?"

"Why? Why? Are you asking me why?" said a dumbfounded Michael.

"Ah, yeah, why?"

"You left me alone and didn't say where you were going."

"You are not my daddy. I don't owe you any explanation on what I do and where I go," she said.

"For all I know you left me out here all alone in a place where I have no idea where I am."

Vicki remained silent. Finally, she spoke. "Are you done with your drama?"

"Yes. Yes. I'm done," Michael said in frustration.

She approached him. "Put your weapons or whatever you call them down. Look at me. We haven't known each other for very long. But from what you know about me, do I look like someone who would leave you behind?"

Michael lowered his head, a bit embarrassed over his tirade, still angry and sore and hurt.

"I know how much Adriel means to you," Vicki said. "I have people in my unit just like that too. We have each other's backs."

He lifted his head. How he longed to hug her now, just for a moment.

Vicki gave a glare. "Let's go find Adriel."

"Thank you," he said.

Vicki hesitated and winced. "Thank you, too, for taking good care of me."

"Always will and have."

Vicki gave a confused look. "You need to be prepared for the worst. He might not be…"

Michael cut her off. "I can't think of that. I need to have hope."

"There isn't much of that in this world."

"I can't bear any more loss."

"We all have lost a lot here." She handed him the bayonet. "You'll need this more than me."

"What about you?"

Vicki sneered. "Do you think I'm just some weak-kneed girl out here in the country that needs a man's help?"

"I didn't say that."

"Don't worry about me. I have enough weapons to carve up a battalion of Umbra thugs from the top of their arrogant heads to the bottom of their spineless toes."

Michael scanned her body. She wore a heavy brown coat that stopped at the top of her knees. She wore thick pants and black army boots. Torn and bloodstained, she went outside and dug and placed mud on her shoes.

"You must hide your weapons well," he said.

"I have places you could never guess where they are," she replied, giving him another glare.

"And I'll use these weapons on anyone. Do you understand, Michael?" She slammed the door behind them before adding, "Anyone."

Chapter 43

T hunder roared, and lightning flashes like bright lasers zipped around them, some striking the sky-reaching trees of the dense forest. The weight of the moisture dampened Michael's light coat and pants. His socks were soaked, and his shoes were waterlogged. The sharp tree branches smuggled inside his jacket and pants were poking him as he tried to keep up with Vicki's quick pace.

It was obvious to him she had spent a great deal of time trekking in outside environments. She navigated the terrain smoothly and without any signs of stress, guiding him through the brush and tricky parts of the journey.

"Don't you think we need to stop somewhere and wait out this weather?" Michael said, rushing to her, out of breath.

Vicki stopped, the downpour drenching her blonde wig through her hood. A tiny waterfall spouted from the top of her head to her nose. She wiped it away. "Where? Where do you want to stay? Look around!"

Michael shrugged. "I was just saying to wait it out until it lightens up."

"How much time do you think Adriel has?"

Michael shrugged again. "This is your world."

Vicki shook her head and started walking. "It's your world too. You should start living in it. Because this is all there is."

"There's much more than what you see and what is here."

Vicki stopped again and scowled. "Where is there more? Look around, Michael. What do you see that I don't?"

"In another place. In another time."

"You must be from a different world because I have no idea what you are talking about."

He thought about telling her where he came from and what his life was, and yet his brain planted red flags each time. He had hoped Vicki would be more open-minded than Adriel.

They were coming to the edge of the forest. A big, dark brick building, oddly shaped like a semi-castle, stood before him. Michael shivered. Vicki grimaced.

The torrential rain was blinding. No guards were standing at the castle's entrance. The wind picked up and blew Vicki's hood back. Her wig was quickly soaked, and her coat was drenched. She grabbed and made sure the wig stayed secure. Vicki waved him forward and found some cover to the left of the entrance.

"Stay behind me. At this time most will be sleeping," she said. "If we need to split up, meet me halfway into the forest." She pointed back in the direction of the trees.

"What does Adriel look like?" she asked.

"Big. Strong. Wide shoulders. A few inches over six feet. Black hair. Mention me, and he'll know you're not from the Umbras."

Vicki nodded.

They scrambled in silence into the dreaded dungeon, finding no resistance on the stairway down. The smell of sweat, mold, blood, and death polluted the air.

"Come on, big boy," she said, noticing Michael slightly bending over. "My cooking wasn't that bad. We have our mission. You can throw up your egg omelet later." She smacked him on the back.

Michael smiled, realizing this was still Vicki being Vicki, no matter what time period, remembering her dry sense of humor. "Yes, sir."

She stopped. "Shhh!"

"There," Michael said in an excited voice. "That's him."

Adriel was chained to a wall, beaten, his head hung, kneeling. There was widespread blood on the cement floor. "I will go first. Cover me. If there's a guard who comes up behind me, wait until he's on me," she said, grabbing the bayonet, "then use this."

He nodded.

She tiptoed a few steps forward.

"Vicki," he said in a whisper.

"What?"

"Be careful."

She turned away and didn't answer. Vicki went to the cage, took out a hairpin, and worked on the first lock. Within seconds, she opened it.

Man, she's good. Who would have thought? Heck, she'd always did lose her keys.

Vicki knelt and said a few words to Adriel. He lifted his head slightly, his face bloodied, his left eye shut, his lips swollen. He watched her dismantle another part of the chain.

Michael heard a voice shouting in the distance. Vicki stopped and pointed to her left. A guard emerged and shouted inaudible words and entered the cage. She defended herself, pulling out a long knife. Michael raced up behind and plunged his bayonet deep into the back of the guard. He fell to his knees, and Vicki slit his throat. The guard dropped his weapon, grabbed his neck, gargled, and fell face first.

"Work on the other chain," Vicki said. "Where's there's one, there's always more behind them."

Michael pulled at the lock. He could hear another voice calling in their direction. "Move quicker," Vicki implored. "Take this," she said to Adriel, giving the soldier's bayonet to him.

Vicki pulled Michael away and struck the last hold on Adriel. It broke, and Michael lifted him up. "You came back," Adriel said.

"Don't be surprised. We're in the same unit now."

"You are a good man, Michael," he said as he took a few wobbly steps up the stairway.

"You are a better man. Can you make it?"

"No worries. Faced worse."

"I'm sure you have."

Vicki was behind them. "Can we keep the chatter to a minimum?"

"Yeah, yeah," Michael said. "We're moving as fast as we can."

"Faster, ladies. Faster."

They made it to the top step and heard several voices screaming from below. Two guards shouted some untranslatable words at them. A couple of shots were fired. They fell and crawled their way out. They stood quickly and Vicki pushed them to the left. "Go into the forest. Get to the safe house. I will take them in another direction."

"What?" Michael said, stopping.

"Go," Vicki insisted.

"Not without you," Michael said.

"Go. Now." Vicki yelled. She raced to the right, and Michael and Adriel scampered left, ducking into the thick brush to hide, both catching their breath. Michael coughed. Adriel put his hand over his mouth.

Vicki called out, luring the Umbras her way. They heard her scream but weren't sure if it was intentional or real. She screamed again. Michael shivered, much like the night when he was told by the doctors Vicki had died.

"She'll be fine," Adriel said. "She's a warrior."

"She's my Vicki. My wife. Always."

"She isn't the same Vicki you knew. And wife? I still don't know what that means."

"Unit. Okay. She's in my unit. I spent time with her in a unit. Does that make sense?"

"Now you're making sense," Adriel replied.

They walked several miles and located the familiar river. Both fell to their knees and cupped water, drinking feverishly. Once quenched, Michael guided Adriel to the old house. He gathered up several pieces of wood and made a fire. They lay near the warmth and didn't speak for much of the day.

As nighttime approached, Michael was glued to the jagged window, his eyes fixated on their surroundings. He felt Adriel's presence behind him. "She's out there," Adriel said. "She's a fighter."

"How do you know?"

"I saw her eyes. They had a fire in them. I felt her heart. It was like a wolf."

A scream echoed through the dense forest.

Michael turned to Adriel. "Did you hear that?"

"Sounded like a wolf."

"Wolf? That was a woman."

A second scream shook Michael. He opened the door. Adriel joined him. There was some rustling not far from them. Adriel pulled Michael back inside and gripped a knife.

Chapter 44

Michael huddled near the window, vigilant. Ferocious winds rattled the tiny foundation as an approaching storm shouted its fury. He pulled over the only available chair and sat, his chin resting on the windowsill. His eyes fluttered several times from exhaustion, only to be alarmed from his light slumber by nocturnal animals scouring for food.

Adriel offered to watch, nudging him several times. Michael refused. Adriel eventually gave up and lay near the fire most of the night, still healing his wounds.

As night turned to early dawn, the sounds of the forest awakened. Birds chirping, squirrels hunting for food to store, and an occasional deer slipping in and out of view in a matter of seconds decorated the forest. Michael did not leave his makeshift post until thirst overwhelmed him. He saw Adriel was in a deep sleep, so he went to the river to drink and hunt for fish.

He quenched his craving with several gulps of water. A strong breeze shook the sky-reaching trees, swaying them back and forth as if they were toothpicks. It wasn't long before he was joined by Adriel.

"I can't wait any longer to see if she's safe," Michael said to him. "It's driving me crazy. I need you, Adriel. If she's captured, we must help her. But where can she be? I didn't see any females in that prison."

Adriel cupped some water and drank. He plunged his head into the river.

"I realize no matter what I do or what I change…it has consequences for everyone," Michael said.

Adriel wiped away some moisture from his eyes. "What happens if you change it? What changes here in this world if you don't do anything?" he asked Michael.

"It isn't good. For Vicki. For me. For Elizabeth." Michael paused. "For you."

"What about for me? For everyone here. Would this world change for all humanity? My world can't get any worse."

Michael reflected for several seconds, realizing the scope of what Adriel was saying. *He's right. There's more. Much more than what happens for me. For Elizabeth. For Vicki. For anyone I know. What about Adriel? And everyone here? Millions. Billions of people it would change for the better. Yes. Billions.*

Michael turned toward Adriel. "Do you believe this can happen if I go back to that tunnel?"

Adriel didn't answer and left.

Forlorn and suffering from deep sadness and depression, Michael cupped more water and rammed it against his face, trying to shake himself from his self-induced sorrow.

Despite falling into his mental black hole, Michael wandered to the deeper part of the river, prepared to hunt fish. He waded to the middle of the flowing water and scanned the area. One fish wiggled past him, and he raced to catch it, thrusting his bayonet down several times in the stream only to strike rocks.

Michael slammed his bayonet down hard in frustration, muttering angry words. He fell to his knees, stayed frozen, and kept his bayonet stationary in a downward position for several minutes. He made several attempts, resting in disappointment over his lack of fishing skills. *I am not going back to that place without something to eat. I will prove Adriel wrong. I can be an outdoor man like him.* Michael laughed. *Listen to yourself. The old ego is rearing its ugly head. Be patient. Fishing is about being patient. That's what your cousin Scott told you on the last fishing trip. I did give him a big laugh the way I struggled with the pole. Okay. Focus. Concentrate. Patience.*

A longer and fatter fish wiggled a few feet from him. Michael dove, his bayonet out in front. "I got it!" his voice echoed. Feeling triumphant, he marched back toward the house and stopped. He pulled the fish off his bayonet and pointed it forward. The door was open slightly. He pushed it wide.

"Adriel, you here?"

There was no answer.

"Oh, no."

Michael walked in and stood before a pool of blood by the fireplace, the last of its wood breaking and burning out.

"Oh no, no, no," he said, dropping the fish. He went outside and lurked around the house. He heard a shovel sound digging in the distance. He snuck behind a thick oak tree and squinted through a dense brush.

He saw a man on his knees wearing the old World War II uniform pushing a body into a deep hole, then covering it with a mound of dirt.

Michael moved closer. *Strangle him. Do not hesitate. They are evil. They deserve death. Make it quick. Show some mercy. He's big. Bigger than you. Think like an animal. Like a bear. Like a tiger. A lion. Surprise him. Don't let him see you. He has a weapon too. Kill him. Kill him until you can't hear him breathe. Kill him. Now.* Michael jumped him from behind the tree and slammed the soldier down with his bayonet.

The soldier held his hands up in surrender. "Stop, it's me."

Michael turned the soldier over. "Adriel? What the...what are you doing?"

"Sometimes what you see isn't what is."

Michael helped him up. "What happened?"

Adriel wiped away the mud from his pants and face. "While you were out fishing, I had a visitor. I think it's a rogue soldier. Looking to kidnap for some money."

"Go on."

"I sent him to another world," Adriel said. "Maybe he went to your world. And I picked up this uniform. He's my size, though the pants are rather small."

Michael took a quick glance and covered his eyes. "Looks like you are ready for the ballet."

Adriel smirked. "Funny."

"What do you have in mind?" Michael said.

"It's our way out of here."

Michael agreed. "We at least have a better chance now. Hey, I caught a fish."

"Leave it."

"Why?"

Adriel pulled a communication device out of his pocket that looked like something out of an old *Star Trek* episode. "The soldier sent a message before I killed him from this location. We can't stay here anymore."

Michael waved his arms. "What about—"

"Vicki?"

"Yes."

"We have to get out of here first. Now. I wish I could give you a better idea. I have none."

There were a few seconds of silence between them.

"Do you have any better ideas?"

"I don't," Michael replied. "We can alter our plans if needed. We need to get back to the lighthouse where we first met…but Vicki…are we out of time?"

Adriel looked away. "Yeah. We need to move fast." Adriel faced him. "And you are going to change this all?"

"Everything. All of this. For billions of people."

Adriel seemed bewildered.

"You just have to trust me. I know where I have to go and what I need to do."

Adriel looked more confused.

"Look around, does any of this make sense? Oh, right, to you it does because you've been living in it. But take my crazy word—this, all of this, shouldn't be."

"Whatever you say. Let's find transportation."

"I hope we aren't taking bikes."

"No. We travel like them. On the rails." He pointed to the uniform. "Because of this."

"Then what?"

"You're my prisoner. For some Umbra money. That will be my story."

"Okay, that's half the plan."

"I guess…."

"You don't sound confident," Michael countered.

"It's my only idea."

"But Vicki?"

"She's a survivor."

Michael froze.

"We either go catch that ship back or you can stay behind. I am going."

Michael grimaced. "I will not make it back alone."

Chapter 45

Still feeling the injuries from his prison torture, Adriel wrapped his legs with some bandage Vicki gave him. She stole it from a nearby residence a few days ago before they met. It seemed Vicki was always a few steps ahead of him, more prepared for the worst, and it was understandable given that she lived in this environment for her entire life.

She had never mentioned any specific people in her unit to Michael. "It's better this way," she'd explained to him one morning. "If you don't know them, you will never be tempted to give them away if the Umbras torture for information."

Michael was disappointed that Vicki thought this of him. "I would never do that."

"Their torture makes the toughest men and women talk," Vicki had added.

"You don't trust me?"

"It's not about trust. It's about reality."

Michael eventually understood why Vicki kept certain parts of her life private. She was a warrior first, confined to a world he couldn't fathom. Loyalty and secrecy were the most important characteristics of their movement.

He realized he would never be a part of her unit. It stung him.

"Can you walk, Adriel? Do you need my help?"

"I've been through worse."

"We need food," Michael said.

"Won't be able to get anything until we get to the railroad," Adriel replied.

"Not good enough." Michael's strength waned, and his stomach growled. "I'm not sure I can make it."

"It's not far from here. We need to walk faster."

"Any faster, and you'll be walking alone. Where are we headed?" Michael asked.

"To what was the Norwich train station."

"Was?"

"Yes. Things have changed here and everywhere. Europe is not what it once was. Not after the big war."

"How much farther?"

"Not far at all," said Adriel, not being specific.

Michael slumped and struggled to keep pace with Adriel. "I'm feeling lightheaded," he said, stopping and bending over. He saw stars and black, then light and more stars.

"Michael, Michael!" Adriel's words grew faint.

Michael awoke in a railcar, laying among numerous dead bodies. He stumbled, wobbled, and fell on a corpse. "What in...where am I?"

The train wasn't moving yet. Michael peeked out through a tiny open window and saw Adriel pointing his bayonet at several people. They were being lined up against a brick wall, hands tied behind them, and hoods placed on their heads.

Then six Umbra soldiers marched forward. A man yelled untranslatable words, and he lifted a shiny, long, thick gold sword high in the air. The six soldiers raised their weapons forward, cocked their guns, and fired, the shots echoing. The hooded people dropped to the ground.

The soldiers picked up a body, laughing. They built a fire and hung the unclothed man over a raging fire. Then turned him like a hog on a campfire. *My God. What are they doing? Adriel, stop them. Stop them.*

Minutes later, a man with a long sword cut up the body, placing parts on plates. He handed it out to the other soldiers, who sat and ate.

Michael gasped and backed away from the peephole.

Stunned, he stared at no place in particular for several minutes. *Bang, bang, bang!*

Pounding on the car door startled him.

"Michael. It's me, Adriel."

He opened the rail door. Adriel hopped on board, grabbing Michael's hand to board the train. Blood marked his uniform.

"What's going on?" Michael asked, shaken. "You're bleeding."

"I'm fine. I had to do some Umbras' work."

"Why? Why would you do that?"

"To save my life. To save your life."

Michael wanted to argue with him. He thought of the entire impact of his journey. "This is not what we planned."

"We didn't plan anything."

"We sure did."

Adriel approached him. "We are here. The plan or whatever you want to call it got us here. Stay here. This is the only safe place on the train."

"Are you sure?"

"Look around," Adriel said, putting ammunition in his gun. "Who wants to stay here? No one will look."

"I don't."

"Do you want to live?"

Michael grudgingly nodded.

"I have to do one more thing. I'll be back soon. Be ready to open the door."

Adriel hopped down, giving a wave. "Close this."

Michael did and watched Adriel move swiftly toward the execution wall. An Umbra soldier was kicking at the rest of the bodies, laughing and spitting on them. Then he bent down and was taking rings, bracelets, valuables, and any mementos he could find off the dead.

"What is Adriel doing?" Michael said to himself, watching him hide behind a barrier, not far from the Umbra soldier. The soldier continued to dig through the pockets of the murdered.

Adriel tiptoed up behind the soldier, slit the man's throat, and plunged his bayonet into his heart, twisting it. The soldier fell backwards. For good measure, Adriel popped him a couple of times with bullets.

Michael withdrew in horror, hand over mouth, eyes wide open and glazed. The train moved, jolting him backward onto a pile of dead people. He sprung right up.

Bang, bang, bang!

"Open, Michael. Hurry."

Michael struggled to hold his balance as the train picked up more speed.

"Open. Now," Adriel demanded.

"I'm trying," Michael said. "I can't budge the bolt."

"Push down on the latch first and then pull it up."

Michael did, and the door opened. Adriel grasped Michael's leg and then arm, jumping back onto the car.

"What did you just do?"

"I told you, taking care of business."

"You didn't have to do that. They'll be after you and me now," Michael said in fear.

"So what?"

"So what? So what? Have you lost your common sense?"

"Big deal. I killed a murderer."

Michael shook his head. "Isn't there enough bloodshed?"

"I had my reasons."

"Well, what were they?"

"None of your business."

Michael stormed to the other side of the car. "Really. Wow. Is that all you have to say?"

"Yes. You saw what they did. Did you not?"

Michael looked down, furious at Adriel for attracting more Umbra soldiers and yet understanding.

"I'm not going to say anything more about it. If you were me, you'd do it too."

Michael didn't answer. He realized Adriel was right. And then wondered. "Did you take this trip to seek revenge?"

They glared at each other for several seconds. "Did you? Tell me you didn't. I thought you did this for me."

"It's not all about you."

Michael was stunned, shaken.

"We stay quiet," Adriel demanded. "When the train stops, we get off, preferably before we stop. So be prepared to jump when I say so."

Michel looked away in disgust, shaking his head and waving his hands in frustration.

"You have a problem?" said Adriel in an annoying and defiant tone.

Michael turned around and pointed his finger at him. "I get it. I do. I understand your rage. I have it too. But you only made our situation worse."

"What do you care? I did it. You can feel all good about yourself that you didn't."

"Hello," Michael said, sarcastically. "I've had to go to the gutter in this cesspool of a world too."

Adriel waved him away.

Michael pushed some bodies to the other side of the car, the growing stench overwhelming him. "I can't stay in this hellhole much longer."

"We have no choice."

Michael stayed silent, staring at Adriel, wondering who this man was. He knew the rules of this world were more barbaric. Yet he'd created a vision in his mind of who this person was, and it was violently butchered with one act.

What good feelings he had of Adriel dissipated. He was on guard, making sure he was mentally and emotionally prepared to deal with even worse. Though what he witnessed a short while ago would be mild in comparison to what he would likely see soon. Adriel tossed him a piece of candy. It was red. It was a well needed distraction for both.

The candy was mint, much like the ones he bought at Christmas. Candy cane mint, it tasted like, Michael thought.

A taste he had forgotten until now. He settled his mind down, closed his eyes, and allowed his emotions to simmer. Always a dreamer, he ventured into one about Vicki. Their last time together back on Long Island. It was a cold day in December. He remembered the sparkly Christmas lights illuminating the cozy neighborhood. A brisk wind shook the leafless trees. Michael admired how he set the lights upon their first live Christmas tree. It was exquisite.

The smell of turkey and stuffing in the oven swept him away in an aroma frenzy, luring him to taste test everything being put out on the table.

She smiled. Oh, her smile. So young. Hopeful. Full of dreams. Nesting. Preparing. Ready to be a first-time mom. Checking on the crib in the baby's room, painted pink with Disney characters plastered on the wall, they stood in complete bliss.

Everything was new. Fresh. A new life to welcome. The overwhelming responsibility. He put his arm around her and twirled Vicki around. "Summer Wind" was playing on the stereo.

They slow danced in unison until the song ended. Michael played it again, took her hand, and danced once more. They danced for over an hour, playing "Summer Wind" until the oven's bell dinged.

"This was like that snowstorm," Vicki said. "At the diner."

Michael smiled. "I remember."

"Do you? That wasn't me you were dancing with. Are you forgetting me?"

Chapter 46

The train shuddered and stopped and restarted several times, zipping around steep curves at high speed, rattling their insides. Adriel was standing, bayonet at his side, glancing through the narrow rectangle opening. "We need to jump soon," he said.

Michael stood, spitting out the stench that filled his throat.

"You ready?" Adriel said, giving Michael a stoic look.

Adriel whipped the door open and jumped, rolling down a big embankment near a spacious farm filled with cows, goats, and sheep.

Michael followed, tumbling several times before smacking face-first into a thick metal fence. A cow greeted him with a loud moo and swat with her foot.

"Oof, ugh, back away, Bessie," Michael said, half angry, half laughing. *Vicki. Yes, Vicki, I'm remembering. I remember that day at the store when we dared each other to have a drink of milk. Your chocolate mustache. My vanilla mustache. I recall what you said. I do. How strange I remember that now.*

"Got milk," Michael said in a low tone. He stood, wiped wet grass off his knees, and pointed at the cow. "Got milk?" he laughed more.

"What's so funny?" said Adriel, wiping blades of grass off his uniform.

"Got milk? Get it?"

"No."

"Oh, right, right…before your time…or is it after your time? Whatever."

"We don't have far to catch the next boat back," Adriel said. "Remember, you're my prisoner, and I'm taking you back to Otomamay."

"Where?"

"Otomamay. Where we came from."

Michael shook his head. "No. The name is America."

"Here we go."

"It's America to me."

Adriel shook his head. "Brother, where we met. Otomamay. The Umbras control what it's called. Not you. Not me. Not your imagination."

They stopped at the nearby farm to eat. Adriel took what he wished. Wearing an Umbra's military uniform had its advantages. Soldiers ate for free, took what they desired, and were feared.

Michael enjoyed a pear, peach, and apple. "I needed this," he said.

"Quiet. I told you before prisoners do not talk to Umbra soldiers. You need to have a look of fear."

They arrived not a minute too soon as the last of the prisoners were being loaded onto the vast vessel. Some soldiers had one male prisoner; others had three prisoners each. "Most of them will be sold into slavery or prostitution," Adriel said.

Young women, hands bound behind their backs and bandanas covering their eyes, were taken to a lower compartment. Many were weeping softly, scared, some showing black and blue marks on their faces, arms, and legs.

The brutality reminded Michael of Elizabeth. The women couldn't have been much older than her.

"The younger, the better," Adriel said. "That's how they think. They believe younger women can be brainwashed for monetary gain."

"How do we stop it?"

"Stop this? No way we can do that."

Michael sat.

"Get up," said Adriel, kicking at him.

Michael stood. "Why?"

"You wait for the commander's order to sit."

Adriel continued. "Pay attention to me. It's your only hope to get back safely."

Two more hours would pass before the commander shouted on a ship speaker to sit. Michael was exhausted and kept his head down, not making eye contact. Adriel did the same as they huddled in a far corner, distancing themselves from the rest of the soldiers and prisoners.

The ship moved rapidly, not feeling the effects of a brief but windy storm. The moon brightened the top deck. Adriel fell asleep. It was an eerie night. Then there was a heavy fog and a blinding rainstorm. Then calm. Peace.

Michael dug into Adriel's pocket and grabbed the key to his chain. He unlocked it and tiptoed down the steps. He stopped in disgust. Women and young girls were chained together, laying on top of each other.

He listened for a moment. He could hear people laughing and talking. *Must be the guards. Stay quiet.*

Michael raced up the stairs and nudged Adriel.

"What? What?" Adriel said, rubbing his eyes. "What is it?"

"Downstairs. The women. The girls. They've been abused. Beaten. Raped."

Adriel straightened up. "Okay—wait a minute. You're supposed to stay in your chains."

"Forget that, Adriel. We have to help them."

Adriel stood and dug into his pocket. "The key. Give it back to me."

"No."

Michael turned, took a few steps toward the railing, peeked down at the ocean below, and threw it into the water.

"Have you lost your mind?" said Adriel, slapping Michael in the head.

"Maybe. But I'm not going to stand by and watch them be tortured. I have a daughter."

Adriel smacked Michael in the chest, sneered, and pulled him into a corner. "You don't think I want to stop that? I've lived a lifetime under them and their savage ways. I've paid the ultimate price with my unit. You have to learn when to pick the battles you can win. This isn't one of them."

"How do you know?"

"I know. I have lost many in my units, including the woman who I was with forever. I'm here with you for many reasons. One being hope, Michael. Hope. You had hope. I had none. You gave me that with who you were trying to find. I don't want to lose any more people close to me."

"Don't con me. You wanted to come here to take revenge."

Adriel sat, dejected and resigned. "True. But now this trip has more meaning. Because of you. And your unit."

Michael saw for the first time a soft side. He sat beside him.

"I understand," Michael said. "I do. I see my wife—the woman who I wanted to be with forever in my unit—I see others in my unit too, like those young girls...."

Adriel did not answer. He hung his head and wiped away a lone tear.

"We must never be silent," Michael said.

Adriel lifted his head. "We move soon."

"Tomorrow night."

Adriel nodded. "But we have a dilemma."

Chapter 47

Michael ate little of his allotted bread given to him for dinner. Adriel was vigilant, also keeping a low profile among the other guards, refusing to participate in their all-night parties and torture. Adriel walked the big deck several times, checking the area and the number of guards working in the various parts of the big ship. He seemed satisfied that the weather was cooperating too. The sky was clear, and the waters were calm.

"When do we get off this ship?" said Michael.

"We have an issue. There are about thirty-five females, give or take, and we only have ten lifeboats. Three females, depending upon the weight, per boat. It doesn't add up."

Michael shrugged. "So what? We put four to a boat on a few of them."

"And us? How do we get off this ship?"

Michael dismissed Adriel's logic. "We make it work. Put the lightest women together with four per boat."

"We may not have the time to do this. We have to lower them without making any noise and get away as soon as possible."

Michael went to the railing and looked back at the boats. He approached Adriel with a big smile.

"What?"

"How drunk are the guards?"

"Not very."

Five Days and Nights Later

Michael slapped his hands together. "Let's do this."

Adriel grimaced.

"Still not sold?" Michael said.

"No."

"We have no other choice. When will we be back there?"

"You mean Otomamay?"

Michael grew angry. "No. Back there. I refuse to call it that."

"We should arrive tomorrow."

Michael sighed. "We do this tonight, or those women and girls will have a life of abuse."

Adriel loaded up his gun. "I will cut the rope on the lifeboats. The females are all in a cage in the far corner to the left as you come down the stairway." He handed Michael a key.

"For the cage?"

"Yes."

"I'm impressed."

"Don't be," said Adriel, looking at him. "I had to kill another man and dump him in the ocean."

"Oh."

"Do you approve?" Adriel said though Michael knew he wasn't asking.

"Whatever it takes."

"You lead the females up the stairs only when you hear me whistle," instructed Adriel. "*Only when you hear the whistle.*"

"Got it. How do we get to the boats?"

"That's my worry. It's near the Captain's Quarters."

"Not good."

"More people are going to die," Adriel said. "Even us. There is no easy way of doing this."

Michael turned back to Adriel. "What if some of the females don't want to go?"

"Take whoever wants to come."

Michael nodded. "I'll head down once you leave and wait for the signal."

"May the fire of today give you the strength to carry on this evening's war."

Michael stayed silent, deep in thought, wondering if this was wise. Images of females being tortured and assaulted convinced him there was no other choice though. He watched Adriel close his eyes and whisper some words—perhaps a prayer. It was then reality hit. Do or die. "It's showtime," Adriel said.

Michael yelped.

"Huh?"

"You finally said something familiar to me."

"Showtime?" said Adriel.

"Yes," Michael said with a nervous smile.

Adriel left.

Michael peeked out to see if anyone was awake on the deck. He saw a couple of guards slumped over at the far end of the ship. *Clear. Stay quiet. Don't bump into anything. Stay calm. Do not argue with the females. You know how that can be. Follow the plan. Wait for the whistle. Move quietly and quickly.*

He took the first few steps slowly, then accelerated his pace as paranoia swept through him. *Was that a guard I heard? Did one of them wake up? Did either of them see me? Did they recognize me?* Michael hid behind a tall crate of medical supplies. He managed to nudge open a little viewing area between the boxes and the cage. *Looks like most are sleeping. I think the one with dirty blonde hair moved. She might be awake.*

Michael tiptoed over and put a finger to his lips as one of the females spotted him.

"What are you doing?" she asked.

Michael opened the cage. "I'm here to get all of you off this ship."

"No. No. We'll all be killed."

"There's no time to argue."

"I have plenty of time, as you can see," she said.

"We only have a few minutes to make this work. My unit is preparing the lifeboats. When he whistles, we go. Wake up the others. "

The dirty blonde woman stared. She gave him an unconvincing look.

"Believe me." Michael listened for a few seconds and heard nothing. "Wake the others up. Now. If I wake them up, they might scream or be frightened. They need a familiar face to do this."

The dirty blonde-haired woman nodded. She woke up almost all of them, whispering instructions. Michael heard the whistle. His heart jumped. Some of the females were refusing to join him.

"We have to get out of here now," Michael said. "Follow me."

The dirty blonde-haired girl gathered those who wanted to leave. Some needed help. There were more than the thirty-five females. Michael couldn't see the entire group, which caused him anxiety.

He changed his plans. "Those who can walk by themselves, head up the stairs now. My unit is waiting and will get you to a lifeboat."

The healthiest ran up the stairway, and Adriel started loading the boats, pointing to the ladder. Michael waited until the last wave of females had gone. Four women, battered and fearful, refused to leave. "Let us help you."

They refused.

Five other women were too weak to walk by themselves. Michael went to the remaining healthy ones. "Can you help them up?" he said to them. They nodded.

"That one over there," another woman said, pointing to her, covered in bruises with a tattoo of an Umbra warrior on her back.

A lone female sat in the corner, covering her face.

"She's badly hurt," the woman said. "I told her to not fight the soldiers. She wouldn't listen. They...they..."

"No more," Michael said. "I know. Take everyone else upstairs. Don't wait for me." Michael fixated on the injured woman. "Tell Adriel, my unit, to go if I am not up there soon. Save yourselves."

The women didn't hesitate. They helped the others up the stairway. Michael went to the injured woman, kneeling down beside her. "I'm here to help you. Can you stand?"

The woman didn't answer.

"My name is Michael."

The woman lifted her head, her face bloodied and bruised, her right eye shut.

"Oh, my God," Michael said in shock.

The woman wept and lowered her head into his chest.

"Vicki. Oh my, Vicki."

She fell into his arms.

"What have they done to you?"

Another whistle sounded, giving him chills.

"That's Adriel. We have to move."

Vicki mumbled a few words that Michael didn't understand.

"Can you walk?"

She shook her head.

Michael took a deep breath and picked her up, struggling to climb. He managed to get to the top step and took a deep breath. Adriel waited, calling up to him.

"The boats are ready. Hurry!"

"Vicki, get on my back." Michael bent over, and she managed to fall on his back. "Hold on tight."

Michael started to descend the long climb down. "Let go and fall back, Vicki."

She let go, and Vicki fell six feet back. Adriel caught her and secured her body with rope. "Hurry," he said.

Michael jumped the rest of the way down to the boat. The others had already made a good distance, rowing. "Take one," Adriel said, handing him an oar.

Another woman was in the boat beside Vicki. She was slumped over, dazed. Her nose was swollen and her lips bloodied. It was then Michael knew they had made the right choice. They rowed as fast as they could, separating themselves by one hundred or so yards from the ship. Gunfire filled the air. Shots zipped short of them in the water.

"Keep rowing!" Adriel yelled.

Two guards were yelling and pointing their guns from the ship. Then they left and came back with one of the women who stayed behind. They picked her up and dangled her from the railing.

Michael stood. "Oh, no."

"Sit." Adriel waved his arm. "Do you want to give them an easy target?"

Distraught, Michael sat.

The guards dropped the woman into the ocean and shot her as she struggled to swim away.

Michael could still hear the woman's screams as they rowed, shrieking in the once quiet night.

Chapter 48

A lighthouse shone brightly through the darkness cloaking most other landmarks, its outlines casted in shadows. They caught up to the other nine boats. Adriel instructed everyone to stop rowing, leave the boats behind, and walk to the beach. Michael held onto Vicki, guiding her against the current, occasionally stopping to catch his breath.

Once upon the beach, he rested, gathering a dose of strength he did not know he even had. Adriel led them to the lighthouse, smashing the door lock off and barreling it open. "In," he said in a rushed whisper.

One by one, some being helped by another female, they moved up the narrow stairway, finally resting on the top floor. There were only two beds.

Michael helped Vicki down. "This is going to be quite cramped."

"We need to map out our next move," Adriel said. "Everyone," he added, moving to the center of the room. "Let's rest for a couple of hours. We will have to find another place before dawn."

Adriel came over to him.

"Where can we go?" Michael asked.

"I have a good idea where our next destination will be. An island—small, not far from here to the northeast."

Michael pulled Adriel away from the crowd of females. "I need to go south. Back where I met you."

"That's dangerous. There are more Umbra soldiers there than here. I'm going to get these women safely north across to our old country."

"Canada?"

Adriel gave an odd look. "Besides the mountains, it's a place many of my units have fled to. I'll get them to an underground tunnel that leads up there. It's not far from here."

Michael paused for a few seconds, mulling over rational options. "I need a boat."

"What you see out there is what you get," Adriel said.

Michael went to the lone window and scanned the dock. "I need something bigger than what we had."

Adriel joined him. "This is your only choice?"

"It's the safest way to get there without being spotted. I know what I need to do."

Adriel nodded.

"Can you help?" Michael asked.

"Of course."

Michael gestured to the group of women. "Can you manage with them?"

"I will be fine."

Michael hugged Adriel, surprising him. Adriel eventually relented and returned the favor. "I wish you had been part of my unit," Michael said.

"You are my unit now," Adriel replied, hugging him tighter.

Michael pulled away, taking a picture of Adriel's face in his mind. "I will need to go in a couple of hours," he said.

"Rest. I will rest too."

"I will be ready."

"Never doubted it."

They sat side by side, each in their own lonely thoughts. Michael was busy mapping out how he would get back to the tunnel and how he would reverse the history of mankind. It was too much for him to absorb, so he genuflected before the hardship and closed his eyes.

It wasn't long until his shallow sleep failed. He awoke to see Vicki kneeling before him. He wondered briefly if he was in a dream. Seeing her bruises alerted him to reality.

"Um, how are you?" he said.

"I've been better."

Michael stared, sad from what he saw and angry he could not do anything about it. He flushed hallowing images from his imagination.

"You got my back. I am grateful," she said, moving closer.

"I owed you."

Vicki rested next to him. "Where are we going next?"

"You will go with Adriel. I am going south. Back to where I came from…."

She put her hand on his, giving Michael chills and a feeling of melancholy. "No. I feel I need to go with you."

Michael gave a surprised look. "You're hurt."

"I'll be fine."

Michael hesitated.

"Something is telling me we were meant to do this together."

"What is telling you this? Or is it *who* is telling you this?"

Vicki remained silent for a few seconds. She shook her head. "I don't know. We helped each other. Fate, maybe? A calling? Something or a voice from another world giving me a subliminal message?"

Michael gave a forlorn smile. "I believe it all." He gripped her hand. "We will steal a boat and leave soon."

"My kind of journey."

Michael and Adriel exchanged a final handshake and left in opposite directions. He figured there would be about five more hours of darkness before the sun ascended. It was paramount to hit the shore by the lighthouse of Otomamay before the sun rose.

They were weaponless. Vicki was not completely healthy. Her legs were littered with gashes and bruises, but she managed to limp to the shore by the dock.

"How are you at hot-wiring a boat?" he asked.

"Um, like most people here…quite good. Why?"

"Well, I'm not good."

"Really?" she said in a surprised tone.

"Where I came from, we respect each other's property…well, for the most part, we do. I guess my world…" He shook his head, remembering what he left behind. The chaos. The hate. The incivility. Innocent people's properties being destroyed. Their businesses burned to the ground. Their livelihoods ruined forever. "I guess respect reached a low point where I lived too."

Michael took a few steps ahead of her and pointed. "This one?"

"Good enough," said Vicki, struggling and needing a hand from him to get on board.

The name "Ojot" was painted on the exterior of the boat. Vicki opened the cabinet filled with tools and a safety guide. She grabbed a thin screwdriver and wiggled it in the ignition. A spark erupted, and another spark flashed, and the motor started.

"Easy cheesy," she said.

"Nice job," said Michael, resisting an urge to hug her.

"You driving or me?"

"Me," Vicki said. "This baby can really scoot. Who wouldn't want to take this honey for a ride?"

"It's not like a racing car."

"Nooooo. It's much better. No traffic out here."

"You've got the wheel." Michael went to the back and untied the boat. "All ready, Captain."

Vicki gave a salute and revved up the boat. *Zoom.* The boat took off like at the start of a NASCAR race. Michael fell back against the railing, spiking his back hard. "Ow," he said.

Vicki looked back and laughed. "You okay, sailor?"

"Ha ha," Michael responded, massaging his lower back and injured ego.

They sped farther out to sea to keep the noise of the boat at a minimum so no Umbra ears could hear. Michael and Vicki didn't speak much. She was focused on guiding the speed of the boat while he worried, pacing front to back and side to side, checking on would-be intruders. *Too dark to see. Listen. That motor is way too loud. Is there any way she can lower it? Forget it. She knows what she is doing. Just focus on your job.*

Vicki quickened the tempo, testing the power of the motor. Michael wobbled a few times as choppy waters bounced the boat up and down.

"How much farther?" he asked. He joined Vicki at the wheel.

"About thirty minutes. What is your plan when we reach Otomamay?"

Michael frowned.

"What's your plan?" she repeated.

"Find a tunnel not far from the Bay."

"And?"

"Take the tunnel and hope I'm coming out on the other end at the right time."

"Michael," Vicki said. "For me to buy into this, you will have to be clearer than that. What is the purpose of going into this tunnel?"

Michael looked away, searching for a rational response, noticing some tiny glowing lights beyond the shore, alarming him. "You wouldn't believe me."

"Try me."

"I'm afraid to tell you because you'll think I'm crazy."

"I already think that," she said with a quick laugh.

Michael pondered giving her the abbreviated version. "Let me say it this way—"

"The truth, Michael. The truth. Just give me the truth."

Exasperated and desperate to tell his incredible story, he spoke in detail. "I can travel back to first-century Jerusalem. The window of time is narrow every trip I take. Only during the time of Jesus."

"Who? Jesus? Time travel? You read too many European novels. Have you lost your mind?"

"No."

"Time travel? Ha."

"I can. I do. And I have done it a few times."

"Whatever."

"Believe me. I can."

"Sure, you can. Who is this Jesus person?"

"Jesus…yeah, well, you don't know about him. I will explain more at another time. But what happened the last time I traveled is I changed, or someone changed, the history of the world."

He paused and reflected. "What you see or what you have been living in or through…shouldn't be."

Vicki shook her head. She slowed the boat, looking pensive. Michael wasn't sure if she believed him or was ready to jump overboard and swim for her life.

"Any thoughts?" Michael asked.

"That's a lot to digest," she replied. "I need time. I was born at night but not last night."

"We don't have time." Michael placed his hand gently on her shoulder. "Vicki, believe me. I wouldn't tell you a fairy tale. Not to you."

"What makes me special?"

"Everything."

"Too vague, mister."

Michael let out a deep breath. "We were married, or…oh, jeez, you're not going to understand…we were a unit and we had created a female for our unit. Her name is Elizabeth."

Vicki turned off the motor and stared at him, her mouth open and eyes wide. "You *are* crazy."

Michael shook his head. "I'm not. All this brutality around us…it's not supposed to be."

"Okay, Mr. Fortune Teller, how long were we part of a unit?"

"Not long," he said.

"Oh, great. We couldn't even stay together."

"It wasn't that," he said in a solemn tone.

"Don't tell me any more about it. What about Elizabeth? Where is she? Where is this female we created?"

Michael slumped into one of the two chairs on board. "I don't know. It's why I need to go back and try and fix whatever needs to be fixed. Maybe she isn't here because we haven't even…"

Vicki sat next to him. "I'm not sure what to believe. I do know you and Adriel in your unit saved me. You didn't have to do that with what you say now is at stake. Other than that, your story sounds like those novels people read."

"What I said was the absolute truth."

"Sure, it was." Vicki nodded. She stood and restarted the engine again with the thin screwdriver. "Let's find this tunnel."

Chapter 49

Vicki slowed the boat to a crawl and turned the motor off. Michael gathered up some tools and anything sharp he could get his hands on including forks and steak knives. He grabbed a small hammer and positioned it under his shirt at his back.

Vicki did the same, meticulously concealing a large carving knife.

"The people who own this boat must have had some big parties," Michael said randomly with no purpose other than to calm his nerves.

"Look at the name on this boat," she said. "Who knows what they did with this? The Umbras are evil—ten times more evil than whatever you have faced."

"You don't think they used it for any other intent but recreation?"

Vicki held up a military manual.

"Oh."

"Are you ready?" Vicki asked.

"As ready as I can be."

There was a glimmer of light painting the early morning horizon, adding to Michael's anxieties. She threw the rope to the dock and limped out. Michael joined her and tied the rope to a wooden pole. "The Bay looks the same," he said. "Nothing else. Nothing else remains. No more stores. No more trolley tracks. No more statues honoring our 9/11 victims. No more churches."

"Trolley tracks? 9/11? What is that—some cult reference? And churches? What are they for?" Vicki asked.

Michael hesitated. "We were in a chur—" He broke off mid-sentence. "No time to discuss it."

There were scattered soldiers near a big brush fire, mostly smoldering. He could see faint outlines of their uniforms and weapons. Bottles littered what was once Main Street in Northport. It reeked of alcohol and blood, the pavement grungy and stained. There were two tanks on each side of the street. But trees stood high and the first signs of spring were in the air, giving Michael confidence the timing may be right to take the tunnel. Or so it seemed. Michael hesitated.

"What's wrong?" Vicki asked.

"It needs to be timed right. Perhaps it's not here that has to be right. But over there?"

"It's your show," Vicki said to him. "Lead the way."

"I know a way if it's still here," he said, getting on his knees.

"What are you doing?"

"Looking for something very few know about."

"On the ground?"

Michael crawled several feet north and to the left where the park once was. The surrounding landscape was still familiar. He got up. "Follow me."

He remembered how in the men's bathroom by the swings and slides there was a janitor's door that led to one of the tunnels below the village. It was built by the Native Americans to escape persecution. Later, the residents helped slaves escape from the south as a means of relocating, back when there was an America.

"Stay behind me. Is anybody around?"

"All clear," Vicki said.

Michael dropped to the ground again and wiped away a bunch of dirt and ripped out some weeds. "There," he said, banging his fist on what looked like a small-sized metal door. "Found it." He dug deep with his fingers and yanked at the rusty metal, embedded in the ground. "Help me."

Vicki got to her knees, and they used all four hands and twenty fingers and pulled it up, both falling backwards.

"Where does it lead?" she asked.

"To the tunnel back to Jerusalem."

Vicki sat back and looked around. "We don't know what's down there. Do you?"

"This is our best chance to make it to the tunnel alive."

"It's your show," she repeated.

"I'll go first. If there's resistance, do not hesitate. Go back to the boat and leave."

"Are you serious?"

"Very serious."

Vicki shook her head. "I'm not leaving you here. I thought you said in some other world and time we were in the same unit? Whatever that means. And we had a female?"

"Yes."

"What would she think if I left you behind?"

"She already thinks you're wonderful."

Vicki smiled for the first time. "No more talk about separating."

Michael started to descend the ladder. It was a longer trip to the bottom than he previously remembered. The brackets to place your feet on the way down were more unstable. "Close the door."

He reached the bottom. There was an inch or two of water, murky and cold. He could feel the frigidness of it soaking his torn shoes. "Stay behind me."

"How far is this tunnel from here?" she asked.

"No more than twenty minutes. I will take it slow. Just keep in contact with me. The tunnel will divide into different chambers."

They'd sloshed their way a mile or so in when Michael stopped. He turned and put a finger to his mouth. "What is that?" he whispered.

"I didn't hear anything. The noise from my feet in the water is distracting enough," Vicki said.

Michael halted again and turned to her. "There, I heard it again. The same sound. My eyes are awful, but my hearing is pristine."

"I heard it too."

"What did it sound like to you?"

"A rifle loading."

"What?"

"A rifle…"

Before Vicki could finish her words, a bright light blinded them. Michael shielded his aging eyes, and Vicki turned away.

A voice barreled toward them, deep and forceful. "Do not take another step forward. Lay down your weapons."

"We have no weapons," Michael shouted back.

"Do not lie to me. You wouldn't have taken this tunnel without any. So you're either lying, or you're just plain dumb."

"Listen to him," Vicki advised. "I heard a few sounds of rifles loading." She pulled a couple of screwdrivers and a medium-sized hammer out of her garment and tossed it to the ground, making loud splashing sounds.

Michael did the same, throwing what he had a few yards forward.

"Anything more? I suggest you do what I say."

"You have everything we had," Michael assured. "Can you drop the light? I can't see."

The bright light was shut down. Several men and women approached with flashlights, some dressed up in Native American garments, others in Japanese attire or German and Italian uniforms. And another group stood behind them; they wore yarmulkes and tallis. Michael recognized some Japanese. "I hear German," Vicki said. "And Italian. Umbras!"

"Run!" Vicki shouted.

"Stop!" They fired shots over their heads and Michael and Vicki froze.

A burly man stood before them. He had long black hair, a wide jaw, and a chiseled nose with a scar-like lightning bolt on the side. His arms were big like those of someone who spent a few thousand days in a gym. "We are not Umbras. We fight the Umbras. These men and women have joined us. From the other countries. They know what was done many sunsets ago was wrong, even knowing they are fighting the ideas of their native countries which were passed down for many generations. We are all brothers and sisters here. We are now one. Forever fighting the injustices of this world." He paused. "What is your purpose?"

"To get to the other side of this tunnel and escape," Michael said.

"Are you an Umbra?"

"No."

"Are you an Umbra spy?"

"No."

"Of course you will say that. No smart man will admit that with guns pointing at them."

Vicki stepped forward. "It is us who should question you. I see many from the Umbras here. Their languages."

The man looked at her. "And who might you be?"

Vicki hesitated. "I am in his unit. We are trying to find our female."

"Your name?" the man said.

"Vicki."

"Vicki...what?"

She gave Michael a quick glance.

"Well..."

Vicki put her hand to her face, staggered and wobbled, falling to the ground.

"Vicki." Michael pulled her out of the shallow water. "Can you hear me?"

The man signaled to a woman. She stepped forward and opened three small tubes. She knelt down as Michael held her up. She massaged the bottom of Vicki's nose with an ointment. A few minutes later, after three ointments were administered, Vicki opened her eyes.

"What happened," she mumbled. "Where am I?"

"You fainted," Michael said. He looked up at the woman. "Thank you."

He gazed at Vicki. "You scared me. I can't lose you again."

Chapter 50

Michael aided Vicki as they followed the big, wide-shouldered man. His supporters were behind them, their rifles pinned to their heads. The group splashed their way through murky, shallow water for another mile or two, navigating without much hesitation despite the musty smell polluting the thin air.

They came to a large opening, and the big man stopped, turned around, and gestured to an old, run-down, dirty couch. "Put her there," he instructed.

"Sir," Michael said as he lowered Vicki onto the couch. "We are running out of time. I need to get to another tunnel."

The big man gave a puzzled look. "There are no other tunnels here."

"I'm telling you, I came from it not long ago, more south from here. Where the church was."

"Church? What is that?"

"I don't have time to explain. Please, sir, help me," Michael pleaded, seeking an explanation that would resonate with the big man. "I know it doesn't make sense to you. But it's south. I promise you. I am telling the truth."

Vicki stirred, opening her eyes.

Michael went to her. "Sir, can you get her some water... some food? She's not well. We haven't eaten or drank anything in days."

The big man gestured to a woman standing beside him, perhaps part of his unit. She was beautiful, without makeup, and with long braided black hair and dark brown eyes. She left and returned moments later with a cup of water and a piece of raw meat. Michael took the cup and helped Vicki, holding it to her mouth as she drank. She made an appreciative gesture but turned away the raw meat.

"Is that the only food you have?" Michael asked.

The big man took the raw meat and ate it before wiping his hands on a cloth. "We do not have the luxury of a big menu. We eat what we hunt. We are given nothing by the Umbras."

"What the people you keep company with? Are they not Umbras?"

"No. They fight with us. They realize what their leaders did was wrong. Their people were led astray. Conditioned to hate and fight and destroy. We are all part of the same unit here."

Michael nodded and gave Vicki another sip of water. "Sir, I beg you. We need to leave now. It's time for us to take the tunnel."

The big man shook his head. "You are telling tales. A white man is good at telling tales like the Umbras."

Michael stood, and the other men locked their rifles. "I have no choice in how I was born and how I look. At least let me show you where this tunnel is."

The big man walked away and engaged in a whispering session with a woman and a man. Then all of them gathered, speaking in many languages. It lasted for several minutes, and he returned. "We will go when the moon is at its apex. I will bring two of my best men. Perhaps even more are needed. You can show me. If you cannot, we will have to keep you prisoner. We cannot allow you to leave and give away our hiding place."

Michael nodded. "I understand."

The big man gestured to another man. "Bring him some food and water." He turned to Michael. "Eat. Drink. You will need it. Though we have the cover of darkness, if caught, we will never return."

Michael stayed by Vicki's side throughout the evening, insisting she drink every hour. He still couldn't interest her in any food. He drank and managed a painful bite or two of the raw meat. Hunger changes a man's appetite, and Michael could only endure the strains of starvation for so long. *How do these people survive this way?*

The big man returned a few hours later. "Are you ready?"

"Yes."

"I am Ernest Evans."

"I'm Michael Stewart."

Two more men and women joined them. They extended their hands. "I am Oyama." Michael shook his hand. "I am Wasuo." Michael did the same.

Two women did not introduce themselves but shook his hand. One German man and woman did the same. "We are the resistance against the Umbras," Oyama said. "What was done many decades ago against this world can no longer be accepted. So we are all brothers today and forever. Are you a brother too? Are you part of our unit? Ready to fight the Umbras."

Michael nodded. "Whatever is necessary."

"You will lead us," said Ernest. "Do you know where this tunnel is precisely?"

"I have an idea."

"If you come upon some area that is unfamiliar, stop and tell us." Ernest gestured to the two men with rifles. "Make no mistake," he added. "If you deceive us, they will kill you."

"I have no plans to do so," Michael said.

"We have an understanding then."

Michael tapped Vicki on the shoulder. She opened her eyes. "I'll be back soon. Rest. I...I...lo..."

She closed her eyes and fell asleep.

Michael turned to Ernest and gave him a fierce look. "I'm ready."

He led Ernest and the group, then stopped. "Point me south of here?" he asked.

"This way," said Ernest, gesturing to the right.

"If anyone notices anything unusual, alert the group with taps to shoulders," said Wasuo.

Michael stepped in front of him and began the trip. The men and women each had flashlights providing plenty of vision. They came upon two tunnels, one to the left and one to the right. Michael guessed and went right. "We need to go a bit west to get there."

"We're right behind you," Ernest warned.

"I know. I know. I can feel the barrels of the rifles on my neck."

"Good."

It wasn't more than a hundred yards or so before Ernest jumped in front of Michael. "Stop."

Michael did.

Ernest turned off his flashlight and gestured to the other two men to do the same. "Cover me," he said to them.

Ernest tiptoed forward, froze, loaded his rifle, pointed it forward, and fired....

Thud.

A man fell face first.

Ernest turned to Michael and the others. He was distraught. "This isn't good."

He demanded everyone run back. Michael stood frozen, slowly walking forward. Ernest called back to him. "Michael, run. There are Umbras up there."

"I can't. I need to get to the tunnel now. Before it's too late."

Ernest and the others disappeared into the darkness, their flashlights zigzagging in the distance. Michael came upon the fallen soldier. Blood flooded the ground around him. A light shone in his face.

A soldier pointed a gun at his head. "Drop your weapon," he said in broken English. Three more soldiers surrounded him; two had automatic weapons.

Michael threw the bayonet to the ground and held his arms up.

"Go get the others," the soldier said to the three. "I will take care of this one."

The three soldiers raced into the darkness. Rapid shots were fired. Yelling echoed in the tunnel. Michael turned in time to see flashes of light illuminating the narrow pathway. Automatic gunfire erupted in a fury.

A hand grabbed Michael from behind, and he was pushed forward, up a stairway and outside onto what was once Main Street. A thump on his head and a whack on the back of his knees crippled him for a few minutes. Michael tried to shake off some of his dizziness. A soldier grabbed his hair and pulled his head back. "Open your mouth," the soldier demanded.

Michael spat at the soldier. *Thump.* The soldier smacked Michael in the face, splitting his nose. Blood flowed down to his mouth and to his chin. Drips fell to the ground as he hung his head.

"Where are you from?" the soldier demanded, threatening to hit him again.

"Here."

Thump! Michael bled more, swallowing and coughing on his blood.

"You are a lying dog."

Michael pondered his next response, not wishing to get another blow to what already felt like a broken nose. "England."

"Why are you here?"

"I got lost."

Whack! Whack! The soldier hit him on the side of his head, damaging his right ear. He grabbed it, wincing. A dull whistle muffled his hearing. He could see the soldier yelling but couldn't understand him. He turned to see several soldiers dragging Ernest and Vicki.

"No," Michael said, reaching from his knees to stop the soldier manhandling Vicki. "Leave her alone!"

Wham! Michael fell to the ground, his arms spread wide like an angel serenading the heavens. Dazed, he saw blurry images of Vicki screaming.

Chapter 51

M ichael labored to free himself from the chains, both
arms tangled in a metal mess, his body tattered with
bruises. He was alone, secured to a frosty, reeking
wall in the darkness. The smell of death and dried up gore was
unsettling, circulated by a lone small fan hung in the top right
corner of his cell.

Beyond the steel bars that confined him, he could see shadows of men and women also shackled and stirring slightly, their
feeble pleas echoing in this dungeon of doom. A soldier was
dragging a wide synthetic line before cannon-shooting the prisoners with water.

Michael closed his eyes and waited for the impact, welcoming some cold relief. There was none, to his surprise.

He opened his eyes. Three Umbra soldiers stood at the cage
door. They laughed and said some unfamiliar words, yet the
translation was clear by the way they mimicked him.

Faint screaming provoked him. He swung his arms wildly,
the adrenaline rousing him into a fury. The shrieking pierced his
soul. The soldiers hooted louder. Another Umbra spit at Michael,

his wicked expression giving him chills. The soldier opened the cage and kicked him. Then kicked him again. Michael cringed. The soldier kicked and kicked. Michael lost his breath, gasping. He looked up and scowled. The soldier smashed his face, throwing Michael's head back into the wall. He wheezed a few breaths and hung his head, throwing up little of the raw meat he had digested.

"We have a present for you," the soldier said in rather good English. "Your female in your unit."

The words were barely audible from the ringing in his ears. "What?" Michael said, lifting his head, still puffing.

"Your female."

The screaming grew.

"What have you done?" Michael said in a weak tone.

"We have a show for you. You Europeans can appreciate that. I'm sure you heard of Shakespeare." He laughed, evil in tone, arrogance on full display.

The Umbras dragged Vicki into the cage and dropped her. She struggled to go fight back. Michael yanked on the chains. "Leave her alone!" he shouted.

"Shut up, English dog," the soldier said, smacking him in the head.

Michael managed to muster up a curse or two at his attacker. The soldier gestured to the two other Umbras. They entered and each whacked Michael in the face, leaving his right eye almost swollen shut.

One soldier took a knife out from his belt. Michael kicked at him, missing. The soldier tore Vicki's pants with the knife. The other soldier ripped apart her shirt, her breasts bare. They turned to Michael and made mocking macho man gestures before pulling off their own pants.

Michael cried out. Vicki turned to him, her eyes glazed and weeping. Michael absorbed her sadness, then felt his rage surge. "Don't you dare touch her."

The Umbras made more lewd gestures and jumped on top of Vicki, tying her hands.

Michael spat blood at the soldier, splashing his face.

The Umbra sat up on Vicki, laughing, playing with his lower body, taunting Michael. He yelled some words and put his hand over her mouth. He pulled her legs apart. Vicki struggled, her cries muffled. Michael shouted. The Umbras laughed some more.

As the soldier pulled his pants lower, Vicki swung her legs backward and hooked the soldier's neck, stunning him momentarily. The Umbra fell. Vicki jumped up and managed to move her hands to the front, held together. She kicked another soldier in the groin. He collapsed, and Vicki came up from behind and choked the soldier. She removed the rope.

The other Umbra soldier staggered, taking a few steps toward her. Michael flattened out and swung his feet, clipping the soldier. He fell face first and then got to his knees. Vicki grabbed the bayonet and pierced his neck and then sliced it, sending him into a free fall.

She recovered a key and unchained Michael. "Are you okay?" she said.

Stunned, he could only reply, "Yes."

"Good. Let's get out of this hellhole."

She slapped him on his cheeks with both hands, then pulled up her pants and adjusted her shirt. "Snap out of it."

Vicki picked up one gun, retrieved the second, and handed it to Michael. "Get a hold of yourself," she implored. "Kill if you have to."

Michael nodded.

Before they left, Vicki turned both soldiers over on their backs. "This is so you never attack a woman again." She took the sharp blade on the bayonet and sliced each men's groin area. Michael joined her, plunging his bayonet into the men. He plunged and plunged the bayonet over and over until his arms could do no more.

She looked at him. "That, Michael, is how justice is served in our world."

They raced up the stairs and confronted two soldiers. Vicki handled the first with a whack to the face, knocking him unconscious. Michael knocked down the second and battered his head seven or eight times before Vicki pulled him away.

"How far to that tunnel?" she asked.

"Not more than a hundred yards," said Michael, scoping the area. "This way." He stopped. "You should go back home."

"No way. I'm with you. I want to see this amazing world."

"It's not so amazing," Michael said. "It's actually a cruel world too."

"As cruel as this world?"

Michael hesitated. "Now, I'm not sure."

They arrived at the tunnel, which was hidden by a square piece of wood and covered by some crabgrass. He pulled it up and turned to Vicki. "Please go home. This isn't your battle."

Vicki hugged him. "I wanted to do this a while ago. I can't let you go alone. Something in my heart is telling me to go with you."

Michael sighed and pulled back from her. As he did, he stuck a piece of paper in her pocket.

Chapter 52

Michael raced two steps at a time down the stairway followed by Vicki. After spitting up blood, he took a moment once he reached the tunnel to collect himself and tried to settle down the adrenaline whipping through his body. *We made it. But what about Vicki? What should I do? She's stubborn…like me. I do need to change time back. It's not just about me. About Vicki. About Elizabeth. It's about us all. Everyone here in this world.* He looked at her. While some of the old memories were fading, new ones were beginning.

"Why are we stopping?" Vicki asked.

"I just needed a moment to think."

"More like rest," she said with that infectious smile.

"Did you pull the cover back over the entrance?"

Vicki's eyes widened.

Michael retreated up the stairway and peeked out from the opening. He squinted as a glimmer of light sprinkled the horizon. Dark outlines of the men battling and falling to the ground alerted him.

Michael took another step up to catch a clearer view. *Is that Adriel? Can't be. I thought he went north. No. I'm not seeing right. It can't be him.*

Michael hopped up two more steps, his face visible for anyone to see. "Adriel!" Michael shouted.

The man turned back to him, catching his eyes.

"Adriel!"

Michael hurtled up the final three steps, ran to the skirmish, and speared the soldier in the back, twisting it 360 degrees. The Umbra collapsed, blood gushed from the deep wound as Michael left the bayonet's blade in his back.

Adriel got up and hugged him. "We are a unit."

"I've got to go," Michael said, pulling back.

"Where are you going?"

"This way. To that other world."

"Your world?"

"No. Another world."

"I'm going with you," Adriel said.

Michael shook his head as he started back to the tunnel. "Your world is here. Go to the mountains."

"I have nothing left."

Michael didn't respond. Who was he to stop him? He took a few steps down the tunnel stairway and turned around. "Pull the cover over."

"You mean you're not going to debate me?" Adriel said in a surprised tone.

Michael shook his head again. "I have seen your world. I thought my world was cruel."

They reached the bottom and Vicki greeted them. "Better to have another warrior with us," Michael said.

Vicki agreed, and Michael led the way through the dark tunnel. It wasn't long before they reached the end, sunlight coming through the sewer crate leading up to the street.

It was déjà vu for him.

The palms were being laid, and the man they called Jesus was on a donkey riding past them.

"Oh, my..." Vicki said, covering her mouth. "What in...are you seeing what I'm seeing, Adriel?"

"Woah," said Adriel. He rubbed his eyes and shook his head.

"What is this?" asked Vicki. "This is not like any place I've been to...."

"Same here," Adriel agreed.

"Who is that?" Vicki asked, pointing. "Why are they treating him like he's some royalty? This place looks...awful. Old. Dirty."

"This doesn't look bad at all—actually looks like a beautiful place," Adriel disagreed.

"That's Jesus," Michael said. "Jesus is unlike any other man who has lived on this planet. A name never forgotten. A man's teachings often repeated."

"Not where I live," Vicki said.

"And this is the man you spoke about before? All those stories you told me?" Adriel said.

Michael nodded. "That man will ignite a revolution of sorts."

Vicki gave a look of disbelief. "Where's his army? Where are his weapons? From what I can see, he's just a simple man riding on a donkey. I can take him myself. Big deal."

"He has no weapons. He has no army...well, no army that you'd know."

Michael continued, "He has apostles—people loyal to him, probably twelve or thirteen."

Vicki laughed. "You've got to be kidding me. You said twelve or thirteen, not twelve or thirteen thousand? I have more in my group. And this is the man you have so much hope in?" Vicki said incredulously.

Michael sighed. "Stop thinking literally. Think spiritually."

"In our world, there are many gods we are forced to worship under the Umbras," Adriel said. "So what you say would not fit into what we have to believe."

Vicki stepped between them. "Adriel's right. I think we're wasting valuable time here. This man looks like any other man. No army. No weapons. He has no chance of, as you say, 'igniting a revolution.' Adriel, what about going back?"

Adriel shrugged. "He does look like any other man. Not even the face of a warrior. No scars. No marks. His hands appear to never have handled a weapon. Too many questions haven't been answered. Vicki makes good points. Why would we believe this...story of yours?"

"I know none of this makes any sense to you both," Michael said. "When I was here the last time with my daughter...my daughter, yes, our daughter...our unit, our female we created...Elizabeth," Michael said with a big burst of joy. "She's already here. We must find her first. She is the key to this all. Now I know."

"Know what?" said Adriel.

"Michael," Vicki said. "My patience is running out."

"We first have to locate my daughter. I mean, our female, Vicki. Our daughter."

Michael grew excited about the possibility of Vicki meeting Elizabeth. *Could this happen?* All rational thoughts and emotions left him. He refused to consider the alternatives, thinking only that if he changed the world history back, every event as he knew it would occur.

"We wait until the gathering ends," Michael said to them.

When the last of the Roman soldiers dispersed, Michael pushed the grate up and climbed onto the street. Adriel followed Vicki. They were amazed at the ancient structures surrounding them.

Vicki turned to Michael. "Is what you said back there true?"

"What part?"

"That Elizabeth is our female?"

"From another time and world. She is."

"Why haven't I met her?"

Michael gave a forlorn glance and looked down at the ground, his heart nearly at rest. "It's too hard to talk about."

Vicki placed her hand under his chin, lifting his head. "Look me in the eyes and tell me the truth."

"You didn't make it. It was a car accident." Michael hugged her. "I'm so sorry."

Vicki stood, arms down at her side. "Car accident? I've never driven a car. We aren't allowed to drive cars where I am." She pushed him away. "You're lying."

"Michael," Adriel said, interrupting. "Romans."

A trio of Roman soldiers were cleaning the area of drunks and vagrants, some with brutal, unforgiving force.

"We need to get to safety," Michael warned.

"Where are we going to?" Adriel asked.

"To a friend's house. I mean another unit I know."

Vicki walked slowly, her face ghost white.

Chapter 53

Heavy wind-swept rain drenched Michael, Vicki, and Adriel. It didn't stop their progress. It only made Michael more determined as he was feeling refreshed from nature's gift. Residents emerged from their small stone homes with buckets in both hands to catch the rain running off their rooftops. They were quite skilled in maximizing their trips back and forth into their homes.

Michael smiled while Adriel and Vicki marveled at the self-sufficiency of the citizens. *What other choice do they have?* Michael thought. They literally had nothing living under the brutal regime of the Roman Empire.

There were not many Roman soldiers around, as they prepared for possible uprisings during this holy time. Michael tried to explain what was at stake, yet he wasn't convinced either Adriel or Vicki understood the significance.

Vicki still seemed out of sorts, asking question after question after question about Elizabeth. "How old is she? What does she look like? Does she look like me? Is she tough like me? Does she go to school? Where did we live? What did you do? What did I do?"

The questions piled up as they approached Leah's house. Michael stopped not far from the front door. "She's not going to remember me," Michael said.

"What? Why?" asked Vicki.

"Explain," added Adriel.

"We have time traveled. I haven't met my friend Leah yet."

"You need to explain more," said Vicki.

"I have time-traveled a few times to this place. Around this time, I can visit and see certain important historical events. I become…part of her unit…after I meet her. At this moment, I haven't. Today is the day I meet her for the first time."

Adriel sighed. Vicki raised her hands up in the air in disbelief.

"Michael," Adriel said. "I have run out of words to say to you."

"I know," he replied. "But I'm here for a big reason. To make everything right again. For everyone. For this world." He looked at Vicki.

"Lead the way," she said.

Michael stopped at the opening of the home, peeked his head inside, and called out. "Hello, Leah," he said.

Leah slowly approached, the shadow of her face recognized by him.

"What do you want?" she asked in a timid tone. "How do you know my name?"

"My name is Michael. We've met before…. You may not remember me."

"I do not. Are you a Roman?"

"No."

"Then what do you want?" she asked.

"I am looking for my daughter. A female in my unit."

"I do not know this person."

Michael sighed. "I'm not with the Romans. The female is about this big." He placed his hand to the top of his eyes. "And she has long hair to her shoulders. She has the tips of her hair colored pink."

"What do you know about me, if you do know me?" she asked.

Michael reflected. "I know your partner was killed by the Romans. I know you talk to him at night on your rooftop. I know your partner's name. It's Yohannan."

Leah's eyes widened.

"How do you know my Yohannan?"

"We became friends. In another place. I am so sorry for your loss. I wish I could have helped."

Leah looked down and wiped a tear. She straightened up, brushing some hair away from her eyes. "I do not know you. Are you talking to my neighbors?"

"I am not. Please believe me. I would not deceive you."

"Many men here lie. Many are with the Romans. They seek silver. Rewards. Blood rewards."

"I am not that man."

Leah hesitated. Her eyes wandered all over Michael. She paused and stopped speaking. Then she stepped out of her home and looked around. She pushed Michael inside to the living room and gestured to Adriel and Vicki to join them. She put a finger to her mouth. "What is the girl's name?"

"Elizabeth."

Leah pulled them into the center of the house away from all the windows, the rooms sparsely decorated with a lone table and two wooden chairs. Michael could see her bedroom. Two beds were placed together. There was a pot of water on a metal grill in the kitchen.

"Elizabeth was here," Leah said.

"What? I thought…"

"I had to be sure," Leah replied.

"When was she here?"

"Not long after the sun rose."

"Do you know where she might have gone?"

"To be with the rebels."

Michael shook his head. "I thought so." He turned to Adriel and Vicki. "We will have to find her soon."

"How much time do we have?" Vicki asked.

"Not long. Maybe a day. But getting around in town will be difficult. We will need a change of clothes."

Michael went to Leah. "We need your help. Elizabeth needs our help. The world needs our help."

Leah gave him a confused look.

"Can you find some clothes?"

Leah gave a pensive look. "I will go to town. The woman can take some of my clothes in my bedroom." She looked at Michael.

"I'm sorry. I don't have any money. Hold on…" Michael pulled a necklace off him. "Take this."

"I cannot."

"It will help pay for what we need."

Leah placed it down on the table. "We will discuss it later." She stopped at the door before leaving. "I should tell you one Roman soldier came here and asked about this girl."

Michael grimaced. *He's back. Great. I'll kill him if he touches Elizabeth and put an end to this finally.*

"Marcus?"

Leah gave an incredulous look. "You know of him?"

"I do." He sat on one of the two wooden chairs. It creaked and felt shaky.

"What's wrong, Michael?" asked Vicki, sitting down next to him.

"Our unit is in danger. This Roman soldier is big trouble. He's real big trouble. For Elizabeth."

"No one is going to hurt her," Vicki said in a defiant tone.

Chapter 54

Michael expertly baked bread while waiting for Leah's return, impressing both Vicki and Adriel. He remembered how Leah taught him the last time he visited. He'd keep the pan of dough a certain distance from the flame and maintain the heat at a simmering level. It was a practice he brought back to Long Island for the few parties he had. It was often a request from Elizabeth for her birthday that he would bake some.

He placed a piece of the warm delight on three plates, handing one to Adriel and one to Vicki. He left his alone. Adriel and Vicki chewed slowly, assessing each bite carefully.

"Well, what do you think?" Michael said with both hands wide like he was opening a Broadway show.

Vicki smiled and swallowed. "I'm not sure what to think. It's chewy. Yes, that's the word…chewy. What about you?" she asked Adriel.

He laughed. "Should I give him the truth?"

"He can handle the truth."

"I don't know," Adriel teased. "He does have a temper."

"Oh, he does?"

"Okay, guys, enough of the banter."

"I'll give it to you straight," Adriel said. "Don't quit your day job."

Vicki gave a slight smile. "What is your day job?"

"I write."

"Really? What do you write?" Vicki said, turning her chair around to see him.

"I write on a number of subjects that deal with emotional pain and joy."

"Why would you write about pain?" she said, her eyebrows raised.

"It's therapeutic."

Vicki shook her head. "Isn't there enough pain in this world?"

"Sometimes you need to write about pain so that you don't feel the brunt of it all."

"I would love to be a writer," Adriel said.

"What stopped you?" Michael asked.

"The Umbras. There's no room for any honesty to be shared where I live. Do you think the Umbras would allow someone like me to write such a book? They wouldn't allow the truth to be published. If I wrote the truth, they would try to burn it. We live in a society where if someone disagrees with you, *you* should be canceled. No..." Adriel sighed. "Freedom of speech only applies for them. Not us." He looked at Michael. "Not even you."

Michael and Vicki remained quiet. He looked away, knowing the truth about his world and the world they just left. In some ways, it was the same for Adriel. In many ways, it would end up the same too.

"I wouldn't even be able to write a book if I lived where you are," Adriel added, gesturing to Vicki.

Michael cut two more pieces of bread and gave it to them. "For two people who didn't like my cooking, you both sure devoured it." He smiled, proud of his small culinary accomplishment.

"I surrender," Vicki said.

"Then again, there's an old Indian saying," Adriel said. "Beggars cannot pass up a meal on an empty stomach."

"I might have heard of that in parts," Michael replied.

"Really? I find that hard to believe," Adriel said.

Michael poured three cups of water. "Drink up."

They all did and rested in silence. Michael went outside where the lamb, so aptly named Cassie by Elizabeth, was sleeping. He recalled how on their first visit to Jerusalem, Elizabeth fell in love with this proposed sacrificial lamb. Passover was near. *I need to convince Elizabeth to stand down, to allow history to take place. But Elizabeth sees oppression, hatred, and injustice. Who am I to deny her these honorable and noble thoughts?*

Michael wrestled with the morality of it all, worried about trying to change everything back, knowing many rebels would die if he did. He would mind-wrestle until the anxiety spun him around emotionally. He waved Vicki and Adriel away. "Go rest."

Vicki and Adriel did not argue and lay down on a spare bed, head to toes, toes to head.

The uneasiness of Michael's decision was relentless. He paced and paced around the room, finding brief comfort in walking outside in the cover of darkness.

After some time, Leah returned.

"Michael, what troubles you?" Leah asked.

Michael noticed her eyes, light green, sorrowful, and sad, still grieving and stricken over the loss of her Yohannan. "My worst fears are for my people in the world."

"You cannot carry the world's burdens," she said.

"Would you mind if I sat on your roof?"

"Sure. Let me show you...."

"I know where to go," Michael interjected.

"You do?"

"I told you I met you before...."

Michael located the stairway leading up to the roof and climbed to the top. He sat, admiring the clear dark sky. Leah joined him.

"This is so beautiful," he said. "Picturesque."

"God's most magnificent painting," Leah said.

"Agreed." He sighed, took a deep breath, and exhaled.

"You carry many burdens," Leah said. "Your eyes tell me this."

"I do."

"Let your burdens be carried away on the shooting stars we see in the sky."

Michael gave a slight smile. "It's not easy to do."

"You will never know until you try."

He nodded and gazed at the twinkling stars enlightening the night. The moon was making a bright appearance. He would have some time before morning to rest. He leaned back and saw the moonlight's glow sweeten Leah's face, her anguished eyes more profound, swollen, and red from recent weeping. It tugged at Michael, drawing him closer to her. She was his friend. Forever.

Leah, weakened from the day's chores, leaned her head down. He lay back, eyes open, heart slowing, soul uncertain, ready to give his mind and body some much-needed rest.

Michael leaned over and kissed her forehead. "I'm kissing your soul."

Leah smiled and closed her eyes.

He fell into a trance, watching the stars take unending journeys. She whispered, "I am blessed to have met you."

"I am too."

The silence of the night was captivating. Only the echoes of wolves in the hills many miles away disrupted the night.

Leah turned over. "Pray with me, Michael. Pray for my Yohannan. Pray for my people. Pray for peace."

Peace. What a wonderful thought. Peace. It's not here. It's not in Vicki and Adriel's world. It's certainly not in my world. Would peace actually be there for Leah in my world? Would her people ever have peace? It's actually worse. There's no peace anywhere.

Michael turned over to his side, back-to-back with Leah. He tried to will himself to sleep. Restless, he sat up several times and looked at the heavens.

A big day lay ahead. Sleep.

Michael lay down once more on his side. He was antsy, scared for Elizabeth. *She could be anywhere, knowing her. She spoke a lot about what Leah and her people suffered after studying Jewish history in college. I should have known. I should have paid more attention to her intentions. She wasn't just a talker; she believed in taking action.*

His anxiety climbed. Leah reassured him like she had done so many times before, though she wouldn't recall them all. "Sleep, Michael."

"I'm worried."

"I know. Sleep. Elizabeth will need to you be rested."

Michael sighed. "You're right."

"Of course I am. Women always are."

Michael laughed.

"Was that funny?" she said.

"In a way. What you said I have heard in many places and many times and from many…"

"Women?"

Michael hesitated, not sure how far he should go in revealing more details of his past and her past. He deflected the conversation.

"Leah, I am ready to do anything to protect Elizabeth."

"Anything?"

Michael pulled a knife from under his pants and showed it to her.

Chapter 55

Michael hid behind a towering, wide marble pole attached to a majestic structure. The crowd howled in delight as each Roman soldier took turns whipping a man holding onto a short wooden stump. The cracking of the whip against the man's back brought forth exploding bursts of blood.

Michael moved closer, wincing from the sound of the metal balls attached to a thin string that were smashing against the man. He stayed behind two women weeping.

He could take it no more and took a few steps forward, planning his move to stop this madness. He looked back at the women, and seeing their grief, Michael was enraged. "Do you know that man?"

A woman, small in stature, covered in a light blue cloak and hood, her hands trembling, slowly turned her head toward him. "Yes. He is my son."

Michael squinted, and clarity drenched him in sorrow. *It's happening again. What do I do? He's in so much pain.* "I am so sorry, Mary. How can I help your son?"

Mary did not answer. The other woman dressed in white removed her hood, her eyes drained in red, and spoke. "Because he speaks the truth, the truth for all of us, what we see must be."

He took several more steps, pushing his way through the mob, giving himself a clear view of the brutality. Exhausted, one Roman soldier handed his whipping weapon to another who was sitting and eating some fruit. The soldier put his steel helmet on and stretched several times, extending his arm upward and behind his back.

The soldier strode toward Jesus like he was on a runaway for an awards show. Another soldier planted a wooden crown complete with thorns on his head. It pierced his forehead and blood trickled down into his eyes.

The Roman winded up and struck him, puncturing the right side of his back. Jesus called out, groaning in pain.

"Stop this madness!" Michael's words were drowned out by the rabid mob, demands being shouted for the Romans to do more.

The soldier obliged, swinging his metal menace three times in rapid fashion. Jesus passed out, his head hung. Splatters of blood littered the Roman's face. He kicked him twice in the back of his legs.

The mob mocked Jesus, throwing objects at him until the two women appeared, falling to their knees. They wiped him, helped him regain his consciousness, and gave him some water to drink.

The Romans ushered the women away. They unchained the man, lifted him, and pushed him a few yards toward a big wooden cross lying flat on a rocky road.

One Roman soldier picked it up and placed it on Jesus' back. His legs collapsed, and he fell to the ground. Michael raced to Jesus and lifted him up. "Let me carry this," he shouted at the Romans.

A soldier flogged Michael behind his legs. He fell to the ground, the sting snaking its way up to his neck. He staggered to his feet, grabbed the Roman's whip, and struck the soldier in the face. The Roman did a face plant. Several more soldiers moved forward to confront Michael.

People surrounding them turned on the Romans, chucking all sorts of objects, rocks, and pieces of concrete. A riot ensued, and Michael picked up Jesus and led him away, sequestering him in a room not far from the chaos and bedlam.

He scoured the areas outside the room to make sure they weren't followed. He ripped a piece of cloth from his own shirt and pressed it against Jesus' wounds. He removed the crown of thorns and kicked it away in anger.

"Don't talk. Rest. Let me try to help you," Michael pleaded.

Distraught, Jesus had a glazed look. "Stay here," Michael said. "Let me see if I can get you more help."

The fighting between the Romans and citizens of Jerusalem escalated. Rocks were hurled and bloodied faces on both sides wrestled on the rocky grounds. From a distance, Michael could see massive Roman enforcements gathering with shields and spears.

Find Mary. She can take him home where they live. Keep him safe. Heal him. Michael found the women huddled in a corner away from the melee. He raced to them. "Come. Come with me. I have your son, Jesus."

He guided them back to the room where Jesus sat dazed in the far corner, his head resting against the wall. Mary and the women went to him, gently wiping his face. They spoke in a whisper, and Jesus listened.

Then Jesus said a few words to them. "Mother, do not weep for me. Weep for this world. Weep for the oppressed. Weep for the poor. Weep for the hungry. Weep, Mother. Weep, for we have much to grieve about in this world."

Mary cried and hugged him. The other woman pleaded with Jesus to leave. He shook his head, held both of their hands, bowed, and whispered some more words. "Leave, women. This is not a place for you. Pray for me. Let me live up to the word of God."

The women approached Michael. "Are you leaving?" he asked. "Where are you going? Look at what they did to him. He's in so much pain."

Mary held Michael's hand. "It is written for the Son of God will suffer for us, for each of us. He will spill his blood and give his life for all."

Michael would not listen, walking to Jesus, gesturing to him. "He is in pain."

Mary joined them. "No. He is not in pain. It is you who is in pain. My son, on this day, is here to forgive you."

"Forgive me?"

"Yes. Forgive you for what you have done."

Michael sighed. "Why does he have to suffer this way?"

"If he does not endure pain like this, how would you know how much he has suffered for you?" Mary touched Michael's heart.

She gave a forlorn look of acceptance and they embraced. "You must go home. You must go home and be with your family."

Mary stepped away. "We all need to feel the pain my son is going through so we may understand the power of his sacrifice. Do not fight it. What you want to change should never be."

Michael watched the two women pick up the crown of thorns and lift Jesus up, bringing him back to the whipping area. The riot simmered, and the Roman's massive presence restored order. Michael watched from afar as Jesus carried the cross. The beating continued. Michael winced and wept. The mocking was fierce. He could watch no more. He ran and ran and ran until he could not run anymore.

Michael turned back. *Marcus.* He put his hands up in self-defense. "No!"

The Roman soldier pierced Michael's heart with a long spear and twisted it. Michael held onto the weapon before falling backward and breathing heavily.

Marcus stood over him, sneering. "I am going to rape and kill your daughter."

Chapter 56

Michael flailed his arms, swinging wildly at the air. He felt the soft touch of her hands on his shoulder. Unsure of where he was, Michael staggered to his feet and fell down. "Where am I? Is this Northport? England?"

"Calm down," Vicki said. "You had a bad dream, or I hope it was a bad dream."

She sat next to him, holding onto his arm.

"It was horrible," he said, trying to settle his racing heart. "But is what I saw in my nightmare going to come true?"

Vicki squeezed his hand gently. Michael took a few minutes to shake off the terrifying cobwebs, retreating from what was his first sustained sleep in weeks.

"What time is it? Where are we?" he asked again.

"You're on the roof of Leah's house," Vicki said.

"Good morning," said Leah, peeking her head out onto the roof from the ladder.

"I've been up here all night? Sleeping?"

"You sure were," Vicki said.

"Come on down for some breakfast," Leah called to them.

Vicki and Michael went down the ladder and entered the living room. He could smell the fresh bread from the kitchen, and he caught a glimpse of Adriel sitting at the table chewing on a piece.

"Do not be shy," Leah said, waving to them. "Join us. You will need to eat and drink. What are your plans today?"

"To find Elizabeth," Michael said, joining her at the oven. The heat from it warmed him.

"What do you think of my clothes?" Vicki said. She was wearing a bright white garment over her head and a long white robe that extended to her ankles. "This is so comfortable. Better than the clothes the Umbras forced us women to wear."

Michael let his eyes take a stroll over her from head to toe. "It works."

They joined Adriel at the table. He was already in his Jerusalem attire. "How are those shoes fitting you?" Michael asked.

"A little tight." Adriel jumped up and down several times, adjusting his feet.

Leah came over to Adriel. "I can make them fit better," she said.

Adriel smiled. "Thank you. I'll be fine."

"You won't be able to run quickly in those shoes, so get used to them," Michael interjected.

"I'll outrun you any day or night," Adriel boasted.

"Okay, boys, it's time to lower the testosterone levels and use our collective minds to come up with a plan," Vicki interjected.

"I'm sure my unit buddy here has one," Adriel said, slapping Michael on the shoulder as he stood.

"There is a place where the rebels are planning an attack on Pilate."

"Number one. That's crazy dangerous," Vicki said. "Number two from what I remember reading back home when Pilate was assassinated, the Romans burned this town down and expelled the Jews from this area. If my history tells me right."

"Yes. Your history," Michael said. "Not the right history."

"How is history wrong? History is our past reality," Vicki argued.

"I've been trying to explain we changed history from what was intended to happen," Michael countered.

Vicki sat next to Adriel while Michael stood between them. "Go ahead, what's the plan?"

"Elizabeth is with the rebels. She is convinced the rebels can beat the Romans and remove their brutal regime. And she is right. But not at this time. Or, more accurately, it cannot happen now. It needs to happen years later."

"So we stop Elizabeth?" Adriel said.

"We stop her and the rebels."

"How?" Adriel asked.

"That's the part I'm still working on."

Vicki shook her head. "This can go all wrong."

"I know." Michael glanced at Adriel, wishing he would suggest a solution. He looked toward Vicki. She was silent too.

"My other choice is to alert Pilate," Michael said, measuring his words.

Vicki frowned. "That's a suicide mission."

"No way," added Adriel. "Pilate will think we are involved. I can fight a few of these Romans but not an entire army."

"That is ultra-dangerous," Vicki added. "Michael, what you say may endanger our Elizabeth."

"Let the rebels crush the Romans. They deserve it," Adriel said.

"We aren't sure that will happen at this time," Michael countered. "Vicki, we are all in peril. There will be blood and death no matter what happens. It's just a matter of time."

Leah joined them. "Michael, eat. Drink. Here are your clothes." She handed them to him.

"Thank you," he said, taking the garments. Michael sat, ate some bread, and drank three cups of water, feeling refreshed. His mind circulated many options. None seemed to satisfy him. He sought the most peaceful plan. Calculating that they were a couple of days away from the crucifixion, Michael knew he had some time to figure out how to avoid the enormous bloodshed.

Leah interrupted his thought trance. She sat next to him at the table. "I need to say this to you," she said. "What you are planning and with that Roman soldier coming by here and asking about your Elizabeth..." She paused. "You do not have much time. I know how the Romans treat women."

Leah's eyes told a more tragic story. Michael remembered listening to how Yohannan died at the hands of the Romans.

"I understand," he said.

Leah gave a sorrowful glance. "I am glad. There has been enough death and bloodshed with my people. May strength and peace be with you."

Michael got up and went to an outside stall where he could clean himself. He took his clothes with him and washed. It was a clear day, the heat and humidity building in the early morning hours. He changed clothes and returned to Adriel and Vicki. "We need to first go find that Roman soldier."

"I think we might find him looking for your daughter," Adriel said.

"Bingo. Are you ready?"

Adriel nodded. Vicki looked down, not answering.

Michael leaned into her shoulder. "Are you okay?"

"I'm nervous."

"The Romans are a vicious army. They take no prisoners."

"No worries there. I've faced Umbra soldiers my whole life with better weapons and numbers."

"What is bothering you?"

"Meeting Elizabeth. Will she like me? Is she mad at me for not being there with you both? You said I never met her."

Michael nodded.

"I'm not sure I want to."

Michael walked Vicki into another room that was a guest room Yohannan had built for Leah's extended family to visit. "I'm sorry. I never should have said anything. Maybe all of this happening right now is supposed to be happening? Maybe... you are supposed to be here at this very moment? Helping me. Helping me help billions everywhere. I certainly don't know. Nor do you."

Vicki went to the lone window in the room and gazed at the pomegranate tree sitting in front of Leah's house. "And if you are wrong about it all?"

"Then we are giving our lives for the better."

Chapter 57

Michael parted ways with Leah. He knew if they were successful in convincing Elizabeth to abandon the plans to overthrow Pilate and the Romans it might be the last time they see each other. Leah stuffed a piece of bread in his pocket.

"Take this," she said. "It is a long trip to where they are hiding."

"Thank you for everything."

"You are welcome back here, you and your friends," she said. Leah had a worried look on her face.

"We'll be okay," said Michael. "They're warriors."

"I know they are. Are you?"

"For my Elizabeth, always."

"Be careful. I have not known your daughter long, but she is determined and wants justice for people like me. I support her and the rebels."

"It won't be easy. Unfortunately, what we have to do will hold off justice a little bit longer."

"Why should justice ever be delayed?" asked Leah.

She stepped back. Michael knew any explanation he provided would not satisfy her, a woman who was grieving and angry about how the Romans murdered her Yohannan. What could he say? If he was in her situation, Michael would feel the same way.

He gave a kiss on her forehead and walked away.

"Were you kissing my soul again?"

"Always."

Leah gave a short wave. Michael did the same. He rejoined Adriel and Vicki. "Look at us, the three amigos," he said, wrapping his arms around both, trying to deflate the seriousness of the task.

"It will be hot," he continued. "Let's wear our hoods to protect us from the sun and give us some more cover. Just blend in with society. Women are submissive here, Vicki."

Vicki did not acknowledge Michael's advice. "Vick, did you hear me?"

"I hear you. Women are submissive. I got it. Can't promise you that."

"Vicki, please…"

"Yeah, I told you I got it. Be submissive." She gave a short, sarcastic laugh. Adriel laughed too.

"Don't encourage her," Michael said to him.

"Far be it for me to get in the middle of your squabble. She is much like me. A born warrior."

Michael ignored Adriel's comparison. "We have about an hour before we reach the wall surrounding Jerusalem. We need to go past it and into the hills. Tensions are high. Stay away from any skirmishes. The Romans will be everywhere. Look away if you run into them. Don't make eye contact."

He looked back at Adriel and Vicki, walking side by side. "Did you hear what I said?"

"Sure did," Vicki answered.

Adriel winked.

"In another couple of miles, we should stop by a well and get some water," Michael suggested.

Vicki caught up to him. "I'm just giving you a hard time," she said.

"I understand."

"You aren't alone in doing this. Adriel is a good man. He is a fierce fighter."

Michael stayed silent.

"What's your biggest worry?" she asked.

"That we fail."

"I don't believe in failure if any man or woman with a heart tries to overturn an injustice," Vicki said.

"People here live such short lives because of the brutality," Michael tried to reason. "They all had plans...like so many millions and billions of people. We must do this and not fail."

They walked in unison for another mile in silence. Michael suppressed the emotional turmoil carving up his heart piece by piece. He glanced at Vicki and saw a numb look. *I must convince her. Any doubts she or Adriel have won't help us. I must have them believe what I believe. I need them to see what I see.*

Michael continued his one-on one-debate with his thoughts.

"Hey, I'm fine," Vicki said, breaking up his emotional tug of war as if she was in his mind.

Surprised, Michael fumbled for a cohesive response. "Um, sure...um, what are we talking about?"

She leaned into him. "I'm fine with what you've told me. I'm glad you did. You have told me everything, right?"

"Of course. Do you believe me?"

"I know you don't belong in this world," she said. "And I know you certainly don't belong in my world."

"Our world," Adriel called out. "I'm not sure what world you belong to, Michael. But you do belong in my unit."

They reached a well hidden by three big trees and flush with ripe fruit. "I don't recommend eating any of this," Michael warned.

Adriel immediately grabbed a piece from a low-lying branch. He took a big bite and chewed several times and swallowed. "I don't see the harm."

Michael shook his head. He reached down into the well and pulled a bucket full of water to the top. He dunked a cup in it and handed it to Vicki. Michael waited until she finished before dropping the bucket down once more and pulling up another one.

He turned to Adriel, who had devoured the fruit. "Don't say I didn't warn you."

He handed Adriel a cup of water. "You may want to take a few more drinks."

"Why is that?"

"I'm just giving you some wise advice having visited this place before and eaten the very same fruit you did while it was ripe."

"Ha." Adriel laughed. He took the cup of water and drank it. He handed it back to Michael, who did the same and then poured water down his back and on his neck.

We're not far from where we need to be," Michael added. "Can you see the wall in the distance?" He pointed.

"I see it," Vicki said. "Where we came from before?"

"Right. But we are going past it, as I said. Past the big temple into the hills and mountains but not far beyond that."

"A perfect place to plan a rebellion, I'd say," Vicki said.

"Agreed," Adriel added.

"Let me do the talking," Michael interjected. "I know the language and customs. We are not to acknowledge Elizabeth."

"Why?" Adriel asked.

"Because I know her. She is stubborn. She never listened to me when she was a child. And oh, those teenage years."

"Sounds like someone I know," Adriel said with a short laugh.

Vicki laughed too, but hers was half-hearted.

It would be their last lighthearted moment. Danger lurked in the mountains, Michael knew.

"We have to convince the rebels we hate the Romans."

"That's easy to do," Adriel said.

They picked up a brisk pace as they approached. Michael steered them away from the wall, creating enough distance for an escape if necessary. Beyond the wall, they walked a few more miles, their steps laboring in the heat and humidity. They were heading up a trail when a voice called out.

"Stop," yelled a lone man, sword in hand. "What is your business here?"

Michael approached the man, standing about twenty yards from him. Adriel and Vicki were another twenty yards behind him. "We are here to support the rebellion," Michael said.

"What rebellion?" the lone man sneered.

"Hmm...I'm not sure. Perhaps we are in the wrong place."

Several more men surrounded them, coming from neatly disguised holes.

Chapter 58

They were taken up the mountain, each step taking its
toll on Michael. Vicki and Adriel were more fit, accus-
tomed to the rigors of such a brutal atmosphere, and
they had no difficulty keeping up with the group.

As they climbed higher, Michael wheezed slightly, stopping
momentarily. "We need to move," said a man several inches
bigger than him. "We are vulnerable at this altitude."

Two other men pushed Michael forward, and he staggered
and stumbled over a small rock. He fell.

"Get up," demanded the leader of the group, jabbing at
Michael with his long spear. "David and Jeremiah, pull him up."

The men lifted Michael and dragged him another hundred
yards up the mountainside. They reached an opening camouflaged in deep brush and makeshift covering of branches, full of
green leaves that disguised it from even the sharpest eyes.

Michael was yanked deep into the cave. He figured two or
three hundred yards. Still weak, he welcomed a wooden bench.
He sat, caught his breath, and asked for water. Michael was
given a small cup. He swallowed it in one gulp.

Vicki and Adriel sat about twenty yards across from him. Adriel was holding his stomach. They had two men on each side with Roman-made spears pointing at their heads. Neither looked shaken or fearful.

A man complete with Roman armor approached Michael. "What is your purpose here?"

"We want to fight with you in the rebellion," he answered, trying to sound believable.

The man turned to Vicki. "And what is your purpose?"

"The same."

"What is a woman doing in this rebellion?"

"I hate the Romans," she said, sounding more convincing than Michael.

"Why are you not with your man?"

"I am a warrior first."

The man looked skeptical. "You? A woman? A warrior?" He sneered. "What would any woman know about fighting the Romans?"

Vicki stood. "Do you want to test me?" she said in a defiant tone.

"Vicki, no," Michael shouted, standing up. He was pushed down by two men who pinged him in the chest twice.

"Stay seated," the man with Roman armor said. The man turned back to Vicki, walking to her, his smile wide and confident. "So you, a woman, want to challenge me?"

The man spun around in a circle slowly, his hands wide open, grinning from ear to ear, and snickered. The crowd enveloping them roared in laughter.

"Are you afraid you'll be beaten by a woman?" Vicki asked, taking two steps forward, clearly invading his space and testing his macho stance.

"Be careful what you wish for, woman."

"Try me," Vicki demanded.

Michael stood again. "Vicki, please."

"I wouldn't test her, mister. I've seen her in action," Adriel said, leaning over.

"Adriel," Michael yelled. "This isn't our plan."

The man in Roman armor confronted Michael. "What is your plan?"

Michael stayed quiet, looking down at his red-stained feet, the blood still trickling down from the small puncture wounds.

The man stared at him for several seconds. Michael took a quick glance up and looked back down, fearful of any more conflict. The man walked back to Vicki. "If you want to challenge me, then you will have your death wish." He turned to several men standing behind Adriel. "Give her a Roman spear. We will make this a fair fight. If there can be such a one when dueling..." he sneered again, "a woman."

The men mocked Vicki. She took the spear. Michael lifted his head and yelled, "No! No. Vicki. Why? No. No." *I need* to stop this. I cannot lose her before we find Elizabeth. Not now.

The men behind Adriel and Michael pulled them up and dragged them several yards back. The benches were removed to give adequate battlespace.

The man took off his Roman armor. "To make this fair," he said with a boastful smile. He tossed the armor away.

"Simon, where shall we bury her body?" a man shouted from the back.

The men roared louder. "Natan, I already have a place picked out for this foolish woman," a man yelled from the back. "We'll bury her where we bury all the Romans and traitors."

The men whistled and cheered as Natan spun around to face Vicki. "Make your move, woman."

Vicki did not respond, standing still.

"Well, make your move," Natan repeated.

Vicki took a few steps toward him, keeping her spear straight and forward. Michael struggled to free himself from the grasp of the guards. Vicki poked at Natan's face. He defended.

Vicki dropped her spear down and feigned another poke at his face. He defended once more. Vicki dropped her weapon down and jabbed his stomach, catching flesh and drawing some blood.

The men holding Adriel and Michael gasped, moving forward.

"Let them fight fair," Adriel demanded, bending over again.

"I am not hurt," Natan reassured his supporters. He went on the offense, weaving in and out like a boxer avoiding a big punch, charging and retreating three times before attacking once more. Vicki maneuvered away from his weapon.

Blood dripped from his stomach. He tended to the wound with a quick swipe of his hand, covering it in blood. Adriel gagged and threw up. Men scattered.

Michael stood. "I told you not to eat that fruit," he said to Adriel.

"Are you okay?" Vicki asked, walking toward him.

Natan charged again, striking her in the calf with his spear. Michael struggled to get loose from the men. "No!"

Vicki smiled. "Ouch. You hurt me. I got a boo-boo. How about you come here and kiss it?" She mocked Natan, taking some blood on her fingers and flicking it at him.

Natan raged. His face reddened. The men whistled and hooted. Michael thought this woman who he married in another time and another world was downright crazy. Natan hurled ahead, the spear at his side pointing forward and bouncing from his speed, blood falling from his stomach to his feet, splattering in all directions.

Vicki glared and moved slightly, nudging her foot out, tripping Natan. He fell, and his spear went flying into the crowd, causing the great divide. Vicki jumped him, her foot on his stomach, her spear pressed against his neck. "I could kill you. But I hate the Romans more. Are you interested in killing them together? I'll be your best worst enemy."

The men surrounding the two were silent. Michael could not believe what he just witnessed. Adriel was nodding and smiling. "I told you so. I told you."

"Let us go kill some Romans," Natan said, out of breath.

Vicki threw her spear away, extended her hand, and lifted Natan up.

"You are a true warrior," Natan said. "It will be an honor to fight beside you."

Chapter 59

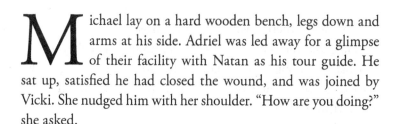

Michael lay on a hard wooden bench, legs down and arms at his side. Adriel was led away for a glimpse of their facility with Natan as his tour guide. He sat up, satisfied he had closed the wound, and was joined by Vicki. She nudged him with her shoulder. "How are you doing?" she asked.

"I'm fine. I'll live."

"Good. Sorry you got hurt. I feel like it's my fault."

"What were you doing?"

Vicki pulled back. "What do you think I was doing?"

Michael threw his hands up in the air. "I don't know," he said flabbergasted.

Vicki pointed her finger at him. "I was saving us. We needed to show them we are worthy of fighting with them. In my world and in their world, we think the same. Force equals respect. Why do you think the Romans hold power?"

"Numbers. Weapons."

"That's partially true," Vicki agreed. "But their power is respected up here and here." She touched her head and heart.

"I had to do something so that they would respect us," Vicki continued. "These men only know two parts of life—war and death. They do not fear death, Michael. They feel if they do not win, they'd rather die. I had to get to their level."

Michael grimaced. "I'm sorry you're living in that type of world."

"Why are you sorry?" she asked, puzzled. "You've had nothing to do with that."

Michael didn't respond and realized a piece of cloth was sliding down to his ankle. He pulled it up and tightened it once more.

"Do you need help?"

"No."

"What's bothering you now? They trust us."

He gazed into her eyes. They were unlike what they looked like back on Long Island. They were kinder there. "It's great we have their trust. You're right. But we have to make sure they fail to overthrow Pilate."

Vicki objected. "Why? History shows he was killed and overthrown."

"No. No. No. That was your history. He must remain in power...for now. The Romans must be successful. It's not the right time."

"Who is to say what time it should take place?" she continued to argue.

"I've tried to explain this before, probably not in an effective way."

"You've given it in bits and pieces," Vicki agreed.

"I know it's difficult to understand because we are living at this moment, and you truly don't know what has changed. I get that."

Vicki moved closer to him.

"You must trust me," Michael said. "For a better world...
for us all."

"And to keep the Romans in power at this time will change
the world...and it has something to do with Elizabeth?"

Michael scrunched his lip under his top one. He searched for
possible clarity that would convince Vicki. *She only knows her
world. Brutality. Oppression. She's right. The Romans only know
war and death. Like the rebels here. How will I convince her? How
will I convince Adriel?*

Michael sighed. "You have to make up your mind. Find what
your heart is telling you but more importantly, what your brain is
telling you. And then re-examine what I said. I'm not a nut case."
He paused. "But we can both agree we need to find Elizabeth first."

She agreed and Michael described her again to Vicki. "You
will be able to get around this place better than me. They respect
you now. You did make the right move," he said after summarizing the choices.

Vicki concurred with the strategy. She gave him a half hug.
"How much time do we have to make this all possible?"

"A couple of days. Maybe."

She released her slight embrace and stood. "Let me look
around. It's going to be easy to spot Elizabeth. There's so much
testosterone in this place I feel my voice deepening." Vicki
smiled, and Michael laughed.

"I guess," he said with an uncertain tone.

"You don't think so?" she questioned.

"I'm guessing she will be here."

"Where else would she be?"

Michael gave a look of exasperation. "I can't say. She's strong-
willed. Smart. Resourceful."

He hesitated. "Like you. Like her mother."

Chapter 60

Natan returned with Adriel from the tour of the rebels' facility. He offered Michael some bread and a cup of water. Michael welcomed some nourishment despite its paltry size. Adriel sat with him.

"How are you feeling?" Michael asked, half grinning.

"No worries. Just a little indigestion."

"A little?" Michael laughed. "You dumped your whole lunch on a couple of those rebels. They weren't very happy with you."

"Nothing they couldn't handle."

"Where did you go?" Michael asked.

"I took a look around where they form their strategy. It's nothing compared to what the Umbras have. Even we had better weapons than these rebels. I'm skeptical about their chances against the Romans."

"No surprise," Michael said. "We are talking a difference of two thousand years of technology and progress."

Adriel's eyes widened. "Progress? What kind of progress is it when a man can kill a man at a quicker pace?" He shook his head in bewilderment.

Michael pondered what he said. "It isn't progress."

Adriel pulled out a knife. It was shiny and unique for this time, bent at an angle with strands of gold. It was nothing Michael had seen when traveling to Jerusalem.

"Where did you find that? It looks like something I've seen back in my world," Michael said.

Adriel leaned over and whispered, "I stole it."

"What?"

"I stole it. They have a weapon-making room far back into this cave."

"Show me."

"Wait until everyone rests. I want to take some more. We'll need them. We'll go when there less activity here," Adriel said.

"How much time you figure we have to wait?"

"Not long. These rebels are up early and rest late. So there's a little window of time to do this. And we must be quick."

Michael strolled near the opening of the cave. It was guarded by five men, all with the best weapons of the times. They each wore Roman armor, likely taken from their victims, Michael figured. The sun descended behind the mountains, giving everyone a small period of peace.

He calculated it would be the last free evening for Jesus. The Last Supper was supposed to take place tomorrow night.

Michael returned to his resting area, wondering where Vicki was. He knew she would not back down from any confrontation, making her a high risk for something to go awry.

He was jittery for another hour and finally lay down on the hard wooden bench and closed his eyes. It wasn't more than another hour when the beginning of a dream was disrupted.

"Hey, time to get up," Adriel said, jolting him.

"I'm ready."

"Let's hustle."

Michael scanned the surrounding area. It was vacant. "Vicki. Where is she?"

Adriel shook his head. "No idea."

"We have to find her."

"She can take care of herself."

Michael sat up. "No. The way they treat women here…it's unscrupulous. Dangerous. Even for her."

"No different here than fighting the Umbras."

"Even so," Michael said, still alarmed. "We go find Vicki first."

"Whatever you say. You're stubborn. I thought you would have more confidence after seeing her kick the crap out of that rebel?"

"I guess I will never get used to seeing my wife, my unit partner, battling those vicious soldiers," Michael said. "I can't think about it anymore."

"Michael," Adriel said.

"What?"

"She's not your wife here, or partner, or whatever you call it."

Michael took a few steps away from the bench. Adriel caught up to him. "In your mind, you feel that way," Adriel added. "But is she the same person you knew when you were together? Back in that wonderful world you described to me?"

"I never said it was wonderful." Michael raised his hands in frustration, racing five steps ahead, and ran straight back to Adriel. "No, of course not," he whispered. "But I will never get used to her fighting these maniacs or the Romans."

Adriel nodded, validating Michael's feelings. "It's much like how I felt watching my last unit fight for their lives."

There was a long moment of silence between them. "I'm sorry, Adriel," Michael finally said.

Adriel ignored the apology and walked ahead of him. "Follow me."

Michael joined him as they faced three narrow pathways. "Which way?"

"Straight ahead."

"Why this way?"

"Because it's the only direction I didn't take with Natan."

The tunnel was dark and musky. Torches lit the pathway every twenty yards or so on alternating sides. The tunnel narrowed further about a mile or so. Michael stayed behind Adriel.

"Stop!" a voice called out.

"Natan?" Adriel shouted with not much confidence in his tone.

A man came forward, carrying a raging torch. He waved and flashed it in front of them. Michael backed up from the strain of the oppressive heat.

"Adriel," the man said.

"Natan. Good to see you again."

"What are the two of you doing here and at this time of the evening?"

Michael stepped around Adriel. "We are searching for my wif—I mean, Vicki."

"The woman who fought me?"

"Yes."

Natan lowered his torch. "This is a concern. I thought she returned to you."

"No. I couldn't find her," Michael said.

Natan pointed back in the other direction. "She's not back there."

Michael hesitated. Natan gestured to go back.

Adriel slapped Michael on the shoulder. "Maybe she got past us."

"She didn't," disputed Michael.

"Let's go see for ourselves."

They returned to their resting area. "Where is she?" he whispered. "Where? Where could she have gone?

Adriel went to the opening of the cave and returned minutes later. "The guards said no one got past them. They were sure too."

Michael paced the area in a circle, muttering several times, "Where could she have gone?"

Chapter 61

Michael could not get comfortable. He twisted and turned on the wooden bench, even stretching out on the dirt floor. He sat up, leaning back against a wall. *Why is she so stubborn? Why won't she trust my plan? She has to do everything by herself. Why won't she trust my ideas? She drives me so crazy sometimes. Like she's always done. She's always pushing my buttons.*

He grew tired of his rambling thoughts. "Shut up, mind."

Michael stood and extended his arms as high as he could. It was early morning. He took frequent walks to the opening of the cave, questioning the guards to see if Vicki had been seen. Frustration grew, then anger, splashing with a soaring level of anxiety. *What if she's hurt? What if she was captured by the Romans? What if she were lying in a ditch somewhere? Now I sound like my mother. She'd be proud. I have to stop thinking "what if?"*

"Vicki, get your ass back here. Now," he said under his breath.

He finally gave up on any sleep until a big hand gripped his shoulder.

"You are driving me loco," Adriel said. "Sit or lay down, I don't care what you do. But running around and muttering whatever you're muttering isn't helping me to get my rest. It's like you are expecting…like my unit. I paced much like you."

Michael sighed and looked away. "I know. I know. Each time my unit—I mean partner—was expecting…wondering whether we made the right decision to bring another human being into this crazy, messed up, wicked world."

He added. "So you were the same way?"

"I was a wreck for sure."

Michael smiled, realizing Adriel was doing what Vicki did when they were together—taking his mind off his anxiety. Michael went with the flow.

"There was one night Vicki was sleeping upstairs, and I went downstairs to paint. She wanted to use the dark green for the shed outside, but I felt it would look great in the kitchen. Keep in mind I made this decision when I was half asleep."

Adriel sat on the bench. "Go on."

"I painted and painted and painted, dead on my feet, barely able to lift the brush to the wall…. My arm was ready to fall off by the time the sun was coming up. I was so proud of my masterpiece, or at least I thought it was a masterpiece."

Adriel grinned ear to ear.

"Then Vicki wakes up. I give her morning coffee in bed and a bagel with cream cheese. I could tell how grateful she was."

Michael sat next to Adriel. "I walked her down the stairs and pleaded for her to close her eyes. She finally did. I guided her into the kitchen and told her to take a look."

Michael continued. "She does and just as quickly…she closes her eyes."

Adriel laughed, slapped Michael on the back, and fell sideways off the bench.

"It gets worse."

"How?"

"She runs into the bathroom, holds her stomach, lifts the toilet cover, and promptly throws up that bagel."

Adriel lay flat laughing, holding his sides. "Michael, men are not color-coordinated. I learned that the hard way when I painted our unit's room red and blue. Didn't you know that?"

"It was at that moment I knew," Michael said with a resigned wink.

"Oh, you kill me sometimes."

Michael smiled, almost completely forgetting about his anxiety. Adriel finally stopped laughing.

"I guess you never forget your loves," Michael said in a sorrowful tone.

"We have choices. Be angry and bitter—vengeful in my situation—or be grateful for what you had or have."

"I don't know how you got through your days."

"I'm getting through by helping others survive theirs."

"Like me?"

"Like you." Adriel closed his eyes. "Don't take this the wrong way. I love your stories. But I need to sleep. The rebels rarely rest. I'm not a young man like them. I need to have the same amount of energy."

"I understand."

"Rest, Michael. Vicki is strong. She isn't the woman you knew in your world. She is who she is because of where she is."

Michael lay down, hands folded on his chest as if ready to say a prayer, and stared at the jagged stone ceiling. He squinted to catch glimpses of spiders weaving wide webs. One particularly big one seemed ready to set his trap for prey.

So disciplined. Spiders do not attack until they are totally prepared. Completed their defense first before they go on the offense.... That's it! I must speak to Natan later. Convince him to wait until they are more prepared. Maybe reasoning with him can change their plans.

He continued to gaze and admire the spiders. "Thank you, Charlotte," he whispered.

Adrenaline rushed once more through Michael, who was excited about his idea, repeating some thoughts in his mind on what he would say to the rebels. He grew confident as the early morning hours evaporated. Finally, he closed his eyes and drifted for a short while.

"Get up, Michael," a voice said.

He sat up. "What's going on?"

Michael rubbed his eyes. "Vicki. You're okay. Where were you? You scared—"

"We can talk about that later."

She helped him up off the bench.

"Where are we going?" he asked.

"To find Elizabeth."

Chapter 62

The guards hoisted their weapons in a threatening position, giving menacing glares. "Easy, guys," Vicki said, stepping in front of him. "He's with me. We will be back. Tell Natan."

The guards lowered their weapons and stepped aside, letting them pass. Vicki and Michael walked halfway down the mountain where they met Adriel.

"I told you she would be fine," Adriel said, rather proudly.

Michael scowled, embarrassed. "How's your stomach doing? Did you make any more deposits on rebel soldiers?" he needled.

Before Adriel could respond, Vicki interrupted. "Was he worried about little old me?" she asked Adriel.

"No," objected Michael. "We need you to get back to home. That was my concern—whether our plan would be successful."

Vicki turned to Adriel. "Is my future partner or is it past partner...telling the truth?"

Adriel laughed.

"Stewart," Vicki said. "Tell me the truth."

Michael sheepishly looked away.

Vicki gave him a short hug. "It's okay to admit you have a crush on me and worry about me and…even adore me."

"That's a bit presumptuous," Michael said. "You do push my buttons."

"Ha!" Vicki laughed, enjoying herself.

This was Vicki being Vicki. Michel wasn't sure whether to enjoy this moment or dive deeper into the melancholy feelings he had being around her.

"I hate to break up this fun fest," Adriel said, "but where are we heading when we get to the bottom?"

"Depends," she responded.

"Depends on what?" Michael said. "I thought you knew where Elizabeth was."

"I said I have an idea," she replied.

"Well?"

"What's your recollection of today's events? Historically speaking?" she asked.

"What is of importance happens after the sun sets."

"Then that's when we'll make our move."

"Why wait?" questioned Adriel.

"There's too many Romans around," Vicki said.

"They party at night. Less attentive," Michael added.

"What about Natan?" asked Adriel.

"What about Saul?" Michael interjected. "Did either of you meet anyone by that name back up there?"

Adriel and Vicki shrugged.

"We go back tonight to be with Natan…with Elizabeth."

Michael stopped walking. "Hold on. If we find Elizabeth, we go home."

Adriel stepped between the two. "We cannot leave here without helping the rebels. That's a betrayal."

"There's going to be more than one betrayal to keep history the way it should be," disagreed Michael.

Vicki concurred with Adriel, frustrating him. "They need us. They helped us get this far. Leaving would be cowardly."

Michael deliberated the opposing views. "Let's first find Elizabeth."

"Then we go back to Natan," pleaded Vicki.

Michael didn't respond. "Where to?"

"Let's scout the area where I think she is," Vicki said, leading them toward the wall of Jerusalem. "It's on a dense, narrow street full of fruit and vegetable markets. It's hidden by the fruit stands. You'll see mangos and watermelons. We must be coy in dealing with the owner. He's looking to get paid off."

Michael jogged and limped, facing her. "We can't pay off anyone. I don't have my silver anymore. What would we pay him or anyone else with?"

"I will distract him," Adriel volunteered. "I can steal something. You both get past him while he chases me."

"Are you fine with that?" Vicki asked.

"I'm ready."

Vicki pulled her hood over her head. Michael and Adriel did the same. The sun was high; only a smattering of clouds painted the blue sky. The humidity began to build as midday approached. Not far from the wall, Michael abruptly halted the journey to grab water from the public well.

Vicki and Adriel drank their fair share. "Those structures are impressive for this time," Adriel said.

"I wouldn't spend too much time admiring the Romans," Michael added.

They sat. "I recommend we rest and drink until nighttime is near," Michael advised.

Adriel looked unsure.

Vicki grabbed her stomach.

"What's wrong?" Michael asked, leaving the well and leaning over.

"A slight pain. Been this way since I've been here. I'm not used to the heat. The air. And the food is atrocious, too, and the water repulsive."

"Why are you smiling?" she asked.

"Because my tough warrior is having a hard time adjusting to Jerusalem."

"Ha. You mock me. I'm fine. I'll be okay. Just a little discomfort."

She closed her eyes. Adriel grabbed another cup of water and drenched his head. "Perhaps it would have been better to wait until evening before we left the rebels?"

Vicki opened her eyes. "We had to leave. The guards were about to change shifts. The guards in the morning were sympathetic to us looking for Elizabeth. The daytime guards aren't."

"How do you know?" Michael questioned.

"Because I asked them," Vicki said.

There was a cool breeze accompanying the final hour of the sun's light. Michael alerted Vicki and then joined Adriel for one last cup of water. "What are you thinking?"

"I don't like running around this strange place at night," Adriel warned. "It's uncomfortable not knowing where everyone is. How do we know who is with the Romans and who isn't?"

Michael sipped his final cup of water. "We don't."

Vicki joined them. "What's the problem?"

Adriel stepped away and pointed at the wall of Jerusalem. "That," he said, "we don't have a map or anyone we can trust."

"Oh, but we do," Vicki replied.

"What?" Michael said. "Who? How? Where?"

Adriel walked back to them. "Is your informant trustworthy?"

"As trustworthy as someone here can be. I gave him what they all want here," Vicki said.

"Oh, no," Michael said, placing his face in his hands. "Don't tell me."

"Tell me," Adriel said.

"Gold."

"Gold? How did you get gold?"

"I have my ways," she said with a grin.

Adriel laughed. "You either robbed someone or made a withdrawal from the Temple."

"Like Pilate," Michael added.

"To beat Pilate, you have to play by the same rules," Vicki said.

Michael frowned. "Don't say any more."

"Better not to know," she added, adjusting a knife in her pocket.

Vicki led the way to the wall entrance, passing two disinterested Roman guards playing dice. Market stands were closing as vendors hurriedly secured their fruits and vegetables.

Roman soldiers standing side by side cordoned off most of the market.

"That's a problem," said Vicki.

"Why?"

"They're blocking our way."

"Let's go around them," Adriel suggested.

Vicki gestured to follow her to the left, cutting through to a narrow vacant street. She pointed to the right and straight forward. "It's over there."

In the distance, a lone Roman soldier stood guard.

"What is that building?" Adriel asked.

"Detention center for women," Vicki replied.

Michael grabbed her arm. "And you know she is there?"

"We are about to find out."

"Who is this informant? What's his name? Or her name?"

"All I know is he's a Roman soldier."

"Woah," Adriel said, stopping.

Chapter 63

Marcus hoisted his long spear, pointing it at Michael, the jagged tip pressing against his neck. The Roman soldier adjusted his steel helmet with one hand while his other gripped his weapon tight.

Adriel distracted Marcus, knocking over a fruit stand and looting several pieces of fruit. "Halt," Marcus shouted, his voice deep and firm, echoing throughout the empty streets of Jerusalem. He pushed Michael to the ground and stepped on his leg, keeping the tip of his spear on his neck, drawing a trickle of blood.

Marcus kicked Michael. "Stay." He removed his spear from his neck and chased after Adriel. Vicki lifted Michael off the ground and raced inside the jail, stopping at a dark, steep stairway, leading down.

"Quiet." Michael listened for any sound. "Now."

They jumped down the stairs, two and sometimes three steps a time, putting pressure on Michael's aging knees. He winced twice, but the adrenaline carried him with speed, keeping pace with Vicki. Then they stopped at the bottom in horror.

Disgusted. Repulsed. Scantily clad women, their garbs ripped and torn, lay in dirty, filthy cells. Some were weeping. Many were young, no more than twelve or thirteen years old.

"My God." Michael picked up his speed, checking each cell. "Elizabeth."

Vicki put two fingers against her lips to hush him.

"Screw that," Michael shouted. "Elizabeth, are you here? Speak up if you can hear me."

"Michael, look out," Vicki screamed.

Thump. Michael fell to the floor in a thud, his head hitting the concrete. Woozy, he got to his knees in time to watch Vicki jump the Roman soldier, falling on top of him and onto the ground. She retrieved the spear and punctured his neck. The soldier lurched slowly to his feet, stumbling several yards until Michael sideswiped him. The soldier collapsed, and Vicki finished him off with one sharp blow to his heart.

Michael staggered to his feet. "Thanks."

"Hold the gratitude until we get out of here," she said.

"Stay quiet," she added. "Pay attention."

They whisked past several more cells. Michael grasped Vicki's arm. "Oh, no."

"What?"

"There," he said weakly.

"Elizabeth?" Vicki walked toward a darkened cell, a lone light shining on her ravaged face. Vicki sprinted back to the dead Roman soldier and pulled his key chains off his body. She raced to open the cell. She unlocked the chains, and Elizabeth fell into her arms.

"Oh, baby, baby, I'm here now," Vicki said, pushing Elizabeth's hair away from her eyes. They were black and blue. Scratches, some deep and some not so deep, littered her face. Her hair was moist and grimy from sweat and drops of blood seeping from a gash on the top of her head.

"I'm here for you," Vicki said.

Michael stood over them, never imaging such an encounter would happen, let alone in such horrific conditions. He was distraught over how Elizabeth looked, anger building inside of him, his mind planning a violent vengeance.

Michael picked up the spear. "Take her out of here."

He kept his weapon straight like Leah had taught him the first time he visited Jerusalem, ready to fight the Romans once more if he had to.

Vicki held onto Elizabeth. "Step, sweetie. Lift your legs. Step, honey. Lift your legs—step. Lift your legs high. We're almost there. You're doing great. Few more steps."

Michael paused, his head peeking out into the hallway, which led to the jail door. Slowly, he stalked, his eyes glued to the little light illuminating from the moon's glow. He stopped, holding up his arm. "Stay until you see me wave," he said to Vicki.

Elizabeth rested her head on Vicki's chest.

Michael went up two more steps, his entire frame visible. In the distance, Adriel battled Marcus. Michael waved Vicki forward. "Do you remember where Leah's house is?"

Vicki nodded, dragging Elizabeth, her feet scraping the ground.

"I'll meet you back there," Michael said. He turned his attention to Marcus, sneaking up behind him. He jabbed the back of his spear into the Roman, stunning him. The distraction helped Adriel push Marcus away. He stood and dodged back and forth, taunting the Roman.

Marcus stung Adriel, hitting him in his ribs. He winced. Michael swung his spear like a baseball bat, striking Marcus in the back of his head, cutting him. Blood gushed from the gash, and Marcus turned and ran away, shocking Michael.

"What a coward," Adriel said.

"Oh, okay. It looked like you were in trouble."

"I was taunting him," Adriel chided.

"You don't fool me. I saw fear in your eyes."

Adriel didn't respond.

"You're human. Everyone has fear."

"I don't think Vicki has it."

"Oh, she does," Michael said as they made their way through the Jerusalem city wall opening.

"How do you know?"

"Because I saw it."

"When?"

"When she saw what happened to Elizabeth."

Chapter 64

Michael whetted a spear against a big rock outside of Leah's home. It was near midnight. The moon slipped behind a cluster of clouds, creating an eerie darkness outside of Jerusalem. Blisters formed on his hands as he ground a point wicked enough to pierce any Roman's heart. Adriel watched him, seemingly lost in thought. He walked to the well nearby and returned. "Why are you doing this?"

"I told you—I need to end this now."

"End what?"

Michael put the weapon down and rubbed the blisters together to deflate the annoying swellings, not even flinching from the sting. "You don't understand," he said, looking up at him.

"I may not understand why you are doing this, but I do know vengeance only leads to more vengeance."

"Maybe you can understand this. I'm a dad first. Anyone who threatens my daughter is going to pay the price."

Adriel approached Michael. "Your unit? Correct?"

"Yeah. Yeah. Yes. My unit."

"Got it. I did take revenge on some. I was sure of who killed my unit. But you don't know if this soldier did anything to Elizabeth."

Michael sighed. "He will."

"How do you know?"

Michael gave him a forlorn look. "He already has."

Adriel frowned. "Sometimes you speak with a strange tongue."

Michael picked up the weapon, feeling the tip of it with his pinky finger. Satisfied when he drew some blood, he joined Adriel sitting against the back wall of Leah's home.

"It's complicated," Michael said.

"Explain it to me."

"We've confronted that soldier, Marcus, the one you were fighting before. On other trips. Other times. Marcus will not quit. Not until he has Elizabeth. He's likely to be more motivated because we took what he believes is his. It's how a Roman soldier thinks. They do not look at women as people, as human beings. They believe they are possessions to claim. I cannot let him touch or hurt Elizabeth." Michael paused. "If he hasn't already."

Adriel gave a sorrowful look. "All these years later and…" his words trailed off.

"And what?"

"The way we treat each other," Adriel said. "This world, my world…"

"My world too."

Adriel grimaced. "I'll go with you."

"No. Stay here."

"You know Vicki can take care of herself."

Michael stood and shook his head. "This is between Elizabeth's dad and that bastard."

He took several steps to the front of the house with Adriel trailing. "What do I tell them?" Adriel asked.

"Tell them I took a walk to calm my nerves and will be back shortly."

"May the courage and fire of the wolf rage in your heart," Adriel shouted.

Michael turned and hoisted a clenched fist.

He covered his spear with clothing, camouflaging it like he was walking gingerly with a cane. His hood covered most of the top part of his face. He walked, hunching over, past two drunk Roman soldiers.

The betrayal occurred in the garden, and the city was percolating. The jails in the dungeons stirred with fervor. Prisoners yelled and banged metal cups at the steel cages, singing a chaotic song.

Michael theorized Marcus was somewhere nearby. He was unlikely to be in the dungeons. He believed the room to find him in would be where wounded soldiers rested. He also knew the Romans would be together en masse tomorrow for the public crucifixion. He figured he could get lost in the crowd and blend in with the mob, and hopefully he would not be seen as a threat to the Romans as he appeared old, walking with a cane.

Michael heard a ruckus nearby and headed in that direction. Where there was chaos, there would be Roman soldiers. He waded through the crowd, using his cane to poke and move people out of his way, disguising his voice as an old man, hunching down slightly, keeping his eyes up and focused straight ahead.

He came to the outer portion of the crowd. There were high scream cries for torture reaching a fever pitch. Michael hesitated, knowing he could try and stop this brutal pain Jesus was enduring. He regained his reasoning and crawled a few steps, leaning on his makeshift cane to create more deception.

He came upon a drunk Roman, laughing and telling his fellow soldiers a dirty joke. Michael staggered forward.

"Hey, old man," the drunken Roman shouted. "You are going in the wrong direction."

"My apologies, sir," Michael mumbled in his weak old man's voice. "I am looking for someone I know, Marcus."

Another Roman stepped forward. "What is your business with him?"

"Sir, my apologies again. I have information on who may have attacked him today."

"How do you know this?"

"I saw this man running and bleeding earlier this evening. Marcus has been nice to me. I want to repay this good man."

The Roman laughed. "Marcus? A good man?" He laughed louder.

The soldier put his arm around Michael, giving him chills of discomfort. "Take the next left at the end of the hallway. He is there healing from his beatdown."

All the soldiers laughed.

"Much gratitude to you, sir."

The soldier left to join the other Romans. Michael walked slowly, occasionally looking back to see if he was being followed, his adrenaline building and heart racing. He gripped his weapon tightly.

He made the left, and beyond it an empty room was lit by two torches hung on both sides of the entrance. Michael dropped his hood to get a better view. His head peeked into the room. Marcus was sleeping, his snore light and staggered. Bandages covered both legs and arms.

Kill him.

His armor lay on the floor beside him. *Perfect. One swift plunge into his heart will do it. It's been a long time coming—too long, you bastard. This is my justice for you…for what you've done to Elizabeth. No one touches my daughter. No one.*

Michael stood over him, rage savaging his heart. He raised his spear high. *It's time I sent you to hell.*

His spear came down, and Michael nudged him slightly. *I want to see your eyes open when you die.*

Marcus woke.

As the spear clipped his chest, Marcus grabbed it, sitting up. "What are you…" he said, wincing.

Michael struggled to remove the spear from Marcus' grip.

The Roman stood, his hand on the weapon and his other hand on Michael's neck. He pushed Michael into the wall, stunning him, knocking the spear to the ground. Marcus took a knife from his pocket. It was long and thick and shiny like it was polished recently. He battered the side of Michael's face; Michael slumped, falling.

Marcus sneered, towering over him, blood dripping from the small gash in his chest. "Any last words, Jew?"

Michael closed his eyes, his hands up in front of his face, and prayed some words. He waited to die; his body tightened, and his heart skipped beats. *I'm coming, Mom. I'm coming, Annie. I'm coming, cousin Mary. I'm…*

Clang. Thump.

Chapter 65

Leah helped Michael to his feet. She wiped some blood off his face with a cloth and Michael pulled back from her. "I must finish what I came for."

Leah shook her head. "You may not get out alive if you do. Did they know you were seeing him?"

Michael ignored her question. He grimaced and picked up his spear. He went to Marcus, who was sprawled on the floor. He turned to Leah. "He will never leave Elizabeth alone. He must die." Michael took a deep breath. "This is for all the women you raped. All the families you destroyed. All the lives you ended. All the innocent people you oppressed." He plunged the spear into his heart and turned it 360 degrees until Marcus' eyes opened. He gasped, took a deep breath, and then there was silence.

"I saved my daughter," he said, pulling the spear out of Marcus' body. "I did what any loving father would do." He took the cloth Leah had given him and wiped the blood off his spear. He bent over and placed the cloth over Marcus' face. "Rot in hell."

"We must go," Leah said. "The crowd is growing. Soldiers are everywhere. I can sense it is going to get worse."

Leah and Michael pulled over their hoods to cover the top part of their foreheads, their eyes barely peeking out. "Leave the weapon," Leah demanded.

"I'll use it as a cane. It's how I got past the Romans."

Leah shook her head. "I cannot argue with you. Put your arm under my shoulder. Pretend I am helping you."

He lowered his shoulder.

"Walk slow," she demanded.

The city streets were alive. The crowd was drinking, many huddled together in clusters, laughing and slurring words in conversation. A high murmur of gaiety.

"Stay close to me," she said, pulling him tight against her body.

"Stop!" a voice called out from behind.

Michael refused, breaking from Leah's grip.

"Michael, come back," Leah pleaded.

The Roman raced to him. "Old man, did you not hear what I ordered?"

Michael turned around, hunched lower. "I am of old age. My hearing is limited. I cannot hear above all this noise," he lied.

"Stay." The Roman went to Leah. "Woman, what are you doing out at this time of night?"

"My apologies, sir. He's my father. His memory is faint, and his mind is frail, not what it used to be many sunsets ago."

"Take him home," the soldier demanded. "Keep him away from here for the next sunset."

"I shall," Leah said, bowing.

"Old man, next time you wander, it will be the last time."

"Yes, sir," Michael said, holding up his middle finger and then moving under Leah's shoulder.

"What did that mean?" said Leah as she grabbed hold of his arm.

"Better not to explain it, but it's a gesture many make when driving…"

"What? Driving a chariot?"

"Yeah. When someone cuts you off while driving your chariot."

Leah gave him a confused look. They weren't more than fifty yards away from the Jerusalem city wall when a brawl in front of them erupted. Bodies smacked bodies. Men swung wildly in drunken stupors. Michael looked up slightly, noticing Natan was being beaten.

Oh, no.

Natan was flat on his back, a man's hands gripped his throat. "Leah, I need to help him."

"No. Stop," she demanded.

Michael left her and swatted the man in the back of the head. He fell off of Natan. Michael lifted him up. Natan gave a confused look. "What are you doing here? Where did you and the others go? Are they safe? We need you all."

"A long story. I needed to kill a Roman soldier."

"Good man," Natan cheered.

Michael was neither proud nor ashamed hearing Natan's praise. "You must rethink attacking the Romans tomorrow."

"Why?"

Leah tugged on Michael. "We must leave. More Romans are coming."

Michael gripped Natan's arm. "Think about it. Now is not the time to do this. There will be a right time soon. But not now."

Natan left without acknowledging Michael's advice. Leah helped him walk through the city wall exit. "You are endangering yourself, me, and Elizabeth," Leah said.

"I know, but to do nothing now would be even more dangerous."

Leah stayed silent, picking up the pace in a brisk fashion. She threw her hood back, her brown hair bouncing in the moonlight's glow.

"Are you angry at me?" Michael asked.

"No. I expected it from you."

Leah remained quiet. They slowed down as they came to her home. She stopped before going inside. "Michael, men have an instinct for violence. Being a woman here, all we have is each other. I have lost many. The Romans killed Yohannan. He gave up his life so I would not be raped. I did not want you to end up the same way. Or I did not want Elizabeth to go home without you."

Her eyes moistened, and she wiped a tear from her eye.

"We are tired of the Romans and their vicious rule," Leah continued. "We do not have much. Perhaps a meal every so often. But we only have each other. And I worry someday we will not even have that...." Her words trailed off in sorrow.

She turned and headed through the front yard, past the fruit tree, and into the house as Michael followed. Adriel and Vicki greeted them, their faces distraught.

"What's wrong?" Michael said.

Vicki wept.

Chapter 66

Michael stalked the perimeter of Leah's home, screaming in silence, aware not to alarm any neighbors but so furious his body tightened into a knot, and he needed to take a deep breath.

He ignored Vicki offering him a cup of water from the well. He paced several more times, stopping and looking for any sign of her.

Vicki trembled, again offering a cup of water. Michael swatted it, sending it flying into the wall.

"We will go find her," Vicki said, trying to reassure him.

"When did she leave?" Michael asked in an angry tone.

"You need to contain that anger and keep it down," implored Adriel.

"Well?!"

"It couldn't be more than an hour ago," Adriel said, sharpening his knife against the big rock.

"How? How did she sneak out? How did you not see this happen?" Michael said in rapid-fire succession.

Adriel joined Vicki. "Elizabeth is smart and determined. She had us believing she was sleeping, hurt, not being able to stand up. She woke up for a minute, asking questions."

"What questions?"

"She asked where you were," Vicki said, interjecting. "She's resourceful. She duped us like any experienced warrior."

"What did you tell her?" Michael asked.

"That you were taking a trip to the city to see someone," Vicki said.

"Why did you tell her that?"

"I told her what you said to tell her," Adriel explained, stepping forward.

"And?"

"She didn't believe us. She kept insisting 'my dad just doesn't take walks in the night here.'"

Michael kicked at the fallen cup, then picked it up and threw it against the side of the house and stood. "I will find her."

"I'll come," Adriel said, putting his knife under his shirt.

"I will too," Vicki said.

Michael didn't argue, knowing full well it was going to be a tumultuous Friday, the day Jesus was to be nailed to the cross. He knew he would have to stop Elizabeth before she got to Pilate.

"Thank you," Michael said to Leah. "You saved my life. I owe you."

"You do not owe me anything," she said. "If you need help, call upon me."

Michael bid goodbye, and they hugged. Leah gave him a Jewish blessing, holding his hands. He gave her a kiss and waved and stayed in his own thoughts walking with Vicki and Adriel.

"What are you thinking about?" Vicki asked.

"Not much."

"She's stronger than any woman I know."

Michael nodded.

"You've done a great job with her," she said.

Michael forced a smile. "That means the world to me."

She gave him a half hug. "We will find her and help you get home."

"What about you?"

"I want to come back with you and Elizabeth," Vicki answered.

Michael paused and sighed in sorrow.

"What's wrong?"

He hesitated again. "I...don't know if it's possible."

"Why?"

Michael didn't answer. "Adriel, how many weapons do you have?"

Adriel pulled out a short knife with a black handle, an image of a Native American carved into it. "Take this."

"You didn't answer my question, Michael," Vicki said.

Frustrated, he glared. "Because I don't know."

Vickie's eyes widened. "What? I'm surprised you wouldn't have any knowledge on whether I can go with you."

"I don't. It's why it's probably better to go back through the tunnel with us, and whatever happens, happens."

Adriel looked back. "That would include me."

"It does. I would not know where else we would go. We go together. We may end up in different places, different times."

There was a long moment of silence among the three.

Finally, Vicki spoke. "If we make it back."

Chapter 67

R age smothered the city streets. The Romans amassed during the holy time. The trial began. Jesus courageously faced Pilate. He was displayed in front of the rebellious mob, thorns from the crown embedded in his skull and blood seeping into his eyes. Pilate urged the crowd to calm down. People were whipped into a frenzy by rebel leaders, which spiked the already frantic atmosphere. The mob spewed words of hate, tossing stones at the stage. Several Roman soldiers thwarted the attacks with their shields drawn.

"What in this world is going on?" asked Vicki.

"They are going to execute Jesus," Michael said.

"What did he do?"

"He taught his followers to love everyone: beggars, thieves, your neighbor, good or bad…and those who sin even more," Michael said.

Adriel interjected. "No man is without sin. Not here. Not anywhere."

"Adriel, you would be the ideal apostle."

Vicki flinched, as a Roman soldier assaulted Jesus. Pieces of his skin exploded off his back. "We can't do nothing," Vicki said.

"Let's stop this!" Adriel said.

"Find Natan and the others," Vicki said to Adriel. "I'll help Michael track down Elizabeth."

"No," Michael said, stopping Adriel from leaving.

"We have to help this man," argued Adriel. "I'm not going to stand here and do nothing."

"This is supposed to happen," Michael countered.

Barabbas was paraded out as cheers and jeers rained down upon him.

"Who is he?" Vicki asked.

"Killed a Roman, a bandit, a hero to many," Michael answered.

"You killed a Roman too."

Michael nodded, feeling chills. "I had no choice."

"Maybe he didn't either," said Adriel.

"So this is what they would do if they found you?" Vicki said.

"Worse."

"I'm not just going to watch this take place."

Michael dismissed her thought. "If my memory serves me right, we will have a small window of time to stop Elizabeth. She's going after Pilate. Soon he will make his decision. Natan and the rebels are going to make their move soon too. Saul will be there as well."

"Who is Saul?" Vicki asked.

"Someone I met before. Someone who wants to kill Pilate too."

"This man had done no one harm nor murdered any man nor stolen anyone's money," Pilate shouted over the angry chants. "I see no reason to execute him."

The crowd booed and hissed. Barabbas and Jesus were taken away. The mob raged and tossed more rocks toward the podium. Once gone, the crowd milled around the courtyard, striking up conversations like old fraternity brothers.

"What's going on now?" asked Vicki.

"Pilate is putting off the decision. Or perhaps he already sent him to Herod, another Roman leader. But Herod will send him back to Pilate."

"I'm not just going to watch," Adriel insisted.

"We have to."

Adriel gave an angry look.

"Pilate will be pressured to put Jesus up on a cross."

"How cruel," Vicki said. "What do they hope to achieve with this?"

"They want to silence the word of love for everyone, bad or good," Michael replied.

"Seems unrealistic in any world," Adriel added.

Michael sighed and adjusted his hood. Sweat was building on his forehead. He wiped some of it away with his sleeve. "We should go to Pilate's room."

Michael paused, dejected. "Pilate must live."

They moved through the dense crowd, nearing the entrance-way to Pilate's stronghold overlooking the courtyard.

"Natan," Vicki said, tugging on Michael's arm. "There."

"I see him," Michael replied.

Natan was with a group of rebels, hiding among the civilians. "We must stop them," Michael insisted.

"There's more of them," Adriel said. "Let them kill the Roman rat. He's about to kill an innocent man who is teaching love for all. Right? That's what you said. Right?"

"I know. I know. It's in all our hearts and instincts to try and stop it. We can't."

Adriel's eyes widened. "I don't know what to say. Every part of me is not feeling good about this at all."

Vicki stepped between them. "What do we do?"

"Follow me," Michael said. He went to Natan, stepping in the middle of his followers.

"Michael, Vicki, Adriel," Natan said with a surprised look. "Are you here to help us kill Romans, or are you on some love gathering mission like that mad man who is going to be hung high?"

"I'm here to convince you what you are hoping to accomplish cannot happen and will not happen," Michael said.

"Oh, is that so?" Natan said, pawing at Michael's neck. He squeezed hard, and Michael choked.

Vicki slapped at Natan's grip, and Adriel wielded his knife at the rebels, spinning around in a circle.

"Try me," Adriel threatened.

"Take your hands off of him," Vicki demanded.

Natan released his hold. A Roman soldier intervened, gripping his sword, pointing it out straight. "Break it up, Jews. Or I will throw you all in the dungeon."

Natan sneered and retreated, backing a few steps from Michael. The Roman soldier left.

Natan came back to him. "Do not interfere with me, or your blood will spill too."

"I can't let you do that," Michael said.

"Do you want to die with the Romans?"

"If it means stopping you, I will."

Natan attacked Michael, knocking him into several rebels. Bodies fell everywhere. Adriel slit a rebel's arm. Vicki defended herself with a knife.

The mob surged toward the brawl, cheering and jeering. Michael got to his feet and was dragged away with Natan, Adriel, and Vicki by a horde of Roman soldiers and into the blackness of the lower bowels of the Roman prison.

Chapter 68

"Shut your Jew mouth," the Roman shouted, threatening Michael with the tip of a long spear.

Michael was separated from Adriel and Vicki. Unchained, he went to the steel door and shouted out, "Can anyone hear me?"

Barely audible words shrieked down the darkened hallway, unnerving him. There was a murmuring in the cage nearby, so he leaned against the steel bars, his left ear peeking out, listening.

"Are you all right, sir?" Michael asked. "Do you need help?"

"Yes," the man's voice whispered.

"Do you need me to call a guard?"

"I do not need a guard. Pray with me. Pray with me to our Father."

Michael sighed. "What am I praying for?"

"For your redemption," he said in a measured tone. "Pray. My time is short."

Michael peeked out further through a bigger opening between the steel bars. Jesus stood, his arms chained to the ceiling, his head hung. Blood trickled down from the gashes on his head.

Michael grew angry. "I'm so sorry."

"You do not need to be sorry," Jesus said. "It is my Father's will."

"But you're going through all that pain."

"I accept the pain because it is my Father's will."

Michael closed his eyes.

"Pray with me, Michael. For we both have much to pray for."

Michael's eyes widened.

"Let us pray for our daughter, Elizabeth," Jesus said. "May my Father protect her and keep her safe from what will happen today. May my Father give her peace and forgiveness, forgiveness from her anger she has at you."

Michael struggled to say some words. "Jesus?"

"Yes, Michael?"

"I've carried anger in my heart for too long. I'm exhausted from my resentment. I have not loved with all my heart. I've wasted your greatest gift—yesterday's and today's."

"Let your heart be free of all your failures. Let your soul feel the warmth of my Father's love."

Michael wiped a tear away. "I have sinned so much, Jesus. Shut loved ones out. Raged at hearts who only wanted to love me. I have run from people who cared for me."

"My Father sees what is in your heart. He sees a flawed man but a good man. A man who wanted to love his family. A father who loves his daughter like no other. A man who wants to help his neighbors. A man who is without judgment. You are a good man, Michael. Accept who you are, what your heart feels—your sorrows, your joys. You are my Father's perfectly imperfect work."

Michael fought back more tears. "Jesus, my daughter, I need to help her. Stop her from making a bad decision."

"Let us pray for her now."

Michael's eyes were transfixed on Jesus.

"Pray to our Father, Michael. Pray with me. Open your heart. Open your soul. Ask our Father to guide Elizabeth and help her find a way home."

Michael repeated Jesus' words. "I need to stop her. She is angry. The Romans hurt her. The Romans destroy women and children here. They killed my friend's husband."

Michael could hear Jesus take a deep breath. His words were now methodical, sometimes staggered, and melancholy. "My word will be misunderstood for thousands of your years to come. Do not misunderstand me. The Romans will be conquered until the next army is spawned for mankind's hate. What is in your heart can never be taken, for it is my Father's treasure. Let your heart rest from the hate. Go to your daughter. Pray with her, teach her, and guide her. But most of all, Michael, love her for who she is."

Michael closed his eyes and said the Our Father, whispering it. Jesus was doing the same. "I'm not sure how I can help her now," Michael said, rattling the jail cell door.

"Go, Michael. Why do you doubt me? Go to your daughter. Go to Adriel and Vicki. Keep me in your heart and prayers."

Michael was confused, knowing the reality of where he was and what he was up against.

"Why do you wait?" Jesus asked.

"I do not understand. I can't go."

"Keep faith in your heart. Why do you not keep it?"

Michael looked at him. The strain in his arms chained to the ceiling was evident. "I don't understand. I don't see any way I can help my daughter from here."

"Faith, Michael. Faith. Do you have it?"

Michael hesitated.

"You can."

Michael shook the steel door again. He glanced at Jesus, his bloodied body trembling, his scars glistening from a nearby torch shining a sliver of light into the cell. Their eyes met for a moment.

"Faith, Michael. Faith. Believe."

Michael closed his eyes and shook the cell door once more. It opened. At that moment, he understood the depth of Jesus' faith.

He ran down the hallway, locating Adriel first. Michael closed his eyes, whispered a few words of prayer, and opened the cell door, astonishing him.

They raced to Vicki. Michael did the same, shocking her. Vicki shook her head. "I don't believe what I just saw."

"Sometimes seeing is believing."

Chapter 69

The stench of suffering poisoned the hot Jerusalem air as the beating of Jesus resumed, his hands bound and chained to a man-made wooden stump. Bent over on his knees, his back swinging wildly from the metal whipping balls penetrating his skin, Jesus winced in pain.

"This is unbearable," Adriel angrily said. "I will not stand here and pretend this is for the good of all mankind. I don't care what you say, Michael."

"Roman," Michael shouted, pointing at a soldier.

"Michael, what are you doing?" Vicki asked.

Adriel gave him a wicked glance. Michael whispered in his ear. "My brother, I say that from the deepest parts of my heart, I am trying to let the real history of this world unfold."

"By him dying? Like this?" Adriel said.

"Yes. By him dying. Like this."

Michael stepped back for a second. The Roman soldier he gestured at was engaged, talking to Vicki. He went back to Adriel, again whispering. "It's our only chance to have a better world. Our only chance to defeat the Umbras. The only chance to win World War II."

Adriel gave him a confused look. "And this man, this man being beaten and whipped and mocked and about to be put to death, according to you, will save us?"

"Faith. Adriel. Faith," Michael said, without hesitation. He gripped Adriel's hand holding his weapon. "We must stop Elizabeth, now," he added. "Will you help me?"

Adriel looked back at Jesus being lashed, the Roman soldiers sitting down from exhaustion from the strain of swinging the long metal balls into his body. "Here lies the King of the Jews," one Roman soldier yelled.

Blood gushed from his back and down his legs. The thorns embedded into his skull and forehead created a red river over his eyes.

"None of what you say is believable," Adriel said. "None of it." He looked at the weeping women nearby, then glanced at the raucous mob thirsting for a more blood. "What you ask goes against everything I believe in," Adriel reasoned.

"I'm asking you to believe in something that you can't see right now but will see soon," Michael replied, releasing his grip on Adriel's hand. "It's our only chance to save this world and your world and my world."

"I only know my world," Adriel countered. "How do I know if your world is any better than the one I've been living in my entire life?"

"You don't. All we have right now is each other," Michael reasoned.

Adriel reflected for what seemed like forever.

"I beg you, Adriel."

"I will help you with Elizabeth," Adriel answered.

They left and slipped through the unruly crowd and into the mansion. "You need to create a diversion. Faint," Michael said.

"What?" said Adriel.

"Faint. Fall. Pretend you are having a heart attack. Now."

Adriel collapsed, unconvincingly at first.

"Help. Help," Michael yelled. "Stay down. Grab your heart."

Three Roman soldiers scurried toward Adriel. "Help this man," Michael urged the soldiers.

"What is wrong?" one Roman soldier asked.

"His heart. He needs medical attention right away," Michael implored, his face showing concern.

"What's wrong with Adriel?" said Vicki, frantic.

"Adriel is having a heart attack," Michael shouted.

"Oh no," yelled Vicki, leaning down and feeling Adriel's wrist. Adriel winked at her.

Vicki stood back up and looked at Michael, baffled. A moment later, it settled in with her. "Oh, no," she said, dropping to her knees again, holding his hand. "My partner. My partner. Please help him." She teared up.

"Go fetch a doctor," one Roman soldier said to another.

Vicki remained next to Adriel while Michael slipped away past some soldiers sitting down playing dice. He ambled up the stairs and into Pilate's bedroom. "Where is he?"

Michael raced down the marbled hallway, peeking into every room. "Where is he?" he called out quietly. *Did Elizabeth get to him first? Oh, please, God, don't let that happen.*

As he approached the last room, Michael heard a conversation. He silently walked to the edge of the opening, his eyes darting into the room.

Chapter 70

Elizabeth held a knife to Pilate's neck, the tip of the blade nicking his skin. A trickle of blood snaked its way down to his chest, touching his grand armor and attire. Saul was nearby holding a long knife.

"My men will come for me soon," Pilate said between short, straining breaths.

Elizabeth took a few steps back, startled. Pilate struggled to shake loose. Elizabeth tightened her grip, her eyes wide open. "Dad?"

"You know her?" Pilate interjected.

"Yes," Michael answered.

"You may be wise to tell her to drop her weapon and surrender, or there will be two who will not make it out of here alive."

"Shut up," Elizabeth said, pressing the edge deeper into his skin. "You are the reason why Jews are suffering in poverty. You murder. You steal." She paused. "Your men," she said with defiance, "kill children and rape women."

Pilate sneered. "You know so little, child."

"Dad, do you know what the Romans did to Leah's husband?"

"I know, I know."

"An eye for an eye, Dad."

"Now is not the time for that, Elizabeth."

"Kill him," Saul insisted.

"Saul, your instructions were to take Pilate hostage," Michael said.

"How did you know that?"

"Mensah told me. Leave, Saul. Now. Before you are killed. I will make sure Pilate is taken to your hideout."

Saul gave a baffled look and left.

Elizabeth shook her head. "I don't know what you're trying to do, Dad, but I'm not taking Pilate anywhere. You know what he does. You know how brutal he is. How many more must lose their lives and families because of him?"

Michael took a few steps toward Elizabeth. She tightened her grip on the weapon and backpedaled a few steps. Pilate winced as the sharp edge pricked him again, cutting his flesh.

"I know all of what he does. I know how history will treat him."

"How?" said Pilate. "Are you a prophet? Tell me. I will give you a hand full of gold. Tell me."

Michael pondered Pilate's request. "I am a prophet," he assured the egotistical Prefect.

"What?" Elizabeth said.

Michael glared at her, putting up his hand. "Prefect, you will be revered," he lied. "You will be praised by hundreds of future generations for condemning that man Jesus to death. The future generations will admire your courage for silencing his voice, his words. Your death sentence will be viewed in history as the single act…" Michael hesitated, confident Pilate was arrogant enough to believe his untrue words. "You will be remembered as the greatest man in history."

"Dad? What are you saying? You know…"

Michael stopped her. "I tell the truth, Prefect. It's why I am here to stop my misguided daughter from committing an atrocious sin against history."

"What are you saying? Have you lost your mind?" Elizabeth said.

"Release the Prefect," Michael demanded, taking a couple of more paces closer to her.

She gave a confused look. "I can't do that. I have no idea why you are saying what you are."

Elizabeth dragged Pilate to the edge of the outdoor balcony. "Don't, Elizabeth!" Michael pleaded. "Don't. Please. Listen to me."

"Listen to the prophet," Pilate shouted.

"Elizabeth, I am doing this for us, all of us, for the Prefect, for the people everywhere."

"Dad, you've lost your sanity," Elizabeth shouted.

"No, he hasn't," Vicki said, stepping into the room.

"Oh, look who it is," Elizabeth said with skepticism.

"Who is she?" Pilate asked.

"Another liar," Elizabeth raged.

Michael looked at Vicki. "What?"

"She refuses to believe that we are all part of the same unit."

Elizabeth grew angrier. "Stop it," she yelled. "What is a unit? You're crazy. Anyway, the only person I've known in my family is my dad. My mom died the night I was born."

Michael approached Elizabeth, putting his hand on the one holding the weapon to Pilate's neck. "This is your mother."

"What? How?"

"It's complicated, but somehow we changed history, and two worlds collided," Michael tried to explain. "We still are in our existence because we are here right now. But in another world for your mom, it's different."

Elizabeth gestured at him and Vicki. "You're both crazy. What have you done to my dad?"

Michael sighed. "You know the history, Elizabeth. I'm not lying to you. Many more will be saved. Please. Please, Elizabeth."

She stayed frozen. Michael put his hand on her shoulder while containing Pilate with his other hand. "Please, Elizabeth. Now is not the time," he repeated. "Believe me."

Elizabeth glanced at Vicki and Michael.

"We aren't crazy," Vicki said. "You don't have to believe me. I understand that. But your Dad. Believe him."

Elizabeth looked away. "This is all too hard to believe. My mom. My dad. We're here, and we are changing the world?"

"You know me best, Lizzy," said Michael. "I wouldn't con you about this. You know how I study history. Please. Believe me."

Elizabeth sighed. "What about him?"

"Pilate," Michael said. "You must let us go if we release you."

"You have my word," Pilate agreed.

"As much as I want to believe you, I need something more," Michael countered. He scanned the room and picked up several pieces of jewelry.

"Those are mine," Pilate said.

"You'll get it back if we get our freedom," Michael replied.

Pilate simmered, trying to wrestle himself away from Elizabeth. Vicki came over and helped restrain him.

"Elizabeth," Vicki said. "Listen to him."

"Prefect, do we have a deal?"

"We do," he said.

Michael pulled out a knife and wielded it in front of Pilate's face. "I will kill you if I have to."

Chapter 71

Michael and Elizabeth tied up Pilate, wrapping a piece of the garment around his mouth, making him kneel in a corner face first looking at the wall. "Listen closely, Prefect, once we are free to leave Jerusalem, I will have someone alert your men where you are," Michael said.

Pilate mumbled some sounds.

Michael pulled the garment down. "What did you say?"

"Leave the jewelry behind."

"You know I can't do that."

He pulled the garment back over his mouth. "Open wide, Prefect." Pilate begrudgingly did so. Michael stuffed it into his mouth and tightened the grip.

"Where is Adriel?"

"He was taken to the 'ill room,' as they call it here," Vicki said.

"Where is that?"

"This way," Elizabeth instructed.

They followed her up another flight of stairs into a small, narrow area, secluded from the rest of the third floor. A Roman guarded the entrance.

"Vicki," Michael said.

"I know. Go get my partner."

"What?" said Elizabeth. "I thought she was…" She looked at Michael.

"Long story," Michael said.

"Another lie?" Elizabeth added, walking away from them.

Vicki spoke to the guard. He dropped his weapon down to his side and stepped away from the entrance. She went to Adriel.

"Stay here," Michael said to Elizabeth. "Sir, I am looking for a man named Adriel."

The Roman maneuvered his weapon chest high. "What is your business here?"

"To see how he is doing," Michael said, turning to look away from the door.

The soldier followed his movement. Vicki peeked out from within the room and gestured to Michael. Adriel was behind her. Vicki snuck up on the Roman. Michael kicked the soldier in the groin, and he doubled over, dropping his weapon. Vicki choked and held him upright. Adriel grabbed the weapon and whacked the soldier in the head. The Roman buckled and fell to the floor.

"Bring the weapon," Michael said.

"I certainly wasn't going to leave it here," Adriel mused.

"Where is Natan?" Michael said.

"Still chained up," Vicki answered.

"Should we help him?" Adriel asked.

"No," Michael said. "He needs to stay there."

"To die?"

"Some must die so many millions, or should I say billions, more will live."

They blended into the courtyard crowd. The mob milled around, growing frustrated over the lack of Pilate's appearance. Michael whispered to the soldier, "We have Pilate. Stay silent. This is your reward." He handed him some jewelry and ran off. Another Roman soldier rushed to a group of six, and they raced off the stage.

"They know now," Michael said.

A Roman dressed in bright political garb took the stage. "The Prefect will be here soon. Bring the prisoners."

Jesus was dragged to the stage broken and bleeding with his eyes barely open. Barabbas danced with his arms high in a victory gesture, igniting a big cheer.

"I should have killed Barabbas," Elizabeth said.

"What stopped you?" Michael asked.

"What you have said to me my whole life," Elizabeth responded.

Michael gave a baffled look. "And…"

"You've always lectured me that every man deserves a second chance."

"Did he touch you? Hurt you?"

Elizabeth didn't answer him. She turned to Michael. "See, I do listen."

"What about Pilate?"

"No man like Pilate deserves any chance," she answered angrily. She paused, her face turning red. "What about the people here?" Elizabeth argued.

Michael was unsure if anything he said to her would be convincing, so he didn't try.

The crowd surged toward the stage as Pilate spoke. His voice was grainy and low, likely from the tightness of the garment that was tied around him. The mob raised their voices to support the release of Barabbas. Pilate tried to hush the crowd. They jeered him and cheered on Barabbas.

A rebel tossed a rock at Pilate, grazing his head. Pilate stepped back. His glare could be seen even from the deepest depths of the crowd. Michael leaned down and ducked behind a raging man who was spouting epitaphs at the Romans.

"That man! Back there!" Pilate yelled, pointing to where Michael was. "Seize him."

Roman soldiers pushed and shoved and inched their way toward him. Michael took a few pieces of jewelry and threw them up into the air, pocketing the rest for insurance. The mob swelled and knocked over the soldiers, causing chaos again.

Chapter 72

Authoritarian rule clashed with rebellious defiance, and skirmishes broke out, igniting turmoil and mayhem. The Romans fought with clusters of renegades, who were small in size and numbers yet relentless. Barabbas was given his freedom.

Jesus was being prepared to face his final fate. Pilate strode across the big podium, his head high, his bright red garment flapping in the soft, warm wind. He said a few words to Jesus as Michael glanced back, ducking behind a group of men looking at their newfound jewelry.

Adriel hesitated when they reached the outer portion of the throng, now breaking up and going in all directions. Michael yanked on his arm, not wanting to lose physical contact with him. "We need to leave," he said, pulling harder, trying to move an immovable object.

"Adriel, we can't stop this," Vicki chimed in.

"But we can help these people," Adriel suggested.

Michael looked at Elizabeth, irritated. He could see the frustration in her face. He understood what her heart was saying to her.

He turned back to Adriel and Vicki. "It's your choice," he said. "I've got a bullseye on me now."

Michael and Elizabeth sped away from the bedlam of the courtyard and toward the fruit and vegetable market, its streets unevenly lined with carts and tables full of produce and the desserts of the day. Most of the Roman army was preoccupied, lining the pathway for Jesus to carry his cross.

"I'm sorry I disappointed you," Michael said to Elizabeth.

She stayed silent, her eyes staring straight ahead.

"It's our only chance."

"Only chance at what?" she said.

"To get back to our world."

"What made it different from the last time we traveled here?"

"Don't you remember what happened when we came out of the tunnel during the previous visit?" he asked.

Elizabeth threw her hands up in the air. "No. I don't remember anything. Or I think I don't. One second I was walking up the stairs."

"And you saw?"

"Nothing," she said.

"Right. Then what did you see? Or feel?"

"I floated. I saw you then. Reaching for me. I reached for you...."

She paused.

"Anything else?" Michael said.

"Nothing. Nothing else. It was like a dream. Then I was back here. Running like I was before with the others. Looking for you."

"It all makes sense now. I think."

"Why? What happened?"

Michael put his hand on her shoulder. "We changed history. Or what we did changed history."

"How?"

"Killing Pilate."

"So? He deserves to die for what he has done here."

Michael thought perhaps what he was concluding wasn't the right way to express his reasoning. "I'm hoping when we go back, it will be what we have lived in before."

"Why wouldn't it be?"

"Because I also lived in Adriel's world and...Vicki's world."

"What was that like? Was it as bad as this world?"

"Worse."

Elizabeth shook her head in disbelief. "That's just...crazy."

Michael sighed.

"How does it compare to our world?"

"I thought our time was better. But after seeing what we have seen over the past year back home, Lizzy..." He wavered. "I always thought the human race had evolved emotionally and intellectually since the time of Christ...I'm not so sure. It's been two thousand years and... "

Michael sighed. They kept walking. "Any educated guess on what world we are about to enter?"

"Your educated guess is as good as mine," he replied.

"That's not a comforting thought." She turned to him. "Was that my mom?"

Michael hesitated, unsure what to say.

"Tell me the truth."

"That's your mom."

She didn't break stride, passing the remaining outdoor stands, and then stopping briefly past a pile of abundant fruits on a small table. Next to the fruit stand, an old lady was selling bread. Elizabeth put down a couple of Roman coins, thanked the woman, and offered a piece of bread to Michael. He turned it down and Elizabeth ate it.

"It's a lot to handle," she said. "I was finally at peace over what happened that night."

"I never should have said anything to you," Michael acknowledged.

"Dad."

"Yes."

"You can't protect me my whole life." She hugged him. "I was worried about you."

I get that, Elizabeth. I do. It's taken a good many years. You worry about me as much I worry about you.

"I'm not that scared girl in grade school, Dad. I can take care of myself."

Michael backed away from Elizabeth. Her eyes were moist yet filled with confidence. His little girl has grown into a wonderful and brave young adult.

It was at that moment Michael's heart beat with unabashed pride. But he was melancholy, too, realizing his role as a parent had changed.

It was joyful yet painful. He embraced her tighter. "I love you. I can't lose you. Ever."

They released the hug. "Are you ready to go home?"

"Absolutely!"

They reached the street they had traveled many times, the same path that Jesus rode along on the donkey, preaching peace as the palms were laid down in front of him. For Michael, there was relief in seeing such a familiar sight. Yet he knew there wasn't going to be any until they took that long stairway back to Long Island.

He stopped for a few seconds about fifty yards from the tunnel. Michael looked back at the bustling streets, the hustling at its peak. Surreal, he thought. Not far from this area and scene, the single most written about event in history was underway.

"What are you looking for?" asked Elizabeth.

Michael grew quiet, and a feeling of acceptance drained his soul.

"Are you worried about Mom? Your friend?"

Chapter 73

The skies darkened and a strong, cold breeze whistled through the marketplace, sending would-be customers scurrying for cover. The wind blasted ferociously, causing fruits and vegetables to tumble off tables, and the tops of the stands flapped. Michael and Elizabeth ducked under a short façade. Water dripped onto his shoes, easing some of the pain. They shielded their eyes from the swirling dust mixed with moisture.

The sunlight tiptoed above the black clouds, illuminating a narrow path up to the hill where three men hung on wooden crosses, their shadows casting eerie images of death. Michael squinted to see the hallow view, then preferred to turn his back to the elements and the excruciating moment.

He wrapped his arms around Elizabeth, tightening his grip as the storm picked up strength. Another cluster of fruit tumbled down the street. One Roman soldier scurried past them and into the distance as Michael looked back to see where he was headed. Elizabeth lay her head against his shoulder. "I'm drenched," she shouted above the wicked weather. "Let's make a run for it."

"Just a few more minutes," he said. "Let's see if it dies down."

Elizabeth lifted her head off of his shoulder, staring at him. "What about Mom? Your friend?"

"I wouldn't know what to say. They are warriors from their world. I knew I wouldn't be able to stop their instincts. And they are good instincts for sure."

Elizabeth nodded. "I understand their language. Do you think they know where the tunnel is?"

"They do."

"Do you think they will come?"

"I've learned a few things on this journey," said Michael. "Your mom is one amazing woman. Whether she was married to me or not, your mom will always be Vicki, that strong woman I am attracted to. She's much like you—fierce with a big heart, wanting justice for everyone."

Elizabeth nodded and a smile finally emerged. "She is my mom."

Michael and Elizabeth stepped out into the storm, still raging. They inched their way toward the street with the familiar grate opening. Michael lowered his head, struggling to make it across the final yards to the tunnel. Elizabeth reached the grate first, pulling it up and sliding it a few feet away. Michael waved to her to go down. She did.

Exhausted, Michael rested against a nearby wall, gathering some much-needed breaths. "Come on, Dad," she shouted to him.

The wind howled more, and sheets of rain lashed his face, blinding him as he took a few more steps. He reached the opening and turned around, shielding his face, wondering where Vicki and Adriel could be.

"Dad, let's go," Elizabeth yelled.

He saw that she was several steps down.

Michael began to descend, taking two steps as debris drifted down the narrow street. He took couple more steps until a hand grabbed the top of his shirt, stopping his momentum. He fought to free himself. Looking up, he saw a Roman soldier growl, sneering in anger. His hand held tightly onto Michael's garment.

"What's wrong, Dad?"

"I need help!" Michael yelled.

She raced back up the ladder. "Leave my dad alone!" Elizabeth tore at the Roman's hand, tugging and then biting his arm.

The soldier maneuvered his other hand to grasp Michael's neck, choking him. He released his grip on Michael's shoulder and clenched his throat with both hands.

"This is for what you did to my brother, Marcus," the Roman said.

"Oh, Marcus' brother," shouted Elizabeth. She swung and struck the Roman in the face, causing her to fall back and down a couple of steps. She hurtled back toward him.

Michael coughed and slumped, wincing.

Elizabeth groaned and screamed. "Let my dad go, you bastard!"

"Die, Jew! This is a Roman's right: revenge. Die, Jew—"

The Roman's face turned white; his eyes glazed over and widened.

He released his hold on Michael and staggered backward. Michael regained his breath and climbed up to see what happened. The Roman sat, his face stunned. Elizabeth joined Michael at the top of the stairway. The soldier staggered to stand, stumbling. He fell.

"My God," Michael said.

The Roman's eyes turned sheet white, a knife deeply implanted into his back.

Leah stood over him holding onto to another knife—the one Michael had given her before he left. "Do you see this knife, you rat?" she said to the soldier.

The Roman struggled to speak. Leah leaned down and lifted the soldier's head. She glared, years of pain and anger in her eyes. "This is for every Jew you killed. Every woman you raped. Every child you hurt. Every man and woman you starved."

Leah kneeled beside him and plunged another knife into his neck .Then she stood, took a deep breath, and kicked the Roman in the back. Leah went to Michael and Elizabeth. "I remember now," she said to them. "I remember the other times."

"How?" Michael asked.

"When you handed me this," she replied. Leah showed the shirt to him. "I remembered."

"How did you know we would be here right now?" he asked.

"I ran into Adriel and Vicki in the courtyard. They told me you were leaving."

Michael sighed and nodded, not saying a word.

"Did they say where they were going?" asked Elizabeth. "No."

The Roman tried to get up once more, then keeled over again.

Leah looked back at him. "My work here is done."

Michael embraced her. "Thank you for everything you have done for me. For Elizabeth."

"It is I who should thank you," she said.

Michael pulled back slightly. "Why?"

"You showed me that I should fight for the life I want, the life I deserve. We live here in a world where Jews are expected to be servants and not control what they wish in their lives."

Michael forced a melancholy smile and released the embrace. "Your victory will come soon."

Elizabeth hugged her. "Goodbye, Leah."

They wiped tears from their eyes. Michael descended the stairway. Elizabeth followed. They hesitated, walking into the tunnel and taking a final glance at Leah.

She pulled the grate over, touched her heart, and left.

Chapter 74

The storm strengthened, thunder rumbled, lightning lit up a portion of the tunnel, and rain tumbled down the steps like a slinky on Michael's childhood stairs. The moisture rolled and rolled until it formed a small-sized puddle at the bottom.

Elizabeth was ahead of him, talking about everything at random. "I'll never take for granted getting together with my cousins and friends."

"I sure could use a barbeque." He sighed. He was no longer the young man he'd been when they first found the tunnel in the old church's basement.

He was sad about meeting Vicki in her other world. Devastated when he recalled Adriel's story of losing his unit.

Michael wondered if they perhaps could have been friends in his world. Would it have been possible? Knowing the history of both worlds?

Winded, he stopped and leaned against the concrete wall. "I need to catch a breath," he said.

Elizabeth came back to him. "Are you having problems again?" she asked, leaning down.

Michael took a deep breath. "I guess I'm not that young dad anymore," he answered.

He looked at his hands, which were much more wrinkled now. He glanced up at Elizabeth, catching another breath. Her face was more mature, full, and grown like she had experienced some life-changing adventures. And she had.

Michael noticed more brown spots too on his hands, which dismayed him.

"We have to take care of each other," she said to him.

Michael nodded and straightened up with one more deep breath. Elizabeth wrapped her arm around him. "We can make it together," he said.

"Is there any room for me?" a voice called out from behind.

Michael and Elizabeth slowly turned around. It was still dark in the tunnel, so neither could see who was behind them.

"What's your answer?" the voice said.

"Vicki?" Michael replied. "Is that you?"

"Mom?" Elizabeth added.

Vicki appeared in front of them, her smile wide and a bit bloodied, which no longer fazed Michael but slowed Elizabeth.

"Mom," Elizabeth said, rushing to her and giving her a big hug.

"I am starting to learn what a 'mom' means," Vicki said. "I so want you to call me that."

"What happened?" Michael asked.

Vicki looked at him over Elizabeth's shoulder. "We were able to free Natan," she explained. "But we couldn't help that man. It was awful."

Michael breathed a sigh of relief, his body resting momentarily from the anxiety. "Adriel?"

Vicki smiled.

"Someone asking about me?" a firm voice called from behind them.

"Adriel!" Michael shouted. Vicki and Elizabeth released their grip and stepped aside. Michael and Adriel gave a quick hug. "I thought I would never see you again."

"We wanted to help him because of what he did for us," Adriel said, giving a sorrowful look. "But we couldn't stop that execution. What a messed-up world."

"As bad as the one you came from?" Michael asked.

"They were pretty comparable. It's hard to imagine humans truly haven't evolved after all these years."

Michael agreed. "Are you ready to see our world?"

Vicki and Adriel exchanged glances. Neither looked convinced.

"Dad, do you think they can come back with us?" asked Elizabeth.

"I guess we are about to find out." The four walked two by two—Elizabeth and Vicki in the front chatting like two sisters at a long-awaited reunion with Michael and Adriel behind them.

"Do you have a partner in a unit?" Vicki asked.

"What is that? What's a unit?"

"A unit. You know. The people you are close to."

Michael laughed. "She means a family. A boyfriend. Do you have a boyfriend? And no, her boyfriend isn't part of our unit."

Elizabeth looked back at him. "Oh." She turned to Vicki. "A partner. Yes. But don't tell Dad. He never likes the boys I bring home," she said in a whisper.

"I can hear you," Michael said.

Vicki and Elizabeth giggled, a sound Michael never thought he would hear. As they got closer to the stairway, he stopped, glued to the writings on the wall. They were still there. An odor nauseated him. He gave a dejected look. Elizabeth frowned. "What's wrong?" asked Vicki.

Michael shook his head. "Let's see what's there."

They approached the stairway leading back up to the church's basement, or at least Michael hoped it would be. He stopped at the first step and looked back.

"In case we are back in your world, Vicki and Adriel, we will have to be extremely careful. We'll have to find shelter quickly. They are likely still looking for us."

"Should we go back then?" asked Elizabeth.

Michael hesitated and looked at Adriel and Vicki for any sort of guidance. They stayed silent. He turned and continued; the only sound was his feet squishing the mushy terrain in the tunnel. Up the stairway he went, taking each step at a methodical pace. He reached the top step and discovered he was not inside the church basement. He bent over, closed his eyes, and said a prayer.

"What's the word?" Adriel asked.

Michael reached down, extending his hand. Adriel grabbed it and reached the top step, taking a few steps toward Michael. He looked out and moved in front of him…and faded, his confused expression the last Michael saw of him as he floated away.

Michael's heart sank. "No!"

Elizabeth joined him. She turned around to watch Vicki take a step toward them, a big smile warming her…then evaporating, her image floating away as Elizabeth chased her. "Mom! Mom, Mom!" she cried.

Elizabeth fell to her knees. "Mom, Mom, Mom…come back! Please come back!"

She wept. Michael dropped to his knees and embraced her. "I'm so sorry, Elizabeth. We have to move. It's too dangerous to stay here."

"I lost Mom. Again."

Chapter 75

Michael sat next to Elizabeth on the top step of the stairway, consoling her, her cries muffled from her head pinned to his chest. "We have to get out of here before we are spotted," he said. "We have to get to a safe place."

It was sunrise. The light streaked across the vast landscape.

There was a scream. A woman and man were being beaten by an Umbra soldier.

"Dad!"

Michael sprinted toward the assault. "Stop!" He could hear Elizabeth behind him, screaming. His eyes got fuzzy, and his pace slowed. The soldier lifted his bayonet high above the fallen man and woman. Everything seemed like it was in slow motion.

"No!"

There was a rumbling and a roar.

Michael wobbled and grabbed onto a tree.

Elizabeth caught up to him, holding onto his arm.

The Umbra faded. The woman and man jettisoned off the ground, both smiling and holding hands.

Behind them, the rumble grew louder. They all stared in disbelief. The toy store emerged from the ground. Across the street, bells rang as the church rose high into the sky. People appeared all around him. Cars zoomed down Main Street.

"Am I daydreaming?"

"You're not," Elizabeth replied. "Right?"

"I guess…"

"We are home."

"Again."

Elizabeth nodded.

There was a brief moment of silence.

Elizabeth wiped her eyes full of tears.

"We should go home," Michael said, weakly.

He put his arm around her.

"Michael, are you all right?" shouted Pastor Dennis, who stood on the church steps.

They strolled across the street, Michael's arm wrapped around Elizabeth.

"My God, what happened to your feet? Your clothes. Elizabeth, you're bleeding?"

Michael and Elizabeth exchanged glances. "It was a rough journey," he said.

"You're telling me," Pastor Dennis said. "It's been one crazy strange week here."

"In what way?" Michael asked.

"I thought I blacked out a few times. I was in the middle of doing a sermon, and then I wasn't. I dreamt I was back in the country of my great grandmother, Ireland. Or I think I dreamt."

"Really?"

Pastor Dennis laughed. "Sometimes I don't know whether I am going or coming. It must be my age. I feel like I am losing my mind! Am I going crazy, Michael?"

Michael forced a smile. "No. You're as sane as we all are."

Pastor Dennis laughed. "Look who is telling me I'm sane," he needled.

"Ha."

Pastor Dennis gripped his shoulder. "Are we still on for some pool?"

Michael nodded.

"I need to go. I have a big wedding to perform."

"How nice," interjected Elizabeth.

"Who's the lucky couple, Pastor?" Michael asked.

"I believe you may know one of them."

"Really? Who?"

"Your neighbor, Susan."

Michael's mouth dropped. "What?"

"Your neighbor, Susan. You know her, right?"

"Yes, but…"

Michael stood silently. Elizabeth urged him to join her. "Dad. We shouldn't go there."

He bid goodbye to Pastor Dennis and then walked with his head down. Michael rejoined Elizabeth outside at the bottom of the concrete stairway. The sun was strong. Spring was in early bloom. There was a freshly cut grass smell in the air, forcing Michael to sneeze twice.

"What did we do to change this time?" Michael questioned, looking down Main Street.

"It looks the same as before," countered Elizabeth. "All the stores are here."

They strolled down Main Street. Michael stopped at the lip of the Bay on the wooden dock. Boats filled the cold water. Children played in the park, riding high on the swings and tumbling down the slides. Boys were playing basketball across the street. A dad was tossing a frisbee to his daughter. Old and young held hands, some walking dogs.

Michael sat on a bench, grateful to rest his weary legs. Strangers stared at them both. "Nothing really to see here," Michael said, causing Elizabeth to laugh.

Elizabeth sat next to him. "Yeah, move along. You'd think they never saw people bleeding before...." She grinned. "Are you okay?"

He gave a forlorn look. "I don't know what to believe and what not to." He got up and offered his hand to her. They walked side by side back up Main Street. A big black limousine arrived for the couple's mystery ride in front of the Lady by the Bay church. A woman with striking red hair got out, her wedding dress pearly white and sparkling. A crowd gathered around her, lining the stairway.

"Dad, don't go there," Elizabeth said.

Michael continued his straight line to the church, climbed the concrete steps, and sat in the back row.

Elizabeth joined him. "Does this mean that...and Paul... what about him?"

"It's changed. Again."

"Why are you doing this to yourself?"

Michael remained quiet, staring straight ahead. Susan was with her groom. Pastor Dennis asked the couple to recite their vows. Michael didn't hear a word. The rings were exchanged. Michael looked at his vacant ring finger. The couple kissed, and family members and friends clapped as Pastor Dennis introduced them for the first time as a married couple.

The music started and the crowd stood. The happy couple walked arm in arm with smiles from ear to ear. Cameras clicked as Susan and her husband acknowledged the well-wishers with words and waves.

"Who is the guy?" Elizabeth asked.

"That reporter who came to the house not long ago," Michael said.

"You've met him?"

"Yes."

He slumped down into the pew, his hands covering his face. "What did I do wrong? Think. Think, Michael, think. What didn't I do right?" he continued. "Should I go back now?"

"Why do you have to change anything?"

Michael sat up. "I don't know. I just don't know what to do anymore."

"Maybe we've spent so much time trying to make everything so right and perfect, we've forgotten how to be just grateful for what we have now."

Michael grabbed a deep breath. "When did you become so wise?"

"I guess we are starting to listen to each other more."

"Let's go congratulate the bride and groom."

Elizabeth went ahead and met Michael on the congratulatory line. He wished the groom well. "My best to you. May you have many years of happiness." They exchanged a handshake.

Susan glowed, smiling. "Michael, your feet! What happened?"

"Too much jogging around Northport...you know the hills and trees and bushes...." Michael smiled. "You look beautiful, Susan. Congratulations. I hope you have endless moments of happiness."

Susan leaned over and gave him a kiss on his cheek. "Thank you always for encouraging me to give my sweetheart a chance."

Chapter 76

The crowd lining the stairway roared with screams of joy and clapping. Susan and her groom waved their approval. The flower girl lifted the bride's gorgeous, long white wedding dress as she walked arm in arm with her husband. Birdseed was tossed from all angles, sprinkling the couple.

Michael stood on his toes to find a clearer view. Susan caught his eye and gave a big smile and threw a kiss to him. He smiled back. Elizabeth gently nudged Michael with her shoulder. It was much like a gesture he would do to her when she'd had a hard day at school or was going through boy troubles.

Michael appreciated the shoulder bump, realizing it was another example of Elizabeth taking a different role in their lives. They trekked up and down the steep hills of Northport, resting occasionally. Michael pretended he wanted to look at the blossoming spring flowers and aura of beauty growing around them. Elizabeth giggled a few times when Michael halted the trip back home.

"Come on, old man," she teased. "Only a few more blocks to go. Want me to get you a wheelchair? I can push you, you know. I am strong. I am woman."

Michael waved her to go ahead. He stopped not far from the old three-story colonial. Its wooden frame was aging, the once bright brown and orange shingles worn down from the sea air smashing into it on many winter nights. He found peace, standing at the top of a hill with a view of the Long Island Sound. It was majestic. He could see the many boats sailing. It was a crystal-clear day—not a cloud in the sky, much like it was in Jerusalem over two thousand years ago. *That first journey. Wow. We were so scared. What a frightening time. The Romans. Marcus. The crucifixion. How blessed are we? So grateful for everything. My life. Thanks, Mom and Dad, for believing in life. Vicki. Oh, Vicki. How I miss you. How I wish I could take all those mistakes back. I wish I could redo it all. Thank you for giving me my greatest gift: Elizabeth. You would be proud. I know you're proud now. She loves you. She misses you. I miss you. Thank you, God. Thank you for letting me spend more time with her.*

He closed his eyes and said a prayer he often repeated when tucking Elizabeth into bed as a child. *Dear God, thank you for today. Thank you for my daughter. Thank you for my home. Thank you for my bed. May I never forget the gift of life you've given me. Most of all, thank you for loving me.*

Michael opened his eyes, wiping a few tears away. He laughed to himself, recalling how Elizabeth would always add a line or two. *Thank you, God, for chocolate. Thank you, God, for candy canes. Thank you, God, for cake....*

He walked the next mile up steeper and deeper hills. He reached the Crab Meadow Golf Course. Golfers were busy teeing off and putting on the greens, enjoying the first warm days of Spring. He recalled the day he and Elizabeth stood near the fence surrounding the course. How a golf ball landed a few inches from them. Michael frowned. *We were lucky. So lucky it didn't hit us. Thank God. I never would have forgiven myself if anything had happened to Lizzy. Maybe that's why I refuse to play? Nah.*

Michael was not one for playing the game, yet Elizabeth was showing unusual interest in it. She never had as a child. She certainly enjoyed sledding down the hills the course provided during the winter. Michael was suspicious of her motivations. He speculated her newfound curiosity was because she was smitten with a boy on the high school golf team. She had dragged Michael to the Sporting Goods store on three occasions to buy clubs. *You don't fool me, Elizabeth. I'm your dad. Can't pull the wool over my eyes. Ha.*

He journeyed up the final hill and stopped in front of the home he first bought with Vicki.

"Hey, Michael. How are you?" his neighbor Vinnie called out, running over. "Where did you walk today?" he added, pointing to his feet.

Michael blushed, turned, and waved. "To a place where I'll never go again, I hope."

Vinnie gave a concerned look. "What are you doing for Easter?"

"The same old, same old."

"Stop by if you have some time. We'd love to see everyone."

"Well, it's just Lizzy and me."

Vinnie laughed and slapped Michael on the back. "I get it. When you've been married that long…I do get it." He winked. "I hope your family has a great day. Can't wait to see what she comes up with today. I loved her vegetable lasagna. I left her a note in the mailbox, I hope she got it."

"What? Vegetable lasagna? Note?"

Vinnie had already gone back inside his home before Michael could pursue the conversation in more detail. *How weird. Maybe being a new dad is making him a bit off-center? He's usually so grounded.* Michael strolled around the house, noticing the bushes were almost full. The apple tree was growing nicely. He pulled the water hose out and sprayed the grounds before returning to the front.

I love this block. I love the neighbors. I love everything about this town. Michael closed his eyes once again and took a deeper breath than before, enjoying the aroma of the ocean air.

He opened his eyes and pulled some bills out of the mailbox, noticing the envelope from Vinnie. It read on the front: "To three of my favorite people..."

I guess he has lost his mind.

He struggled to open the envelope. It had been taped shut, which frustrated Michael. He placed the envelope and mail in a pile on the table as he entered the vestibule. The smell of turkey cooking seduced his senses.

"Elizabeth, how did you put that in so quickly?" She came running down the stairs, a big smile stretching from ear to ear.

"Are you cooking a turkey?" he asked.

She refused to answer.

"What is going on?

"Hurry," she shouted up the stairs.

"Who are you shouting to? Is your—Oh no, is your aunt here?"

"No."

"One of the neighbors? Are you and Vinnie playing a joke on me? I'm totally not in the mood for this."

"No, Dad."

"Who then is here cooking? I told you I don't want any charity. Did you call ahead or plan this?"

Elizabeth laughed.

Michael grew frustrated.

"I'm the guilty party," said a voice from the top of the stairs.

"Vicki?"

"Where have you been?" Vicki said, limping.

Michael raced to her, two steps at a time, and barreled into Vicki, embracing her. He kissed her forehead, her cheeks, her lips. Vicki teared up.

"How? How are you here?"

"Did you forget what you did?"

Michael gave a confused look. Vicki pulled out a piece of paper.

Vicki, you may think I'm a nutcase or that I have lost my common sense or that I am a crazed lunatic. Just read this. Think about it. Remember everything you have seen. It doesn't make sense, right? It seems impossible. But it is possible. Faith makes it possible. Somehow, our daughter changed the history of what once was. Strange, right? Keep reading. We were married. Then on the night of December 24th, when you were pregnant with our daughter, you went out to get something to eat. Do not go out on this night. Do this for me. Do this for you. Do this for our daughter! I love you. Always. Forever. Michael

"Yes, yes, yes!" Michael shouted. "But—but I didn't think you would see it. I wasn't sure about doing it. I didn't want to... for you to think I..."

"Lost your marbles?"

"Yes."

"I'm glad you did it because I wanted to give you something you gave away a long time ago…to save our daughter."

Michael gave a puzzled look. "What?"

"Put out your left hand," Vicki said.

Michael did. Vicki placed his wedding ring on his finger.

"How did you get this?"

She pointed to the cross hanging on the wall. "He gave it to me when I went to him on that awful day."

Michael was dumbfounded. Stunned. He got chills and hugged her tighter.

"Okay, kids," said Elizabeth. "It's time to eat. "

Michael gave Vicki several more kisses.

"Come, let's sit down," Vicki said.

They entered the dining room. The extension was inserted into the polished wooden table. There were eight plates. Knives and forks were neatly placed on bright purple napkins.

"Sit, Michael. Elizabeth, help me."

"Sure will, Mom."

Vicki smiled.

"Who else is coming?" Michael asked.

Vicki returned with a bowl of mashed potatoes. Elizabeth brought in green beans and stuffing.

"I see there's room for more. Anyone else joining me?" Michael said again.

Vicki put her hands on his, a touch Michael had longed for many years. Was he living a dream? Was right now really his reality? Was the journey he took to the world of the Umbras and First Century Jerusalem real or a mirage he invented?

"A friend from our past."

"What? Who? Why the mystery?"

The doorbell rang. "I got it," said Elizabeth with a burst of joy.

Excitement erupted as adults and children's voices clashed and climbed high. Michael stood and turned.

"Adriel?"

"Brother."

They hugged and didn't let go for what was only a few seconds but felt like a lifetime for both.

Adriel stepped back. "Brother, my family," Adriel said, introducing his wife and three children.

"Brother, my family," Michael said.

The End

Acknowledgments

Every so often, authors dig deep inside their hearts and souls and write a story out of desperation. During the pandemic, my choices were to write the next story or keep the emotional downward spiral descending.

So here I sit, in front of my laptop, inside my home, giving thanks to those who were there during a dark time and helped me move this book forward. I thank my family, who have always endured my flaws and still love me to this very day. Thank you Debbie, Caitlyn, and Jackie. My greatest gifts, our children.

I'm grateful to have such wonderful friends, such as Shelley Larkin, who sat on the opposite coast, reading out loud this story numerous times. She endured my moods, my angst, and the times where I was ready to toss this aside. The encouragement is never forgotten, nor was it ever conditional.

My former publisher, Lou Aronica, was kind enough to spend many hours on the phone and some in person, helping me give birth to this idea.

Thank you to Lena Robinson for her editing skills and phone discussions. She has been an incredible help in the time travel series, including the books *An Angel Comes Home*, *Everybody's Daughter*, and *The Greatest Gift*.

I am grateful for Anthony Ziccardi for giving me the opportunity to have this book published. It is what I consider my most ambitious story.

In conclusion, this is the fifth book of the time travel series—*Necessary Heartbreak*, *An Angel Comes Home*, *Everybody's Daughter*, *The Greatest Gift*, and *The Shattered Cross*.

I hope you enjoy this story, for it was the one I originally wanted to tell in *Necessary Heartbreak*.

I'll see you in our imagination.

About the Author

Michael John Sullivan is an author living in Florida. He has previously published *Necessary Heartbreak*, *An Angel Comes Home*, *Everybody's Daughter*, and *The Greatest Gift*.